THE
VALKYRIE'S
DAUGHTER

ALSO BY TIANA WARNER

The Mermaids of Eriana Kwai series

Ice Massacre
Ice Crypt
Ice Kingdom

THE
VALKYRIE'S
DAUGHTER

TIANA WARNER

Entangled Publishing, LLC
644 Shrewsbury Commons Ave., STE 181
Shrewsbury, PA 17361
rights@entangledpublishing.com

Entangled Teen is an imprint of Entangled Publishing, LLC.

Visit our website at www.entangledpublishing.com.

Edited by Amy Acosta
Cover design by Bree Archer
Stock Art Credits Nerthuz/Gettyimages, stereohype/Gettyimages, RedKoalaDesign/Gettyimages, Mykhailo Skop/Shutterstock, Nanashiro/Shutterstock
Interior design by Toni Kerr

ISBN 978-1-64937-148-5
Ebook ISBN 978-1-64937-153-9

Manufactured in the United States of America

First Edition July 2022

10 9 8 7 6 5 4 3 2 1

entangled teen
an imprint of Entangled Publishing LLC

To Bailey

At Entangled, we want our readers to be well-informed. If you would like to know if this book contains any elements that might be of concern for you, please check the book's webpage.

https://entangledpublishing.com/books/the-valkyries-daughter

CHAPTER ONE

THE QUICKEST HOOVES
IN VANAHEIM

Sigrid urged Hestur into a gallop, tearing across Vanaheim's grassy hills while the other girls flew drills atop their winged white mares on the training field. As valkyries, their job was to serve the nine worlds and be battle-ready at all times.

As the only girl in Vanaheim paired with an ordinary horse at birth, Sigrid's job was different. *This* mission was hers and hers alone.

She bent low in the saddle, heart racing in anticipation of the flat-out, barely controlled speed that sucked the breath from her lungs. Hestur might've been the most ordinary of all horses—plain brown with no dapples, no markings, and no wings—but this realm had no faster animal.

"Let's go, Hestur."

With a toss of his head, he seemed to surge into another world, his strong hindquarters carrying them up the hill at a pace that sent his mane lashing across her face.

A grin pulled at her lips as her stomach swooped at the incredible speed. This feeling, like teetering on a stone wall that separated control from chaos, was the best in all the nine worlds.

They galloped toward Vanahalla, the royal hall whose

shimmering gold towers touched the sky, reacting to each other's movements with an instinct born out of sixteen years of partnership. While Hestur focused on navigating the divots and molehills, Sigrid directed them around the larger obstacles, like boulders, bushes, and —

"Watch the sheep!"

Hestur expertly wove through the fluffy white herd, barely slowing. The sheep raised their heads, tracking the pair up the hill with beady eyes.

"Nice work, buddy."

Her breaths came fast, the dull burn in her thighs signaling that her body was growing tired from the gallop.

She checked the sun's position. A thrill of dread coursed through her chest. *Is it past noon?*

She crouched lower. "Faster."

Hestur's ears turned back, listening, and then he pushed on.

They crested the hill and arrived at the base of Vanahalla's stone steps. Sigrid held her balance and let Hestur sort out his footing, trusting him to find his path. He checked his speed, cantering smoothly up.

At the top, he powered over the bridge in three long strides, hooves rattling the wood. The moat churned below, deep and murky.

"Good boy."

The courtyard sprawled before them, double the length of the training field. Gasping for breath, Sigrid found their target and nudged Hestur into a canter. "Make way!"

Sigrid and Hestur barreled over the cobblestones, courtiers diving out of their path, yelling and cursing.

It was internally cursing not their first mission.

Hestur's clattering hoofbeats masked the softly trickling fountains, and Sigrid's dirt-smudged skin and clothes contrasted spectacularly with the pristine marble. Sunlight glinted off the gold towers, always snagging her attention and tempting her to check the empty windows and closed doors as she raced past. Growing up in the stable beyond the courtyard walls, she'd heard stories of what went on inside Vanahalla. Sorcerers lived there with the royal family and courtiers, and enough magic filled the halls to give Vanaheim its status as the closest world to Asgard. Some said close enough to kiss the gods.

The same way Odin had given his eye for a drink of wisdom, Sigrid might just surrender hers to know everything that went on inside those golden towers.

But now was not the time.

They blew by the polished gold statues lining the perimeter. Sigrid saluted the figure of a valkyrie as they whipped past. A sculpted, winged helmet dangled from one of the woman's hands and a spear from the other. Three braids ran front-to-back along the right side of her head, so the bulk of her hair fell heavily over her left shoulder.

Although she wasn't a valkyrie—*yet*—Sigrid kept her blond hair in the same style beneath her helmet, only mirrored. Braiding back the left side freed her fighting arm, while keeping her hair long and thick protected her light skin from the sun on long journeys. Not that she ever traveled far or had reason to fight.

When they arrived at the open door, Sigrid leaned down from the saddle to look inside. "Gregor!"

"Up here." Overhead, Gregor's broad shoulders filled the window as he leaned out from the second floor. Except for his dark eyes, his face was masked beneath his thick beard. "Running a bit early today?"

Sigrid grinned and held out her arms. "Record time."

Gregor's booming laugh echoed as he heaved a linen bag through the window.

She caught it and laid it over Hestur's wither, allowing the surge of satisfaction.

Now to deliver it in even less time.

"Get going!" Gregor shouted and waved her off.

Hestur took his cue and spun on his haunches, leaving Sigrid scrambling to collect the reins. He carried her back over the bridge, down the stone steps, and down the hill, picking up so much speed that all she could do was grab his mane and clamp her legs tighter. Their new target was the valkyrie stable midway down, a village in itself with all of its barns, pastures, and outbuildings.

Twenty-one junior valkyries soared around the training field as Sigrid approached, their snow-white mares like a lightning storm in the clear sky. They were an image of poise and perfection, spiraling up and down in *V* formation, taking turns throwing golden spears at airborne targets.

The familiar twist in Sigrid's gut had her drawing a sharp inhale. She barely had time to jam her heels down to stay in the saddle as Hestur slid to a stop in front of General Eira. The woman spluttered and waved her arms to dissipate the resulting cloud of dirt.

"Sorry," Sigrid said, panting and internally cursing herself for not paying better attention. Antics like this would not send the message that she was serious about joining the valkyries. She clapped a hand on the linen bag draped over Hestur's wither. "It's all…here… On time and…undamaged." She hoped.

While General Eira wiped dirt off her forehead and cheeks, the junior valkyries landed behind her, hooves thumping, wings sending up another whirl of dust. Just not in the general's face. They all looked dignified, with their fitted white training clothes, winged helmets, and hair fixed in elegant knots and long braids.

Sigrid dismounted, hoisted the linen bag off Hestur, and passed it to the general, who narrowed her eyes. Her dark hair was in a tight bun, as usual, and her pale face in her most disapproving expression, also as usual.

While Sigrid clutched a stitch in her side, General Eira reached in and pulled out the first item.

"All right, who ordered ham and cheese?"

Mission complete.

CHAPTER TWO

GROUND TROOPS
COULD BE USEFUL

"Took her long enough. I'm starved," Ylva said, swinging a leg forward over her mare's neck and sliding off the saddle. She moved like a swan, tall and poised—not to mention likely to hiss and bite.

Behind her, Edith dismounted, cracked her neck, and began her usual lunchtime stretching routine—once again the most composed of all the juniors. Where the others were shiny and blotchy from exertion, Edith had but a single bead of sweat on her temple and the faintest hint of flattering pink beneath her amber complexion.

The rest left their mares and pushed past Sigrid to claim their lunches, moaning about how hungry they were. Their lack of thanks was nothing new, but she huffed to dispel the iciness in her chest as they failed to give her so much as a glance.

You're welcome, your royal highnesses.

The mares' wings twitched as they fanned themselves, cooling down after the flight. Sigrid carefully checked over them, receiving some gentle nudges as thanks. It never failed to send a trickle of warmth through her.

Sigrid would never say it aloud, but it was obvious how much the mares loved her. Runa's mare, Tobia, didn't affectionately nibble just anyone's hair, and Mjöll's favorite part of lunchtime was a butt scratch from Sigrid while her rider, Edith, stretched.

Sigrid paused as she checked Oda's leg wraps. "Gunni, Oda might have landed hard. Her knees are a little hot. You should—"

"I know," Gunni snapped, mouth full of sandwich. She studied her mare's legs as if trying to see whether this was true. Her round, pink face was permanently scrunched up, like someone was about to hit her in the nose.

Sigrid gritted her teeth but chose to disregard the snark. It was more important that Oda got the help she needed. "She doesn't seem sore, but we can cold-hose them tonight."

"I know how to take care of my horse." Gunni squinted at the mare's knees and nodded, like she'd come to a decision. "Cold-hose them for me when we're done here."

Of course Gunni found it beneath her to do such a simple task. Sigrid stifled a sigh. "Sure."

Apparently still affronted, Gunni took an aggressive bite of sandwich and wrinkled her nose at Sigrid. "Why have you got so much dirt on your face?"

Sigrid raised a hand to her cheek and immediately regretted it.

"Raised in a barn," Ylva said in sing-song. She narrowed her dark eyes and set her lips, looking even more swan-like.

A rush of heat crawled up Sigrid's cheeks at the laughter from the other valkyries. *Nothing new.* But she hated giving them fuel for their taunts.

Besides, being raised in a barn wasn't so bad.

If she forgot to tell Gunni about the lettuce stuck in her teeth, it was because she had more pressing things on her mind, like caring for the mares.

"Did you see her trying to practice with the hoops the other day?" Ylva continued, clearly not done. She jumped and flailed as if trying to reach something, dark braid swinging.

Everyone laughed. Even Runa's mouth twisted in a little smile as she turned the page of her book.

General Eira heard none of this, or at least pretended not to. Why would she interrupt the valkyries' favorite team-bonding activity?

The heat in Sigrid's face increased, along with the burning anger in her stomach. She knew how she must have looked attempting their drills, galloping over the turf instead of soaring above it—but she also knew how many targets she'd hit. More than Ylva, even.

Finding satisfaction in this, she cast them a tight-lipped smile and went back to work.

As the girls returned to their sandwiches and she checked the last of the mares, footsteps stopped beside her. She lifted her gaze from General Eira's leather boots, to her breeches, up to her face, apprehension building.

"You're not going to trick me into it, Sigrid," she said in a volume for Sigrid's ears only.

Sigrid stood, blinking innocently, even as her heart raced. "What? I was just doing my—"

General Eira pushed the empty lunch bag into Sigrid's chest. "Next time, trot. Nothing you ever do is urgent enough for galloping."

Sigrid squared her shoulders and clenched her jaw. She hadn't been trying to *trick* General Eira into anything, but fine, she'd spent most of her sixteen years trying to prove that it was a mistake not to let her be a valkyrie. It was time to get creative with her methods of proving herself.

Sigrid clenched the bag harder to keep her hands from trembling and then said, "General, I wondered if I could show you what I've been practicing. I've run your drills and know the formations by heart. I think I can handle enemies on the ground as well as any of them—maybe better. If you'll let me—"

"Enough, Sigrid." General Eira rubbed the crease between her eyebrows, an all-too-familiar gesture. "Valkyries are sky troops, not ground troops. You'd be a hindrance out in the field. A distraction. Stop wasting my time and focus on your duties."

Sigrid snapped her mouth shut. Her eyes stung, and the anger bubbling in her gut rose like acid.

Behind the general, Ylva and Gunni peered over, apparently trying to listen in. Runa absently chewed her sandwich while reading. Edith, who had yet to claim her lunch, made slow spear-throwing motions like a dance ritual.

Unwilling to give them more fuel, Sigrid dropped her gaze. "Yes, General."

"You should be content with your place among us," General Eira said, keeping her voice low.

Sigrid swallowed hard. It wasn't about hating her place. It was about wanting to do more with her life. She was so ready to serve Vanaheim among the valkyries. Why couldn't they see that?

When Sigrid remained silent, the general sighed and walked away.

Hestur approached and nosed the bag in Sigrid's hands as if hoping to find an apple. She rubbed between his big brown ears, willing the churning in her gut to go away and not develop into a roar of frustration. No sense in losing her temper over this. Again.

Leaving the valkyries to chat about the amazing stunts they'd practiced that morning, she led Hestur back to the barn.

"We'll just have to try again, buddy," she whispered.

Whether Hestur was a winged mare or an ordinary gelding, Sigrid refused to accept that the valkyries didn't need a ground team. Not all battles had to be fought from the sky. She just needed a way to prove it.

"Sky troops," she muttered.

Hestur snorted—in indignance, probably. If only General

Eira had seen the stunts they'd practiced before her lunch run.

She might not have attended valkyrie school, but she was as good as any of them. A lifetime of heaving a pitchfork had made her strong, and she'd gleaned generations of horsemanship wisdom from the stable hands. What would it take to convince General Eira that she deserved to join the ranks? It wouldn't be much longer until the juniors were sent on their inaugural mission, and Sigrid was set on becoming part of their team.

Sigrid patted Hestur's neck. "We'll just have to find a way to convince her before then."

CHAPTER THREE

PESKY COMPANIONS

The hundred-horse barn was nearly empty, with most of the senior valkyries helping to tame the civil unrest in Jotunheim and the juniors on the training field. Chickens scattered as Sigrid marched inside with Hestur in tow. The muted lighting and cooler temperature eased the sweat dampening the back of her neck.

Morning chores had been completed a while ago, but a few stable hands remained sweeping the aisle and carrying feed to the storage room. Sigrid nodded to them and headed to the farthest end of the barn with Hestur following close.

Hestur's stall was her home—an independent, self-reliant cube, with everything she needed stacked under her hammock at the back. It wasn't much, but stable hands earned low wages.

Sigrid rolled her shoulders, disappointment still weighing on her, but she needed to focus, since there were only a few minutes left before the afternoon chores began. She quickly tended to Hestur—a routine as familiar as brushing her teeth, washing her face, and combing hay out of her hair before bed. When she massaged him with the curry comb, he arched his neck and wiggled his lip, a reflex that never failed to make her laugh.

It helped dissipate the remaining tension in her limbs and

the post-gallop adrenaline. Calmer, she stood back to admire her work. All the dirt and hair had relocated to her wool tunic and trousers, but at least Hestur's brown coat gleamed like Vanahalla's towers.

"One more pass with the rag should do it," she said, reaching into her brush box. The rag wasn't there. She checked around her feet. "Where'd it go?"

With rising suspicion, she looked up to find Hestur holding it in his teeth, smugly bobbing his head and waving it around.

"Give me that!"

She pried it from his mouth, laughing. Stealing handkerchiefs was one trick she maybe shouldn't have taught him. It had become more pesky than useful.

She kissed his soft nose. "Cute, though."

Roland, a fifteen-year-old annoyance who'd been a stable hand for as long as she had, paused on his way past Hestur's stall. He peered in with a wry smile. "Aw, shucks, Sig. You think I'm cute?"

She appraised him with mock seriousness. He'd taken to wearing his white hair in a high ponytail to accentuate his ears, which he said was a conversation starter with the ladies. He insisted their pointed shape proved that his father must have been a Light Elf.

Charming ear shape or not, Sigrid was not interested. "Maybe if you didn't have the fashion sense of a potato."

He ran a hand over his burlap shirt. "You can hardly keep your paws off my alternative style."

She threw a brush at him, and it bounced off his chest and clattered to the floor.

This sass was a recent development. Somewhere in the last year—and much to her irritation—some of the stable hands had seemed to finally notice her. She returned the snark in equal measure, but only when the junior valkyries weren't around. They became waspish when Sigrid bantered with any of their crushes.

It was completely unfair. What was she supposed to do? Isolate herself from the only friends she had? It wasn't her fault she was a stable hand and spent all day working alongside them. She obviously would have preferred to be a valkyrie.

Roland picked up the boar-bristle brush. "Whose brushes are you using?"

Sigrid huffed. "Mine, potato-sack. Now give it back."

"Oh. Oops."

Sigrid froze. Coming from Roland, the word could indicate disaster. "What?"

"Well, you were busy fixing divots on the training field earlier, so I thought I would help you out by brushing Hestur, and…"

Sigrid groaned, skin prickling from the disaster he'd just created for her. "You used the wrong brushes?"

"I'm sorry! But at least he was clean, right?"

She narrowed her eyes. "I did notice he seemed unusually non-disgusting."

"You're welcome."

Sigrid bit back her frustration, not wanting to be mean to her friend after he'd tried to do her a favor. With forced calm, she said, "Did you at least put the other brushes back properly?"

"I'll make sure. Don't worry. No one will ever know." Roland clapped a hand over the stall door in farewell before continuing down the aisle toward the tack room.

She huffed. He'd better get all the brown hairs out of whoever's brushes he used, because her horse was the only non-white one in the barn. If the valkyries found out, they'd get her in trouble faster than she could explain herself to the general.

Sigrid didn't want another lecture.

Wiping an arm across her gritty face, she sat in her hammock at the back of the stall. Thinking of General Eira's rejection made her chest tighten. A lunch mission wouldn't have been the tipping point in proving she could become a valkyrie, but couldn't General Eira at least give her the chance to prove she could run drills just as well as the others?

What else could she possibly do to prove that—?

Boots scuffed on clay. Peter leaned over the stall door, a smile crinkling his brown eyes and sweat dampening his deep brown skin. As one of the older stable hands, he was strong and broad-shouldered from a lifetime of barn chores. He always stood with his head tilted a little, as if listening thoughtfully. Once, when Sigrid was ten, he'd used his day off to build her a fort out of hay bales. Another time, he'd grabbed a wasp with his bare hand to stop her from getting stung. He was twenty-nine years old and the closest person she had to a big brother.

"Hey, lightning bolt," he said. "Are we under siege?"

She pursed her lips. He must have seen her gallop past. "The juniors needed lunch."

"Ah. Wouldn't want them to waste away."

Sigrid didn't want to talk about it, but her expression must have revealed something, because his smile faded. He had a way of catching the subtlest glint in her eyes, which he kindly called light blue but which were, in fact, a colorless gray. He said they always made her emotions plain.

"You know those girls just can't stand to see a stable hand who is better at riding than them," he said, using his sleeve to wipe the sweat from his brow.

She crossed her arms and leaned back, letting the hammock swing. "I don't care what they think of me."

"Then what's wrong?"

"Nothing. I'm here, Hestur is here, what more could I want?"

He nodded knowingly. He'd seen her cry the first time they'd denied her request. And all the other times that followed as well. "Foiled again, huh?"

Swatted away like a fly, more like.

She dug her paddock boot into the shavings, rocking the hammock harder.

"Why do you want to be a valkyrie so badly, anyway?" Peter said, tilting his head a little. "You really want to fight alongside those girls?"

"It doesn't matter who I'm alongside, as long as I get to be more than just a stable hand."

"Ouch."

Sigrid winced, regretting her bluntness. "Sorry."

"Teasing you. I get it." Peter sighed and ran a hand through his tightly curled hair. "But we're all more than the job, and you don't need to be a valkyrie to know it. Take me, for instance. I'm also a blacksmith, and a Svenson, and if I do say so myself, I'm a pretty good painter. You just need to find your version of that."

Ignoring the familiar ache in her chest, she grunted. "I'm a Nobody's-dottir with no art skills."

Peter smiled. "You're Sigrid. And you're good at training Hestur."

He pointed to Hestur's nose, and on cue, the horse curled his upper lip as if in laughter.

She scowled at both of them, not feeling any better.

Peter came to sit next to her in the hammock, jostling her about on purpose until she elbowed him in the ribs, refusing to smile. He sat back and got them swinging again. "Sigrid, you've been thinking of life as either being a valkyrie or not being a valkyrie. Maybe there are other options. Maybe there's another destiny that's perfect for you."

It was a nice idea, but that destiny was nonexistent. She had no interest in becoming an ordinary villager, like a smith or a tailor. The gods created the valkyries to maintain balance and peace in the nine worlds, and that purpose called to her more than anything. She wanted to travel with them through the upper and middle worlds, to provide help in emergencies, and to fight and defend innocent lives from the evils of the lower realms. She wanted the reverence that came with being a guardian, a protector, a valued member of the best warriors in the cosmos. Most of all, in her heart, being a valkyrie was her destiny.

Without parents to confirm or deny this, it pained her to think that she was missing out on her cosmic purpose.

There *had* to be more in life for her.

A chorus of *clip-clops* rose in the barn entrance, and Sigrid and Peter jumped to their feet. The valkyries were returning from training, and it was a stable hand's job to help.

Peter nudged her. "Anyway, if you were a valkyrie, who would shine their boots?"

Sigrid stuck out her tongue and left the stall in time for the usual bombardment of, "Sigrid, where's my halter? Sigrid, take my bridle. Sigrid, get my shoes."

They liked watching her scurry like a barn rat.

While the riders removed their sweaty helmets, shook loose their braids, and peeled off their gloves and boots, Sigrid and the dozen other stable hands untacked and groomed their mares.

All the while, Sigrid strategized.

What if Roland pretended to be in danger and I saved him right before General Eira's eyes? She can't say no to a hero.

Except putting him in danger might result in actual danger, so that was no good.

"Sigrid, pass me an apple for Mjöll," Edith said, nuzzling her mare's mane. "You were so good, weren't you, boo-boo?"

Sigrid fetched her an apple, stifling the suggestion that maybe Mjöll could use a diet. The mare's belly hung low enough that she looked pregnant.

What if I built a contraption that lets Hestur fly?

She nearly snorted at the impossibility.

Buried under a mound of saddles, bridles, and helmets, she put everything away and started removing Mjöll's leg wraps. The mare nudged her persistently for more food, and Sigrid slipped her a tiny piece of carrot out of sympathy.

"I'm so sore," Ylva said, arching her back and stretching her arms. Her fitted riding shirt lifted to reveal a tease of her midsection, possibly on purpose, as Peter walked by. "When do you think we can stop practicing that stupid barrel roll?"

Sigrid forced her attention back to Mjöll's legs, doing a worse job than Peter of ignoring Ylva's skin-flaunting.

The barrel roll was their latest stunt, one that Sigrid had been practicing in secret on Hestur. The rider had to pull herself under the horse's belly and up the other side of the saddle while the horse was moving at full speed. For a valkyrie, the risk was slipping and falling from the mare's belly. For Sigrid, the risk was getting trampled under Hestur's galloping hooves. Either way, it was the most advanced saddle stunt that the training program taught—short of the full barrel roll, in which the mare tucked in her wings and rolled over in the sky without losing her rider. This trick, Hestur would never be able to do.

Maybe General Eira would finally be impressed if I galloped circles around her doing barrel rolls.

"Ugh, I hate those," Gunni said, scrunching her already scrunched face. "My arms aren't strong enough."

"Same!" Ylva said.

"It's not about arm strength," Sigrid said automatically. "It's legs and core."

She winced at the resulting silence. Why did she have to say that? She knew better than to chime in on their conversations, even if it was to share useful information.

When she looked up, the nearby valkyries stared back like she'd cursed at them.

"Like you know anything, stable hand," Ylva said.

Sigrid's face burned. She bent lower to finish removing Mjöll's leg wraps, fumbling the ball of material so it nearly unraveled across the floor.

"Don't forget to take care of Oda's legs," Gunni snapped, as if the mare's condition was Sigrid's fault.

"Tobia's legs, too," Runa said, pulling her book out of her saddlebag and planting a kiss on her mare's fuzzy neck. "She landed hard on that last flight."

They liked to see her scurry, yes, but it was obviously more than that. None of them would ever admit that Sigrid did the best job caring for their mares. But they knew it, and they hated her more for it.

Peter might have been right that jealousy was a factor. But what did they think was going to happen—that the general would force one of them to switch places with Sigrid? A valkyrie and her mare were a blood bond formed at birth. It wasn't like Sigrid could just take one of their mares. Her mount was Hestur, and it would always be Hestur. They were a pair. An oddity. They'd both shown up in this world with no explanation, no parents, no bloodlines—a mystery that nobody was bothered to solve.

"Roland!" Gunni said, unscrunching her face to break into a smile.

Roland, on his way past with a wheelbarrow, paused. He waved back tentatively, looking confused. "Did you, uh, have a good training session?"

"The best," Gunni said, breathless. "We practiced barrel rolls."

"Right," he said, stretching the word. "Hey, did you know you have something green in your teeth?"

Gunni's face turned as red as the apple Sigrid had passed her.

Roland continued on with the wheelbarrow and gave Sigrid a wink. She had to bite her lip to keep from smiling. Unfortunately, Gunni caught their exchange, and her face darkened so intensely that it was as if a candle had been extinguished.

"Sigrid, stop taking so long—"

A clatter rose at the far end of the aisle. Everyone turned.

Hestur gazed down at a pitchfork lying in front of his stall, which he'd evidently just knocked over.

Good boy.

"Anyway, only three days until the seniors are back!" Edith clenched her fists, beside herself with excitement. "Wonder what our first mission with them will be."

Sigrid seized the chance to hurry to the next mare, continuing to remove tack.

"Bet they're going to send us to fight something awful to test our skills," Runa said, eyes still fixed on her book. "Like Garmr."

Everyone cringed. Even Sigrid and the other stable hands cast her looks of horror at the casual mention of the monster who guarded the underworld. Garmr's job was to keep the living and dead where they belonged, and fighting him wouldn't be so much a test as a death sentence.

"Well, maybe not quite that bad," Runa said, scanning their worried faces.

Sigrid opened her mouth, hesitated, then plowed on. "Are you definitely joining them on the next mission, then?" She held her breath.

Runa eyed her for a moment, then said in a haughty tone, "That's what General Eira says. She thinks *we* are ready."

Sigrid exhaled, choosing to ignore the jab. *Three days.* Could she convince the general to let her join them before those three days were up?

She couldn't imagine a scenario in which General Eira would say yes.

What if, when the seniors returned, another general would be more willing to give Sigrid a chance? She could go behind General Eira's back and ask them.

And it'll be the last thing I do before getting murdered by General Eira.

More likely, Sigrid was going to watch them depart, and the

next round of valkyrie trainees would come through, and she would continue down the same path she'd been on for sixteen years.

The thought had her chest feeling hollow and cold.

Dreaming was the closest she would ever get to being a valkyrie. She often imagined galloping beneath their *V* formation on Hestur, hurtling into battle in some misty, shimmering world, making friends as they all talked about the day's adventures over bowls of stew.

"Sigrid, you're dragging my reins!"

Sigrid jolted to attention. Ylva's bridle, which she'd put over her shoulder while removing the saddle, hung lopsided so the reins touched the ground.

"Sorry," she mumbled, tugging them straight.

"Ugh, there's brown hair in my brush," Gunni said, voice cutting like a knife. "Sigrid, you stole it!"

Everyone turned. Even Runa lifted her gaze from her book. Gunni plucked a short hair from the brush and held it up for all to see.

Sigrid's stomach swooped, and not in the fun, exhilarating way. She was too far to tell if it was actually brown—but she looked at Roland, who grimaced.

Maybe if she played ignorant. "I've never used your brush. I have my own."

"Then why is Hestur's hair all over it?"

She swallowed. "Maybe a cat rubbed against it."

General Eira swept in. "What's going on?"

"Sigrid has been using my brushes," Gunni yelled.

"I haven't!" Sigrid said. And it was the truth. *She* hadn't.

Gunni thrust out her brush, showing General Eira the hairs stuck in the bristles. "Look! This is Hestur's hair. She's going to give my mare a disease."

Sigrid clenched her fists, ready to yell back, but froze when

General Eira whirled around to glare at her.

"There's a single brown horse in this barn, Sigrid," the general said. "We've been kind enough to let you keep Hestur here, but if you're going to start using valkyrie gear without permission, we need to talk."

Sigrid bit her tongue, her face and neck burning from the effort of keeping her words in. They didn't *let* her stay, as if she were a cat they let sleep in the hay room in exchange for catching mice. She paid to be there. She used her wages to pay board, sharing the stall with Hestur instead of renting a room or a house like the other stable hands did.

Roland stepped forward, opening his mouth to speak, but Sigrid couldn't let him take the fall. He'd made an innocent mistake.

"It was a cat," she said. "I swear, I haven't used anyone's gear but my own."

Gunni stamped her foot. "General, she's always trying to sabotage my stuff!"

Sigrid's insides roiled at how blatantly untrue this was. But she knew from experience that there was no winning an argument against a valkyrie. Her purpose was to serve them, and they would always have power over her.

"I cannot allow this behavior, Sigrid," General Eira said. "If I catch you one more time—"

Thump. Thump. Thump.

A sound rose from outside. Everyone turned toward the barn doors as an old woman hobbled toward them, leaning on a crooked wooden walking stick. Her face was more wrinkled than any Sigrid had seen, her tawny-brown skin speckled with age spots. Her waist-length hair shuddered in the breeze, as white as a valkyrie mare's. She was dressed like the dead of winter in a fur cloak over a brown wool dress.

Whispers passed over the group like a breath of wind.

"Vala. It's Vala!"

Sigrid gasped, running a hand down her tunic in an effort to appear presentable. Of all the royals who lived in the hall—all of the masters of sorcery and magic—none were as gifted as Vala. Every generation, a Seer was granted access to the Eye of Hnitbjorg, the stone that showed visions about the nine worlds. Vala had seen more visions than anyone else since the beginning of time—but even then, she only emerged from the Seer's tower if something critical was shown. And in Sigrid's whole life, she'd never had cause to come down to the valkyrie stables.

General Eira stepped forward, dusting off her jacket. "Vala. What brings you here?"

"The Eye," she said, voice as brittle as if she hadn't used it in years.

Every valkyrie, every stable hand, even every horse seemed to hold their breath.

"A vision?" General Eira whispered.

Vala's icy blue eyes were wide. "General, Vanaheim is about to be attacked."

CHAPTER FOUR

THE EYE
NEVER LIES

In all of Sigrid's sixteen years, Vanaheim had never been invaded. Except for the attack that happened months before she was born, the valkyries had always fought for peace in other worlds.

The idea was so inconceivable that her body went numb as her mind flew with questions. Who was attacking? Why now? After sixteen years without attacks, what was Vanaheim about to face?

Thump. Thump. Thump.

Vala stepped farther into the barn, leaning on her walking stick. Nobody spoke as the old woman raised an arm as if to throw a handful of dirt into the air. From her palm burst a white light that hovered in the barn aisle. Ylva's mare startled, backing away. The light expanded, shifting and flickering, until it formed a scene—like a window into another place.

It showed the field beside the stables, where a two-story stone wall encircled the hill to prevent foot soldiers from getting to Vanahalla. Then the view soared up and over the wall, stopping before descending into the valley. The village, which Sigrid often rode to for the market, sat at the base of the hill. Beyond it, the forest stretched to the edge of the world, each tree as clear as if she were seeing it for real.

Amazing. What did Vala do to release the vision like that? It was an incredible display of the magic contained in the walls of Vanahalla. If a Seer was classified as a sorceress, maybe she could do other magic, too—

In the vision, a shaggy black animal crested the hill, snarling, looking around as if calculating its path.

Several valkyries gasped. The mares snorted, raising a clatter of hooves and gusts of wind as they tried to skitter away.

Sigrid's pulse spiked as she recognized the creature.

A dire wolf.

She had only seen illustrations in old history books, which had left her with nightmares. The live version was worse. Sucking in a breath, she took a step closer to the vision. The creature had intelligent eyes, strings of saliva glistening on its long teeth, and coarse fur that emphasized the swollen muscles beneath it. The wolf moved as if time had slowed, its fur blowing at a slower pace than was natural.

"The attack is by dire wolves?" General Eira said as the drooling wolf charged past and out of sight.

"They were sent," Vala said in that faint, brittle voice. "Do you see the shadows?"

Dark shapes crested behind the wolf. At least a hundred blurred figures charged toward the wall, also moving at a time-slowed pace.

They came into focus, and Sigrid gasped.

"Night Elves," General Eira said through her teeth.

Vala nodded. "I fear they are after the royals again, General. We have to protect King Óleifr and Princess Kaia."

The valkyries and stable hands exchanged knowing looks. Peter caught Sigrid's eye, and though he gave a reassuring nod, he couldn't hide the fear tightening his face. Sigrid was sure it matched her own expression.

Last time Vanaheim was under siege, the attackers had also been Night Elves, the wicked inhabitants of the realm of night. The elves had broken through the gate and reached Vanahalla, where they kidnapped the king's eldest daughter, Princess Helena, and she was never seen again.

The memory remained like a fresh wound in people's minds. Vala's request made sense—the valkyries' priority should be to protect the royals.

The vision shifted again, snagging Sigrid's attention.

The elves vanished, and a flash of white plummeted through the haze. A mare plunged toward the ground, wings pulled skyward, body limp—and the vision blinked out.

Sigrid's heart lurched. Everyone gasped. The valkyries clapped hands over their mouths to stifle their cries.

A mare, dead.

All the blood seemed to drain from Sigrid's head. She grasped a stall door as she swayed. Losing one of the mares she loved and cared for would destroy her. It would destroy all of them. And did the loss of that mare mean something would happen to her rider?

Sigrid looked around at the junior valkyries. Who would it be? The vision had been too hazy to tell.

"How long do we have?" General Eira broke the silence. She stood taller, looking twenty years younger and ready for war.

Vala shook her head. "Not long now. No more than an hour. The vision came white hot."

Everyone—even the general—seemed too stunned, their faces taut with worry.

Vala furrowed her brow, studying the valkyries, horses, and stable hands. "I beg you not to lose hope. If we act now, we can alter the vision before it is fulfilled. Now, I need to get back to my tower."

"Ylva will take you." The general snapped her fingers toward the huddled valkyries.

Ylva jolted to attention. "Y-yes, General Vala. I mean, General

Eira—and Vala."

Sigrid stepped forward, her heart hammering. That was all? They needed to know more! How would the battle play out? How would they win? She wanted to stop Vala and blurt all of the questions, but the fear of being scolded by General Eira for the thousandth time that day held her still.

While frantic whispers broke out among the valkyries as they tried to figure out which mare was in the vision, Peter and Roland tacked up Ylva's mount in seconds. Vala hobbled over to be helped up.

Sigrid couldn't make her feet move to help or even to—she swallowed hard—get ready for a Night Elf attack. How could they even help? Stable hands didn't have spears like the valkyries or magic like the sorcerers. Going against dire wolves and battle-thirsty elves with pitchforks and horse brushes would get them slaughtered.

Sigrid closed her eyes, hoping none of it was true. But...

The Eye of Hnitbjorg never lied. Vanaheim was about to be attacked. A winged mare was going to die, and a valkyrie might go with her.

Her eyes snapped open.

Vala said the future could be changed, and if they acted now, they could affect the outcome. Maybe there was hope of turning that army around. There *had* to be hope.

Sigrid gave a sharp exhale and shook out the tension in her hands.

Valkyries trained to protect their world at all costs. If she wanted to become one, she had to stop overthinking and get moving.

Sigrid would use her training and skills to defend Vanaheim just like any other valkyrie.

Those Night Elves wouldn't win this time.

Not if she could help it.

CHAPTER FIVE

WASTING MY SKILLS

In a flurry of saddles and bridles, Sigrid and the stable hands tacked up the winged mares again. The junior valkyries donned their golden armor—winged helmets, breastplates, and greaves over their shins. Looking as spectacular as the towers of Vanahalla, they mounted up, while Sigrid wiped layers of dirt, sweat, and horse hair from her skin and clothes.

"Division one," General Eira shouted, tightening the girth on her old mare, "stay at the gate with the stable hands. Don't let them get past you. Division two, up to Vanahalla. Get the royals to safety."

Half of the valkyries took flight out the open barn doors, shooting toward Vanahalla to protect the royals, while the other half assembled by the gate. With the senior valkyries off-world, everything rested on the junior valkyries' shoulders.

Sigrid's pulse raced. She could help them. She *would*. From the far end of the barn, Hestur watched her, ears perked, plainly wondering about all the commotion.

"Reinforce the gate with hay bales!" Peter shouted to the stable hands. "Let's go."

As they all raced for the hay room, Sigrid ran for Hestur.

She hadn't yet opened his stall when General Eira shouted over the din.

"Sigrid! I know what you're doing, and you're going to get yourself killed. Get over there with the stable hands."

"I can help!" Sigrid shouted back, unable to keep the heat out of her words. They needed all the warriors they could get, and this was her chance to prove she could fight as well as any valkyrie.

The general put a foot in her stirrup and mounted Drifa. "You don't have the training. You'll get in the way."

"But, General, I've been—" She hesitated over the confession, but this moment was too urgent for secrets. "I've been practicing with spears."

General Eira's brief surprise melted into a withering glare. In any other circumstance, Sigrid would definitely have been shouted at. The spears were the expensive property of the valkyries, forged out of gold and enchantments in the towers of Vanahalla—not a toy for a stable hand to play with during her off-hours. Instead, the general said through gritted teeth, "Work on the barricade with the other stable hands. I forbid you to try and fight."

"But I can—"

"*Now, Sigrid.*" She took flight, her mare's wingspan touching the stalls on either side as she left the barn.

Sigrid's harsh breaths made her lungs ache as she tried to tamp down the hurt. Did the general think so lowly of her abilities that she wouldn't accept an extra warrior in battle? But her word was absolute. She ran the valkyries, and so she ran the stables.

Biting back a curse, Sigrid set her jaw and left the stall. "Stay here, buddy."

Hestur snorted and stomped his hooves, responding to the frantic energy.

Sigrid stormed into the hay room, grabbed a pair of thick leather gloves, and hurried to help move bales. *Waste of my skills.*

Outside was a flurry of activity as the stable hands rushed to secure the area. The weakest spot in the stone wall was the wrought iron gate, which could open to grant passage to anyone wishing to climb to Vanahalla, like merchants, messengers, and the occasional haughty group wearing fur cloaks who came from other worlds to do business with the royals. The gate was strategically placed outside the stables, so anyone who tried to pass without permission would have the valkyries to answer to.

Sigrid scowled and grabbed a hay bale.

By the time she carried the fifth one out to the gate, sweat rolled down her face and neck, her arms ached, and her nerves were as taut as the twine holding the bales together. The stable hands shouted orders to each other, arguing with rising volume about what else they could do to fortify the gate.

Tension clogged the air as they waited for the first signs of the elf army to appear.

Sigrid shivered at the cold unease sliding down her spine. She hated sitting still, so she climbed on a bale and looked over their wall of hay, through the wrought iron gate, down to the sprawling village. Villagers wove like ants through the thatched-roof houses, no doubt hurrying to secure their own places and hide. Cows and goats had been left to graze in a pasture full of buttercups. Why hadn't the people rounded up those poor animals? What if the dire wolves got them?

A bell's clanging carried faintly up the hill, usually chiming a suppertime song but now used as a signal.

"Peter, how long do you think we have—?"

A hand closed around her ankle, and Sigrid screamed. Her heart jumped, and she turned to kick the monster away.

Only it wasn't a monster.

On the ground, Roland had dropped his bale and collapsed. He reached for her, trying to grab her again. Sweat trickled down his face. "Sigrid," he croaked. "It—hurts—"

"Roland!" She climbed down, pulse picking up, and knelt at his side. "What happened? Where does it hurt?"

Had he been shot by a hidden enemy?

"I—need—mouth-to-mouth resuscitation," he said, rolling dramatically on his back.

Sigrid gaped, absorbing his words. Then she cuffed him on the head, irritated at where his thoughts went at a time like this. "You turd!"

He reached for her, mustering up the most pleading expression she'd seen in someone who wasn't a dog. Muted laughter came from the other hands. No wonder they hadn't come closer to help.

She ignored them all, refusing to laugh and play games right now, and climbed again to adjust the hay bales.

When something grazed her ankle again, she kicked out. "Stop it, Roland."

"I didn't!"

The touch came again, and she growled. "I said stop!"

When she looked down, a huge black paw with claws longer than her fingers swiped through a gap in the hay. For a moment, Sigrid could only stare as the paw retreated.

"Look out!" Peter grabbed the collar of her tunic and hauled her backward. She toppled over, landing unsteadily on her feet.

The black dire wolf rammed into the gate with rattling force, making a couple of hay bales tumble off. It closed its jaws around the iron bars with a loud *clack*. Its teeth, as big as Sigrid's fingers, glinted in the sunlight. A whiff of its putrid breath made her stomach roil.

The wolf from the vision.

Sigrid's heart thrummed. She looked past it to the empty field, breaths coming fast. How would they stop one wolf, let alone an entire pack? The animal was as big as Hestur, and judging by the swollen muscles underneath its shaggy coat, alarmingly more powerful.

"Peter?" Sigrid whispered. "Wh-What do we do?"

Why was there only one? Was this the start of the attack?

Around them, the stable hands backed away slowly, as if trying not to be seen. Roland whimpered and stepped closer to Sigrid.

Then the wolf threw its massive head back and howled.

In the distance, more howls answered.

This was it.

"We're under attack!" Sigrid's voice boomed across the yard, loud enough to reach every ear.

Everyone exploded into action, the valkyries responding first. With a collective cry and a whoosh of wings, those on the ground took flight, armed with their golden spears.

"Barricade the barns!" Peter shouted, and the stable hands ran to lock every door and window—except for Roland, who stayed at Sigrid's elbow.

More dire wolves appeared at the gate, now trying to climb and jump over it.

Sigrid wrapped her gloved hands around the nearest weapon she found—a sharp stone at her feet.

"Sigrid!" Roland pointed at the rock wall above their heads, where a gray snout and two paws peeked up. The wolf scrambled, snarled, and disappeared with a thump.

When it appeared again, nails scraping as it tried to get over the top, Sigrid hurled the rock. The beast yelped and fell back.

"Ha! Take that, beast!" Sigrid shouted. "Come on, Roland, find more rocks with me."

Peter ran over to them. "Fall back." The alarm in his voice was clear as he pointed. "We have to fall back."

Through a gap in the hay bales and beyond the gate, a pack of thirty or more dire wolves charged at them. At least two hundred Night Elves followed, maces and swords drawn. They moved like shadows, swift and silent, with an insubstantial air about them. As beings from the land of night, the elves had completely covered themselves from the sun with animal skull masks, clothes of black leather and chainmail, and thick boots and gloves.

No one knew what a Night Elf truly looked like.

Sigrid did *not* want to find out, so she followed Peter and Roland away from the gate to where the other stable hands were gathering near the stable.

The vision had shown that the army would bypass the village at the base of the hill, too intent on reaching their target—Vanahalla. The junior valkyries would be waiting for them, ready to defend the hall with everything they had.

When the sky darkened and the sound of wings shuddered through the air, Sigrid stopped and looked up. Her skin tingled, and she gasped at the fleet of winged white mares. It wasn't the juniors. These mares were flying *toward* Vanahalla in *V* formation.

Had the senior valkyries returned from Jotunheim?

A closer look revealed the riders' weapons were raised, and though they wore the same armor as the Vanaheim army, theirs was rough and tarnished. Some were painted black.

Sigrid's heart lodged in her throat.

Enemy valkyries.

CHAPTER SIX

THE ENEMY VALKYRIE

Sigrid shook her head, mouth dry. Valkyries fighting against Vanaheim? This was unheard of. Valkyries were supposed to serve this world, not attack it. But another world must have had valkyries—a place allied with Night Elves and dire wolves.

Peter shielded his eyes with a gloved hand. "Those aren't our troops!"

Sigrid's stomach roiled, and she covered her mouth with one hand.

"Where did they come from?" Roland asked, sounding more confused than afraid.

Sigrid's pulse picked up. If enemy valkyries were in the air, that meant the junior valkyries would be too busy to fend off the Night Elves and dire wolves on the ground.

"You three, get inside! Now!" General Eira roared from above, pointing to the barn with her spear.

Peter pulled Sigrid's arm, and they ran after Roland.

The enemy valkyries cast a shadow over them, and their own valkyries met the attack head-on. The sky became a clash of winged horses and valkyrie war cries.

Sigrid kept running.

She looked back in time to see the army collide with the iron gate. Elves attacked the hinges with maces. Wolves reached through to tear apart the hay bales. The junior valkyries had to multitask, hurling spears downward while fighting the opponents in the sky. After every throw, they summoned their spears back with open palms.

When they reached the barn, they closed the main doors and joined the others in peeking through a window. Sigrid panted as the battle unfolded outside.

Frustration churned inside her, making her hands tremble with the need to take action. As she watched, the girls missed too many shots. They might have spent their lives in training, but they were still juniors, and they hadn't experienced a real battle.

She should be helping. She practiced every night, and she could run a spear through a target and summon it back as well as any of them. How pissed would the general be if Sigrid grabbed a weapon and galloped out there?

Sigrid hissed. "They're firing too slowly," she said, waving an arm. "If they break formation once in a while, they'll be able to hit more."

"They're more effective as a team," Peter said, keeping calm as always. "See how they're keeping everyone contained?"

Yes, they'd formed a half moon around the attackers, but they were wasting time trying to stay in formation when they could have been hitting more targets.

Sigrid rolled her eyes. "They're acting like they're doing training drills."

"It's not about getting more kills. It's about strategy." Peter pointed through the window. "Do you see how big that army is?"

As if the god of mischief had heard him, a metallic groan rent the air, and the gate broke, falling over the hay bales to form a ramp. The elves wasted no time climbing up. The black wolf from the vision leaped over and hit the ground on its shaggy paws. It took in the scene and charged onward, snarling.

"No!" Sigrid stepped toward the barn aisle, but Peter blocked her way. She tried to sidestep him, but he moved again. "Let me get Hestur."

"Don't be reckless."

"Look," Roland said. "They have it under control."

The valkyries swooped lower, their mares' wings beating a windstorm over the dirt and turning the field into a brown haze. The wolves and Night Elves had to use the gate to get through, and with that as a bottleneck, the valkyries could focus their efforts.

"We can help stop them from getting past the stables," Sigrid said. "We can use pitchforks, hammers—anything!"

Roland was already shaking his head.

Peter looked into her eyes, the way he'd done many times before when she wanted to do something reckless.

"We *can* help," Sigrid pleaded.

Someone screamed near the gate. A white wolf charged past Ylva and went for Gunni. It leaped into the air, snapping at her mare's belly. The mare snorted, striking back with such fury that Gunni was nearly unseated.

Sigrid gasped. "Oda!"

Bile rose up her throat at the reminder of the vision. It had shown a mare falling from the sky. No matter how vile the juniors had been to her, none of them deserved that fate.

Forget what Peter thought. The valkyries needed help.

Sigrid bolted down the barn aisle to search for weapons. Peter let out a resigned growl.

At the far end, Hestur whinnied, no doubt recognizing her footsteps. He probably wanted to know why he was alone here while something exciting went on outside.

"You've got to stay here, buddy. It's not safe—ha!" Sigrid's eyes fell upon a metal shovel. Swinging this at someone's head would do damage. Plus, it was encrusted in years' worth of horse poop, which would make it more satisfying when she hit a Night Elf in the face.

"I've got hooks," Peter shouted from the hay room, and a rush of fondness filled Sigrid at his change of heart. She ran over with her shovel. He held three hay hooks in each hand, like he'd sprouted metal claws. "Want one?"

"You fight like that. I've got a poop shovel."

"Perfect. Let's…" He faltered, gaze snapping toward the wooden wall.

Beyond it, a gust of wind and a clatter of hooves rose—the sound of a valkyrie landing. Footsteps pounded, and several voices spoke at once, too muffled to discern words.

Sigrid and Peter raced for the grimy window, ducking low. Right outside, a valkyrie wearing tarnished armor stood before two elves, shouting them down.

When Sigrid caught the word "princess," she sucked in a breath. Peter's eyes widened. Just like Vala suspected, and like so many years ago, a mysterious army had come to kidnap the princess of Vanaheim.

They will fail.

Hands clenched around the shovel, jaw set, she took in their opponents. The elves appeared more substantial while standing still—like stout, strong humans, made more imposing by the animal skulls covering their heads. Their black leather, chainmail, and thick swords looked heavy enough to make them sluggish, but Sigrid knew better after seeing them move.

As her gaze fell to the valkyrie, her insides swooped, like the girl had caught her off guard. She had a cunning, calculating look, with black-lined eyes and a downturn in her lips. Beneath the tarnished valkyrie armor and helmet, her skin was a warm beige, and her long black hair rippled in the daylight.

The winged mare beneath her pranced in excitement, and the

girl reined her in with lean, muscular arms. There was an unusual marking on the mare—a reddish-brown patch sweeping down her shoulder, like a dense cluster of freckles.

"I'll lead the others around back," the girl said. Her voice was low, rough. "Keep them occupied here…"

Her words became muffled by her mare's stomping hooves and the distant clash of battle. Sigrid pressed her face as close to the window as she could manage, trying to hear.

One of the elves said something, which she again missed.

"…horse, and probably among these valkyries…" the girl said.

Sigrid's heart beat faster. What were they planning? Carefully, she reached up and seized the handle on the window.

Peter inhaled sharply and shook his head. She put a finger to her lips and turned the latch. The window was sticky. She pushed harder. It opened with a *pop*.

Through it, the Night Elf nearest them snapped his head toward the sound.

Sigrid jerked back out of sight and held her breath.

"Klaus," the valkyrie snapped. "You listening? I can't go for the Eye unless you've got everyone's focus on you. Don't let me down."

Sigrid peeked back out the window.

The valkyrie carried herself proudly, chin high like Ylva and Gunni—born with a sense of entitlement, hardly living in a way that earned it.

Sigrid's insides soured. The way that girl snapped at the elves, rolled her eyes at them, looked down at them from her perch, was no different from the way the juniors treated her.

The elf rubbed the chin of its skull mask. "Uh, do you know which tower the princess is in, Mariam?"

"For gods' sake, it doesn't matter. It's enough that they think we're going after her."

"Right, right."

"So keep the fight at the gate, even if you break their defense, all right?" She waited until the others nodded. "Don't mess this up. We're not going back to Helheim without it."

Sigrid's gasp was masked by a war cry somewhere distant.

The valkyrie, Mariam, whirled her mare toward the hall. "Go!"

The two elves dispersed, blurring as they picked up speed.

Helheim. The vast underworld ruled by the goddess Hel. The army was from the realm of the dead, and they were here to steal the Eye of Hnitbjorg.

"They're not really after the royal family?" Peter said, voice high.

Sigrid leaped to her feet. "We have to tell someone. They'll be guarding the princess, but it's Vala who's in danger."

He stood, hay hooks between his fingers. "Who? Everyone's fighting!"

Sigrid let out a harsh breath and paced. Without the Eye of Hnitbjorg, what was Vanaheim? The Eye's visions and prophetic wisdom were what gave Vanaheim significance in the nine worlds. The stone was made from the rock salt of the legendary mountain Hnitbjorg, and nothing else like it existed in the cosmos.

They couldn't allow it to fall into enemy hands.

Valkyrie or not, Sigrid was from Vanaheim, and she had a duty.

She dropped the poop shovel, flung off her thick leather gloves, and ran for the tack room. *Time for a real weapon.*

"Hestur, come!"

Peter groaned. "Sigrid, don't…"

While she grabbed her helmet and a golden spear, Hestur leaned his head over his stall door and unlocked it. He let himself out and stepped into the aisle in time for Sigrid to run over and vault onto his back. No time for tacking up.

"If General Eira catches you, she'll feed you to the dire wolves," Peter said—though he was helpfully putting on Hestur's halter.

"Just open the door, Peter."

He hesitated for a fraction of time before passing Sigrid the lead rope and running to the rear barn door—respecting her choice and maybe even believing in her. Gratitude warmed her chest as he grabbed the handle and heaved it open, rolling it along its track.

Hestur snapped to attention, skin quivering beneath Sigrid's legs.

"Yah!"

Sigrid barely had time to clench her calves around his ribs as he lunged into a gallop. Jolted by the power, she tried to hold steady as his hooves clattered over the barn aisle.

They burst into the sunlight, the sounds of battle rushing past her ears, and raced toward Vanahalla. Hestur was as alert as ever, responding to the subtlest turn of her body.

Overhead, Mariam and her oddly marked mare soared toward the hall's golden towers, as silent and unnoticed as a barn owl leaving to hunt. She would reach the hall before them, and it would be too late to spread the warning to protect Vala.

Not too late to stop Mariam.

Sigrid grinned, adrenaline sparking through her veins. With the spear in one hand and Hestur's lead rope in the other, she leaned closer to her horse's neck.

"Let's get her."

CHAPTER SEVEN

REFURBISHING
THE SEER'S TOWER

Sigrid and Hestur left the battle behind, where dust whirled and war cries rose as the valkyries fended off the flow of attackers. Flying ahead, Mariam and her white mare disappeared among the golden towers of Vanahalla.

No one else knew this was all a decoy. They wouldn't be ready.

Sigrid asked Hestur to go faster, gripping the spear and hoping they made it on time. He was fresh and responsive as he powered up the hill for the second time that day, each long stride flowing from his limbs into hers.

In the courtyard, she pulled the lead rope and reined him to a stop. All courtiers had barricaded themselves inside the hall, every door shut tight. The golden statues lingered like ghosts, the sky devoid of signs of Mariam. The valkyries who had been sent up here were obviously elsewhere, bringing the royals to safety or guarding them somewhere secret.

Only the sound of Hestur's blowing nostrils filled her ears.

Then a gentle clatter above snagged her attention.

Mariam's winged mare stood on the conical roof of the Seer's tower. A pure white vision with that strange reddish mark on her shoulder, she splayed her legs on the steep slope, beating her wings left and right for balance. Her rider was gone.

Burgundy curtains flapped through an open window right below.

Mariam must have climbed inside.

"Go," Sigrid said, urging Hestur to gallop the last few strides across the courtyard.

At the base of the tower, she jumped off and ran to the wooden door. It was locked and barred with iron. No amount of pulling, rattling, and kicking would budge it.

Sigrid cursed, frustration tightening in her gut. Whether or not she was allowed inside, she had to get up there. Mariam was about to steal the most valuable relic in Vanaheim, and no one was here to stop her.

Hestur stood waiting for command. His tricks had always been for fun, not for battle. They were an excuse to say to Peter, "Look what Hestur learned today!"

Heart pounding, she seized the lead rope and backed him toward the wooden door. "Ready to put your skills to use?"

He nickered.

With the spear, she tapped his hocks. "Kick!"

Hestur kicked his back legs, slamming them into the wooden door with enough force to make the hinges groan.

"Good boy. Kick!"

She tapped his hocks again. The second kick popped the lock and sent the door crashing open.

"Good, Hestur! Wait here." She patted his haunches on her way past and left him looking pleased with himself.

Inside was dimmer than expected, with dark stone walls instead of shimmering gold and only a square of natural light coming through a rectangular window across from her. Beyond it, the moat churned, muddy and opaque. The air clung to her skin, damp, chilly, and smelling like soil.

Sigrid shivered. *Grim.* Was this all the legendary hall

amounted to?

Something thumped overhead.

She hurried silently through the space, spear in hand. When she found the spiral stairs that led up the tower, she climbed them two at a time. The hollow silence rang in her ears and made her tense.

At the top landing, she stopped with a gasp. "Vala!"

The old woman was slumped on the stairs, clutching her stomach. Blood oozed between her fingers.

Sigrid made to drop to her knees, but Vala shook her head. Her icy blue eyes were wide and protuberant, her face as gray as death. She pointed to the nearby door.

"She's—taking it."

The wooden door sat open, leading to a candlelit room.

"The Eye?" Sigrid whispered.

Vala nodded.

Sigrid nodded back and then raced through the doorway, spear ready. "Stop!"

Warm air wafted at her, spicy with incense. Overflowing bookshelves lined the circular room, tapestries hanging between them on the stone walls. A threadbare, dark red rug covered most of the wooden floor. A desk full of trinkets, scales, and books sat beneath the far window.

At the window, burgundy curtains flapping on either side of her, Mariam spun and sank into a half crouch, spear at the ready to defend herself. Something about the graceful movement froze Sigrid in place. It was the way the daylight illuminated Mariam from behind, framing her like one of the gold statues in the courtyard. She narrowed her eyes, her fiery expression at odds with the soft curves of her face.

For a moment, Sigrid forgot why she was there. But the pale pink, semitranslucent stone dangling from Mariam's hand snapped her focus back. Though Sigrid had never seen it before, she knew what it was—the Eye of Hnitbjorg.

Sigrid pointed her spear. "Don't move."

Mariam's gaze traced over her. Her lips curled into a haughty sneer that sent a blaze of some unnamed feeling through Sigrid's middle.

"Sorry. I've got somewhere to be." Mariam spun back to the window, nimble on her feet.

Sigrid tightened her grip on the spear. The prospect of using it and drawing blood twisted her insides, but she had no choice. She wanted to be a valkyrie, and a valkyrie didn't fear blood.

With a roar, she threw it, aiming for the vulnerable space between the armor at the back of the girl's leg.

Mariam leaped onto the windowsill, pulling out of the line of fire just in time. The spear hit the stone wall and clattered to the floor.

Sigrid cursed.

Mariam teetered over the courtyard, hesitating. She looked back at Sigrid with her brow furrowed. "Who are you?" she said in that low, rough voice.

Sigrid opened her palm to invite the weapon back. It soared into her hand. "I'm a defender of Vanaheim. Here to stop you from stealing what's ours."

She raised her arm to throw again, but Mariam hurled her own spear, and she had to duck to avoid the pointed tip. When Mariam opened her palm, Sigrid lunged for the weapon, catching it before it could return. Mariam's spear was finely honed, sharp enough to draw blood if she wasn't careful. The hilt was scratched, the raw layer beneath the polished exterior threatening to show through.

Sigrid held tight, resisting its pull toward its owner.

Mariam rolled her eyes. "I meant, like, what's your—"

Sigrid hurled both spears at Mariam, aiming higher this time.

Mariam ducked, falling back inside, and flung her hands over her head. The weapons flew past her face and out the window. Her glare could melt iron. "What is wrong with you?"

Sigrid ignored her and summoned the spears back with a shaking hand. She had to finish this battle, and the only way to do that was by incapacitating the girl who was trying to steal the Eye. If they could capture her, question her, they could learn where this army came from and why they wanted Vanaheim's most precious relic.

Her golden spear whipped through the window and back into her palm. It felt *good* to use a weapon. But where was the second one?

"First rule of spears," Mariam said, opening her hand. "You can't summon one that belongs to someone else, unless it's given willingly."

When her chipped spear flew through the window, she swiped it out of the air like a cat catching a butterfly and twirled it over her forearm for show.

Sigrid didn't give her time to settle and simply fired.

Mariam dove behind the desk, and the weapon smashed into an hourglass, sending a cloud of sand into the air.

Not good enough.

Sweat prickled on Sigrid's forehead, and her lungs screamed for a rest. She opened her palm, but not before Mariam got to her feet and threw her spear.

Sigrid flattened on the rug to dodge it. The sound of rock cascading to the floor filled the room, followed by the *whoosh* of the weapons soaring back to their owners.

From the floor, Sigrid aimed at Mariam's exposed shoulder, but her shot missed, carving a chunk out of a reading desk.

Mariam scanned the destruction. "A passable effort for a girl who isn't a valkyrie."

"I could say the same to you." Sigrid jumped to her feet, snatched her spear from the air, and fired another shot.

Mariam ducked, and it cracked the shelf behind her. Several

books and a glass figurine crashed to the floor.

"Why aren't you one? That's your brown horse down there, right?"

Heat rose to Sigrid's face so fast that when she threw, her poorly aimed attack impaled a leather-bound book several feet away from Mariam.

Sigrid's arms trembled as she recalled the spear. The fight had drained her too fast, like blood gushing from an open wound. But she couldn't give up. She had to retrieve the Eye.

She paced to the side, hoping to get closer. "I wasn't aware valkyries had joined forces with dire wolves and Night Elves."

Mariam's expression hardened. "And *I* wasn't aware Vanaheim had ground troops," she said, wiping sweat from her brow. "Yet here we are."

Sigrid ducked in time. The spear made a *zing* across the top of her helmet. She held back on throwing another shot. With her aim getting worse, it would be better to save her energy for one final throw.

"What does Helheim want with the Eye?" she asked, desperate to figure out what was going on.

Mariam's mouth opened in surprise, but she regained her composure. "What makes you think we're from Helheim?"

Sigrid cheered inside at having caught her unaware. "I know more than you think, *Mariam*."

Mariam studied her, a flash of confusion on her face, which she quickly covered up with a taunting smile. "Wish I could stay and explain, but—" She bolted for the open window.

"No!" Sigrid lunged for her, crossing the room with long strides. She wrapped her arms around Mariam's waist from behind, and they toppled to the floor.

One of the burgundy curtains tore in Mariam's grip as she tried to haul herself up. "Gah! Let go!"

"Give—me—that." Sigrid held her tighter and grabbed for the

stone, nails scraping the girl's wrist.

Mariam held it out of reach, using her other hand to push Sigrid's face away.

Sigrid dodged her hand and shimmied up, pinning Mariam with her knees. She grabbed both wrists and slammed the girl's arms to the wooden floor. They were both sweaty, Sigrid's palms slipping on Mariam's skin.

They paused, gasping for breath.

Their eyes locked on each other.

Then Mariam looked toward her spear, which she'd dropped in the scuffle.

Sigrid held tight. With her hands pinned, Mariam wouldn't be able to throw it. But Sigrid couldn't grab her own spear, either, not without letting go. She tried to reach with her boot and drag it closer. "Give me back the Eye and I won't poke yours out."

Mariam's nostrils flared. "Why should I be afraid of a girl who isn't even a real valkyrie?"

Sigrid ground her teeth, the taunt igniting something inside her like flint on steel. She let go, snatched the spear, and held it to Mariam's face before the girl could react. At her stunned expression, Sigrid's insides coiled with pleasure.

Though she had no intention of poking Mariam's eye out, she brought the spear closer to the girl's face. Mariam squeezed her eyes shut as the spear touched her cheekbone.

Sigrid snarled, pressing until a droplet of blood came out. "You tell me."

With a shriek of pain, Mariam let go of the Eye. It fell from her hand and rolled across the floor.

Sigrid dove for it. Her fingers closed around the cool, rough stone.

Relief was short-lived as the stone started to burn hot in her hand.

At once, her vision honed to a point, a whoosh of light.

The room dissolved, and in its place, a dark, dry landscape formed. Red sand steamed. Lava bubbled. Black rock blistered the sand like battle scars.

A fleet of valkyries appeared mid-charge, mouths open in silent war cries—Gunni, Ylva, Edith, Runa, and the rest of Vanaheim's junior valkyries. Their spears pointed forward as their winged mares carried them above the fiery ground. They moved as if time had slowed, each flap of wings taking many times longer than normal. And with them, flying in their midst on her red-marked mare, was Mariam. The mare's nostrils flared with the effort of the charge.

Below the army, several strides in the lead, a stallion galloped over the sand, his coat steel gray, his mane and tail coal black. He was sure-footed over the rough terrain, balanced on eight legs. Stretching out his four front legs, he made long, powerful strides that tore divots in the stone beneath his hooves. His nostrils flared, fiery-red on the insides. His eyes rolled wildly.

Odin's infamous eight-legged horse, Sleipnir, led the charge with a valkyrie on his back.

Sigrid's chest constricted, air leaving her lungs.

It's...it's me.

Sigrid was riding Sleipnir. She was leading the valkyrie charge.

CHAPTER EIGHT

THE WORST
VALKYRIE EVER

With the same whoosh of light, the vision disappeared. Sigrid gasped for air on the dark red rug in the Seer's tower. The Eye of Hnitbjorg lay on the floor nearby, a tendril of smoke rising from it. Her palm stung where the stone had burned her skin.

Mariam sat up, shaking her head as if to regain her senses.

"What was—? Did you see that?" Sigrid said.

Mariam's expression clouded. She pushed a hand to the droplet of blood on her cheekbone from where Sigrid had pressed her spear. "Very funny," she said, glancing at the floor.

Sigrid followed her gaze and dove for the Eye.

Mariam swiped a leg and kicked her hand out of the way.

"Ow!" Sigrid ignored the pain and reached for it again.

But Mariam snatched up the stone first and backed away. She yelped, tossing it between her palms as she made for the window. "This thing is scorching—Aesa!"

Sigrid scrambled to her feet. "Don't!"

On the window ledge, Mariam gathered her legs under her like a frog and leaped from the tower.

Sigrid ran across the room and leaned out to see her land

on the back of her winged mare. They made a sharp turn away from Vanahalla.

Far below, Hestur waited by the tower door. She could whistle him over, but no way could she jump out the window and land on him from this height. Besides, she would never catch up to Mariam. Hestur was lightning fast, but galloping full-out would be impossible on the rough landscape and steep slope.

Don't let her get away.

Not now, when she'd come so close to proving she could defend their world as well as any other valkyrie. If she caught this enemy, brought her in, and saved the Eye, the act of heroism might finally earn her respect from General Eira and the valkyries.

Sigrid opened her palm, and her spear slapped into it. Mariam was halfway across the courtyard. Knocking her off her mare would require perfect aim. But surrendering wasn't an option. Her future as a valkyrie was at stake—and possibly the future of Vanaheim.

Her arms ached and twinged in spasms that ran all the way up to her shoulders. She'd worked herself to exhaustion.

One more. You can do one more throw.

Valkyrie or stable hand? Firing this shot was the only option if she wanted to change her fate.

She gripped the spear tightly in a trembling, sweating palm.

Mariam fumbled the Eye, the stone evidently still hot after the vision.

Sigrid aimed, focusing with everything she had, and—

She threw it as hard as she could.

"No!" She gasped.

The shot was wrong. It was too low, too hard.

Her knees weakened as it soared over the courtyard.

The spear struck Mariam's winged mare in the haunches. The horse bellowed. It wasn't a whinny, a snort, or any other sound Sigrid had heard a horse make. It was the most terrible sound she'd ever heard. It was a wail of pain, fear, despair—an animal that knew it had been fatally shot.

Sigrid choked back a sob, holding onto the windowsill with shaking arms.

The mare went limp, wings pulling skyward as she plummeted. Mariam screamed, separating from the mare as they fell.

Sigrid ran, heart in her throat, sweeping past Vala and bumping into the stone walls, descending the steps as fast as she could. Her insides plummeted alongside Mariam and her horse. Any moment, she would hit the cobblestones, and she would close her eyes and slip into unconsciousness.

"I didn't mean to," she said, gasping back her horror. "Please don't be dead. Please."

She'd meant to incapacitate. She wasn't a killer.

Sigrid burst through the door and shielded her eyes from the blinding daylight. The courtyard was empty—except for the bodies lying at the far end.

She sprinted over.

I can help. I can make this right.

Mariam lay on the cobblestones, propped on one arm, wheezing for breath. *Alive.* She coughed, wiping her bloody nose with a trembling arm.

But beside her…

Sigrid covered her mouth, remorse cascading over her.

Mariam's dark eyes locked onto her mare—her lifelong partner, her closest comrade, a piece of her soul. Gone.

Sigrid grasped at her chest, a painful tightness forming there. She couldn't breathe. A valkyrie never killed a winged horse. Never something so pure. Without their mare, a valkyrie was empty and broken, the purest part of them gone from this world.

The silence broke when Mariam screamed, her agony ringing in Sigrid's ears. She fell over her horse's head, shaking with sobs. "Aesa! No! Come back!"

A weight settled over Sigrid and threatened to send her tumbling onto the cobblestones. Her brain went hazy and detached. The sun beat down on them, but her skin grew cold the longer Mariam sobbed.

Footsteps pounded closer.

A Night Elf in a fanged mask stopped before them.

Sigrid observed him, feeling disconnected from what was happening. She had no energy left to fight and no intention of retrieving the weapon that had taken a life. Would its summoning magic even work? The hilt looked dead, dull, where it was embedded in the mare.

The elf closed his fingers around the small and pink rock at his feet. The Eye of Hnitbjorg. It had been lying next to the fragments of Mariam's spear, which must have shattered on impact. The elf turned his mask to the mare sprawled over the cobblestones and then to Mariam, who heaved with sobs over the body.

He did not move to help her.

A shout split the air overhead. Two valkyries descended. Ylva and Gunni dove at the elf, their mares' hooves aiming to strike him on the back and head. But they missed. The elf moved in a blur, rolling away from the attack.

He took one last look at Mariam, then fled with the speed and silence of a shadow, taking the Eye of Hnitbjorg with him.

"The Eye," Sigrid said, too quietly. "He's got the Eye."

Her voice was broken, her body weak.

Somewhere distant, a dire wolf howled. The long, chilling sound swelled across the hillside as more wolves joined in. A signal. They'd completed their mission and were no doubt retreating.

The army was leaving Mariam behind. Was she as good as dead without her mare?

Hooves clip-clopped and wing gusts blew Sigrid's cold, sweaty tunic against her back.

"What happened?" General Eira said, addressing the gathering crowd.

Sigrid hadn't noticed their approach. She couldn't bear to look at anyone.

I killed a winged mare. And nearly her rider.

A valkyrie wasn't supposed to be bloodthirsty.

A gruff voice said, "That elf just made off with something. Your junior valkyries chased him—"

"He took something?" General Eira said. "What was it?"

Sigrid stepped closer. Sweat dampened her clothes, making her shiver, and her brain floated in a haze. "The Eye of Hnitbjorg," she said, lips numb. "Vala needs help. She's injured near the top of the Seer's tower."

Footsteps scuffled as people ran to give aid.

General Eira turned her attention to Mariam, who lay sobbing over her mare. The girl trembled, her skin bloody and raw from hitting the cobblestones.

"Lock this girl in the lower ward," said the general, lip curling in disgust. "Keep her there for questioning. Nice work, Ylva and Gunni."

Ylva and Gunni sat taller on their magnificent white mares, noses turned up with pride. But Ylva's mount pawed nervously, trying to back away from the dead mare on the cobblestones.

Sigrid drew a ragged breath. It didn't ease the pain in her chest.

Armored guards grabbed Mariam and hauled her off. She struggled, trying to get back. Her screams were hysterical, rupturing as they passed her lips. Her legs swung and her black hair flew. "No! Let me go! Please don't take me away from her—"

A guard punched her in the gut, making her splutter.

As they dragged her away, her eyes found Sigrid's. Behind her tears came a flash of deep, murderous hatred. The words tore from her throat like a clap of thunder. "I'll kill you! I will kill—"

The guard silenced her with another punch to the gut.

Sigrid gasped, like she'd received the same punch.

Mariam's stuttering breaths and sobs faded as the guards dragged her away. She continued to scream, the word "*Aesa*" echoing off the gold towers, pummeling Sigrid from every direction.

General Eira turned Drifa, looking down at Sigrid from what seemed like a mile up. "This is what happens when you don't follow the rules. You're lucky you weren't killed."

Sigrid had no words. She stood trembling and sweating, heavy with exhaustion.

"Return to your duties, stable hand." With a last hard look, the general took flight.

Ylva and Gunni leaned into each other, whispering and shooting glances in Sigrid's direction. They'd no doubt share what happened with the rest of the juniors and devise new ways to torment her.

But nothing they did or said could make Sigrid suffer more than she was right now.

She stepped back once, then again, until she ran into something. She turned and found Hestur's blurry brown shape behind her tears. He raised his nose to her face, like he was trying to smell what was wrong.

"You'll have to help me get on, buddy," she said thickly, touching his knee with her boot. He bent on one knee, lowering his wither to waist-height, and Sigrid climbed onto his back with shaking limbs.

Moving at a walk, Hestur began the long descent to the stables. They left the scene behind, Mariam's screams rippling like a shiver down Sigrid's back.

The Eye was gone. The Night Elves had taken it.

And despite her efforts, despite spilling the blood of a winged mare in her attempt, Sigrid had failed to save it.

CHAPTER NINE

THE IMPOSSIBLE VISION

The Eye of Hnitbjorg never lied.

So why did Sigrid's vision make no sense?

All night, the impossible image galloped through her dreams—the junior valkyries, Mariam, and herself riding Sleipnir, charging through a red-and-black world.

Sigrid quickly gave up on the restless sleep to try and figure out the details. The barren lava fields could be in Muspelheim, the realm of the Fire Giants. But why would valkyries be there? Maybe it was a dark circle of Helheim. The dire wolf and Night Elf army had come from there, after all. Mariam too. But how could her mare have been alive and unharmed after what Sigrid had done? The dead went to Helheim, and once they crossed the gates, there was no leaving.

Even more shocking, the vision showed Sigrid charging as an ally, even leading them.

And she'd been riding Odin's mount.

Sleipnir.

The most powerful horse in all the nine worlds.

It made no sense for a stable hand to ride him, but Sigrid couldn't stop the thrill that ran down her spine every time she thought about it.

The faint glow of sunrise on the stable's windows meant she had to get up and face the world. She groaned and covered her eyes with her hands, not ready to deal with her chores and whatever the valkyries had to say.

Hestur had other ideas. He persistently sniffed her face until she labored out of her hammock and began her chores. Even with all the daily work and training she did, every muscle screamed at her, stiff and heavy from the fight.

The vision still lingered in her mind's eye as she changed into wool trousers and a loose red tunic. How did the Eye work? Was that vision going to come true no matter what?

Sigrid shook her head and pushed those thoughts down, burning with shame. She'd wanted to help, but all she'd done was create chaos. Yesterday's disaster proved that the gods had given her Hestur and not a winged mare for a reason.

I don't deserve to be a valkyrie. Look what happened when I tried to act like one.

She'd ensured the vision Vala showed them in the stable came true, right to the end, dead mare and all.

Sigrid's eyes stung with unshed tears as she focused on her chores. If this was all she was good for, the least she could do was finish them properly.

Peter stopped by as she pulled an empty wheelbarrow into the feed room. "I heard Vala's going to be all right. Her injuries aren't so bad."

She let go of the wheelbarrow, palm aching where it had been burned by the Eye, and faced him. She swallowed around the gathering knot in her throat. Thank the gods Vanaheim still had its Seer. "That's...that's good."

He nodded, studying her. "General Eira told me to give you more work today as punishment. But given that you haven't noticed the piece of hay stuck to your face, I think it's safe to say you're suffering enough."

He had no idea.

She grunted and rubbed an arm across her cheek. Unsure if she could lift any bales this morning, she said, "I'll feed grain if you do hay."

He tilted his head and cast her a pitying smile before making for the hay room.

The horses pawed and whinnied as Sigrid trudged down the aisle with the wheelbarrow of grain. The chickens followed, clucking noisily and catching any bits that fell. At each stall, she measured a scoop, added that mare's supplements, and leaned over the door to dump it into her bucket. Each horse plunged her nose into the grain with enthusiasm, wings swishing.

A few junior valkyries wandered in groggily with their hair in matching topknots. Their loose, casual tunics and trousers probably meant General Eira had canceled the day's training.

Sigrid kept her head down and set about feeding the mares. Oda was first, and she bobbed her head as Sigrid measured the portions—*a spoonful of mineral salt and a pump of flaxseed oil*—and dumped it in her bucket.

"I hated shooting at another valkyrie," Runa said, and Sigrid almost dropped the bag of supplements. Runa plunked on the clay floor in front of Tobia, hugging a book close to her chest. Her mare leaned over the stall door with her lips flapping and tried to eat Runa's topknot.

Sigrid walked past, ignoring the twinge in her gut at Runa's words. In all the chaos, she'd forgotten that the junior valkyries would have gone through a traumatic fight, as well. Her stomach roiled.

She stopped at Roskva's stall and took a breath before measuring out the portions. *One scoop of valerian root and an apple cut into quarters.*

"We did the right thing," Ylva said, although her voice

trembled a bit before she cleared her throat. "Because of us, the royals are safe. The only thing missing is the Eye."

"The only thing?" Runa said, teary-eyed. "They're probably going to make *us* go get it back!"

Ylva pursed her lips. No one argued.

Sigrid stopped in her tracks. *Of course.* The realm in the vision *was* Helheim, and the juniors were there to retrieve the Eye of Hnitbjorg. But that didn't answer why Sigrid and Mariam had traveled with them or why Sigrid was on Sleipnir. How would she even get Sleipnir?

She hadn't told anyone about the vision the Eye had shown her—not even Peter—and keeping it a secret weighed on her more heavily by the minute. Just as Vala had a duty to share the visions she saw, Sigrid had a duty to share this one. Knowledge of the future was a power great enough to give Vanaheim its status among the nine worlds. Keeping prophetic knowledge to herself was irresponsible, even dangerous.

But she was afraid of what would happen if she shared it. While her actions yesterday proved she could never be a valkyrie, a part of her still ached for the vision to come true. The promise of charging at the head of the valkyries, riding the most powerful stallion to exist, put a longing in her chest like she'd never experienced.

If she followed the vision, it might be possible to find answers to the questions that had burned inside her for her whole life— who she was, her life's purpose, and whether a greater future awaited her. But if she told others that she saw herself riding with the valkyries, they would quash those hopes before she finished speaking.

Besides, what if she hadn't even seen the vision properly? What if it was skewed because she wasn't a real Seer or she missed an important detail?

In the next stall, Drifa whinnied. Sigrid shook her head at the mare's impatience and towed the wheelbarrow the short distance. *Two scoops of senior vitamins.*

Vala had spoken of the stone's temperature, of visions coming hot. When Sigrid touched the Eye, it had burned like a freshly boiled kettle. Did that mean it would happen soon, just like the attack? Was it possible for a vision to not come true at all?

Gunni groaned, breaking Sigrid's reverie. "How are we supposed to get the Eye back when we don't know where that army came from?"

"I thought we already established that they're from Helheim," Runa said. She gently pushed away Tobia, who had nibbled her topknot into a frizzy disaster resembling a mouse nest.

"Are you sure? They looked pretty alive to me."

"They *are* from Helheim." The words burst from Sigrid. She couldn't stay quiet any longer. "I overheard them talking."

Everyone turned to her, irritated as usual that she had the nerve to speak.

"This is a valkyrie conversation," Gunni said, face scrunched up more than normal as she glared.

"And our mares are hungry, if you don't mind," Ylva said, flapping her delicate arms in Sigrid's direction. "Or do you plan to kill them, too?"

The words hit Sigrid like an ice-cold waterfall.

A few valkyries gasped.

They all looked expectantly at Sigrid, apparently waiting for a retort. To her horror, her eyes burned, not just at the cruelty but at the fresh wave of shame crashing over her. She ground her teeth, gave a sharp nod, and continued her duties.

She'd never cried in this company and didn't plan to start now.

Sigrid grabbed the wheelbarrow, ready to move on, when the general appeared in the open barn doors.

"Juniors," General Eira said, marching into the barn with the rest of the junior valkyries in tow. "I've met with King Óleifr, and after much discussion, he's given the order." She paused, the weight of whatever she would say next clear in her eyes. "As this is a time-sensitive mission and we cannot wait for the seniors to return, you are to travel to Helheim and recover the Eye. If possible, find out who sent the army and why."

Runa and Ylva exchanged a dark look.

Sigrid's heart raced. The juniors would be in Helheim—one part of her vision coming true.

"I am confident in your training, but be cautious," General Eira said. "The goddess Hel is fair, but we don't know what happened to cause that army to attack us." She held up a scroll of parchment. "I've borrowed a map to help you find your way. *Do not* lose this."

"Yes, General," several girls said, but only a few managed to do it without their voices wavering.

The general unfurled the map, and everyone gathered close.

Sigrid rocked from foot to foot, the urge to listen battling the obligation to keep feeding the horses. If she told General Eira, even the immutable facts of a vision seemed unlikely to convince her to let Sigrid join the valkyries. Then again, what if she did take it seriously? Maybe the two of them and Vala could discuss what it all meant.

She imagined saddling up with the girls and leaving Vanaheim—the place she'd never left in all her sixteen years. She would take Hestur into the dangerous underworld and find Sleipnir, whatever that entailed. And then…what?

Was she supposed to conquer worlds, like Odin had?

She shuddered at the thought of war.

This is all so confusing.

Perhaps she could just pretend she hadn't seen the vision. The future could change, and maybe altering it was as simple as deciding not to tell anyone about it or follow it. She could stay a stable hand—

A chicken pecked at her trousers. Sigrid frowned at it for interrupting her planning and nudged it back with her boot.

Yes, she could stay here and do this job, where she would continue to get snapped at every day, teased, and treated like she was a class below every valkyrie her age. She would continue to wonder about her true potential.

A fire burned in her chest, and Sigrid almost laughed at the idea of remaining as she was. Now that she knew what future was possible, one where she led the valkyries on the most powerful stallion in the cosmos, she had to pursue it.

This was the destiny she had been searching for.

It was like Peter said. Her destiny was not to be a valkyrie, but something else entirely. It was to be the rider of Sleipnir.

Besides, Mariam's horse had been there, meaning there might be a way for Sigrid to fix what she'd done. If she had to enter Helheim alone and search for the mare, she'd do it.

Ignoring Mjöll, who swung her head impatiently in the next stall, Sigrid edged closer to the gathered valkyries. She craned her neck to see the map over everyone's heads.

"The spring of Hvergelmir will get you there," General Eira said. "King Óleifr has guaranteed you safe passage up and down it. Its mouth is to the north, beyond Myrkviðr. The journey is nothing you haven't trained for, but don't be overconfident."

Over their heads, the top part of the map was visible—Asgard, Vanaheim, and Alfheim, all connected to the mouth of the spring of Hvergelmir. Ylva's head masked the lower part, but Sigrid knew the Bifrost connected to Midgard.

"Can't we get there through Midgard?" Gunni said, sounding nervous.

"That takes too long," General Eira said. "Only go through Midgard if you can't get down the spring. Besides, Midgard or not, you'll still have to pass Garmr."

Sigrid's heart tripped upon hearing the name again. Hel's

guardian was not a creature many survived.

"Told you," Runa hissed. "I told you we'd have to fight Garmr!"

Ylva crossed her arms, nails digging into her biceps. "Do any other monsters guard the route to Helheim?"

She stepped back, and Sigrid had no time to dodge her.

Ylva bumped into Sigrid and whirled around, a sneer sliding in place when she realized who it was. "Are you eavesdropping?"

"General, Sigrid is eavesdropping!" Gunni yelled, her tone somewhat gleeful.

General Eira closed her eyes and inhaled deeply. When her tired blue eyes opened, they pinned Sigrid on the spot. "Sigrid, what are you hoping to hear from this conversation?"

"I just—" She huffed. Despite all the disdainful faces, she had to tell the general. "Can I talk to you?"

"Go ahead," General Eira said, giving no indication that she was ready to put down the map and step away from her team.

Sigrid did not want to unveil this in front of everyone, but given no choice, she drew a breath. "General, during the fight, I...I touched the Eye by accident when I was trying to stop Ma—the enemy valkyrie from taking it, and I saw a vision. I saw the junior valkyries."

The general's mouth fell open.

The valkyries stared at her.

Seizing the moment of silence, Sigrid plowed on. "T-They were charging somewhere that looked like Helheim. I think they were after the Eye of Hnitbjorg."

"Did it show you how they got it?" General Eira asked.

Shocked that she wasn't being dismissed, Sigrid said, "No, but the thing is, I was there, too. I was riding Sleipnir. And no, this isn't a trick to make me a valkyrie," she added fiercely as several valkyries shook their heads.

The general's eyes turned skyward, like she was praying for patience. "Then what are you asking?"

Sigrid swallowed. "I'm just…telling you what I saw."

"Riding with us means being a valkyrie," Ylva said.

"Why would *you* be riding Sleipnir?" Gunni asked, seemingly more confused about that detail.

Edith stepped closer. "Did the vision show you how to get past Garmr?"

"There was no vision!" Ylva flapped her arms. "She's making it up so we'll let her come with us."

"I'm not!" Sigrid said, standing tall despite their resolute faces. Her chest ached with the need to scream. "Ask Vala. She knows everything the Eye has ever shown."

"She knows everything she has *seen*," General Eira said. "Convenient she was not there to see this."

Fury ignited in Sigrid's stomach at the accusation.

"Even if you did see this, we have no reason to try and fulfill it," General Eira said. "For all we know, you saw the beginning of what might have been a lost battle."

Sigrid gaped at her. "But—but it came from the Eye! That means it's going to happen."

"If Sigrid saw us in Helheim," Edith said, twisting her fingers together, "she might be able to lead us there. Don't you think, General? The Eye of Hnitbjorg doesn't lie."

"The Eye doesn't," General Eira said, gazing back at the map.

Heat rushed to Sigrid's face at the implication.

The Eye didn't lie.

But Sigrid might.

CHAPTER TEN

REFUSING TO STAY PUT

Sigrid couldn't find the words to argue. Her arms trembled with the effort of not reacting. *Lie?* She never lied! No matter what they all thought, the vision she'd seen was real.

General Eira continued giving out instructions to the junior valkyries, clearly having finished the discussion and dismissed it as nonsense. Ylva and Gunni didn't miss the opportunity to smirk before turning their backs on Sigrid. Only Edith looked guilty as she moved away.

When Peter came back inside, the general snapped her fingers at him. "Saddle them up."

"Yes, General." Peter's eyes flicked to Sigrid, no doubt noticing her flushed face and rigid posture. The flash of pity in his eyes was infuriating.

"Valkyries," General Eira said over the flurry of activity, "I hope your education has stressed how important the Eye is to Vanaheim. Failure in retrieving it is not an option. The gods trusted us alone with prophetic knowledge. Remember King Fálki, who planned an assault on Alfheim and waited for the Eye to show him the outcome before deciding whether to go through with it. Imagine what the depraved souls from the lower realms might plan with this kind of power, and how vulnerable we will become without a means to see them coming."

With that dire warning, she gave a final nod at the gathered valkyries. "May the gods guide you on this journey."

Sigrid remained where she was, trembling with rage at being called a liar and being denied yet another opportunity. It would never end. No matter what she did, they would never allow her to be more than a stable hand.

She fed the remaining mares their grain, then grabbed the wheelbarrow with a white-knuckled grip and continued down the aisle. The burn on her palm was nothing next to every other feeling eclipsing it.

Around her, the other stable hands came in and rushed around with tack and brushes. The girls chatted excitedly, disappearing to change into their fitted white uniforms and returning to don their golden armor.

Peter kept looking her way, but Sigrid pretended not to notice. She just took her time putting away the bucket and supplements, not sure she should be near any mares with her temper burning hot as lava.

"Hi, Roland!" Gunni called out loudly enough to be heard all the way to the village.

Roland smoothly skirted around her to help Edith.

Sigrid almost smiled, but she couldn't. She was at a loss. She had to get to Helheim to fulfill that vision. But she couldn't force herself upon the valkyries. If she tried to follow in secret, she would lose them beneath the forest's canopy. And where exactly would she hide on the boat ride down the spring?

By the time General Eira rode her mare up to Vanahalla, Sigrid had no plan. She watched the V formation of white mares take flight, watched as they soared over the stone wall, up into the cloudy sky, and were gone.

Gone, without her.

Sigrid marched back to the barn before Peter or Roland, who'd caught wind of her mood, could come talk to her. Without more information about what she'd seen, she wouldn't be able to figure this out.

Vala knew more than anyone about the Eye, but she was probably resting after her injuries. Plus, a stable hand would never be allowed in the infirmary to see her. Unless she didn't need Vala. What about all those books in her tower? A library of knowledge lived on those shelves. Surely, they had information about Sleipnir, Hnitbjorg, and Helheim.

Sneaking into Vanahalla would be risky, but this was urgent. She needed to understand what that vision meant, and the Seer's tower held all the answers.

CHAPTER ELEVEN

BEING SNEAKY

Sneaking into the Seer's tower wasn't bad, exactly. The point wasn't to steal or damage anything. Sigrid just needed some answers, and she couldn't wait for morning or for Vala to be well enough to receive her.

It'll be fine.

Sigrid told herself this over and over as Hestur descended to the water, hooves sliding in the mud. Nightfall, along with his dark coat, provided all the camouflage they needed. The entrance she'd chosen to slip through was a rectangular window at the base of the Seer's tower, which meant crossing the moat surrounding the hall.

The moat was intended to stop enemies from entering the hall unchecked. A natural obstacle in the path of an army. No one would expect to find a stable hand and a little brown horse swimming across at a leisurely pace.

At least Sigrid hoped so. If they had guards keeping watch, they were done for.

Hestur dipped into the cool water and began paddling, taking them confidently across. He loved swimming, and though he seemed hesitant at first about why Sigrid asked him to swim in the middle of the night, he paddled on with enthusiasm.

On the other side, she grabbed his mane as he heaved himself out. He stopped and blew his nostrils, shaking his head.

She clamped her legs tighter. "No, don't shake—"

He shook. His body rattled with such force that Sigrid was sure her brain and guts jostled around inside her. She stifled a laugh. Hestur craned his neck to peer back at her.

Sigrid grinned. "Let's go."

They climbed the muddy hill and stopped at the base of the golden tower. Sigrid didn't see any light coming from the upper windows, but the one she needed to climb through had a faint glow. Hopefully, it was a light left unattended and not someone waiting inside. The window was an arm's length above her head, so she would need to stand on Hestur's back to climb through.

No problem. They'd done this a hundred times, reaching for the juiciest apples, cleaning cobwebs from rafters, and putting baby swallows back in their nests. *Easy.*

She nudged him sideways, asking him to stand parallel to the window. The bank offered no flat ground to stand on, so he ended up splayed as he stood sideways on the muddy slope.

"Good boy," she whispered, letting go of the reins. "Wait here."

She stood on his back, a little wobbly on the slanted ground, and reached for the window. With a grunt, she pulled herself up.

A corridor was on the other side. The glow she'd spied came from the torch at the far end. She held still for a moment, waiting to see if anyone walked by. When no one did, she pulled herself the rest of the way. Her boots hit the stone floor lightly.

Silence.

Stepping carefully, she moved toward the stairs and climbed up to Vala's study.

Her pulse pounded in her ears, and her chest constricted with the fear of being caught. The tower had to be empty, right? No one was allowed in except the Seer, and right now, she was in the infirmary with serious injuries.

Drip, drip, drip.

Sigrid stopped mid-step and followed the sound. Her trousers were leaving moat water all over Vanahalla's floors, an easy trail that anyone could follow. So much for not making a mess.

Too late now.

She'd have to hurry.

At the top, Vala's door was ajar again.

Sigrid pushed it open and peeked inside.

Lit by moonlight, the room was as she'd left it, torn apart by the fight, with books and furniture strewn everywhere. She tiptoed as she moved farther in. The spicy incense lingered, a ghost of what it'd been earlier. A lantern lay sideways on the ground, which she lit, keeping the flame small.

Had the room been this creepy earlier? She shivered, trying to ignore the moving shadows. She placed the lantern on the desk as a reading lamp, grateful that it pushed the shadows away.

Between two bookshelves, a tapestry hung crooked on the wall. It was a diagram of Yggdrasil, the ash tree representing the universe. The nine worlds made up the branches.

Other tapestries hung around the room, depicting scenes from the great poems, with Vikings, elves, valkyries, gods, and monsters running across their threads. Most were embroidered with runes, which Sigrid had never learned to read. She only recognized some of these stories thanks to Peter, but knowledge about veterinary care and horsemanship tended to nudge them aside in her brain.

The shelf to the left of Yggdrasil held books titled *Seer Archives*, with volume numbers painted on the spines. The shelf to the right revealed familiar names of poems and prophecies — Völuspá, Hávamál, and others she'd heard mention of. Those sources would be too old.

What she most wanted to learn about was Sleipnir. Odin was

from Asgard, so maybe starting with a book about that world…

She pulled *World of the Aesir* off the shelf and skimmed the pages for a mention of Odin. The text was a handwritten, ancient scrawl, with simple diagrams scattered throughout. It was probably the only one of its kind. She held it gingerly beside the lamplight, regretting not washing the mud off her hands before touching it.

She skimmed a third of the book before finding a mention of Sleipnir. Her heart thumped as she read the line.

"Of the Aesir's steeds, Sleipnir is the best. He is Odin's, and he has eight feet."

The best. By what standards? Was he the fastest, or did Odin affectionately call him "the best," in the same way Sigrid told Hestur he was a very good boy?

Sigrid couldn't imagine Odin cooing at anything.

The page made no further mention of Sleipnir, nor did the next.

Sigrid's gut churned, and she shivered, feeling icier by the minute after that dip in the moat. At this pace, she would be looking for the information until the sun rose.

She skimmed the pages faster, hoping she didn't miss anything in her haste.

Finally, she came upon a page that made her heart skip. It was an illustration of a stallion with eight legs. The chapter heading was a single word: *Sleipnir.*

"Yes," she said under her breath, reading on hungrily.

"Sleipnir, the best of all horses, was birthed by Loki."

Sigrid drew back. "Ew."

Loki gave birth to a horse? How? Hopefully this was a

metaphor, and Loki just owned the mare who gave birth to Sleipnir. But Asgard was a weird place full of strong magic, so there was no telling what'd happened.

She kept reading.

"Ridden by Odin for millennia, the stallion helped him conquer worlds and thwart great beasts. He took his rider freely across the nine worlds, from the towers of Asgard to the gates of Helheim, through places that none other could pass."

An inked illustration showed Odin riding Sleipnir through a gate. A horde of people behind him clawed and screamed at the threshold. Was this the gate leading to the realm of the dead?

Sigrid shivered, averting her eyes from the grotesquely drawn faces.

The following pages had illustrations of Sleipnir and Odin riding through the nine worlds, fighting wolves and serpents, and victorious against all of them.

"Tell me the stories," she whispered, turning the pages faster.

"After Odin's last conquest, he set Sleipnir free to gallop through the nine worlds. The steed will roam until his heir is born and claims him as her own, empowering her to travel the cosmos as Odin did."

She held her breath and studied the letters carefully. Yes, that definitely said "her" twice. Sleipnir's heir was meant to be a woman.

"While Sleipnir can be tamed and ridden by anyone brave enough to dare, only his heir can use his power to lead armies across the nine worlds."

Another illustration depicted Sleipnir and a faceless new rider. They galloped across the page, an army of Vikings and valkyries behind them.

Sigrid touched the figure of Sleipnir, and it dawned on her that he had no wings. All pictures, text, and even the vision depicted him galloping, not flying. The valkyries had always made her feel like Hestur was less worthy than the winged mares. But Sleipnir was the greatest horse ever to exist, and he galloped over the ground like Hestur did—even if he did have twice the number of legs.

Her pulse jumped. Was Sigrid meant to be Sleipnir's rider? His heir? A lifetime of honing her skills on the ground might finally count for something. She would be able to wield Odin's stallion like the weapon he was. She could use him to take back the Eye of Hnitbjorg and keep Vanaheim safe.

"Sigrid?"

She gasped and jumped so violently that she dropped the book. It hit the floor with a *thump*.

Vala stood in the doorway with her walking stick. "Would you like to borrow a book?"

Sigrid grimaced.

CHAPTER TWELVE

COSMIC PATHS

"I thought I heard someone—ah, I see you've already made your pick," Vala said.

Sigrid followed her gaze to the book lying at her feet, its delicate pages bent and squished beneath the cover. *Oh gods.* She swooped down, picked it up, and flattened the pages with trembling hands. "I-I thought you were in the infirmary, ma'am."

The old woman fixed her with icy blue eyes. "I prefer to mend at home."

Vala's tawny face, which had been rosy and full of life when Sigrid had first seen her, was ashen. Bandages covered her wrists, and she wore a fur cloak over her wool tunic, again dressed too warmly for the summer night. But her eyes twinkled in the lamplight, and her presence remained formidable. Her waist-length white hair cascaded over her shoulders, the brightest thing in the room.

"I'm sorry I couldn't stop them," Sigrid said, not disguising the waver in her voice. "From taking the Eye or from hurting you."

"You tried," Vala said kindly. "You did more than anyone else in your effort to stop them."

Sigrid flushed, unused to compliments. She closed *World*

of the Aesir, taking a moment to gather her thoughts. She hadn't prepared for a conversation with the Seer, but now that the opportunity presented itself, she couldn't let it pass. "Are you okay?"

The woman lifted a hand as if to touch her stomach, then dropped it. The loose-fitting tunic probably hid the more serious bandages. "I'll recover."

Sigrid wanted to apologize for waking her, but Vala spoke again.

"And you, Sigrid? How are you doing?"

"I'm…" Her throat closed up. She'd battled an enemy valkyrie and shot her winged mare from the sky. She'd been called a liar and dismissed by the valkyries *again*. Oh, and she'd had a vision that showed her riding Sleipnir and probably meant she was his destined heir.

"I'm fine." She shuffled her feet, cringing at the small pool of moat water that had formed around her.

"Forgive me for saying this, Sigrid, but I don't normally have guests." Vala swayed, this time clutching her stomach. "Is it knowledge you seek in my library?"

"Oh. Yes." Hoping Vala wouldn't dismiss her as well, Sigrid started with the easy part. "The valkyries are going to get the Eye of Hnitbjorg back. They left for Helheim."

Vala looked past her, out the window toward the stables. "Good. That's good."

"What do you think will happen if they fail?"

"If the Eye remains in the hands of those unworthy of prophetic knowledge, it can become a dangerous weapon. Only a Seer is supposed to have power over the Eye of Hnitbjorg." She looked back at Sigrid, a fearful glint in her blue eyes. "Without the ability to see an attack coming, Vanaheim lies exposed to any who wish to harm us."

Sigrid clenched her fist, where the dull pain from the burn remained. She'd had the Eye in her hands and lost it. "Could a new one be made? Hnitbjorg is a real mountain, isn't it? Can't we just…pick another rock?"

It sounded ridiculous when spoken aloud. If it were that simple, they would have sent the valkyries to the mountain and not Helheim. But the Seer remained quiet, considering Sigrid's words.

Eventually, Vala shook her head. "I have firm reason to believe that no, it is not possible to make a new one. The Eye is a unique object. Replacing it…"

The Seer hesitated once more, but Sigrid was desperate for answers.

"Vala, do all visions come true?"

The old woman winced as she stepped farther into the room, hobbling over the dark red rug toward Sigrid. *Thump. Thump. Thump.* The lamplight flickered in a warm breeze that rolled through the window as she came to stand in front of Sigrid. "The future always changes. We are all following a cosmic path, but at any moment, something could happen to change our perception or to redefine where we are going. A vision shows us what is in the realm of possibility, should its subjects choose to follow that path."

Sigrid frowned. So the Eye had shown her a cosmic path, but cosmic paths could change. Did that mean the vision was slipping further away with each passing moment? What if she'd already missed her chance to pursue it?

The corner of Vala's lips quirked, almost a smile. "I presume you're wondering about the vision you saw of yourself riding Sleipnir?"

Sigrid's eyes widened, and her stomach tightened. "You saw it? Do you know more?"

But Vala was already shaking her head. "General Eira was here. She told me."

Right. The general had flown here after everyone left.

Sigrid sighed and looked out the window. The night cast everything into blackness. A few lights glowed faintly from the stables, and far below, the village twinkled. Somewhere far away, the junior valkyries would be pausing to sleep beneath the densely canopied trees of Myrkviðr.

"Did she also tell you that no one believes me?" Sigrid said.

"She did."

"I'm telling the truth."

"I believe you."

Sigrid's mouth opened in surprise. Those three simple words lifted her more than anything had all day. "You do? But Vala, why does no one else?"

"Because no one understands the Eye as I do." Vala shared a small smile. "And, I suspect, no one understands *you*."

Sigrid crossed her arms. "That's their fault."

"I believe you on that, too."

This encounter was not turning out how she'd expected. If Vala believed her—believed *in* her—then did this mean Vala also believed Sigrid was destined to ride Sleipnir?

Sigrid chewed her lip. "There's no chance I saw wrong, is there? I'm not a Seer."

"If the Eye showed it to you, then you saw correctly."

Sigrid nodded slowly. "So anyone can use the Eye? You don't need, like, Seer blood to be able to…?"

She trailed off at the pitying look in Vala's eyes.

"I don't believe your parents were Seers, Sigrid."

"Oh." The glimmer of hope went out like a snuffed flame, leaving a hollow feeling behind. It was the piece of her that would always be missing. She'd been naive to consider the possibility. "Who do you think they were?"

Vala searched her face, frowning. What was she trying to find there?

Sigrid dropped her gaze.

After a long silence, Vala said softly, "This, I cannot say."

Of course she didn't know. Nobody knew. Sigrid didn't know

a single thing about her parents, and neither did anyone else in Vanaheim. She should never have brought up the topic or gotten her hopes up on a small detail.

"You were able to show us a vision by throwing it in the air," Sigrid said, quickly changing topics. "Could I do that, too? If I can show them the vision, they'll have to believe me."

"That, I regret to say, is a Seer's ability." Vala tilted her head, eyes intent on Sigrid. "I'm afraid they won't believe you unless they see it for themselves."

Frustration churned inside her at Vala's lack of answers. "But they *can't* see it. The Eye is gone."

"I did not mean the vision."

Sigrid stared at her until it clicked. "You mean in real life? Me and Sleipnir?"

Vala studied her, a little frown on her lips. "This is a cosmic path you want to pursue, is it?"

"Yes," she said, failing to mask her desperation. This was a future she wanted, and she had to follow the path that led to it before it changed.

Vala nodded and thumped her cane twice. "I think if you believe in your destiny, Sigrid, then you can choose to fulfill it."

Sigrid's heart beat faster, her limbs itching with the need to move. Vala's words were all the confirmation she needed. If Vanaheim's Seer said the vision could be part of Sigrid's cosmic path, then nothing was going to stop Sigrid from fulfilling it.

Except she was missing one key detail.

"I choose this path. I do, but...how do I get Sleipnir? Where is he now?"

Vala shook her head. "I can tell you about the Eye, but as for the vision's contents, I don't know any more than you do. You have to work from whatever details were revealed."

The vision had shown her people—the valkyries. And a place—Helheim. If Sigrid had been riding Sleipnir already, did that mean he was in Helheim or that they met on the journey there? How soon did she have to find him?

Sigrid exhaled, hating all the unknowns. "The stone was hot. Does that mean it's going to happen soon?"

Vala's forehead became more deeply lined as she raised her eyebrows. "Yes. But with you as its subject, I would expect no less than a hasty timeline. You like to rush, Sigrid. I wonder, is this the result of having the fastest horse in the stables?"

Sigrid dropped her gaze, fighting the urge to fidget. Had Vala really noticed her and Hestur before? Did she really think they were the fastest?

Vala laughed, a dry, choppy sound. "I've seen you galloping to Vanahalla and back for years. You two are the fastest pair that's ever ridden over our lands. But that does not mean you should rush everything in life. Sometimes, it's good to wait for the opportunity to ripen."

It sounded like one of Peter's lectures, and if it had been anyone other than Vala telling her this, she would have rolled her eyes. There was nothing wrong with moving fast. Maybe everyone else worked too slowly.

"If we're so fast, then I should be allowed to go with the valkyries. They could use me and Hestur. We could support them on the ground." She was tired of repeating the same thing over and over. Why couldn't anyone see the logic behind it?

Vala shook her head. "If the valkyries don't want you along, then it would be unwise to force yourself upon them."

"Then I'll go to Helheim by myself."

"That would also be unwise," Vala said, eyes narrowed and tone dry. "The journey is long and riddled with all kinds of dangerous creatures. The path to Helheim is not one for a lone traveler."

Frustration turned her insides. Though she might be able to rally Peter, Roland, and maybe a couple of other stable hands, they would be useless on a journey like this. She needed a real army—or someone who knew what they were doing.

Struggling to keep her voice polite, she said, "Then what am I supposed to do?"

Vala picked at a thread on her tunic. "The valkyrie you took down while you were defending the Eye—what was her name?"

Sigrid's throat clenched with guilt. Lips numb, she said, "Mariam."

"Lovely."

They stared at each other. *Mariam? What's Vala on about?*

"She almost killed you," Sigrid said.

Vala tilted her head. "We all do desperate things when our lives are at stake."

Sigrid blinked, mind churning to fit the pieces together.

"She's in the infirmary," Vala continued. "They have her locked in the lower ward."

Somewhere beyond layers of stone walls and wooden floors was the valkyrie who had returned Sigrid's resentment tenfold, who had threatened to kill her—all with reason. Was Vala hinting that Sigrid should walk in and ask Mariam how to get to Helheim?

Vala turned, wincing, and shuffled out the door of the study.

Thump. Thump. Thump.

"If you'll excuse me, Sigrid, I need some rest." Without looking back, she said, "And I would kindly ask that next time you stop for a visit, you don't drip all over my floor." She disappeared out the doorway, hobbling toward what must have been her bedroom.

Mariam.

It wasn't just about asking her. The enemy valkyrie had been in the vision, too, which meant...

Sigrid raced after Vala and stopped in the black corridor, short of breath. "You really think so?"

Standing in the door of her bedroom, eyes and hair aglow in a sliver of moonlight, Vala said, "Safe travels, Sigrid."

CHAPTER THIRTEEN

THE INFIRMARY
DOESN'T TAKE VISITORS

Finding the infirmary inside the sprawling walls of Vanahalla was the easy part. During a training session months ago when a thunderstorm rolled in, a flash of lightning had split the sky next to Runa and Tobia, making Runa fall and break her collarbone. General Eira had shouted at the valkyries to fly her up to the infirmary, her words echoing across the field, while Sigrid had led a rattled Tobia back to the barn without her rider.

Those shouted instructions had stayed in Sigrid's memory, corralled beside the knowledge of how to stop a bolting horse, how to mend a strained tendon, and other essentials.

Now, she followed the directions, crossing the courtyard to the northwest corner, past a statue of Freyja, and under an archway. She passed a group of little girls and gangly white fillies chasing each other around a grass patch, the foals' wings too small to let them be airborne for more than a few seconds. The valkyrie preschool must have been nearby.

Sigrid's heart swelled at the sight, even as it twinged with a sense of loss at never experiencing that type of cosmic bond. She and Hestur had worked hard to build theirs.

Around the corner, the infirmary's oversize double doors

stood at the end of the walkway. Sigrid barely had time to smile smugly when the doors swung open and out stepped two people—a wispy female doctor wearing all white, and a tall, muscular man whose thick hair and beard were the same color as his gold robes. Atop his head, a delicate, semi-translucent amber crown caught the sunlight.

King Óleifr!

Sigrid dove sideways, scrambling on hands and knees for the first object that would mask her—a fountain of a sorcerer holding an endlessly overflowing goblet. All right, so finding the place had been easy, but sneaking in would not be so. She wasn't allowed up here, especially not to slip into a holding cell and make a deal with an enemy valkyrie.

"More rest, my king," the doctor said. "The stress of the job has you out of sorts."

"I know. I've been getting my sister to help where I can."

Sigrid peered around the fountain. Was King Óleifr sick? He didn't look it. With his muscular build and energetic step, one could even call him lively. Or did his eyes seem a little tired?

A little valkyrie ran up to them, curly black hair flying wildly, a knee-high foal clip-clopping after her. "King Ó! King Ó! Look what I can do."

She ran to her foal, flung her arms over its back, and heaved herself up, swinging a leg so hard that she overcompensated and toppled off the other side. The foal gave a squeaky whinny, its little wings lifting it off the ground for a moment.

"Oh, dear!" the doctor said, stooping to lift the girl to her feet.

"Well, we're still practicing," she said, swiping hair out of her eyes.

King Óleifr laughed heartily. "Very good! You'll be flying in no time. What's your name?"

"Ingrid."

More little valkyries ran up to talk to him, and he took the time to speak to each in turn. It was surprising to see the king being this patient and kind when he no doubt had other things to attend to. It filled her with pride to know such a leader ruled over Vanaheim.

By the time King Óleifr and the doctor said goodbye to the little valkyries and sent them off to their play area, Sigrid's legs had seized up and the stone walkway was bruising her kneecaps. *Ow*.

The moment the king and the doctor left her sight, Sigrid rose from behind the fountain on shaky legs and strode to the infirmary doors. It wouldn't do to barge in, so she ducked into a garden, scratching her arms on rose bushes, and peeked through a stained-glass window depicting the valkyrie goddess Eir.

The red-tinted pane distorted the lobby beyond, where several doctors in white robes chatted by the front desk—blocking any signage that might indicate where Sigrid needed to go. How was she supposed to get to Mariam?

"Get back to work," she whispered and then cursed as her hand grazed a thorn. This was a busier place than anticipated.

A door opened behind the desk, and a woman waved them in. The doctors followed, shutting the door behind them.

Yes! Sigrid raced to the front door, seized the massive handle, and slipped into the empty lobby. The infirmary was decorated with such an immoderate amount of gold that she tripped over her own feet as she entered, gaping at the vaulted ceilings and ornate pillars. She regained her footing, paddock boots scuffing on the marble floor.

The doctors' muffled conversation continued beyond the closed door, but to Sigrid's other side, voices grew louder.

"I tried to get her to stay, but she insisted on returning to her tower."

"They're all like that. Can't be around others for long."

Sigrid ran across the marble and gold lobby, where a sign

with too many words pointed every which way. *Emergency ward—lower floor.* Vala said Mariam would be there.

Sigrid made it to the stairs when footsteps thumped from below. She skidded to a stop. Someone was slowly coming up. She had to move back and hide, let them pass before attempting to descend.

Back in the lobby, the door that all the doctors had gone through swung open, and a horde of people emerged.

Sigrid dove behind a potted shrub sitting beside the steps.

A young male doctor emerged from the stairwell and kept walking, not noticing her. She let out a breath.

Before she could stand, the room across the way caught her attention. Through the window, three newborns slept in their cradles. At the foot of each one, lying on a gold cushion, was a white foal. Their wings, as tiny and nonfunctional as newborn birds, rested against their sides, which rose and fell as they breathed.

Sigrid melted from the cuteness.

How odd she must have looked as a baby—a little orphaned blond girl with the blue-gray eyes, lying in her cradle with an ordinary brown colt at the foot of it. Had the doctors argued about whether to keep her with the valkyrie babies or send her to the village?

When she was a child asking where she'd come from, Peter had explained how a valkyrie and her mare will give birth at the same moment, usually a girl and a filly, born together and paired by the cosmos. But there were deviations. Some, like Edith, were born with the spirit of a valkyrie and the body of a boy. Like others before her, Edith had followed the call of her spirit and become a valkyrie instead of a stable hand.

Sigrid, Peter said, was born with a different kind of duality. She had the spirit of a valkyrie but the horse of a commoner. To his knowledge, this had never happened before. Sigrid and Hestur seemed to have appeared out of nowhere. No doctor had helped deliver Sigrid that day, no veterinarian had delivered a brown colt, and it wasn't like a commoner could walk into Vanahalla and deposit their infant and foal in the nursery.

Was Sigrid's valkyrie spirit a mistake, or was Hestur a mistake? Either way, being half a valkyrie wasn't enough to join their ranks.

Of course, she loved Hestur with all her heart and would never trade him for a winged mare. But it hurt to see what her life could have been. These little girls and fillies through the window would grow up to defend the nine worlds. They would begin training when they were old enough to walk, and they would dedicate their lives to the cause. No one would question their calling.

That destiny was not Sigrid's, and it never had been.

"Excuse me, miss. What are you doing?"

Sigrid let out a squeak of surprise, heart jumping into her throat.

A doctor stopped behind her, brow pinched in an expression reminiscent of General Eira. The woman's gaze swept over Sigrid from top to bottom before coming to rest on her face. When their eyes met, her mouth opened. "Oh!"

Weird. Was Sigrid filthy or something? She wiped an arm across her cheek, sure she must be covered in her usual layer of dust.

As quickly as the doctor's expression had changed, it twisted back into one of anger. "No commoners are permitted here."

"I'm—" *So close.* The emergency ward was at the bottom of this dim staircase. Sigrid lifted her chin in her most valkyrie-like expression. "Visiting a friend."

"No visitors, either," the doctor said, pointing firmly back the other way.

"But—"

"This area is restricted, young lady."

"My friend is sick—"

"Out!" The woman shooed her back toward the marble-and-gold lobby.

Sigrid clenched her jaw and shuffled away, but she wasn't going to give up easily. As the doctor strode away, she whirled around and sprinted down the steps. She hurtled down them so fast that she had to put out her hands to break her impact with the opposite wall at the bottom.

Her pulse raced. She was going to be in so much trouble if they caught her again.

More footsteps came from ahead. She dove into a nook, cursing under her breath. Why were so many staff working? Were royals and courtiers so clumsy they needed a hundred doctors on call? The infirmary might be this busy if valkyries had just returned from a grisly battle, but this was absurd.

Sigrid held her breath as a man strode past pushing a cart full of cleaning supplies. When his footsteps faded away, she checked left and right and kept moving. The dark, candle-lit corridor was lined with stone instead of marble, iron instead of gold. Shivering, she walked slowly, careful not to make noise as she peered through the small window on each wooden door.

And there, on the other side of door number four, Mariam lay asleep.

CHAPTER FOURTEEN

A LOST VALKYRIE

Sigrid's stomach did a strange swoop at seeing Mariam again. She looked smaller under the thick wool blanket, less intimidating, probably because they'd removed her armor. Her face was serene and not glaring at Sigrid.

Or smirking.

Sigrid swallowed.

A moment to compose herself would have been nice, but this busy infirmary left no time for that. She opened the door as gently as she could and slipped inside. The square room was all stone and wood with no decorations and no windows, like a prison cell. The fireplace in the opposite wall made the room suffocatingly hot.

Sigrid was about to shut the door when it occurred to her that Vala had said Mariam was locked in. She tested the handle, and sure enough, it locked from the outside. She removed one of her boots and used it to prop the door open.

Through all the shuffling and scraping, Mariam didn't stir.

Sigrid crossed the room to the cot where she lay. Her face was the only part not covered by the wool blanket. An untouched glass of water sat on the bedside table, bubbles clinging to its sides.

Either the doctors were being kind by offering her water or they were supposed to keep her well enough to answer questions.

Mariam's face was round, like the apples of her cheeks might be her most prominent feature if she had occasion to smile. Her lightly freckled nose drew a straight line to her lips, which had a perfect, pleasing shape. Someone had removed the black liner from her eyes, which made her whole face softer. Like this, with her expression neutral, she almost looked kind. *A mask.* When they'd fired spears at each other, that face had not been kind.

Sigrid's heart pumped faster at the idea of asking this girl for help. But she didn't know the way to Helheim, and Mariam could tell her. Guide her? After all, Mariam would be there, too.

The vision flashed across her mind's eye like a lightning strike, Mariam's mouth open in a silent roar as they charged over that red-and-black landscape.

Sigrid moved a lock of Mariam's black hair off her forehead. If she could wake her up gently, they could have a calm discussion about—

Mariam's eyes flew open, dark and dilated. She gasped, her breaths coming shallow and panicked.

Sigrid jumped back, pulse spiking. "Don't be scared. You're safe."

Mariam's gaze darted around the room before fixing on Sigrid. "What did you do to me?" she said hoarsely.

"Nothing. I'm not going to hurt you." *So much for a gentle wake-up.*

Mariam's arm came out of the blanket to clutch at her chest, as if trying to make a fist around her heart. "She's gone. I feel her fading from me."

A bandage was wrapped around her forearm where the cobblestones had skinned her.

Sigrid's insides twisted. She shouldn't be asking anything of her, not after hurting her like this. But she couldn't back out now.

"Mariam." Again, the girl's name tingled on her lips. She held out a calming hand, trying not to let her voice break. "You'll be all right. I had a vision and—"

"You broke me." The girl sat up and swung her legs over the edge of the bed, swaying, teeth gritted. "You took her from me."

Mariam wore only her undergarments, and Sigrid averted her gaze as a fierce flush invaded her face. Why did she keep having such strong reactions to this girl? It was embarrassing.

When Mariam made to stand, Sigrid gasped and clapped both hands over her shoulders. Despite her obvious strength, the sharp lines between her muscles gave away how dehydrated she was, and it was easy to force her back down.

"Don't. You're... You need rest."

"Let me go!" Mariam threw a punch, which Sigrid easily dodged. Mariam leaped to her feet and swung again, long hair flaring around.

Sigrid moved back, holding up her hands. She couldn't retaliate against someone so weak and injured.

With a growl of frustration, Mariam grabbed the glass of water on the bedside table and hurled the whole thing at her. Sigrid ducked. It hit the wall behind her, shattering, the noise reverberating through the room.

"Shh!" *Gods, she's going to bring everyone down here.*

Mariam ran at her—but between her weakness and blind rage, she tipped off-balance. Sigrid grabbed her around the middle. Her weight was insubstantial, like she'd been wasting away for weeks instead of a day.

"Would you calm down for half a second?" Sigrid grunted, holding Mariam off the ground like she was a bag of grain. This was not the calm discussion she'd had in mind.

Mariam gasped for breath, kicking feebly, as Sigrid forced her back onto the bed.

"Let me go. Let—"

"Shut up!" Sigrid said through gritted teeth. "Do you want the doctors to come in?"

Mariam seemed to think about it and judge Sigrid the lesser of two evils, because she didn't try anything else. Her nostrils flared as she breathed through her nose, visibly trying to calm down. Through her tangled locks, her gaze darted around the room. She lingered on the fire, the red glow reflecting in her glassy eyes. "I have to find Aesa."

Sigrid's throat was tight. She might have had no family, but other stable hands did, and she'd seen what death did to them. She'd also heard about valkyries who had lost their mares. People talked about them in hushed voices, full of phrases like, "poor thing," and "hasn't been the same."

"I know death is hard to accept," Sigrid said, keeping her voice low. "But she's gone. There's nothing you—"

"I'm not in denial. I know Aesa's dead." Mariam's glare burned hotter than fire. "I know her body and soul are gone from *here*."

Sigrid didn't follow. "What are you saying?"

Mariam smoldered at her for another moment, like she was considering whether she was strong enough to beat up Sigrid.

Suppressing the urge to crouch into a fighting stance, Sigrid opened her hands in a gesture of surrender.

Mariam scanned the room once more, not like she was looking for an escape but as if searching for words. "I come from Helheim."

"I know." It was, after all, why she'd come to see Mariam.

Mariam dropped her chin, looking exasperated. "The realm of the dead."

Something clicked into place.

The vision had shown Mariam riding her winged mare, who was dead.

Sigrid's heart jumped. "You think her soul went back to Helheim?"

"Yes." Mariam's eyes darted over the stone floor as she considered. "I'm sure. She'll be waiting for me at the gates."

The thought that Aesa might be waiting for Mariam in Helheim injected hope into Sigrid. If Aesa still existed somewhere in the nine worlds, then they could retrieve her. She could fix what she had done. But how did Mariam know for certain?

"Has she—um—died before?"

"Only the first time."

Sigrid tilted her head. What did that mean? If they'd come from Helheim, that meant...

"Wait. You're dead?" She almost tripped skipping back a step.

Mariam rolled her eyes. "Not really. I'm—supposed to be dead." Mariam pushed her hair back from her face, wincing as her fingers caught in the tangles. "I was killed, but the Queen of Helheim stopped me at the gates of Hel, along with everyone else in that army. She turned us around and sent us here."

Sigrid opened her mouth, then closed it, words deserting her. Mariam had been *killed* once? Not only that, but she had been turned away? Everyone was supposed to be admitted to the afterlife. "You were denied from entering Helheim?"

Mariam narrowed her eyes, bringing back that cunning expression. "Are you shocked and horrified, Miss Self-Appointed Valkyrie Hero, protector of Vanaheim, noblest in all the land?" Her gaze landed on Sigrid's feet, one of which was without a boot given that she'd used it to prop open the door.

Sigrid's cheeks burned. "Just wondering why—"

"I don't want to talk about it," Mariam said, curling her bare toes over the stone floor. She slid off the bed gingerly, leaning on it to help her stand.

"Right, so...Aesa died and is now in Helheim," Sigrid said, squaring her shoulders. "Does that mean you would be headed there if you weren't...?"

Mariam cast her a withering look. "Locked up and wasting

time chatting with you? What do you think?"

A rush of certainty made Sigrid's pulse race, but she tried not to sound too eager when she said, "Well, you'll never be able to walk there."

Mariam glared in silence. "Thanks for the reminder."

Sigrid wanted to pull her hair. Why was it so difficult to talk to her? "That's not what I meant, Mariam."

Their gazes locked. Something about the girl's eyes made Sigrid want to keep looking at them, but at the same time, to look away and break the thread of tension. Maybe it was their color. They were the exact shade of brown as Hestur's coat, so they triggered a warm, pleasant feeling.

"I have no right to ask anything of you," Sigrid said, "but would you just hear me out?"

Mariam released a big sigh and flung a hand, motioning for her to continue.

"Okay, so, when we fought in the tower and I touched the Eye...what did you see?"

Mariam raised an eyebrow. "Nothing. The room went black."

Sigrid nodded. At least she'd confirmed the vision must have come to her alone. "Well, I saw a vision. It was of you and me riding with the valkyries. We were in Helheim, and you—um, you had Aesa back."

Mariam's brown eyes widened. "You did?"

Sigrid nodded, her heart twisting at the way Mariam's eyes filled with tears.

"You're sure it was Aesa?"

Sigrid thought back to that time-slowed image of Mariam, charging with the valkyries, shouting a war-cry. The mare beneath her was pure white with that blood-like marking—the same horse as the one lying on the cobblestones, eyes open and glassy, wings bent.

She swallowed hard. "Positive."

Mariam's solemn face broke into a smile. Her cheeks did have apples, like perfect circles beneath her eyes. She was radiant like this, and so lovely that Sigrid couldn't stop the smile pulling at her own lips.

When Mariam made for the door, it took a second to process what was happening.

"Whoa, whoa. Where are you going?" Sigrid stepped in front of her, hands up. "You won't get past the lobby. And we just established that you have no way of getting there."

Mariam shrugged. "I'll find my way. And what do they even want with me here? You know we're from Helheim, and you know we took the Eye of Hnitbjorg. Didn't you tell them all that?"

"They don't listen to me."

Mariam searched her face, like she was checking if Sigrid was serious. Sigrid would bet anything that when Mariam spoke, people—or Night Elves, as was the case—always listened.

Sigrid tilted her head, going through what Mariam had just said and frowning. "Why does Hel want the Eye?"

Mariam snorted. "Why would a goddess need that lump of rock salt? No, the queen of Helheim wants it."

To Sigrid's annoyance, she looked cute when she cocked her eyebrow in that haughty, stuck-up way.

Sigrid huffed. "Is she the one who sent the army? And why did they leave you behind?"

Mariam shrugged again, seeming indifferent. "We were sent on a mission. They're allies, not friends. Now, are we done here?" She tried to sidestep out the door.

"I can't let you leave," Sigrid said, moving in front of her again. The words had come out sharp, and she tried to mitigate them by dropping her hands.

Mariam glowered, her anger crackling like the fire beside them. "You don't know what it's like to be severed from your mare. You're not a valkyrie."

Sigrid clenched her fists automatically, the words stinging. But she didn't move.

"I need to go to her. *Now*. Before I…" Mariam ground her teeth, tears welling in her dark eyes. "Did you know when a mare dies without her rider, the purest part of the rider is gone from this world? What's left behind is darkness. Nothing is more pure than a horse. Even *you* should know this."

Cold dread ran down Sigrid's spine. Nothing she'd heard about valkyries and their mares had prepared her for seeing Mariam breaking down in front of her. She'd feel the same if she lost Hestur. Even the suggestion put a lump in her throat.

But Sigrid would survive and live with the loss, whereas Mariam's description of a broken cosmic bond sounded like a death sentence.

"The pure part of me is gone," Mariam said, her voice as sharp as the tip of a spear. "What's left is imbalance, wickedness. What's left is the part of me that deserved to be denied entry to Helheim."

CHAPTER FIFTEEN

RELUCTANT
QUEST BUDDIES

Silence filled the room, punctuated by pops from the dying fire. Mariam's tense breaths were the only thing Sigrid could focus on. No matter what had happened or her reasons for joining the attack on Vanaheim, Sigrid did not believe Mariam was evil. Or that she'd succumb to wickedness without the cosmic bond to keep her in balance.

Sigrid would fix her terrible mistake.

She stepped closer to Mariam, who trembled despite the heat from the fire. "I'll help you get to Aesa. We'll travel together to Helheim."

Mariam raised a haughty eyebrow. "Why would you want to go to the realm of the dead?"

"The vision, remember? I'm following its clues. It showed me in Helheim with you and the valkyries."

"Clues?"

Sigrid blushed. It sounded so juvenile when Mariam repeated it.

Mariam narrowed her eyes. "Why do you care so much about fulfilling it?"

"Because it's my destiny." When Mariam simply stared, Sigrid crossed her arms, flustered. "I was... Okay, I was riding Sleipnir in the vision."

Mariam's mouth fell slightly open, but her eyes turned calculating a moment later.

Sigrid's face grew hot as the girl took in every inch of her, from her braided hair to her worn leather boot and wool sock.

Eventually, Mariam said, "The Queen of Helheim has Sleipnir."

Now it was Sigrid's turn to gape.

"If you saw yourself riding him," Mariam said, "that means you took him from her."

Sigrid's heart thrummed, chest tight as the pieces fell into place. Sleipnir was in Helheim. The vision proved true once again, but... "I have to steal Sleipnir from the actual *queen of the underworld*?

Mariam shook her head. "Don't even think about it. Queen Elina is giving me a chance to redeem myself. I'm not about to upset her by letting you steal her horse when she has control over my afterlife."

Queen Elina.

Putting a name to her target made everything more real. Too real. It made her queasy.

"We don't know if I'm meant to take Sleipnir by force. Maybe Sleipnir chooses his own rider." It was a weak argument, but it was all she had. Sigrid had no idea how she would end up riding the most powerful horse in the cosmos, and the more she learned about this vision, the more confusing it became.

When Mariam continued to glare, Sigrid huffed. "If you won't help me, then I'll just go to Helheim by myself. I could find my way."

Mariam gave a short laugh. "No, you couldn't."

"I could learn the directions." It would be tough, but she believed in herself and Hestur. "I already know I need to go down the spring of Hvergelmir to get there."

"And where is the mouth of the spring? Do you know how to get Ratatosk to take you down it? Or do you plan to swim past Garmr?"

Sigrid frowned, her grand plans turning to dust.

Mariam's lips curled into a taunting grin. "Your Righteousness, there are obstacles you couldn't possibly dream of. You need my help getting there."

"Then help me!" Sigrid snapped, annoyance at Mariam's stubbornness boiling over. "I'll help you get Aesa, no matter what. But please help me get Sleipnir."

Mariam furrowed her brow. "Won't your parents wonder where you've gone?"

Sigrid sighed. "If I had any."

Mariam's frown deepened. Her brown eyes roved over Sigrid again, searching.

"And we'd be riding that horse—the brown Midgard one."

"Yeah. Why?" Sigrid crossed her arms. If Mariam said a thing about Hestur, then so help her…

"When we were in the Seer's tower," Mariam said, "how did you know my name and that I was from Helheim?"

Sigrid waved a dismissive hand. "I overheard you talking to a couple of elves outside the barn."

"Ah." Mariam paused again. "That's all you overheard?"

"Why?"

Sigrid narrowed her eyes. What else was she supposed to have heard?

"Just wondering." Mariam looked around at the stone walls, then said, "So can we leave now?"

"I didn't run into any guards down here, but there are too many people upstairs," Sigrid said. One person might have sneaked by, but two would draw attention. "It'll have to be later."

"They station a guard outside my room at night. I had to listen to his awful singing for hours. You would have to get past him."

They would need a distraction. A big one. Something that would cause the guard to run upstairs.

"I've got a plan." Sigrid's stomach flipped in anticipation. "I'll go pack my saddlebags right now and come get you at midnight. How many days does it take to get to Helheim?"

"Two or three, depending on how often we stop to rest. Hypothetically."

Queen Elina had both Sleipnir and the Eye of Hnitbjorg, which meant Sigrid would have to get to her before the valkyries did. If they were willing to do whatever it took in their desperation to get the Eye back, including killing Sleipnir in the process of getting to Elina, then they would ruin Sigrid's chances of fulfilling the vision.

Sigrid stepped closer, twisting her fingers together. "And once we hypothetically get there, do you know how to find—"

The door creaked.

The doctor who'd scolded her in that General Eira-like manner came into the room with a leather medical bag. A step behind her was General Eira herself, hair in a tight bun, expression disapproving.

Sigrid stared at them.

They stared back.

"Uh," Sigrid said.

"You again!" the doctor said sharply. "This is a restricted ward."

"Sigrid, you're going to be the death of me," General Eira said with a sigh, rubbing the crease between her eyebrows.

"General! Glad you're here. I was just—" Sigrid turned back to Mariam and found her lying down, eyes closed. She waved a hand, inwardly scrambling. "I came to see if you needed help questioning this valkyrie. But I guess she's out of it still, so I'll be going now."

She made for the door, but General Eira grabbed her by the elbow, her grip as cold and unyielding as stone.

"Why would you think we needed help with questioning?" the general said.

"Um. See, I was the one to shoot her down, so…" Sigrid shrugged, as if there were some obvious connection.

"And has she revealed anything to you?" General Eira said, her tone icy.

"She's been asleep. Hasn't moved since I got here."

The general's expression was dangerously taut. "What did you learn about her before you killed her mare?"

Sigrid's stomach coiled at hearing the words so bluntly. "She and the army came from Helheim. They were after the Eye."

"We knew this already. What else?"

"That's it."

Sigrid gazed as innocently as she could at the general. No part of her wanted to share what she'd just discussed with Mariam. If they knew what Sigrid was about to do, they would try to stop her, and she would lose her chance to fulfill her cosmic purpose.

"Fine." The general released her grip. "Now get out and stick to your duties."

Sigrid stepped toward the door. "Just so you know, I already tried to wake her up. She's weak. You might have more luck questioning her if you come back tomorrow."

After we're gone.

"Bold stable hands you keep, General," the doctor said shortly, taking her medical bag to the corner. "Thank you for telling me how to do my job, girl, but I still need to check her vitals."

General Eira's face reddened. She drew herself taller, adjusting her riding jacket. "Sigrid, do you need to be escorted out, or are you capable of listening to an instruction for once in your life?"

Sigrid grabbed her boot, dropping her gaze so the general

wouldn't see her flushed cheeks. Arguing wouldn't get her anywhere faster. She rammed her foot into her boot, fuming, and backed out the door.

But before she could leave, the general added, "You've also lost your riding privileges. Turn in your tack immediately."

All the air left Sigrid's lungs. "What?"

"I'm finished with having you embarrass me like this," General Eira said, then addressed the doctor. "I'll schedule the questioning for dawn. We can't predict her rate of deterioration after losing her mare."

Mariam must have had her eyes open a sliver, because as the women turned their backs, she snapped them open and gave Sigrid a little nod.

Sigrid nodded back, grasping the silent agreement.

The general would be disappointed when she returned to the holding room at dawn.

Tonight, Sigrid and Mariam were getting out of here.

CHAPTER SIXTEEN

JUST A STABLE HAND

"You look like you're getting ready to travel."

Peter hooked his muscled arms over Hestur's stall, watching Sigrid tack up. The sun had long set and everyone else had gone home—and rather than settle into her hammock like usual, Sigrid was wrapping Hestur's legs. A set of overstuffed saddlebags already hung across his wither.

"I am."

Poor Hestur looked like a pack mule, but he seemed to take pride in all the stuff he was able to carry for Sigrid. He stood with his neck stretched high, chest puffed out like a cart horse. She hadn't taken armor—first, it was heavy, and second, it wasn't hers to take—but she had packed extra clothes for herself and Mariam. She'd also packed two leather flasks, bread, nuts, liniment for Hestur's legs, and alfalfa cubes in case they found themselves in a place without grass. Hopefully they would find plenty of water and wild fruit along the way, because there was no room for more.

"Wait, did General Eira change her mind?" Peter said, frowning.

Sigrid gave a humorless laugh, her stomach heating up at the memory of the general's last order. "General Eira has made it very clear she's not changing her mind until Ragnarök."

Peter opened Hestur's stall door and stepped inside, arms crossed. "Okay, I'm going to need you to elaborate. What's going on?"

Sigrid would have preferred to not tell him about her plan, knowing what he would say, but the time had come, and she might as well say it outright. "I saw a vision about me when I touched the Eye of Hnitbjorg by accident. I was riding Sleipnir on Helheim and leading a valkyrie charge. I'm going to fulfill it."

Peter's jaw fell open.

She averted her gaze to the dark aisle behind him. When she put it into words, it sounded like a ridiculous dream she'd had after eating too much cheese before bed.

Peter opened his mouth, closed it, then said, "You're going after Sleipnir? *Odin's* Sleipnir?"

"Yes."

"But…" Peter's gaze darted over the floor.

"I know, but the Eye of Hnitbjorg doesn't lie. I'm meant to ride Sleipnir." Sigrid felt that truth inside her bones. "I don't understand how or why, but I'm going to find out. The vision showed it's possible for me to become a valkyrie."

Peter sighed. "Sigrid—"

"Even Vala said that if I feel like this is my destiny, then I should go. This is the destiny you were talking about, remember? You said I had a purpose and that I would find it one day."

"It's not quite what I meant!" Peter's voice was high, desperate. She'd never seen him like this.

He stepped closer, arms crossed tightly, like he had to restrain his hands to stop himself from grabbing her. And possibly trying to shake sense into her.

"If they ask where I am, tell them Hestur and I went on a grain run."

"For several days?"

"Just lie for me, Peter."

He rubbed his head firmly, like he was trying to massage his brain. "This is a bad idea."

"Why?"

"Have you even thought this plan through?"

She clenched her jaw and took a step forward. "I've been thinking about this my whole life. You know I've always wondered what my purpose is—why I have Hestur, and why I wasn't born a valkyrie like the other girls. When the Eye showed me that vision, it was like the cosmos granted me an answer." She raised her chin. "Yesterday in the Seer's tower, I caught a glimpse of my future. And now I'm going after it."

"Sigrid…" His eyebrows pulled down in a desperate, pleading expression. "The road to Helheim is long and dangerous."

"No matter how risky the journey is, the destination will be worth it." Her words came out strong, even as her insides quivered. She *wanted* to do this. She *should* do it. But *could* she? Was her simple life as a stable hand enough to prepare her for what waited along the journey to Helheim?

Peter shook his head. "You're not ready for this."

"I'm sixteen."

"Yeah, I remember being sixteen. You think you know your way around the world, but—"

She stepped toward him. "I've spent my whole life struggling my way through everything, learning about the world by myself. I *do* know my way around."

Peter dropped his gaze.

Sigrid fussed with the stirrups, shame burning in her cheeks. Maybe it'd been harsh to imply she had no one when Peter had spent his youth treating her as a little sister, inviting her over for meals, teaching her life skills like how to go to the market and do her washing.

"You really want to leave home?" he said.

His sorrow trickled into her, but she had to be honest. "Sometimes, Vanaheim doesn't feel like home," she said and was horrified to hear her voice break.

Peter's brown eyes looked so sad that she had to avert her gaze to his chin.

"I've never had a family. And you're the closest I've had to a brother," she said. "But I've never *belonged* here, Peter. And if I don't go now, I will wonder every day if I missed the opportunity to discover where I do belong."

To hide the burning in her eyes, she turned away and tightened Hestur's girth. He pinned his ears at how quickly she tightened it, and she patted him in apology.

"I appreciate your warning about the dangers. I'd probably say the same if you told me you were going to venture across the nine worlds," she said, absently patting Hestur's shoulder. "But you don't understand how much I need to take those risks. You don't know what it's like to live like I do. You go home to your parents and brothers. You have a path in life and feel fulfilled by what the universe has in store. I've never had any of that—a family, a path, a future. I'll always be below the other girls my age. It's not enough. Not for me."

She drew a steadying breath. "I'll come back, Peter."

It was the longest, most excruciating pause before Peter said, "Ride safe."

When Sigrid turned, he was gone.

She ran to the stall door in time to see him stride out of the barn and around the corner.

It was better this way. Saying "goodbye" would be too hard.

CHAPTER SEVENTEEN

BEING SNEAKY...AGAIN

Escaping with Mariam without getting caught would have its challenges. Hestur was faster than a valkyrie mare, but that was when he carried only Sigrid—not Sigrid, an unfamiliar extra passenger, and full saddlebags. If the staff decided the breakout was serious enough to summon the valkyries remaining on standby, they would be in trouble.

Night had fallen by the time Sigrid and Hestur made it back to the infirmary. They'd encountered no one on the way in, with most people gone home after ending their long work day.

Outside the main doors, Sigrid dismounted and peeked through the same glass window as earlier. The entry hall was lit with candles but otherwise dark and vacant.

It was time to put her plan in motion.

From the saddlebags, she grabbed clothes for Mariam, along with the extra helmet she'd taken from the tack room. She unbuckled the reins from Hestur's bit so he wouldn't step on them. He looked back at her, awaiting instruction.

Sigrid bit her lip. She'd never taken Hestur inside a building meant for people, and leading him into the infirmary felt even more wrong. She eyed him and whispered, "Don't poop on the floor."

His tail swished.

"I mean it." Then she heaved open the door and pointed inside. "Away."

Hestur obediently walked away from her, entering the building with the confidence of an animal who did it all the time. His hooves clip-clopped absurdly on the marble floor. With the door open a crack, Sigrid almost laughed at the sight of his hindquarters disappearing down a dark corridor.

Moments later, there was a shout, followed by running footsteps.

"A horse! In the infirm— Wait, come back! Hey, horse!"

At the top of the steps leading to the lower ward, a man appeared, winded. "Did someone say there's a horse?" He turned toward the distant clip-clopping and shouting, hesitated, then ran after it.

The noise receded, echoing off the walls.

Sigrid took a moment to marvel that her plan had actually worked, then sprinted down the steps to Mariam's room. She flung open the door, tripping over the threshold as she burst in.

Mariam sat on her cot, hair braided back, a fresh bandage on her arm, ready to go. She rose to her feet, face barely masking her surprise. "You're actually here."

"Of course I am." Sigrid grinned wickedly. "I said I'd get you out, so I'm getting you out."

"I expected you to change your mind."

"Well, I didn't," Sigrid said, holding out the clothes and helmet.

Mariam took the clothes and looked disdainfully at the helmet. "You're going to make me wear some other valkyrie's lice-filled headcap?"

"Do you like your skull the way it is? Anything could be out there. Hestur might be perfect, but he could still startle."

Mariam scowled, but she fastened the trousers, pulled the

tunic over her head, stuffed her feet in the boots, and took the helmet. The clothes fit her better than they fit Sigrid, who often had to roll her trousers to prevent the bottoms from getting muddy.

"Is everything you own red?" Mariam said, eyeing their matching tunics.

"Hestur looks good in red." And so did Mariam, if she was honest. It complemented her dark hair, not to mention her fiery attitude. Sigrid motioned through the open door. "Are you well enough to run?"

Mariam scoffed and darted past Sigrid. Together, they sprinted up the stairs.

"Hestur!" Sigrid shouted as they reached the top.

She waited, heart thumping. Hestur always came when he was called.

There was a thump, a clatter of hooves, and a shout. Everything echoed off the walls, and it sounded like an army stampeding through.

The clip-clop grew louder, and her horse barreled toward her, ears forward. A leather strap hung from his bit—evidently, the guard had tried to restrain him. And failed.

She laughed. "Good boy, Hestur!"

If she weren't with Mariam, she could have grabbed the saddle and vaulted up as he cantered alongside her. But Mariam was still hurt, so she held up a palm to get Hestur to stop at their sides.

"Quick!" She linked her hands to give Mariam a boost.

Hestur seemed to know what was happening, because without being asked, he bent on one knee to help Mariam get on.

A surprised "*oh!*" fell from Mariam's lips.

Pride surged through Sigrid—and maybe a little smugness—but there was no time to bask in it. Footsteps pounded toward them from the dark hallways. "Come on!"

Mariam swung a leg over the saddle and pushed herself behind it.

Sigrid got on in front of her and clucked to Hestur, who raised himself up. "Ready?" she said. "He's fast, so hold on tight."

Mariam gave a short laugh. "Have you forgotten I'm a valkyrie?"

"No, he's *really* fast. Just hold on."

Mariam sighed, a breath that tickled Sigrid's ear and made her shiver, then slid her arms around Sigrid's waist. Sigrid's stomach swooped, and she tightened her fingers over the reins, blushing and hoping Mariam couldn't feel the heat radiating off the back of her neck.

A man shouted behind them. "There! He's got two girls on his back!"

"Right. Let's go." Sigrid nudged Hestur.

He must have known Mariam needed extra care, because he didn't explode into a canter with his usual gusto. He eased into the quicker speed, keeping his strides smooth and even. He took them through the open doors and out into the crisp night air.

"Nice work, buddy." Sigrid gave him more rein so he could guide them through the darkness.

As they cantered down the hill, she prayed he remembered where the divots were. The ride was bumpy, the slope and the unseen terrain making her sweat with the effort of going with the motion. In spite of her earlier haughtiness, Mariam had a strong hold on Sigrid.

At last, they reached the flat stretch between the training field and barn.

"Slow down for a second?" Mariam shouted.

Sigrid leaned back, cueing Hestur to slow to a trot. "You all right?"

In her periphery, Mariam's bandaged arm stretched toward the barn. Her palm was open, inviting something to her.

"What are you—?"

Two spears soared from the open barn door and landed in Mariam's hand. She let out a cry of delight. "You've got spare weapons!"

"They're not spares. They belong to the valkyries." Which was exactly why Sigrid hadn't grabbed them or the spare armor pieces.

"If they belonged to someone, they wouldn't have come to me. First rule of spears, Sigrid." Mariam secured one to a saddlebag and held onto the other.

"They still belong to the valkyries. We can't just take them."

"Why not?"

"They're not ours!"

Mariam considered. "You took a spear when you came after me in the tower."

"I was borrowing it, not running away with it," she argued, though she burned at the memory of what she'd done with that spear.

"Then consider these borrowed indefinitely," Mariam said. "Never go without a spear. The gods wrote it in Hávamál."

Sigrid huffed in frustration, giving up. If the valkyries had been less horrible to her, defending them might be easier—but the truth was, the weapons would be useful, and she owed the valkyries nothing.

"What are the other *rules of spears*?" It pained her to ask, because if she'd been a real valkyrie, she would know this. But all her skills were self-taught—like a dog raised with a litter of cats, picking up abnormal behaviors by mimicking those around it.

"Only one other. Don't destroy them. Vanaheim's sorcerers only create new ones every few years. Something about the difficulty of adding the summoning enchantment to gold."

Sigrid flushed. She'd already failed at that rule when she caused Mariam's to shatter.

Mariam's hand tightened painfully at Sigrid's side.

"Someone's coming." She pointed to the barn doors where a dark figure appeared, lit from behind by dim nightlights. The shape of his body and the way he stood was familiar—broad shoulders, hands in pockets, head tilted a little.

"It's okay," Sigrid said, heart squeezing with regret. "It's just a stable hand."

When Peter raised a hand in farewell, she urged Hestur back into a gallop.

They raced through the open iron gate, leaving behind Vanahalla and the valkyrie training field. There was no telling how long she'd be gone, and even though she'd never felt part of this world, her chest constricted at the thought of never seeing home again.

The unknown scared her, but a thrilling sensation built under her skin the farther away they got. She was leaving to travel to new worlds and fulfill her cosmic destiny.

"To Helheim," Sigrid said, excitement bubbling over as she nudged Hestur's sides.

He opened up his speed, lengthening his stride until they seemed to surge into that whole other realm.

"Oh!" Mariam gasped, holding onto Sigrid's waist more tightly. "You weren't kidding."

Sigrid couldn't help the full smile tugging at her lips.

Wings or not, Hestur could fly.

CHAPTER EIGHTEEN

NOT BAD, STABLE GIRL

Deep in the dense trees of Myrkviðr, Sigrid slowed Hestur to a brisk walk. As they caught their breath, she let him make his own trail through the darkness. He was sure-footed, taking her and Mariam confidently over logs and roots, hoofbeats muffled on the mossy floor.

Ancient trees cocooned them from the outside world and formed a canopy. The air was heavy, clinging to her face and smelling of dirt and dampness. Their only illumination came from flecks of glowing insects drifting across their path like ashes from a fire.

It was like a new world, one she'd always seen from a distance but never dared to venture into. Now she was riding through it and beyond, and hopefully getting to their destination without ending up lost.

"You definitely know the way to Helheim?" Sigrid asked.

Mariam released her crushing hold on Sigrid's waist, which left Sigrid grateful for the extra breathing capacity…but also missing her touch in a weird way. It must have been because of the dark and lonely forest. "We keep going north to the spring of Hvergelmir. It'll take us all night. Then it's a full day for Ratatosk to bring us down the spring and a few hours more to ride to Helheim."

That was a lot of riding without rest. Good thing Hestur was fit. "Ratatosk is the ship, right?"

Mariam chuckled. "He's the captain of the ship. And he's the only way to get up and down the spring."

All nine worlds were connected by the spring, and although it was the safest way to travel, the journey was riddled with beasts and guardians. General Eira's warning came to mind. "What about Garmr?" Sigrid asked. "What kind of monster is it?"

"Hellhound," Mariam said simply.

A hound? She could have laughed. How much of a monster could a dog be? Maybe she could find a juicy steak along the way to distract him with while they slipped past.

"How'd you get past him when you were coming out of Helheim?"

Mariam stiffened behind Sigrid. "We should be fine if we're with Ratatosk. I mean, we did pay him enough to take us back to Helheim, but…"

But Mariam had been left for dead.

Sigrid chewed her lip, stomach tight with mounting worry. What if Ratatosk wouldn't ferry them? She refused to turn home because a stranger failed to cooperate. "Maybe we could pay Ratatosk ourselves. We could sell my tack."

"You would have to sell ten thousand saddles for that. Elina sent us with an entire cart of gold when we came up. There's a reason only gods and royals travel up and down the spring."

The light from the glowing insects revealed a mossy log crossing their path, as high as Hestur's chest. He paused to decide how to get over it. His ears turned as he thought about it, shuffling sideways.

Mariam grabbed Sigrid again, anticipating a jump, and heat rushed into Sigrid's cheeks at the sensation of Mariam's warm hands tightening on her waist.

"Is it possible to get past Garmr and to Helheim any other way?" The valkyries had mentioned going through Midgard, but even if Sigrid figured out the route, it would be slower. She needed to get to Helheim before they did. Besides, General Eira had said, *Midgard or not, you'll still have to pass Garmr.*

Mariam shook her head, her chin brushing Sigrid's shoulder. "Not that I know of. A few heroes with big fat swords have tried to fight their way past Garmr, but they usually don't last two seconds."

Retracting claws and venomous fangs as long as her arm came to mind. She shuddered and pushed that image aside. "Okay. So our only hope is Ratatosk."

A frustrating conclusion, but they knew no other options.

Hestur found the log's lowest point and stepped over calmly like Sigrid had trained him instead of deer-hopping over like many horses did, which tended to send the rider flying like a pebble in a slingshot. She stroked his neck in praise.

Mariam let out a breath, leaving a cool breeze where her sweaty palms had been clamped on Sigrid's waist. Was she trembling? Maybe it was exertion from the gallop.

"I'm sure we'll be fine," Mariam said. "Ratatosk brought us up here, and he was nice enough. I'll tell him what happened."

If it was true that he usually demanded a cart full of gold, this seemed too easy a solution. But Sigrid let the subject drop for now.

"At least we're armed," Mariam said.

Sigrid glared at the spear sticking out of a saddlebag. Guilt about taking them still churned in her gut. "With weapons we stole."

"We should have taken armor, too. We're completely vulnerable."

"Mariam!"

"What?"

"I didn't think I was making an alliance with a thief."

Sure, she'd known Mariam was dishonorable, but she hadn't put much thought into what that meant. Maybe she should have expected some thieving.

"You regret it? Dump me here, then," Mariam said, as casual as ever. Like she didn't care one way or another.

Sigrid rolled her eyes. "I'm not going to dump you in the middle of Myrkviðr at midnight."

"Then stop being such a prig."

"I'm not a prig!"

Mariam scoffed. "What do you care if the valkyries are missing two extra spears? Are they your friends?"

Sigrid couldn't help letting out a bitter laugh.

"There you go," Mariam said, playfully slapping a hand on Sigrid's thigh and almost giving her a heart attack. "Sounds to me like the valkyries owe you. You have every right to borrow some things from them."

This reasoning was a stretch, but Sigrid found it hard to argue in favor of the girls who'd made her life miserable. Besides, the two of them *did* need spears, and these ones had been sitting in the barn collecting dust.

Hestur's ears flicked to and fro as he marched on. They'd never been this far from the stables, and he was handling the unknown bravely. It was, at least, a peaceful place, with spongy moss covering every surface and silvery moonlight shining through the trees.

Behind her, Mariam shivered but kept silent. She was clearly unwell—maybe from her injuries, maybe from the loss of Aesa, maybe both. Sigrid recalled trying to ride with the flu once, and she'd barely made it out the barn doors.

When they came upon a stream, Sigrid asked Hestur to stop. She swung her leg over the front of the saddle and dismounted.

"What are you doing?" Mariam asked, her tone a little panicked, as if she thought Sigrid was about to bolt.

"You stay on. As long as we're walking, I'll stay on foot so we don't burn too much of Hestur's energy." And so Mariam could sit comfortably in the saddle.

"I'll get off, too."

Sigrid reached out. "No, you need to preserve your strength. It's fine. He's fit."

Mariam glowered, as if she knew the real reason behind the gesture.

But Sigrid couldn't ignore Mariam's clammy face and the tremor in her hands anymore. Her bandaged arm peeked out from the sleeve of her tunic. Did she need to change it?

"You're being a prig thinking I don't have the strength to walk," Mariam said.

"I'm being nice!"

"You're being righteous."

Sigrid huffed and kept walking.

After a drink from the stream, Hestur followed.

Everything about Mariam puzzled her. Though she was a valkyrie, she couldn't have come from Vanaheim, because if that were the case, Sigrid would know her. She was the right age to be a junior. She also seemed to know a lot of their history, which all valkyries were required to learn as part of their education.

"Where did you come from, anyway," Sigrid asked, "before you went to Helheim?"

"I told you I don't want to talk about how I died."

"That's not what I was—"

"I don't want to talk about it," Mariam snapped, her posture stiff atop Hestur.

Backing off from what was clearly an off-limits topic, Sigrid said, "Fine, then tell me about Queen Elina."

Hestur stopped next to an apple tree to clean up the fruit that had fallen around its base. Sigrid plucked a few from above for a midnight snack and offered one to Mariam.

Mariam took the apple without thanks and stared at it for a moment. "What do you want to know?"

She sounded less angry, at least.

"Everything," Sigrid said. "I missed out on history lessons growing up."

Mariam tilted her head, looking down at Sigrid. "About that. What do you do on Vanaheim, if you're not a valkyrie?"

Sigrid's cheeks warmed, and she cursed herself for blushing so easily. "I'm a stable hand."

"A girl stable hand. Wow. Not many of those." Mariam bit into the apple and said through a mouthful, "I bet all the other stable hands have a crush on you. You could probably have your pick of them."

Sigrid's shoulders tightened, even as her stomach tumbled at being noticed in that way by Mariam. "Hilarious."

"What, none of them gets you feeling all fluttery?" Mariam became more animated, like she thrived on the heat radiating from Sigrid's face.

"No," Sigrid said shortly.

"Hmm. Who was that stable hand we left behind looking all morose?"

"Peter. It's not like that. He basically raised me. They all did." She hesitated. "I guess a few of the younger ones have been awkward around me over the last year or so, but…"

She took Hestur's reins and kept walking, concentrating on their path. The stable hands honestly didn't interest her. They were like her brothers, and the idea of kissing any of them tickled her gag reflex. A few other girls certainly were interested, with all their giggling and whispering. Overall, her life had always been too busy to think about who she was drawn to or who made her stomach flutter or who she found attractive. But now…

She glanced surreptitiously to Mariam, with her defined muscles and soft facial features and long, dark hair.

"Don't change the subject," Sigrid said, flustered. "Why does Elina have Sleipnir and why did she want to steal the Eye?"

"I don't know why she has Sleipnir. Born into the family?" Mariam shrugged. "And she made us go after the Eye because it's powerful, I guess."

Sigrid waited for her to go on. When nothing but a crunching apple filled the silence, she snapped her fingers. "C'mon. I saved you from the infirmary. What do you know about her? Where in Helheim does she live? Do you know where she keeps Sleipnir?"

Mariam laughed, a musical, throaty sound that made Sigrid's belly flutter. "It's not like I'm friends with her. I only talked to her for long enough to agree to join her army." She raised an eyebrow and leveled Sigrid with a look. "And you won't be stealing Sleipnir from anyone, stable girl."

"Thanks for the confidence," Sigrid snapped. Ugh, why had she admitted she was a stable hand? Like everyone else, Mariam had already assumed Sigrid's only skills were to clean stalls and carry hay.

Mariam shrugged again. "Just want you to know that up front. Anyway, what do you plan to do with this guy once you get Sleipnir?" She motioned down to Hestur with her half-eaten apple. "You can't ride two horses."

Sigrid rolled her eyes. "Plenty of people have more than one horse."

"You're delusional."

Sigrid didn't justify that with a response. She could have two horses. She was dedicated enough to give both of them care and exercise. Hestur would stay as her everyday horse, while Sleipnir would be reserved for...whatever she was supposed to use Sleipnir for. Traveling the nine worlds or whatever.

"You said his name's Hestur?" After Sigrid nodded, Mariam

leaned forward to stroke his neck. "He's nice. Good horse."

"Thank you." Sigrid tried not to let the surge of pride show on her face. He *was* good. He was amazing. All her years of training aside, Hestur's disposition was sweet. He took care of Sigrid as much as she took care of him.

"So why is he like this? Is he from Midgard?"

A pang of annoyance surged at the question, but she appreciated the rewording of *what's wrong with him*. "I don't know. We were paired at birth, same as a valkyrie and her mare."

"But he's not a valkyrie mare."

"Obviously."

"Weird." A crunchy pause while Mariam finished her apple. "And you don't have any parents to ask about this."

Sigrid stiffened with each question. "Right."

Mariam leaned forward to offer Hestur her apple core. "So you just showed up in the valkyrie ward with a Midgard horse, and no one knows why. You must be dying to know who your parents are."

Hestur paused to bend his neck and take the treat from Mariam.

"It's irked me from time to time."

Or for my whole life.

When dawn brightened the sky and misty beams of sunlight made the forest burst with color, they stopped to rest by a creek. While Hestur drank and happily munched on grass, Mariam sat on a boulder to change her bandage. At least, she was trying to. She wrapped a clean one around her arm and used her teeth and one hand to try and fasten the end.

Sigrid walked over. "Let me."

"It's fine. You're not exactly a doctor."

"No, but I've spent my life wrapping horse legs."

Mariam considered this, then held out her arm.

Sigrid sat next to her, relieving her throbbing ankles, and repositioned the bandage. It was hard to resent her in this state. Without her mare, she didn't have that snobby air that seemed to come with being a valkyrie. Although her snark and fire stayed very much present, making their conversations exasperating, a part of Sigrid enjoyed their verbal sparring.

Sigrid wrapped the bandage more gently than she would have on a horse, her fingers grazing Mariam's soft skin. Mariam's breath tickled her cheek, but she pretended not to notice how close they were sitting. A flutter spread through her middle, like the thrill of anticipation before a gallop—a sensation both pleasant and confusing.

As she pulled the material tight, Mariam gave a little gasp.

Sigrid drew back. "Sorry. Are you okay?"

The daylight revealed beads rolling down the girl's temples beneath her helmet, a pained scrunch between her eyebrows, and every freckle dusting her nose and cheeks.

"I'm fine," Mariam said, her breath tingling on Sigrid's lips. It smelled sweet from the apples they'd eaten.

Heat rising in her face, Sigrid grabbed Mariam's arm again. Maybe she should slide back a little and give her more space. But Mariam didn't lean away.

Sigrid stayed where she was, knowing her face must be as red as a flame, because Mariam was lovely and her perfectly shaped lips were close enough to… *Stop it. What is going on with me?*

"All done."

She finished the knot and slid away a little.

Mariam examined her work. "Not bad, stable girl."

Sigrid didn't bristle at the nickname this time, because the way Mariam said it was less of an insult and more of an endearment.

It made her heart race.

She offered a quick smile in answer and jumped to her feet, needing the distance.

After letting Hestur fill up on grass, Sigrid called him over and had him stand beside the boulder so Mariam could use it to mount up.

Mariam pushed herself behind the saddle and patted it, inviting Sigrid aboard. "Come on. We should pick up the pace for a bit."

Sigrid gulped, her stomach doing that fluttery thing. She used the boulder to climb in front, gathered the reins—making an effort not to react when Mariam clung to her waist—and urged Hestur into a trot.

"Who knew a stable girl would be such good company?" Mariam said, voice bouncing as Hestur trotted over the rough terrain.

The corners of Sigrid's mouth turned upward. "I could say the same about having to spend the day with a valkyrie."

They rode on until at last, Hestur's ears perked and his head rose.

"Oh, look!" Mariam's arm appeared in her periphery, pointing ahead.

Between the trees was a window of blue sky. Sigrid's heart leaped. Could it be the end of the forest?

They pressed onward, moving faster. Hestur whinnied softly, as if calling to a friend. The greenery thinned out the closer they got to the forest's edge.

"The mouth of the spring will be just beyond this point," Mariam said, sounding animated. "Ratatosk should be there with his ship to—oof!"

Hestur balked, pitching them forward. Sigrid would have stayed upright if she'd been on her own, but with Mariam's weight behind her, the abrupt stop sent her into Hestur's neck.

She planted her hands to right herself, but before she could sit up, Hestur tensed. His muscles quivered, and she braced her core. Then came a mental disconnect, like her brain readying for whatever bad thing was about to happen.

"Whoa—"

He shied, darting left.

Mariam yelped, her weight jolting to the right.

Sigrid used all her strength to try and stay in the saddle, clamping her legs tighter, grabbing Hestur's mane. Her arms and legs couldn't hold her. With Mariam sliding sideways, arms around Sigrid's waist, they tumbled helplessly off the saddle.

But Hestur never lets me fall...

She let go of the reins and thrust her hands in front of her as the ground flew toward her face.

CHAPTER NINETEEN

TRAPPED LEMMING

All the air whooshed out of Sigrid's lungs as she hit the ground, leaving her disoriented and gasping. Mariam landed behind her in a heap a moment later. Their limbs tangled over a layer of mud and decaying leaves.

Sigrid coughed and rubbed at her aching chest. "Ow…"

The world was sideways.

Hooves thumped on dirt as Hestur skittered away.

Plucking the wet leaves from her cheek, she sat up. "Told you we should wear helmets."

"I put it on, didn't I?" Mariam groaned as she rose on all fours.

Hestur seemed to realize he lost his riders, because he stopped scooting sideways and looked at them. His tail was aloft, his neck upright, and his ears forward on alert. He blew his nostrils, a harsh sound like a saw slicing through wood—the kind he made when something scared him.

Sigrid got to her feet, wiping mud from her trousers while Mariam did the same. It didn't look like she'd made her injuries worse or gotten new ones, so Sigrid left her to sort herself out and limped over to Hestur.

"Buddy, what's wrong?" She extended a soothing hand.

Normally when he shied, it was a minor jolt, and he took care not to unseat Sigrid—like the time a llama bolted across their path in the village and Hestur reacted by stopping and staring, even when the nearby cart horses spiraled into panic.

After catching the reins, which he thankfully hadn't stepped on and broken, she patted his neck and listened. Nothing stirred in the scary bush.

She shook out the pang in her arm. "Is it a bear?"

Not that he could answer, but talking through the situation was better than the unnerving silence.

"What is it?" Mariam hobbled over to stand beside her.

Sigrid squinted into the bush, waiting for something to move. "I don't know. But I don't think we should go this way."

Hestur was still on alert, tail raised, each blow of his nostrils causing a jitter of nerves in her gut. Mariam swept her gaze over him and nodded.

Sigrid pulled the reins and walked the other way, parallel to the forest edge. They could emerge from the trees elsewhere.

Hestur turned reluctantly, keeping an eye on the bush.

"Hey!" came a voice.

All three whirled around. Hestur snorted.

"Someone there?" the voice said. "Hello?"

It was muffled, coming vaguely from the place Hestur was looking.

Sigrid stepped toward it, heart thumping. "Who's there?"

"My name's Fisk. I seem to have gotten myself into a bit of a pickle."

Had someone gotten lost in the forest? It wouldn't be a valkyrie or a stable hand—everyone knew better than to venture this far out. Maybe it was someone from a neighboring village.

She edged toward the voice. It was difficult to see anything through the dense foliage, so she started to push through the bushes. Mariam put a cautious hand on her arm and followed close.

They came to a stop on the other side.

An arm's length overhead, a Night Elf dangled from a tree. He was upside down in a net, feet stuck in the holes, neck bent sideways as it pushed his head level with his shoulders. Like the elves from the attack, he wore black leather and chainmail, every inch of skin covered. His animal skull mask was…unique. Rather than fierce and predatory, his was round and big-toothed, like it might have belonged to an oversize lemming. And he had none of that mysterious, otherworldly aura of the elves who had attacked Vanaheim.

Sigrid glared back at Mariam. "Do you know him?"

"Why would I know him?" she whispered back.

"You were allied with the Night Elves only a day ago."

"Not *all* the Night Elves."

Okay, so this wasn't one of her evil buddies from the day before.

But Sigrid was still wary. "Are you all right?" she said to the elf.

"I was meandering past, and this thing snapped shut over me. Animal trap, I suppose."

Meandering, or a hasty escape as the army retreated?

Sigrid frowned.

After yesterday's attack, was it wise to help a Night Elf? He resembled the rest of them, heavily armored and insulated— but he seemed like an ordinary boy, with a youthful voice that was muffled beneath his absurd mask and the lanky shape of a teenager who had recently hit a growth spurt.

"You don't have to help me if you don't want," Fisk said. "But I've lost feeling in my legs, so I would really very much appreciate it if you could help me flip upright. I can wait for the next group of travelers and maybe they'll agree to get me down."

Mariam stood beside Sigrid with her arms crossed, studying the situation, her mouth twisted in amusement.

Fisk struggled with himself. He was a pathetic sight, flopping about and tangled in the net. Each struggle wrapped the ropes more tightly around his legs.

Mariam chewed her lip. "I don't get why he would be here in the Vanaheim forest by himself."

"Another casualty they left behind," Sigrid murmured, and she didn't miss Mariam's flinch. Maybe that'd been cold.

"Does either of you have a dagger?" Fisk said. "Even a butterknife would do. I would also accept a fork."

Sigrid didn't like this, but she was also not cruel enough to leave someone hanging from a tree. She walked over to Hestur and took the spear out of the saddlebag.

"You have to promise to leave Vanaheim once we free you."

Fisk nodded quickly. "Oh, yes! I do. I will."

Cautiously, she stepped closer, trying to get a read on the strange elf.

Mariam pulled her to a stop this time. She scrutinized their surroundings, brow pinched. "I don't like this."

Hestur snorted, that same sound that cut the air like a blade. After seeing that the mysterious thing in the bush was an elf, he should have calmed down. But he was still on alert, prancing sideways and looking in every direction.

Sigrid took another step, scanning the surroundings. Maybe there was a scent or sound. "What—"

Something jerked beneath her foot, sending her toppling. She screamed as ropes closed over her body. She thrust out her hands, but before she hit the ground, they lifted her up with a sickening lurch. The world spun as the net carried her high into the air.

Hestur whinnied.

Mariam shouted.

Sigrid gasped for breath, heart pounding, as the bushes rustled and snapped below, as if aggravated by a sudden storm. Black shadows flitted across her vision in all directions. A shot of dread surged through her veins, cold and dizzying. *Night Elves.* "Mariam, run! Get on Hestur and go."

Instead of listening, Mariam sprinted toward her. She jumped and grabbed the net, sending them swinging like a pendulum.

"What are you doing?" Sigrid yelled, fighting against the ropes.

"Getting you out!" With an impressive burst of strength, Mariam climbed the netting. At the top, she grabbed the knot, tugging to untie it.

Hestur whinnied again, his breaths and stomps loud as figures drew closer.

"Mariam, leave it! Run!"

But it was too late.

The elves closed in, swift and insubstantial like shadows. They formed a circle, pointing swords and bows and arrows at them.

"Try anything, girls," an oily voice said, "and you'll have arrows in your heads before you can scream."

CHAPTER TWENTY

YGGDRASIL'S
BIG PROBLEMS

Heart hammering, flooded with enough adrenaline to make her jittery, Sigrid twisted inside the net and scanned the horde of elves, who were all hidden beneath black armor, leather, chainmail, and animal skulls. Once they stopped moving, they'd become tangible. They were all a head shorter than her, but strong and broad. Wind thundered in and out of their masks as they caught their breath.

Even passing through the deepest part of Myrkviðr at midnight hadn't rendered her this small and enclosed.

A hulking female elf wearing a mask with antlers used a blade to cut down Fisk's net, and he hit the ground in a heap. "Nice work, runt," she barked, helping him to his feet. "Dug up some Vanaheim treasure for us. These'll be valuable, these two."

Fisk brushed dirt from his arms and legs and straightened his oversize lemming mask. "Can someone else be the bait next time?"

"Naw. Why would we do that when you're such a good actor? Really good at acting pathetic, you are."

"It's not acting," another elf shouted, to roars of laughter.

Sigrid's insides bubbled in fury. *That lying little scum!*

"We're not worth anything," Mariam called out from her

perch on the net. "I'm from Helheim. She's just a stable hand. The horse is from Midgard."

Sigrid bristled but trusted Mariam's strategy.

"Don't lie to us," the female elf barked. "You're both from Vanaheim. You're both of age to be valkyries. You've even got the helmets and spears. Running away on a commoner's horse, are we?"

Sigrid gripped the ropes harder, jaw clenched. All she had to do was open her palm and summon her spear back. Cut herself free and...

Mariam caught her gaze and shook her head. "Too many," she whispered.

She was right. Sigrid wouldn't be able to take out more than one or two elves before the others knocked her out. But she didn't like being at their mercy.

An elf wearing a mask with enormous, cat-like fangs had gone to retrieve Hestur and now led him into the crowd. Hestur followed obediently, the whites of his eyes visible as he nervously took in the horde. "Nice horse, these girls got. Look at 'im. A good working horse, this is. Big muscle on 'im." He clapped Hestur on the neck with too much force, sending him skittering sideways.

"Don't touch him!" Sigrid shouted, grabbing the net.

Seeing him in a stranger's hands sent acid roiling in her stomach. She should have paid attention to Hestur's body language. He'd picked up on their presence and had been trying to tell her they were in danger. Why hadn't she bolted the other way without a second thought?

The net swung when Mariam let go and landed on her feet below. It swung again when an elf took her place and started sawing the rope. She didn't have a moment to brace herself before the rope snapped.

Sigrid's stomach flipped, and she plummeted to the forest floor, crumpling in a heap with the enclosure tangled around her. Before she could kick free and run, several hands lifted her, forcing her to walk even though the net tripped her with each step.

"Think they're with the ones who got away?" an elf said.

The female elf tilted her head. "Could be. Send a message to Vanahalla to tell 'em we got 'em. We should earn a nice reward."

What did they mean by "the ones who got away"? Had the junior valkyries run into them as well?

A scuffle rose as more elves closed on Mariam and grabbed her arms. She hissed in pain but still tried to punch one in the face.

"They better be worth it," a squat one said. "I don't like being interrupted."

"Ah, shut up, Bjórr! You'll get your turn in a minute."

Sigrid's gut churned, a mix of anger and fear, as the elves pulled them along. They kept a steady stream of loud conversation among them, mostly discussing what sort of reward they would get. They also seemed to enjoy tormenting the lemming-masked elf.

She clenched her jaw. He'd seemed so benign and polite asking for help, but she should have known better than to trust a Night Elf.

The trees gave way to a meadow with swaying, waist-high grass and a river running through it. A wooden longship sat moored to a dock, bobbing gently in the clear water. Big enough to transport a couple of hundred warriors, it was wide, flat, with a blood-red sail that could have blanketed the roof of the barn back home. Ropes hung loosely from the mast to both ends. The front and back of it curved up into the open-mouthed serpent, Jörmungandr. Circular shields protected the sides, their painted artwork indiscernible yet colorful from this distance.

Sigrid's mouth dropped open at the menacing and awe-inspiring sight. She had never seen a real ship before. There was something graceful about the way it moved with the water—but right now, any admiration was smothered by fear. The shields were like teeth; the sail, a tongue; the ropes, strings of saliva.

Her breaths turned quick and shallow.

In the meadow by the shore, the elves had set up camp, canvas tents and belongings strewn everywhere. A fire burned off to the side, sending black-and-white ash into the sky as it roasted something mammal-shaped on a spit.

The elf with the fanged mask leading Hestur tied his reins to a post at the end of a clothesline.

Sigrid could have clobbered him for it. Would it have killed him to remove the bit from her horse's mouth? She tried drawing a steadying breath. There were worse things than her horse being tied up improperly.

They needed to come up with an escape plan, preferably one that didn't involve fighting the elves. But her mind kept being unhelpful and showing her all the bad things that could happen if they failed.

"They're going to sell him," Sigrid whispered to Mariam, unable to cover up the slightly hysterical note in her voice. "They're probably going to sell us, too. Or torture us!"

"They're not selling or torturing us." Mariam squinted at the ship bobbing on the river. "We're hostages."

Sigrid jerked her head back. "For what?"

Nobody in the nine worlds would care to take her as a hostage. She was no one.

The elves led them to a cage meant for transporting pigs. It smelled like the manure pile behind the stables. Mariam gagged before crawling in. Sigrid pressed her lips together and followed, the door slamming behind her with rattling force. Their spears, helmets, saddle, and saddlebags were tossed into a pile of weapons and belongings that were also probably stolen.

The Night Elves kept talking and laughing raucously as they moved to a circle of stumps and rocks. There must have been thirty of them, and they looked ready to settle down for the day.

"What do you want from us?" Sigrid shouted, but even after repeated attempts, they fully ignored her. "Scum," she hissed, gripping the bars of the cage. "I'll gut them if they do anything to Hestur."

"Vicious," Mariam said, sounding bored. "That's the spirit."

Sigrid sighed and slumped back, the cold metal bars jabbing her vertebrae.

How did this happen?

One minute, they'd been arriving at the top of the spring. The next, they were trapped in a cage while Night Elves had a merry time after their successful hunt.

Sigrid gritted her teeth, gut churning with anxiety. They couldn't afford any delays. Never mind ruining her chances of fulfilling the vision, this unplanned stop might make her miss the valkyries completely. With her luck, she would arrive at the gates of Hel only to discover that the team was already back in Vanaheim.

She exhaled a harsh breath and kicked the cage door, hoping it bent. Or better yet popped open. It didn't even budge. "There has to be a way out of here."

Mariam remained quiet at her side, looking out at the messy campsite. Sigrid studied it as well. There were piles of belongings undoubtedly stolen from others who'd come to travel down the spring. Between jumbles of canvas lay fishing nets, bows and arrows, quivers, axes, knives, saddles, bags of grain, even gemstones and coins. The elves had been quite busy.

Sigrid turned her back to the campfire. The smell of cooked meat coming from the pit was enough to make her stomach rumble, but she couldn't imagine eating anything. Wrapping her arms around her knees, she tried to settle.

Mariam sat back as well. She winced as she peeled the dirty bandage off her arm, and tossed it through the cage bars. The skin underneath was raw and oozing.

The sight of it made Sigrid's chest burn with guilt. "You shouldn't have tried to save me."

Mariam's face was drawn, the journey having taken its toll. It couldn't have been easy for her to jump up to the net. "Well, you got me out of that infirmary when they were about to torture me for information. Just trying to make it even."

They eyed each other, some unspoken camaraderie forming between them. Mariam could have grabbed Hestur and bolted, but she'd chosen not to. She'd stayed. For Sigrid.

It would be easy to let Mariam in, to work together. The idea of trusting her fit comfortably, like the way Sigrid's hands slid into her riding gloves, and it made her chest tight with some unnamed feeling. With the future so hazy and metal bars trapping them together, trust sounded like a better option than simply tolerating each other.

Sigrid wanted an ally. She wanted companionship from the girl sitting across from her—and not just because she was the only person in the cosmos who shared her misery right now.

Mariam reached forward and plucked something from Sigrid's braid. "Twig."

Sigrid's scalp tingled as it came free, the sensation traveling down her neck. "Thanks."

"And there's mud on your cheek." Mariam lifted a hand as if to brush it away but stopped. Instead, she leaned back and prodded the scrapes on her arm, like this suddenly demanded her full attention. A faint flush reddened her cheeks.

Sigrid's heart did one of those strange little flips again. The drying mud that Mariam must have been referring to tickled her face, and she swiped an arm across her cheek. She'd probably made it worse, judging by the grit and dampness.

Mariam looked no better, muddy, sweaty, and scraped. Her braid had come loose, frizzy strands sticking to her face.

"We're both a mess," Sigrid said.

Mariam looked up from her arm, the corner of her mouth lifting into a lopsided smile.

Their gazes caught on each other, like the twig had clung

to Sigrid's hair. *Those eyes.* They sent a rush of warmth through Sigrid's middle. Maybe it wasn't their shade so much as their depth. They invited her closer, promising something she never knew she wanted.

Heat rushed into her face as Mariam's brow pinched. Was she wondering why Sigrid was being so awkward? Could she somehow feel the barrel rolls going on in Sigrid's belly?

An elf shouted, "Oy! Wait your turn, Ótama."

Sigrid and Mariam started.

The shout had come from the squat elf they called Bjórr, who tended to the massive roast over the fire. Half of the group had settled on the circle of stumps and boulders while the others dug through the piles of stolen goods.

"Hurry up, then!" the hulking female elf in the antler mask shouted, kicking over a stump.

"I'm seasoning the pork," Bjórr barked. "Do you want bland meat for dinner tonight?"

None had taken off their masks. Not even Bjórr as he seasoned the food. Could they not take them off? Did they spend their whole lives wearing them?

Sigrid didn't know much about Night Elves other than what she'd learned from poems and legends sung by skalds. She hated all these knowledge gaps. To defend the nine worlds, the valkyries were required to learn about each one—their geography, their people, and their gods. Stable hands were not afforded the same opportunities.

It would've been very useful if she'd had knowledge of elf weaknesses.

Sigrid glowered at them before turning back to Mariam. "Do you think they got left behind when the main army left or they stayed on purpose?"

Mariam shook her head. "I don't think they were part of the army at all." She pointed toward the river. "That ship is Ratatosk's.

He must have ferried them up from Svartalfheim after taking the army back to Helheim—or before."

"What? Really?" She'd assumed the ship belonged to the Night Elves, but it kind of made sense. The wooden longship looked majestic as it swayed on the current. She couldn't imagine this rowdy band of elves taking care of it. Sigrid frowned as she scanned the main deck. Something was…missing. In drawings, didn't ships have rows of oars beneath the shields? Could this one sail without a crew? Maybe that was part of Ratatosk's magic and why he was the only one who could ferry travelers along the spring.

There was also another thing missing…

"Where's Ratatosk?"

"Exactly." Mariam's brows dipped. "I haven't seen him around, and they've not mentioned him at all."

The elves' camp had crushed the meadow, flattening the grass and turning the ground into a mud pit. They must have been here for a while, perhaps even weeks before the attack. But if they'd been sent as scouts, why had they stayed behind?

"You think they killed him?"

Mariam hummed. "He's too valuable. They could be holding him captive somewhere else. Or they took the ship from him and left him in another world. Who knows?"

Sigrid clenched her hands. This was bad. If the elves had control of Ratatosk's ship, they could control who traveled along the spring. They could ferry more armies and creatures, spreading chaos across the worlds.

"Runt!" Bjórr bellowed. "Get me the paprika!"

Sitting on the ground—the stumps were all taken—Fisk in his ridiculous lemming mask leaped to attention.

"Unfortunately for them," Mariam continued, "no one cares that they've captured us. They might as well have taken two pigeons as hostages."

Sigrid frowned at being likened to a pigeon but then snorted.

The Vanahalla royals would sooner yawn and return to their supper than send a valkyrie squadron to rescue her from this cage. Still, she didn't like the idea of the elves sending a letter to inform them that they'd found her and their escaped enemy valkyrie.

General Eira would stuff them all into a holding room, Hestur included.

"I still don't get why they're doing this," Sigrid said.

"They're from Svartalfheim. A lower world."

Sigrid blinked. "And?"

Mariam rolled her eyes. She reached through the bars of the cage and picked up a branch on the ground, dead leaves clinging to it. "Let's say this is Yggdrasil. The universe."

"Right."

"Between Asgard and Helheim"—Mariam pointed to the branch's top and bottom—"the other seven worlds have always struggled for power."

Next, she pointed to the topmost twig, below Asgard. "Vanaheim sits here, closest to the gods. Your royals have had control over all the lower worlds since the Eye of Hnitbjorg was created to give them prophetic power. But it hasn't always been this way.

"The Light Elves in Alfheim were closest for millennia before that." She pointed to the branch below Vanaheim to indicate Alfheim.

Then she motioned down the remaining branches. "In the lower worlds, the universe is in constant flux. Every world is trying to secure a place above the rest. Jotunheim, Muspelheim, Midgard, Niflheim, and Svartalfheim, where the Night Elves live."

Sigrid nodded slowly. She knew the other worlds fought wars within their territories and with one another, hence why the senior valkyries were often sent on missions off-world. But no one had explained Yggdrasil to her this way. "So…this is about power."

Mariam nodded. "Essentially. Svartalfheim has always existed at the bottom of the universe, exploited by others and never respected. It's the land of night—the lowest you can go without hitting the underworld."

"How are they exploited?" In poems, the Night Elves were described as master crafters who often made gifts for the gods, including Thor's hammer. She'd thought that meant they were respected, but apparently not.

Mariam rolled the branch in her fingers, examining it from all sides. "The worlds above them have stolen their knowledge, refused to give payment, and even destroyed their creations to keep them down. It was a matter of time before they rebelled."

Sigrid exhaled hard. The unfairness of it made her stomach clench, but at the moment, she found it hard to pity them as the metal pressed into her spine and the manure scent of the cage floor wafted under her nose. "You think they're right for being angry?"

"I don't think they're right to do a hostile takeover of the spring of Hvergelmir—but we can't act surprised that they're sick of being stepped on." She shook the branch, and all the dead leaves fell to the cage floor. She tossed the bald twig aside. "Anyway, I'm starving."

While the leaves blew away in a cold breeze, Mariam rummaged in the pocket of her trousers and pulled out a fat, juicy peach.

Sigrid's eyes widened. "Where'd you get that?"

"Pinched it from one of the oafs that grabbed me. It was in his pocket." She cleaned it against the front of her tunic. "Want some?"

Was it impressive or scary that she had such an easy time stealing?

Sigrid didn't care at the moment. After smelling Bjórr's well-seasoned roast over the fire for some time now, she was already salivating. Her lips puckered as Mariam took a bite that dribbled down her chin. Her cheeks heated up the longer she stared at it.

Shouts rose from the circle of Night Elves, drawing her attention.

Two of them were trying to sit on the same stump.

"You stood up, and now it's mine!"

"I was taking a leak, you boneheaded—"

"Ow!"

One threw a punch, and they toppled, rolling across the mud while others jeered and threw rocks at them.

Sigrid shook her head. When Mariam silently offered her the fruit, she accepted it, and the sweet juice tasted so good that she couldn't help sighing. Mariam's explanation of the nine worlds kept tumbling in her mind, and Sigrid wondered where she'd learned so much. "Will you tell me where you're from?"

"Niflheim," Mariam said, still looking at the fighting elves.

Sigrid's heart jumped as she finally got a confession. She waited for details, but Mariam took back the peach for another bite and licked the juice from her fingers.

All Sigrid knew of Niflheim was that the valkyries dreaded missions there. Banished people from other worlds populated the harsh landscape of ice and stone and, like Helheim, it was ruled by the goddess Hel.

"You grew up there?" Sigrid said, trying to sound indifferent about the fact that Mariam came from a world full of thieves, murderers, and traitors.

"Yep."

"Did you learn about Yggdrasil in school?"

"No school. My mom taught me everything I needed to know."

Sigrid accepted another bite of fruit. Getting Mariam to share details about herself was about as hard as getting Hestur to stop stealing the rag while she brushed him. Still, she tried again. "Like…valkyrie stuff?"

"Like how to survive. How to fight, how to defend myself, how to steal food," Mariam said, her tone lifeless. "A valkyrie has no place in Niflheim. We had to steal most things."

Their fingers brushed as Sigrid gave back the peach. She had the sudden urge to clasp her hand, offer some kind of comfort.

At the circle of Night Elves, the fight resolved with both elves seated on the ground, covered in mud, and the stump in question lying in splinters.

"Where's your mom now?" Sigrid said, watching Mariam eat the last piece of the fruit.

Mariam hesitated, staring at the pit between her fingers. "Home, I'm pretty sure. I haven't seen her in weeks. She doesn't know what happened to me. Probably thinks I'm dead. I mean…I guess I kind of am."

"I'm sorry," Sigrid whispered.

Mariam half shrugged, now sucking every last string of fruit off the pit. "Nothing I can do about it right now. I'll see her again one day."

"In Helheim?"

Mariam gave a humorless laugh. "Or outside the gates. Given that I spent my life thieving, I might never be allowed in."

Sigrid's heart ached for her.

What would life be like, having to steal to survive? Living as a stable hand suddenly didn't seem so bad. Sigrid was paid for her work, and because of that, she could afford essentials. She had food, a bed, friends, and tack for Hestur. And she'd spent her life resentful about it.

Mariam deserved better than what Niflheim had to offer.

"I'm sorry," Sigrid repeated. "No one should have to live like that."

"Thank the royals for banishing my mother." The sourness of her words could have made a lemon taste sweet. "She was a valkyrie on Vanaheim until she was eighteen. That's where I should have been born."

CHAPTER TWENTY-ONE

THE WORST CHOIR
IN EXISTENCE

Sigrid swallowed a gasp, her heart tripping over itself. A storm of questions formed, but she pressed her lips together and kept still. Mariam's mother was from Vanaheim? And she'd been *banished*? Why had she never heard of a valkyrie being banished?

Mariam smirked. "Shocking, isn't it?"

"No, just…" Sigrid shook her head.

"Save it." Mariam tossed the peach pit out the bars of the cage. "I guess it was all supposed to work that way. She wouldn't have met my father if she hadn't been banished to Niflheim and I wouldn't have been born."

An alternate world flashed across Sigrid's mind, one in which Mariam had been born in Vanaheim. Would she have been as nasty as Ylva and Gunni, or would she have been Sigrid's friend?

"Now," Björr barked loudly enough to make them both jump. Sigrid wished he would stop doing that. The elf finally left the roast to join the rest. "If no one minds, I'll have my turn."

The group watched him lumber over to a pile of junk and snatch something, then take his place in the center of the circle. He held the object across his protruding belly and placed a hand over it.

It was a string instrument.

"Ohhh!" he bellowed like a wounded dog, the note carrying across the clearing. In an eruption of sound, he began strumming the instrument and jumping side to side. "When I was a lad, I had a good steed, and I rode him into war!"

"Sweet mother of Odin," Mariam whispered.

The elves clapped their gloved hands and bobbed side to side on their stumps and boulders.

"We slayed the gods, and we slayed the men, and we ne'er picked a side! We swung an axe, and we made some kills, fer a war that weren't our fight!"

"Told you we would be tortured," Sigrid said, and groaned at a particularly off-key note.

Mariam laughed.

They watched and listened, cringing every few verses.

"Gods, I hope they fall asleep early," Mariam said during a small break while the instrument was passed to another elf. "Once they do, let's pick the lock, grab our stuff, and get out of here."

A moment passed before Sigrid absorbed her words. "You know how to pick a lock?"

Mariam shared her now-familiar lopsided smile. Even sweaty and grimy, she looked radiant.

Sigrid absently wiped an arm over her forehead, hoping she wasn't too much of a mess.

Sneaking out of the camp would be a challenge. Their belongings and Hestur were at opposite ends, meaning they would have to navigate through the horde of sleeping Night Elves. They'd have to move fast and hope the elves weren't light sleepers.

"I'll be ready," Sigrid said. "As soon as they go to sleep, we leave."

But the elves sang and danced to song after song well into the night, each piece sounding like it had been written by a flock of geese. Sigrid didn't know if all Night Elves were this talentless or if it was just this group.

Mariam and she could do nothing but cover their ears and cringe.

After a night without sleep, Sigrid's eyes began to drift closed, and she slumped lower against the bars, drifting in and out of consciousness. In her mind's eye, the *V* formation of valkyries soared through worlds, getting closer to Helheim with every minute they were stuck in this cage.

Sigrid woke with a start sometime later. Somehow, she'd ended up resting against Mariam's shoulder. Heat rose to her cheeks, and she quickly moved off. Mariam remained curled on her side, dozing.

The moon was high in the sky, and her mouth was dry with thirst. The elves still sang and strummed, though the tune had softened into a mournful ballad. The roast over the fire was gone, the orange glow from the dying flames illuminating the edge of the campsite. At the opposite end, Hestur's outline was visible, tied to the post, his head low as he dozed.

Mariam shifted at her side, the movement tense. Her chest rose and fell too quickly, and her skin glistened in the twilight.

Sigrid sat up and kept her voice low. "Mariam, are you all right?"

A small whimper was the only answer, but then she moaned. Was she sick? The only thing they'd eaten was the stolen peach, and it hadn't tasted wrong.

Sigrid's heart skipped a beat at another possibility. She leaned forward, examining her. "Are you allergic to peaches?"

Mariam shuddered and sat up. "Aesa," she whispered. "It's like half of me is gone—like my blood dried up in my veins or my insides dissolved. Does that make sense?"

A wave of regret and guilt threatened to drown Sigrid. Only the reminder that they would look for Aesa in Helheim allowed her to breathe again. But she still felt helpless as to how to help Mariam. Her condition was about more than shock and loneliness. This was cosmic. She'd been paired with Aesa at birth by the gods, and the longer they were apart, the more she deteriorated.

And it's my fault.

"We'll get her back. I promise," Sigrid said, her calm tone at odds with everything twisting inside her—panic, sadness, and guilt. Anger too. She clenched her fists and glared at the elves.

If everyone would hurry up and fall asleep, they could get out of this cage and be on their way to Helheim.

Mariam's hands, smooth and slender, rested on her legs. Sigrid had the urge to hold one. She could squeeze it gently and rub her thumb over the back of the valkyrie's hand, letting her feel some comfort even as she lay in pain. But Sigrid kept her hands to herself, nails digging into her palms.

The elf's mournful ballad ended with a long, low note.

"…and they were deeeead."

Everyone clapped their gloved hands gently, a muffled sound like an orchard suddenly shedding all its apples.

"They must be getting tired," Mariam said faintly.

The elf with the fanged mask who'd grabbed Hestur said, "I've got a poem."

The one they'd called Ótama clapped him on the back. "Let's have it, Ábiǫrn."

Sigrid sighed. "Or not."

Ábiǫrn stood, mask bowed solemnly toward the ground, and let out a slow breath. He let a dramatic silence pass before opening his mouth. He spoke at the slowest rate Sigrid had ever heard anyone speak in her entire life.

"Whence Svartalfheim bore 'er fruits, Yggdrasil doomed 'er

to its roots. Now gather 'round, across the land, fer a tale longer than Jörmungandr…"

Sigrid slumped against the cage. "We're going to die here."

Mariam laughed softly, a noise that raised Sigrid's spirits for some reason.

Ábiǫrn's poem cut off and he barked, "Where you going, runt?"

Fisk had risen from his spot on the ground. "To give our captives water."

Sigrid hadn't noticed him approaching. He'd kept to the shadows, clearly not wanting to be seen.

"They don't need any!" Ábiǫrn yelled. "Don't waste our resources."

Fisk gestured helplessly at the river. "We have a lot of it…"

"They won't be worth anything if they're dead," Ótama said.

"Ah…I suppose. Go on, then." Ábiǫrn cleared his throat and resumed his poem in that slow, solemn tone. "Them early elves were tasked to make, three treasures fer the gods to take…"

Fisk shuffled over with a pitcher and two cups. It was impossible to see his expression beneath the lemming-like skull covering his face. Through the eye holes, there was only blackness.

The poem continued in the distance while Fisk poured them water. He casually checked over his shoulder before facing them and whispering, "You're banished valkyries."

Sigrid sat up, ready to scoff at this, but Mariam spoke first.

"What makes you say that?"

He nodded to the pile of belongings, where their spears, winged helmets, saddle, and saddlebags lay. "Between your gear and your training, you're obviously valkyries. But the horse, and the fact that you're fleeing…"

Sigrid followed Mariam's lead and remained silent.

Fisk took his time sliding the full cups through the bars.

After accepting hers, Sigrid glowered at him to let him know she still hated him. Even when the cool water hit her parched throat, she didn't soften. She set down her cup and crossed her arms.

"Why does it matter what we are?" Mariam asked.

His shoulders drooped. "I…I almost drowned near Jotunheim a few months ago," he said in that muffled voice. "Valkyries were passing through, and one of them saw me and pulled me from the water. I guess she took pity on me because I'm so pathetic…

"It's also hard to swim in all this." He opened his arms and tipped his mask, presumably looking down at himself. The chainmail on his belly clanked softly.

Sigrid and Mariam exchanged a glance.

A blood debt.

If Fisk thought they were both valkyries, then he would be willing to help them to pay it.

Mariam shifted, setting down her cup and facing him with her legs crossed. "Maybe we are. Maybe we aren't."

Fisk motioned toward Hestur. "But where are your mares?"

"We lost them in battle," Mariam lied smoothly. "We were on our way to get them in Helheim."

The mask made it impossible to tell what he was thinking or if he even believed them. But after a short pause, he said, words barely audible, "I'll help you get out of here."

Sigrid gripped the bars of the cage, pulse jumping, ready for him to bust them out that very moment.

"You'll betray everyone here because a valkyrie saved you once?" Mariam said, more reserved.

He poked at a beetle crawling up the bars and mumbled something about his conscience.

Sigrid scoffed. "I thought Night Elves didn't have a—ouch!"

Mariam shot her a glare, which Sigrid returned while rubbing her ribs where Mariam had jabbed her. Could she blame Sigrid for being bitter about getting tricked by this lemming?

"What's the real reason, Fisk?" Mariam said in that voice like the tip of a spear. Even in her weakened condition, she was strong enough to break him.

He slumped. "I want to come with you."

"No," Sigrid snapped at the same time Mariam asked, "Why?"

Allying with a Night Elf who'd already betrayed them? The nerve of him for asking. How could Mariam even consider it?

He hesitated, kicking the dirt and turning his mask as if scanning the ground for something.

Sigrid crossed her arms. "You understand that you lost our trust seconds after we met you, right?"

Fisk kept his lemming nose pointed at his boots. "You wouldn't understand. I'm nothing but a servant to them. I'm doomed to be treated this way my whole life."

Sigrid ignored Mariam's nudge. Yes, she got the similarities. No, she would not empathize with him. It was his fault they were in this mess.

Mariam sighed, as if Sigrid were being unreasonable. "I think we do understand. You want to run away. Find a better life in another world."

Fisk's eye holes stayed fixed on her for a long moment. "Not exactly. I…" He sighed, then mumbled something inaudible.

"You what?" Sigrid snapped.

He kicked the dirt and said a bit louder, "I want to find a new mask."

Sigrid opened her mouth, then closed it for fear of laughing.

"What's wrong with this one?" Mariam asked, but her mouth twisted in a way that said she was desperately hiding a smirk.

"I want something that will earn me respect, like a bear. This was all I managed to catch on my own"—he pointed at his lemming nose—"but golly, I know I can do better. If I can find a fearsome mask somewhere in the nine worlds, the other Night Elves won't treat me like this anymore."

Sigrid's anger loosened a tiny bit. Wasn't she on her way to do the same? She wanted to fulfill a vision, become a valkyrie, and find her cosmic purpose, and for what? Maybe wanting respect was part of it.

Seeming bolstered by his own words, Fisk straightened, fists clenched and shoulders squared. "Plus, you need me. I know how to sail Ratatosk's ship and which route to take to the bottom of the spring. I helped navigate on the way up."

Grudges aside, they did need someone who knew their way around a ship. She'd never seen a real ship before today, never mind captained one. Even if they got out of this cage, without a ship they would have to turn back. Fisk was their only hope of continuing to Helheim.

As he stared at them with his empty eye holes, waiting for an answer, he scratched his mask's nose. That seemed like an odd thing to do.

Sigrid grabbed her cup and held it out for more. "Will you give my horse water, too?"

Fisk refilled her cup and looked back at Hestur dozing at the end of the clothesline. "There's a bucket somewhere. I'll fill it for him. I can also give him oats and barley, if you'd like."

Sigrid offered him a tight smile. "Thank you."

She also gave a nod of approval to Mariam.

"Okay, Fisk," Mariam said. "We could use your help."

Fisk straightened up so quickly that his mask clattered against the cage. "What can I do?"

Mariam quickly outlined her plan, leaving Sigrid more than impressed with how easily she took charge. "We'll go as soon as everyone is asleep. No hesitating. We have to move fast before they wake up and realize what's happening."

Sigrid and Fisk nodded.

They watched him return to the others, where Ótama playfully shoved him so hard that he fell over. The group roared with laughter. Bjórr grabbed Fisk's collar and rubbed his knuckles into the back of his head, setting his mask askew.

"Shut up, all of ye, so I can finish my poem!" Ábiǫrn shouted.

Sigrid leaned toward Mariam. "Do you think we can trust him?"

"We'll have to. Without him, we can't get down the spring."

"I know, but we should be cautious."

"Hmm." After a thoughtful pause, Mariam said, "What animal do you think his mask is?"

Sigrid grinned. "I've been thinking of it as a lemming mask."

Mariam giggled, a warm sound that made the cage a little more tolerable. She arched her back, spine cracking, then shook out the frizzy remains of her braid and combed her fingers through the knots.

"Are you feeling any better?" Sigrid asked.

"The water helped." Mariam pulled her hair into a high ponytail, exposing the smooth skin on the back of her neck.

"Oh, um. Good." Fidgety and with a fluttery sensation in her stomach, Sigrid picked up the branch Mariam had used to explain Yggdrasil and began peeling off twigs, tossing them into the dirt.

Mariam nudged her with her shoulder. "Don't worry about Fisk. He might have deceived us with that net, but I think he's harmless. I mean, he said *golly*."

Her gentle nudge and the sound of her laughter made the flutter turn into a maelstrom.

Having a reluctant ally was not so bad, especially when they got along so well. Hopefully Mariam felt the same. Maybe together, they would be able to face whatever awaited them in the underworld.

CHAPTER TWENTY-TWO

TRUSTING A
NIGHT ELF

By the time the elves' snores replaced their singing, it was the middle of the night. The fire had died, wisps of smoke trailing into the inky sky. Ratatosk's ship was a shadowy figure bobbing gently in the water.

Sigrid shifted uncomfortably, cursing the cage for keeping her stuck in a sitting position for so many hours. *When I get out of here, I'm never complaining about standing for too long again.*

Across the campsite, poor Hestur tugged his rope and stomped. She'd sighed in relief when Fisk had approached him earlier with the bucket of water and some oats.

He'd kept that promise, but now Sigrid monitored him. Betraying his kin was a much bigger deal, and she half expected him to change his mind about helping them escape.

He'd better not. Yggdrasil was already shifting around her, obscuring the path she was supposed to take to fulfill the vision. If they didn't get out of here soon, the valkyries would finish their mission and she would miss her chance.

Never thought I would be desperate enough to trust a Night Elf, but here I am.

The elves lay scattered on the ground, and beneath their

shoddy canvas tents like a pack of wolves, cast in the moon's pale glow. Fisk had settled somewhere on the far side, separate from the others.

A long time passed, long enough to make her worry, before movement caught her eye.

Fisk sat up and turned his lemming-like mask in their direction.

Mariam perked up. "Finally. Let's go."

They slid their arms through the bars and opened their palms to summon their spears. Sigrid's gut twisted as hers lifted from the pile of stolen things and something dislodged, clattering away.

She held her breath when a few snores stopped. But no one sat up.

They caught the spears and grinned at each other.

Mariam had crawled over Sigrid earlier—an experience that almost made Sigrid's face melt—so she could be closest to the door. Now she knelt and reached through the bars to pick the lock. The golden hilt of her spear glinted as she moved it.

"If you can't get it," Sigrid whispered, "Fisk might know where—"

Pop.

"—the key is," Sigrid finished.

Mariam cast her a smug smile.

They pushed the door open slowly. The iron hinges let out a short groan, like an angry rodent.

Mariam stepped out of the cage first, smooth and agile. Sigrid followed, feeling a lot less sly as she tiptoed through the darkness, testing the ground with each step so as to avoid twisting her ankle on a rock or tripping over some junk.

Hestur watched them from afar, rigid and alert as he waited for them. Fisk was already at his side, untying his reins from the post.

"Runt?" a sleepy voice called out.

Sigrid and Mariam picked up their pace. They got to the pile where their stuff had been tossed, and Mariam passed Sigrid her spear and grabbed the saddlebags. Sigrid grabbed their helmets.

She was about to reach for her saddle when an elf shouted, "Runt, what are you doing?"

Fisk tossed the reins over Hestur's neck and scrambled clumsily on his back. Hestur pranced on the spot, a combination of anxiety over the unfamiliar rider and excitement that he'd been set free.

"That horse isn't yours, Runt!"

Sigrid's heart pounded. If they didn't hurry up, the whole camp would notice them. They were making too much noise already. She had no choice.

"Hestur!"

He locked onto her across the campsite, ears perked, and sprang into a gallop. Fisk squeaked, nearly rolling backward off Hestur's hind end. Riding bareback, he looked ready to tumble sideways as Hestur dodged around elves and jumped over debris.

Hestur skidded to a stop in front of her, and she wasted no time in passing Fisk their things. "Quick!"

While Mariam heaved the saddlebags over Hestur's wither, Sigrid grabbed the saddle. The sounds of elves stirring awake made her want to drop everything and run. Fisk slid back so she could throw the saddle on, and she hastily fastened the girth.

More elves were stumbling to their feet, wondering what the racket was.

Mariam stepped on an overturned bucket and swung her leg over Hestur's back, settling behind Fisk, who passed her a helmet. She shoved it on, then said to Sigrid, "What, you're not going to make Fisk wear a helmet?"

Sigrid grabbed hers, fingers trembling from the rush as she put it on. "The forehead bulge at the top of his mask should break his fall." She looked at Fisk. "Right?"

Fisk knocked the side of his skull mask. "I'm good."

Sigrid stepped closer to get on when something crunched beneath her foot. Among the weapons, hunting supplies, tack, and food, she'd stepped on a goblet-sized woolen sack. Something clinked inside it. She reached down and confirmed it was full of coins.

She passed the sack to Mariam, who gasped. "Sigrid! Are you really taking something that doesn't belong to you?"

"It doesn't count! It was stolen to begin with." Her mouth twisted into a rebellious smile as she stepped onto the overturned bucket. "Move back—"

A roar split the still night air. "The valkyries are out of their cage!"

Their chance to sneak away evaporated.

They had one option left—fight their way out.

"Get on!" Mariam shouted.

The campsite roiled, elves looming like holes in the fabric of nightfall. They moved more swiftly than she remembered, dark and blurred like nothing on Vanaheim.

A heavy chill invaded her stomach, and she couldn't make her feet move.

This was a terrible mistake.

Ábiǫrn roared, his form going blurry as he moved. "Everyone up! We're losing our—ack!"

Mariam had thrown her spear and somehow knocked him flat.

Sigrid's mouth dropped open. "How did you—"

"It's an illusion when they move." Mariam caught her spear and threw it again. "Stay calm, find a shadow, and aim for its middle."

Sigrid nodded, Mariam's confidence bolstering her. *Basic moving targets.* She'd practiced those. She swung a leg over the saddle and forced herself in front. No way was she letting Sir Lemming Mask try to steer.

With poor Hestur supporting the weight of all three of them plus the saddlebags, Sigrid squeezed his sides and cued him into a gallop.

They surged through the mess of bodies, aiming for the river. The flitting shadows dizzied her, but she still aimed and threw her spear. Even if she hit nothing, it kept them away.

Hestur dodged them as if navigating through sheep.

"Go, go, go," she said, breathless, every muscle tense as she fought to stay balanced. The saddle rocked, threatening to slip sideways with each stride. She cursed at not having tightened the girth properly. The weight of others tipped behind her, and the disorienting darkness kept pulling her off-center.

"They're headed for our ship!" Bjórr shouted, his blurred shape appearing in front of them wielding a terrifyingly large axe.

Sigrid fired her spear and was satisfied to hear a *clunk* as it drove into his chainmail and knocked him over. She summoned it back as they galloped away from the horde.

A small cluster of arrows flew over them, and they barely had time to scream and duck.

"They're trying to kill us!" she shouted, blood pounding in her ears. "Actually *kill* us!"

"Well, they worked hard to steal that ship," Mariam said, voice bouncing. She took care of more elves as they hurtled down the slope toward the river.

Fisk screamed uselessly from between them.

Ratatosk's ship waited, ghostly in the moonlight.

"Hold tight!" Sigrid shouted, and Fisk's arms cinched around her waist.

Hestur hesitated when she steered him toward the river. She clucked, inviting him to trust her, and he pushed onward. He carried them onto the wooden dock, up the gangplank, and jumped over the shields on the ship's railing. They landed with a jolting bump on the deck. Hestur's hooves clattered, but he'd been across the bridge to Vanahalla enough times that the noise didn't startle him.

"Whoa, boy." Sigrid sucked in a breath, sliding sideways as the loose girth finally gave way.

Fisk and Mariam tipped behind her, and all three of them hit the deck with a thud.

Hestur looked down at them, nostrils blowing from the effort of carrying all three, no doubt wondering what they were doing on the floor.

The yelling from the elves got closer, and they scrambled to their feet. Fisk and Mariam ran in opposite directions. Sigrid gripped her spear, ready to fight.

Ótama was the first to appear at the railing, gloved hands wrapping around it as she heaved herself up. "Runt, you traitor!"

Sigrid moved in close and slashed the elf's grip with her spear.

The elf fell into the water with a yell and a splash.

A dark swarm rushed the gangplank, but Mariam kicked it down, sending the elves plunging into the river.

"That's our ship," Ábiǫrn shouted.

"Pretty sure it's Ratatosk's," Mariam taunted back.

"We rightfully stole it!"

More arrows flew at them from the shore, whizzing too close to Hestur.

Sigrid hurried over and tapped him on the knees, pointing at the deck. "Lie down."

Hestur sank to his knees, lowering his front end and sending a tremor through the deck as his hindquarters followed.

A hand closed over Sigrid's arm and pulled her behind one of the big shields lining the railing. Sigrid's heart leaped into her throat when a javelin flew where her head had been. It ricocheted off the mast and clattered to the deck.

"You're welcome," Mariam said and snatched up the javelin. She leaned around a shield and hurled it back at them.

If Sigrid's heart raced any faster, it would pound right out of her chest. She rocked onto her knees and called her spear, ready to help. Most of the projectiles that flew past them glanced off the deck, bouncing across it before splashing into the water. Either the weapons were dull or this was a very well-made ship.

They dipped and swayed, striking where they could, as more elves clung to the railing, trying to climb aboard. Her muscles burned from all the ducking and throwing. They wouldn't be able to hold them off much longer.

"Fisk?" she yelled. "Nearly ready?"

Unease churned in her gut. Had he tricked them again? She checked over her shoulder, scanning the long deck.

Fisk stood at the back of the ship, pulling and securing the ropes that tightened the sail. He gave it a final tug, and the sail caught the wind. The ship shuddered away from the shore, rocking and creaking as the wind and current carried it down the river.

"Yeah!" Mariam shouted.

Soon, the flying arrows and weapons fell short, their splashes echoing from the water.

Sigrid and Mariam rose to their feet, watching the shore from behind the ship's shields.

"Traitor!" was the last word they heard as they sailed away from the campsite.

Footsteps pattered as Fisk left the sail and skipped to the helm, humming a jaunty tune. How could he be so calm and chipper?

Panting and still jittery from all the action, Sigrid invited Hestur to stand. He breathed hard, and the whites of his eyes showed, but a thorough pat-down confirmed he wasn't injured. She kissed his nose and rubbed his forehead before freeing him of the twisted saddle. "Nice work, buddy. We're safe now."

Sigrid stuffed the sack of coins in a saddlebag and tossed all of their belongings by the mast, while Mariam lit the lanterns scattered about the railings. This might have provided comfort, except the immediate light cast their surroundings into greater darkness.

When Sigrid brought this up, Mariam shrugged. "I'd rather be able to see what's in front of me than what's a mile ahead."

Sigrid opened her mouth to argue that seeing a mile ahead might be useful, but Mariam had already moved onto the next lantern.

"It's downright lucky I paid attention to how we got here," Fisk said, heaving on a rope. "And that they made me figure out how to sail on the first night. It should be an easy enough time getting to Helheim."

The sail, an enormous red square of material, strained against what seemed like too many ropes as it caught the wind and pushed them faster.

"You're all right working this thing by yourself?" Sigrid asked, doubtful. Although, despite the enormity of the ship, he seemed to be handling the ropes and wheel without a struggle.

"Sure. It's only a bit of rigging and a bit of magic," he said mysteriously.

She squinted at him. "I can't tell if you're being sarcastic behind that weird mask."

Mariam laughed nearby, and Sigrid grinned. Fisk mumbled and bent to tie down some rope. He bonked his mask's overbite on the wheel, which made both girls turn and walk away, covering their mouths.

As the ship swayed, Hestur refused to stand still and kept snorting and tossing his head as if flies were bothering him.

"Nothing to be afraid of," Sigrid said, scratching his wither. The knuckles of her other hand whitened as she gripped her spear tighter.

Truth? She was trying to reassure herself as much as him.

CHAPTER TWENTY-THREE

THE LONGSHIP'S CAPTAIN

Once Hestur calmed, he walked away to sniff around the deck. He would feel better once he confirmed no predators had snuck aboard.

Mariam had finished lighting all the lanterns and stared out at the fading campsite in the distance.

Sigrid joined her. "The elves aren't following us?" Hopefully, the Night Elves were as attached to Fisk as the valkyries were to her.

"Nah," Mariam said. "Can't do much without a boat."

Thank the gods our escape plan worked.

And thank the gods Fisk knew how to sail. He stood at the helm, mask turned toward them. He seemed to sense Sigrid's glare, because he quickly looked ahead again.

They weren't mistaken to trust him, right? He'd gotten them out and was helping them sail to Helheim, after all.

Still, she would have to keep a close watch on him.

Sigrid leaned over the wooden shields along the railing, which were painted with the emblems of the nine worlds. She ran a hand over the one depicting a boar's head—the emblem of Vanaheim.

This was the first time she'd ever left her world. She never imagined leaving on her own, never mind leaving on a journey to the realm of the dead. A small ache formed in her chest at the thought of her comfortable hammock and the sound of winged mares munching hay all around her, but a lightness expanded around it, like Hestur had sprouted wings and carried her high beyond the clouds.

Vanahalla's stone wall no longer bound her. The worlds were hers to explore, and no valkyrie or general could stop her.

The journey ahead wouldn't be easy, but with Mariam—and Fisk—she bet they could overcome any obstacle. Speaking of…

"You said Ratatosk could get us past Garmr, but he's not here," she said, tapping the wooden railing.

"It's fine. Garmr can't harm this ship," Mariam said. "Perks of being built by the gods."

Hestur clip-clopped by, still sniffing everything.

"And what about us?" Sigrid said.

Mariam leaned back on the railing to study the open deck. "We can hide under the canvas. It's also indestructible. Some people did that on the way up, not really trusting Ratatosk's magic to hide us."

At the ship's nose, canvas stretched from railing to railing to form a small shelter, under which sat barrels, crates, and coils of rope. If Mariam hadn't saved her more than once already, Sigrid might have been hesitant to trust her word. Hopefully getting past Garmr turned out to be that simple.

Sigrid was about to ask more when Mariam's knees bent, and before Sigrid could react, she slumped sideways and fell onto the deck.

"Mariam!" Sigrid knelt and reached for her, setting a hand over her shoulder.

"I'm fine," Mariam said, which wasn't very convincing considering she was knocked flat with an arm resting across her eyes. "Just tired. That escape just took a lot out of me."

"They didn't get you, did they?" Fisk said from the helm.

"No, no."

Sigrid sat beside Mariam, who trembled despite her casual tone. Her skin was hot to the touch and glistened with sweat. "What can I do? Are you sure you're not hurt?"

Mariam shook her head, keeping her arm over her eyes. Her nostrils flared, like she was fighting to keep her breathing steady.

This was about Aesa.

Sigrid bit her lip, at a loss. Mariam needed rest. "All right. Let's get you comfortable and warm."

Mariam didn't argue.

Sigrid jumped to her feet and ran to the front, under the canvas where barrels and crates were stacked. She riffled through them until she found a pile of musty furs, then heaved them back over to the mast and made a bed.

"There," she said, pulling Mariam's arm across her shoulders and guiding her to the furs. Sigrid tucked them in around her. "Like a bird in a nest."

Mariam cracked a smile that made Sigrid's heart soar. After a moment, she stopped shivering and let out a sigh. Her eyes closed.

Sigrid reached out, then hesitated. Mariam looked so frail lying there, her usual fierceness gone. She wanted to comfort her, but would that be welcome?

Bracing for potential awkwardness, Sigrid brushed her fingers through Mariam's hair. The girl's eyelids gave the subtlest flinch at the contact, but she made no other motion. She was sweaty and hot to the touch.

Sigrid stroked her hair until Mariam's breathing slowed.

It seemed that at every turn, invisible strings kept tugging her closer to Mariam. It made her heart do barrel rolls inside her chest. She would do everything in her power to make sure Mariam and Aesa were reunited. Mariam *had* to survive this.

They stayed like that for a long moment, Mariam lying

beneath the furs, Sigrid sitting beside her head, stroking her hair. Fisk remained at the helm, though his attention prickled the back of her neck. What if he tried leading them somewhere else? She wouldn't even notice until it was too late.

Only Mariam knew the way to Helheim. But Sigrid was reluctant to wake her, knowing she needed to rest.

Mariam must have sensed the tension rolling off Sigrid, because she shifted and drew a breath. While her eyes remained closed, she said, "So, Fisk, why are the Night Elves trying to control the spring of Hvergelmir?"

Fisk took a moment to answer, then lifted a shoulder. "No idea. I'm just the runt. I had no choice when they pulled me along."

Mariam opened her eyes, a muscle in her jaw working.

Sigrid didn't quite believe him, either.

Dark shadows loomed on either side, indicating they'd left the meadow and sailed into a forest. The air grew warmer and thicker. Fisk turned the wheel sharply, going left at a fork in the river.

Water sloshed against the hull, and the wind grew louder. They picked up speed, the land whooshing by suspiciously fast for such a gentle current.

"Do you know if the valkyries came through?" Sigrid asked, then corrected herself when Mariam nudged her. "The, um, other valkyries besides us."

Fisk nodded once. "They refused to pay us, and wanted to know what we did with Ratatosk. When things got tense, they turned around, I think to pass through Midgard instead. They were *not* happy about it."

Hope surged inside her.

It would take them longer to get to Helheim now. Maybe Sigrid could still get to Sleipnir in time to join them and fulfill the vision.

A howl rose in the distance.

Sigrid called her spear and clutched it tight. The three of them and Hestur stared into the blackness as a pack of dire wolves formed a chorus.

Mariam sat up. She yelled out to Fisk again. "What did the elves do with Ratatosk?"

Fisk kept his hands on the wheel, silent.

"Fisk," Mariam said in that cutting tone. "Where is he?"

"The king promised a reward to the group who did it," Fisk said. "I don't care about the reward. I wanted to leave camp after, but they didn't let me."

"You mean there are more groups of Night Elves skulking around?" Sigrid said, alarmed.

Fisk nodded. "Not just in Vanaheim. Everywhere."

"What did they do with him?" Mariam said.

He lifted a shoulder. "I don't know. Gone. They don't tell me anything."

Sigrid drew a breath. *What's that supposed to mean? Is he dead?* Ratatosk had controlled the spring since the beginning of time. Yes, she'd grown up in the isolated bubble of the Vanaheim stables, oblivious to the goings-on of the nine worlds, but even she knew about this ship that ferried gods and mortals along the spring of Hvergelmir. A being like that couldn't be killed, right? What would this mean for the nine worlds?

A chill ran up her arms. With the Eye of Hnitbjorg in Helheim and Ratatosk gone, it was like the cosmos turned inside out.

Any inclination Sigrid had about giving Fisk a second chance fizzled. No matter his pledge to help them, he kept telling them half-truths and holding back gods knew what else. He wanted a new mask to get the respect of a group that might have killed Ratatosk! For that alone, he couldn't be trusted. Plus, it didn't help that she could never read his expression or tell where he was looking because of that ridiculous lemming mask.

Sigrid had to find a way to talk to Mariam without being

overheard. And at the first chance they got, they needed to leave him behind.

Fisk kept looking up and checking the stars for guidance. He turned them down another fork. The land sped by faster, the shadows on either side blending together.

An odd thought occurred to Sigrid. "How will we get back up the spring if we have to move against the current?"

"Oh! It's amazing," Fisk said. "The current moves in the same direction as Ratatosk's ship. Wherever I point it to, the water will flow that way."

"Second perk of being on a magical ship built by the gods," Mariam said absently.

Fisk began humming. "When I was a lad, I had a good steed—"

"Don't." Sigrid and Mariam said together.

Unlike the campfire elves, he shut up.

After a short pause, he said brightly, "My dad used to sing that to me when I was a kid, before he was sent to battle in Muspelheim and was killed by the Fire Giants. It's not a great place for a Night Elf, the realm of fire. Darkness is the most flammable substance."

Sigrid and Mariam exchanged an uncertain glance. Pity sparked in Sigrid's gut but extinguished as she recalled the things his group had done.

"I'm sorry," Mariam said.

Fisk turned his focus back to the wheel, steering them rapidly through the blackness. "You two should sleep. I'll keep navigating and make sure we don't crash into anything."

"He's right. Come on," Mariam said, patting the furs next to her. "It'll take hours to get down the spring."

Sigrid let out a breath. True, they couldn't face Garmr exhausted. And she still needed to figure out how to get Sleipnir from Queen Elina, a feat Mariam had qualified equally dangerous and impossible.

Trying to be nonchalant about the idea of sharing a bed, she cleared her throat. "I'll just get Hestur settled first."

Hestur was at the front, aggressively nosing a barrel as if hoping to find carrots. She crossed her arms against the chill, her footsteps echoing in the isolated silence as she went to find a water bucket for him. If she took extra time to calm her nerves before joining Mariam, no one would ever know what was going on inside her right now.

Around them, the darkness accelerated, Ratatosk's ship carrying them into the vast emptiness between worlds.

CHAPTER TWENTY-FOUR

SERPENTS
IN THE SPRING

Sigrid stood like a silent castle guard next to the furs where Mariam lay resting. Her insides were a tangled mess like the ropes at Fisk's feet. She wanted to blame the sensation on the longship accelerating in the last few minutes—she'd never been on a ship before, so maybe this was sea sickness?—but she knew better.

She drew a breath and shook out her braid, doing her best to ignore the flutters.

Ordinarily, she would sleep in something more comfortable than trousers and a riding tunic, but she wasn't about to strip down here. Besides, Mariam had fallen asleep in day clothes just fine.

Sigrid would fix her hair, wash her face, and hopefully calm down.

The sail flapped noisily overhead, straining against its ropes. Fisk leaned all his weight into the wheel as he guided them. They seemed barely in control, but he didn't look concerned, and Mariam's eyes remained closed.

Sigrid knelt over a bucket and tried to palm water on her face, but the swaying ship sloshed the water right out. The contents of her stomach seemed to be doing the same. Was she going to be sick? Wind howled in her ears. The forest on either side of the river blurred into a wall of blackness.

All right, so maybe the ship's speed was not helping her situation.

"Woo!" Fisk shouted, raising a hand. "We're moving now. I *loved* this part on the way up."

The sail flogged and pulled, like an animal trying to break its tether.

Sigrid's pulse quickened as she stood and took a wobbly step toward the helm. "Do you need help?"

Fisk waved her off. "Nah. She's moving on her own now. Isn't it great?"

What was *that* supposed to mean? Was the ship out of control?

Mariam sat up with a groan. "Fisk, are you sure—"

A huff came from the shoreline, then pounding steps.

A beastly growl.

Sigrid jumped to her feet, opened her palm, and her spear slapped into her hand. Her pulse raced as dread coursed through her. Dire wolves again? No. Whatever was out there sounded bigger, meaner.

Breaths coming short, Sigrid tightened her grip on the spear. They weren't ready to face anything. Not when Mariam was too ill to fight and Fisk had to focus on steering.

But as quickly as the threat had come, it fell behind them.

Fisk whooped.

Sigrid shot him a glare but jumped when an orange light swept past, and the roar of a massive fire and a rush of heat forced her back a step. That, too, disappeared before she could raise her weapon.

Fisk grunted as he turned the wheel, leaning back to use his full weight. "Not today, Muspelheim!"

"He's enjoying this too much," Mariam grumbled, expression-less as she braced herself against the mast and stared into the passing darkness. She'd also summoned her spear, though she looked too weak to fight.

Sigrid braced herself on deck, muscles taut as she balanced

against the turbulent water.

A flash of white light. A distant shriek. A brief icy sensation, like they'd plunged through a waterfall.

Hestur whinnied. His hooves clattered, the sound seeming to catch in a vortex and come back to them from all directions.

"I feel so alive!" Fisk yelled.

"I don't!" Sigrid yelled when the ship rolled over a wave, leaving her dizzy enough to stumble. She needed to take control of this runaway ship before they capsized. "Let me steer."

He shook his head, mask wobbling. "No need! I've got it."

The lantern flames on the railing thrashed, threatening to extinguish. The blackness moved faster, the longship swaying until Sigrid's stomach heaved in protest.

She ran to the railing and leaned over, taking deep breaths. Her palms slipped on the cold, wet wood. "We need to—slow down—!"

An icy spray hit her face, the fresh water tasteless on her tongue. The long ship rolled one more time, the jolt sending Sigrid to her knees. Then with a whoosh of air and a subtle lift of darkness, they slowed.

The dense forest on either side had vanished.

In its place, the ship rocked gently on a dark ocean that stretched infinitely in all directions. The sail arced forward in a steady breeze, and the deck glistened where the water had splashed, their items strewn across it.

The lantern flames steadied, and everything fell silent. Too silent.

Sigrid got to her feet, limbs shaking, breaths unsteady, and checked on the others.

Mariam was untangling herself from the furs but declined Sigrid's hand to stand.

Fisk continued to sail, his head swaying to whatever tune he was now humming to himself.

The sea gave no indication of the land they'd left behind.

It was as if they'd dropped from the sky into the middle of an endless pool. Waves spread outward, their caps glinting in the darkness. In place of looming treetops, the sky had opened up to a bright tapestry of stars. A denser streak crossed the middle like a sprinkle of sugar. She searched for familiar constellations but found none.

Sigrid wiped her brow, which was hot beneath the icy droplets. "Please, tell me we're there." She was done with this boat ride. Hestur, too, looked fed up as he stood with his legs splayed for balance, nostrils flaring.

"We're in the space between worlds." Mariam had pushed the fur blankets off her and looked mussed up and vulnerable amid the pile. When she pointed her spear ahead, Sigrid wrenched her gaze away to look. "Get ready."

Sigrid tensed. "For what?"

In the glassy water ahead, a mountain burst through the surface. Waves frothed and hissed around it, the sound filling the air. As the shape rose high above them, long, slow swells pushed out in all directions, lifting the longship with a swooping sensation. Was the sea floor shifting and forming new mountains before their eyes?

Fisk braced himself against the helm. "We need to wait until he sinks."

Sigrid crouched into a fighting stance as they dipped into a trough. "*He*?"

The mountain was barely visible in the starlight—a black hole in the darkness. As it arced from the water, it grew impossibly big, brushing the sky and spreading out to touch the horizon on either side.

"Jörmungandr," Mariam said.

Sigrid heart dropped into her stomach.

It wasn't a mountain.

It was the back of the world serpent.

CHAPTER TWENTY-FIVE

CONVERSATIONS
UNDER CONSTELLATIONS

Sigrid moved next to Mariam without a second thought, ready to stand between her and the serpent — though what was the point, against jaws big enough to swallow the ship? Or maybe that could be a weak spot? She could throw her spear and lodge it between its teeth.

Sigrid grabbed her spear. "Where's the mouth?"

"Could be anywhere," Mariam said, her tone trying for casual, but Sigrid saw through the act. "He wraps around Midgard, so he's, uh, pretty big."

The serpent's back rose high enough to touch the stars, leaving little doubt that this thing circled an entire world.

"What do we do?" Sigrid's legs weakened. Why weren't the others offering advice or instructions? They'd traveled through here once before, so they should know something. Anything? This was so far out of her range of experience. "We can't keep sailing toward it. What do we—"

Mariam's hand landed over hers for a moment, but even that wasn't enough to calm her. "Just wait. Watch."

In the next breath, the rising mountain changed course and began to sink. The waves churned wildly, hissing and lapping.

Sigrid and Mariam had to cling to the mast for support. Hestur had come over, deeming it safer to lie down at their side while the ship rocked.

Lower the serpent sank, until the horizon was visible over its back.

"Hold on!" Fisk shouted.

Before Sigrid could ask for clarification, the ship accelerated. The sail caught the wind of its own accord, ballooning forward and groaning against the ropes.

She screamed. "Fisk!"

As the mountain disappeared below the surface, they sailed right over where it had been. They crossed the turbulent waters, faster and faster. Then a *thud* rattled the hull, like they'd hit bottom.

The back of the ship started to lift.

The serpent's back was rising again.

They all screamed, even Hestur.

The ship's nose plunged beneath the surface, a spray rose high overhead, and they lurched forward. Salt met her tongue and stung her eyes. As the cold deluge splashed over the deck and drenched everyone, the ship wobbled, regaining its balance. Vision blurry and stinging, Sigrid grabbed the saddlebags to stop them from sliding away.

Behind them, the horizon and sky were slowly eclipsed once more.

Fisk whooped. "See why an ordinary boat wouldn't work? Try getting a homemade raft to accelerate over Jörmungandr at the right moment. Ratatosk would've done this more smoothly, mind you. But I didn't do so bad, right?" A pause. "Right?"

Braced on all fours and fighting nausea, Sigrid patted the cold, wet deck. "Good boat."

Miraculously—maybe magically—all of the ship's crates and barrels had stayed put. Their belongings, however, were everywhere. At least all of it had stayed aboard.

And all of us.

They sailed quickly over the rolling waves, Fisk admittedly doing a good job of captaining. Sigrid's stomach threatened to empty its contents, but the swells blessedly reduced to ripples before that happened.

Deeming it safe, Hestur stood and shook himself off, snorting indignantly.

"*Now* are we there?" Sigrid said, leaning against the mast, her legs needing the support.

Mariam pointed across the water, where blurry reflections of the stars above writhed in the current. "A few hours more. That's where we're headed."

On the horizon, another dark mass rose—except this mountain stayed fixed. *Finally, land.* But the relief didn't last as a dark feeling churned inside her. What waited for them beyond that dark, looming landmass?

"All right," she said, trying not to sound like she'd nearly vomited all over the deck. She wouldn't have been able to look at Mariam again if that had happened.

Drenched and shivering, Sigrid and Mariam changed into the spare clothes Sigrid had packed—which, to Mariam's amusement, also happened to be matching trousers and red tunics. Fisk insisted he'd stayed dry beneath his layers of leather.

By the time they hung their clothes to dry and fixed the mess that had become of their bed—which had thankfully stayed dry underneath—Mariam had drank some water and regained some energy.

"We'll be there in the morning."

"About time," Sigrid said, heavy with exhaustion.

The moment had come to crawl under the furs and lay next to Mariam. As she did, there was a rigid, invisible wall of tension between them. Something tingled beneath Sigrid's skin, a spark of heat that roamed from her belly, up to her lips, down to her toes.

"Um, sleep well," Mariam said.

"You, too!" Sigrid said with too much energy. She cringed.

"Good night," Fisk shouted from the helm. "I slept great last night, so I'm fine to keep steering."

Mariam muffled a giggle, which brought a smile to Sigrid's lips.

In the unfamiliar map of stars overhead, she tried to connect the dots. They almost made patterns, but this world was too new to recognize anything.

Beside her, Mariam breathed too fast to be anywhere near falling asleep. What was she thinking? Did she notice how close they lay, or was this normal for her?

Sigrid had never slept beside anyone before. Though she'd have shuffled away if anyone else had been beside her, there was something exciting about being this close to Mariam. She was acutely aware of the position of the girl's body—face inches away, chest rising and falling, hand within touching distance beneath the furs.

Heat rushed into her face.

She was being awkward. The pull toward Mariam was pure instinct, like the way horses gathered close in herds. Humans were pack animals, after all. That was all it came down to.

Besides, this wasn't the right time to entertain what else this feeling could be. They both needed to get to Helheim, and that should be the only thing going through her head—*not* wondering how it might feel to sleep a little closer or what Mariam would do if she moved her hand over so they touched or how soft her hair had felt running between her fingers.

Stop it. This was definitely the last thing Mariam would be thinking about right now.

In the stars, she decided upon her own constellation, visualizing lines to make up Sleipnir's eight legs. On his back was a girl with her hair braided over one shoulder.

She licked her lips, contemplating. Finally, she whispered, "Mariam?"

"Yeah?" Her reply came instantly.

"Do you really think I won't be able to get Sleipnir?"

It had been bugging her since they talked about it. Not that she needed Mariam to believe in her—she believed in herself even if no one else did—but it would have helped to know someone, anyone, thought she could fulfill that vision.

The whites of Mariam's eyes gleamed in the lantern flame. "After berating me for stealing a spear, you're telling me you want to steal the most powerful horse in all the nine worlds from one of the most powerful women in the nine worlds. Do you see why I'm a bit confused?"

Sigrid frowned. "We don't know for sure if I have to steal him from Elina."

"Then how else do you plan to get him?"

Fair point.

Sigrid considered pretending she had a secret plan, then gave up with a scoff. "She has it coming. She didn't seem to have a problem with sending you and that army to Vanaheim to steal the Eye, did she?"

A strange, almost startled expression crossed Mariam's face, like the blankets had been pulled off something she'd hidden. What was that about?

Fisk thumped over in his leather boots. "Do you want me to tie up your horse or…?"

Something clattered at the far end of the ship—probably Hestur nosing around the crates again and knocking something over.

Sigrid waved a hand. "Nah, he can just walk around and sniff things."

"Fisk," Mariam said, businesslike. "You and those elves stole from a lot of people, right?"

Fisk hesitated, then settled cross-legged beside them. "They did. Not me. I was dragged along without a say, more or less. You see, when my family—"

"Sure," Mariam said quickly. "Well, would any Night Elves try to steal something from a queen? Say, a prized possession?"

Fisk jerked back, as though aghast. "Golly, only if they wanted to get executed!"

"Hmm," Mariam said in a tone of mock thoughtfulness, pointedly staring at Sigrid.

Sigrid rolled her eyes. "What if it was written in the cosmos that they were the true owners of the thing they're trying to steal?"

"Well," Fisk said, elongating the word. "The queen probably doesn't care who the true owner is."

"Hmm," Mariam said again.

Sigrid poked her ribs, and Mariam squeaked, apparently ticklish.

Fisk made an odd, stifled noise.

Sigrid eyed him. "Are you laughing or constipated?"

"What?" Fisk tilted his head.

"Maybe if you took that ridiculous lemming mask off, we'd be able to read your expressions better." Sigrid grabbed for it.

Fisk recoiled, slapping his gloved hands to his cheeks. "Don't!"

"Just for a second." Sigrid reached for it again and managed to seize its large front teeth.

Fisk hollered. They toppled to the deck, rolling across it, while Mariam dissolved into laughter.

"Leave me alone!"

"Take it off."

"I can't!"

"Take it—off."

"Stop it!"

As they rolled across the deck, Mariam doubled over with

giggles, and Sigrid made the struggle more theatrical for her entertainment. The sound was like a taste of honey after a day spent eating cabbage.

"Stop! Do you want me to shrivel up and die?" Fisk said, sounding squashed as Sigrid lay halfway over him.

She let go and sat up, panting. "What? Is that what happens?"

"Yes!" Fisk adjusted his mask, breathing hard. "I mean, supposedly. I've never seen it because we were all careful not to expose ourselves to light after leaving Svartalfheim. But that is what we're warned of."

Sigrid pointed up. "It's nighttime, though. It should be okay."

Fisk pointed at the lanterns around them and then at the sky. "Fire. Stars. It counts." He sat up, tugging his leather sleeves and smoothing his chainmail, looking disgruntled even beneath it all.

From across the deck, Hestur stared at them with his ears back, like he disapproved of all the racket at this time of night.

"What do you look like then?" Mariam said, wiping tears of laughter.

Fisk said nothing, continuing to brush himself off. Was he angry?

"Maybe he's never been able to see his reflection," Sigrid said. Then a thought occurred to her. "Can you see through those eye holes?"

His lemming mask turned toward her. "Not in the same way you do. I mean, I have eyes." He pointed to the eye holes. "But they don't see light. They see heat."

"Weird," Sigrid said.

Mariam shrugged. "Sounds useful."

Hestur nickered.

"Now, if you're done trying to kill me, I'll go back to steering the ship," Fisk said, squaring his shoulders. Mumbling about personal space, he stomped back to the helm.

Sigrid frowned. The feeling that she'd done something bad

knotted her stomach, but she brushed it aside. She crawled back to the makeshift bed, and they lay beside each other, watching wispy clouds drift across the stars.

"Do you miss your friends?" Mariam said into the silence.

Sigrid let out a breath of laughter. "You know how the valkyries treated me."

"What about the stable hands? That guy, the one who raised you. Peter?"

Sigrid's chest tightened. Yes, she did miss him. After spending her whole life seeing him every day, she should have left him on better terms. What if Garmr ensured she never saw him again?

It'll be fine. A hellhound is a dog. I'm good with dogs.

Waves sloshed against the ship.

Hestur clip-clopped around the deck.

The silence stretched on.

"I don't get why you left," Mariam said.

Sigrid frowned at the darkness. "Vanaheim?"

Mariam exhaled. "It's the most beautiful place I've ever seen."

The lush vegetation and towers of Vanahalla were beautiful, but Sigrid knew from experience that a place could look as beautiful as Asgard and be as cruel as Niflheim.

"You don't know what it was like," she said, her words clipped.

Mariam was silent for a minute, and when she spoke again, her voice was colder than before. "How many meals did you eat per day?"

Sigrid hesitated. "Three."

Mariam snorted.

Sigrid sat up, glaring at her through the darkness. "Just because my suffering wasn't the same as yours—"

"Only the valkyries were mean to you, right? The stable hands were nice? Other people were nice."

Peter, Roland, Gregor, Vala… The names appeared in Sigrid's mind in answer to the question. But anger still burned in her chest.

How did sleeping side by side with fluttery feelings in her stomach devolve into this?

Sigrid glared at her. "You try being the butt of everyone's jokes for sixteen years!"

"At least you grew up around girls your age," Mariam said, glaring back. "Try growing up with literally no one."

"I'd rather grow up alone than with them," Sigrid snapped.

Mariam sucked in a breath. "Would you?" she said, sounding venomous.

Sigrid crossed her arms and lay back down, facing away from Mariam.

A moment later, Mariam scoffed and shuffled around until Sigrid was sure their backs were to each other.

Mariam didn't understand what it was like to be the only girl who wasn't a valkyrie. Sure, her life hadn't been one of exile and poverty like Mariam's, but she'd had her own struggles.

Hadn't she?

Sigrid's daily chores could hardly be called stressful. Next to living in Niflheim, spending the day feeding winged mares and cleaning a barn sounded luxurious. And she did have people who treated her right. She scowled into the darkness. Mariam's words couldn't make her doubt herself. She had every right to leave Vanaheim in search of something greater.

A long time passed before her eyelids grew heavy. She took solace in watching her constellation gallop across the sky, imagining herself as an unparalleled force in all the nine worlds.

CHAPTER TWENTY-SIX

A TART THIEF

Sigrid opened her eyes and found the longship still smothered in night, though strangely, the stars dusting the sky had vanished. *Did clouds roll in?*

The lanterns on the railing flickered, their flames struggling to cut through the blackness. Hestur's clip-clopping hooves echoed off their surroundings, eerie and hollow. The air was cool and damp, with a *drip, drip, drip* on all sides.

She sat up. It sounded like they were in a cave. They must have sailed right into that dark landmass on the horizon.

Across the deck, Mariam leaned against the helm, chatting with Fisk. A high-pitched giggle drifted toward Sigrid. She knew enough about Mariam by now to know she would never make that sound. It was Fisk, and he clasped a gloved hand on Mariam's shoulder as he buckled over with laughter.

Sigrid kicked out of the fur blankets and stood, suddenly irritated. Between the gloomy cave and last night's argument with Mariam, she found little to giggle about. The worst part was that Mariam was right. Sigrid's life had been cozy in comparison. But was it so wrong to seek a higher purpose?

Sigrid sighed and looked toward Hestur. The echo from his

hoofbeats and the sloshing water below were the only signs of the cavern's boundaries. They could have been sailing through the void between stars, for all the lanterns revealed. They should be on the lookout for anything threatening here, but Fisk and Mariam didn't seem to care. Hopefully this passage was safe—

Hestur blew his nostrils, making that harsh sound he often did when he was scared. His neck and tail lifted, his ears forward.

Sigrid opened her fingers and summoned her spear lying beside their nest of furs. Her pulse picked up.

Mariam, too, turned to Hestur with her spear ready.

But nothing happened.

Hestur wasn't even looking at a particular spot. He seemed to shy away from everything at once. Sigrid approached him with a soothing hand out. He leaned into her, seeking reassurance.

"What does he see?" Mariam said, knees bent as if ready to pounce.

"It's the atmosphere. I'm going to corral him." He was going to strain his tendons or drive himself to exhaustion with all of his pacing.

As she grabbed his mane to guide him, a *pit-pat, pit-pat, pit-pat* came from somewhere between Mariam and Fisk.

On the deck, a knee-high wooden duck wobbled in circles. Its feet were on wheels, little pieces of hide slapping the deck with each turn. It kept momentum, as if propelled by magic.

At Sigrid's puzzlement, Mariam said, "Fisk made it. Isn't it cute?"

Pit-pat, pit-pat, pit-pat.

"Made it out of what?"

Fisk motioned to the barrels and crates beneath the canvas up front. "Scraps."

Right. Night Elves were supposed to be the best craftsmen in the nine worlds.

"I siphoned the mobility enchantment on the boat," Fisk said.

"I made myself a weapon, too. It's not as great as your spears, but at least it's something. It's indestructible, same as this." He patted the wheel.

From a sheath across his back, he drew a wooden sword that had been honed to a fine point.

"Very impressive," Mariam said, beaming.

It's okay, I guess. Anyone could make a sword.

Hestur snorted and stomped his hooves, as if to remind her that he needed attention.

"Come on." She tugged his mane gently so he followed. "Let's make a corral for you."

She guided him to the canvas shelter and barricaded him by dragging the barrels and crates to form a wall. They came to his chest, letting him see over while keeping him safely contained. He snubbed the handful of alfalfa cubes she offered but after a moment seemed to decide he was hungry and closed his lips over them.

She rubbed his forehead. "Easy, buddy. We're almost there."

I hope.

Satisfied that he would be safer in this makeshift stall, Sigrid turned around and bumped into Mariam, who had walked over at some point.

"Is he all right?"

"Just nervous."

The orange glow from the lanterns flickered over Mariam's face, making her expression hard to read. Her lips were parted, her dark eyes deeper than the pool beneath them. Had she come over to check on Hestur, or did she want something? Last night's argument hovered between them like a swarm of flies.

Sigrid backed up half a step so her stomach would stop dancing over how close their faces were. She grasped for something to say. "I thought the underworld would be, you know, populated."

"We haven't reached the gates of Hel yet. This is just a primordial space between worlds."

"I see." She pushed her hands into her pockets, trying to look at ease. At the thought of what might lie ahead, her insides paced and weaved as much as Hestur. "How long before we get to Garmr?"

"Not sure. Like I said, leaving Helheim was easy."

Sigrid nodded. She let her gaze wander, as if there were more to see than blackness.

Pit-pat, pit-pat, thump.

The duck had broken away from its circle and bumped into the railing.

"Cheer up, stable girl," Mariam said, poking her ribs. "You don't need sunshine to be happy."

Sigrid couldn't help the little smile tugging at her lips. Maybe the air between them was clear, after all.

Mariam produced something from behind her back. It was a semla, round and doughy, looking like it had just been pulled out of an oven and pumped full of fresh whipped cream. "I don't know about you, but I'm going to have breakfast."

Sigrid's mouth fell open, all sense of dread evaporating as a more important urge seized her stomach. "Where did you get that?"

Mariam took a big gooey bite and motioned for her to follow. At the mast, a crate had been pried open, and an assortment of food spilled out.

"It refills itself," Mariam said thickly. "Third perk of a ship made by the gods." She stuffed the remainder in her mouth.

A moan of longing escaped. *Bless Ratatosk and his spectacular ship.*

Now, how many sweets could she devour before getting a stomachache?

Fisk left the helm to come eat, too. He hummed over the

contents, blocking Sigrid's view for an irritatingly long time before coming to a decision.

"An apple?" Sigrid said. "All the tarts and pastries in the worlds, and you choose an apple?"

Fisk shrugged feebly. "They're better here than at home." He lifted the sour green fruit to his lemming mask, then hesitated. It seemed that the shape of his mask didn't allow space for him to slide the apple underneath, because he announced that he was going to find a spot beneath the canvas. Lifting the mask would let in light and burn him.

"But we're in a cave," Sigrid said.

Fisk pointed to a lantern. "Fire."

As he skipped off, Sigrid called after him, "Feed the core to Hestur!"

Fisk gave a thumbs-up before slipping between the barrels and disappearing into a corner.

Her stomach growled. She stooped and grabbed the most delicious thing in sight—a tart with a thick pastry crust and blueberry filling.

"Amazing! I haven't had one of these in—"

Mariam swiped it out of her hand, leaving her clutching at air. "Thank you."

"Hey!" Sigrid said, stomach fluttering at Mariam's mischievous grin. Her shock melted into a laugh. *So Mariam is feeling playful.*

Sigrid stepped closer and extended a hand, a smile tugging her lips. "Dangerous move. I'm *very* serious about dessert."

Instead of returning it, Mariam took a bite. It pulled apart in a flaky, gooey way. "Mm, so tasty," she said through a mouthful.

Sigrid gave an indignant cry and tried to steal back the remainder.

Mariam dodged her. "So—mmph—good."

Sigrid couldn't help laughing, relieved to see her feeling better. She reached for the pastry again, determined to get a bite.

"I earned this breakfast! Don't you want me to feel joy?"

They struggled for a minute, a tangle of limbs and hair and giggles, before Mariam bit into it and seized Sigrid's wrists, stopping her. She grinned with the uneaten half of pastry between her teeth.

"How dare you steal my tart?" Sigrid said, attempting her most threatening whisper.

Mariam cocked an eyebrow as if issuing a challenge.

Sigrid's gaze flicked to the dessert between Mariam's lips.

A tendril of heat wound through her middle. Though she could have pulled her wrists free, she let Mariam keep holding them. They both panted from the struggle. The sweet smell of blueberries drifted toward her on Mariam's breath.

Would it be too forward if she leaned in and took a bite? Could she go so far as to think Mariam *wanted* her to do that? Her heart thrummed as she tried to summon the courage. Mariam's brown eyes burned through her, heating up her cheeks.

She could also be completely misreading this situation.

She leaned closer, tentatively, trying to interpret whatever that glint was in Mariam's eyes. Her lips parted with the anticipation of brushing against Mariam's, of tasting her for the briefest moment. If Mariam recoiled or got awkward, Sigrid could just laugh it off and never make eye contact with her again. But if her intent was what it seemed to be...

"Found a dark corner between some barrels!" Fisk called out, flitting back toward them.

Mariam let go of Sigrid's wrists and swallowed the rest. She turned away, patting her cheeks. "I can take over steering for a bit, if you want more breakfast."

"It's all right," Fisk said. "We're nearly there."

Sigrid stayed on the floor, face hot, cursing Fisk's timing.

CHAPTER TWENTY-SEVEN

HELLHOUNDS
AREN'T DOGS

Sigrid's lips still tingled in anticipation as she went back to the crate and looked inside. It had magically replenished the missing tart.

She grabbed it and took a bite.

The flavor was okay, but tasting the one in Mariam's lips would have been better.

Couldn't Fisk have waited another minute before returning to them?

"Nearly there? How much longer?" she asked him, ready to welcome the base of the spring and set foot on land again. The cave was dismally lonely, even with one another's company.

In answer, Fisk pointed ahead through the darkness. A glimmer showed up in the distance.

Sigrid gasped and ran to the railing. "What is that?"

Flames danced on a far-off shoreline—maybe there to guide visitors to port. The cave warmed as they drew nearer.

Sigrid squinted, searching for signs of people. "Is that Helheim?"

A *glop* sounded in the water, like a fish jumping. Did fish live in the spring of Hvergelmir?

Mariam joined her at the railing. "We're close to Garmr. I remember this from when we came through with Ratatosk."

A jolt ran up Sigrid's spine. *Garmr.* The hellhound was here somewhere, ready to defend the way to Helheim. She'd put off thinking about what they would do when they got here, and now her time ignoring the inevitable had run out. Did that crate of food have a steak inside, and would the dog go after it if she threw it?

The cave widened into a massive dome the size of the valkyrie training field, its ceiling too high and dark to see, the rock walls glistening faintly in the glow from their lanterns. At the edges, a rocky shoreline sloped up from the water and wrapped around the perimeter. Opposite them, a black hole in the rock marked the only way out besides the tunnel they came from.

It was big enough for Ratatosk's ship to fit through.

On the shore beside their exit, the heat from the dancing flames intensified, thickening the air like a wool blanket over her mouth. She wiped the beads of sweat rolling down her temples.

"We're sure Garmr is just a hound, right?" Sigrid said, unable to stop the wavering in her voice.

"Just?" Fisk said from the helm. "Mariam, is she serious?"

The distant flames extinguished, like someone had thrown water over them. The shore plunged into darkness. Ghosts of orange light lingered in Sigrid's vision, which she blinked away. *Odd.* Was the cave alive? Did it know they were here?

"Let's make something clear, Sigrid," Mariam said. "A hellhound is not a dog. The only reason for the *hound* in the name is...well, I suppose because of its shape."

Their words drifted on the edge of Sigrid's attention.

Above where the flames had vanished, a spark ignited. A trail of fire flickered across the ceiling toward them, swirling and gathering like the dancing lights that had once illuminated Vanaheim's sky in the dead of winter.

Maybe the cave is showing us the way.

But then why was her body telling her to run?

The ship swayed as Fisk steered them close to the cavern's perimeter instead of through the middle. Their lanterns illuminated the rocky shore beside them and what seemed to be clusters of black-and-white stones piled across it.

Sigrid wiped her face to get the layer of sweat off. What were they talking about, saying a hellhound wasn't a dog? "Does it bark?"

"Yeah," Mariam said.

"If it looks like a dog and sounds like a dog, then why isn't it a dog?"

The clusters on the shoreline became clearer. *Bones.* Skeletons lay all over the shore, charred and blackened by fire. Some formed the shape of human bodies, arms and legs splayed in whatever position they'd died in. Other bones were strewn about, broken fragments that could have belonged to anyone or anything. Every piece was stripped bare, no trace of flesh or tendon left attached.

Her muscles locked tight. The wrongness in the air sucked the breath from her lungs. "Mariam?"

But Mariam and Fisk were gaping at the ceiling.

Sigrid's gaze shot up. The river of fire was gathering into a swirling maelstrom, intensifying, stinging her eyes and forcing sweat through her skin. Its shape twisted and pinched, forming something resembling a—*paw?*

With a *whoosh* like a gust of wind, the blaze shot at Fisk. Sigrid and Mariam cried out and lunged for him, hauling him down and away from the flame.

The three of them flattened on the deck as it swept over their heads. Sigrid's eyes watered from the brightness. Then the blaze was gone, leaving them blinking in the inadequate glow from the lanterns.

Something was burning, pungent and smoky. Sigrid clapped a shaking hand to her scalp to check if it singed her hair, but it hadn't. She sat up along with the others.

"Am I on fire?" Fisk said. "I feel like I am."

A wisp of smoke rose from his back, where his chainmail glowed bright red and seemed to be melting his leather jacket.

Mariam grabbed the water bucket meant for Hestur and doused him.

"What was that?" Sigrid exclaimed, finding her voice as Fisk's clothing sizzled and spat.

"That," Mariam said, pointing at the fire storm on the ceiling, "is Garmr."

CHAPTER TWENTY-EIGHT

PROVOKING A HELLHOUND

A low growl like the rumbling of a rockfall came from overhead, as if to confirm Mariam's words.

Fisk nodded. "If we're calling him a dog, then that was his paw."

Sigrid's head spun. "Garmr is *fire*?"

"More or less," Mariam said.

The flames from around the cavern knitted together, rendering a distinct form that towered over them. It really had the shape of a hound, but it was the furthest thing from one. Garmr's body was a storm of orange-and-red flame, which danced as if wind roared through the cavern. His back reached as high as the barn back home, each leg as thick as a tree trunk.

The darker spots where his eyes would be narrowed, like he was analyzing how best to destroy them. When he snarled, balls of fire dripped from his fangs like saliva.

"Run!" Fisk shouted.

They scattered.

The dripping fire slobbered onto the deck, hissing and dying where they landed.

The hound snapped, fiery teeth closing over the place where they'd been. He lunged again, snarling and biting, until his jaws closed over the pit-patting duck. With a *crunch*, it was gone. Splinters and ashes fell from his jaws and plopped into the water.

Garmr moved like a spreading wildfire, flames jumping between his joints as if moving from tree to tree. He struck the ship with his paws and tail until it careened out of control.

"He's going to burn the boat down!" Sigrid said, heart slamming into her ribs, pumping adrenaline through her body.

The three of them huddled beneath the canvas where Hestur was corralled. He tirelessly pawed the deck, wanting to be let out.

Mariam wiped her brow. "It won't burn. First perk, remember? We just have to stay aboard and not get burned ourselves."

The water in the cavern became a stormy sea as Garmr roamed the dome, looking to attack from all sides. Choppy waves started pushing the ship back the way they came.

Garmr seemed satisfied with their retreat, because he backed off. He crossed the cavern, the water rising to his knees. It bubbled and spat wherever he stepped, sending up tendrils of steam. At the opposite wall, he left the water to crouch defensively in front of the opening.

He'd just blocked their only way to Helheim.

Sigrid worked to calm her breath, but it was impossible. How were they supposed to fight against pure fire? "There's no other way, right?"

Mariam shook her head. "It's a straight shot to Helheim."

Sigrid stepped out from the canopy for a better look, but when Garmr saw her, he let out a bark so loud that she brought her hands to her ears. A blast of heat forced her back a step.

"We need to stay under here if we want to get past him alive," Mariam said. "It won't burn."

"But who's going to steer?" Fisk asked.

Already the wheel spun out of control, the ship rising and falling in the waves. The current pushed them resolutely back the way they came.

Garmr paced between shore and water, keeping his attention on their bobbing ship.

Mariam ran her hands along the edge of the canvas. "Doesn't it stretch across the ship? Where's the rest of it?"

"Ah…" Fisk cleared his throat. "I, um, apologize on behalf of Night Elves."

Mariam's expression fell.

Sigrid put a hand over her mouth, pulse racing. *The canvas tents around the elves' campsite.* It was stolen, like everything else there. Those thieving scumbags had sabotaged their plan for getting past Garmr. Now what were they supposed to do?

She traced a finger where the canvas was fastened to the railing. Could they move the whole thing and hide under it while Fisk steered? She tugged one of the enormous wooden pegs until she was out of breath, then gave a growl of frustration. They would need an axe to separate the canvas from the wood. Given the roughly cut edge, that must have been exactly what the Night Elves had used.

"I thought this thing was supposed to be indestructible," she said through gritted teeth, pulling the canvas with two hands.

"The, um, axe was crafted in Svartalfheim using the same enchantments used to…build Thor's hammer…" Fisk said in a small voice, trailing off at Sigrid's deadly glare.

So they hacked up an indestructible ship. Brilliant.

They had to get into that tunnel. They could try letting the ship steer itself toward the little opening, but the waves were too fierce. The current would push them wherever it wanted, and they would hit the walls and capsize.

Fisk turned his mask to her, as if waiting for instruction. Mariam quivered, gripping a barrel for support. She needed to rest again, not fight a hellhound.

Hestur bumped Sigrid's shoulder with his nose, as if to say, *Do something!*

"All right," she said under her breath, then louder, "All right."

They couldn't let this walking campfire push them back. They hadn't come this far to turn around. What could be used to extinguish fire? He was too big to smother—but could something magical incapacitate him?

Sigrid squared her shoulders, stomach tightening in anticipation. She stepped out from under the canvas, twirling her spear. "If a weapon infused with magic can be used to damage Ratatosk's ship, then one can be used to damage Garmr, right?"

"Sigrid, don't," Mariam said. "You'll destroy your spear."

"She's right," Fisk said.

She shot them a glare. "Anyone have a better idea? We need to force him back, and these are our only weapons. That, and Fisk's toy sword."

Mariam was silent.

"It's not a toy," Fisk mumbled.

When neither Mariam nor Fisk raised any more protests, she focused on Garmr and lifted her arm. A tremor of nerves passed over her, messing up her aim. She had to stay calm.

He's a normal target. You've done this a thousand times.

With a sharp exhale, she threw her weapon with everything she had.

The golden spear flew across the dark cavern like a shooting star. She held her breath, pulse pounding in her ears.

After several long seconds, it hit Garmr in the chest. He yelped, cringing, as fire bloomed like a mushroom from the point of impact. The cavern rattled with a deafening noise.

Before Sigrid could tell if she'd injured him, a wave of heat blasted the ship, sending all of them crashing into each other. She gasped, colliding with Fisk. Even Hestur stumbled, and Mariam fell flat on the deck against his shoulder.

In a jumble of limbs and hooves, everyone got to their feet, struggling against the careening ship. Nothing aboard had reduced to ash, thank the gods.

Garmr shook his head, and the flames that made up his body roared as brightly as ever.

"Well," Sigrid said, wiping an arm across her hot, stinging face.

"Good effort," Fisk said, helping Mariam lean on Hestur for support.

Garmr kept pacing. Balls of fire dripped from his fangs and sizzled when they hit the water. Steam billowed around his legs.

Sigrid opened her hand to summon the spear back, knowing it was hopeless. The thing had been vaporized by hellfire. *Great plan.*

"You're brave for trying," Mariam offered.

Her words were a small comfort. Brave or not, it hadn't worked. Sigrid sucked in lungfuls of air, unable to catch her breath. She refused to come all this way for nothing.

Garmr snarled as the ship drifted closer, his fiery hackles rising. He blocked the whole exit. The flames that made up his spine rose high overhead, casting shadows across the ceiling. Emptiness filled the space between his four towering legs. And beside him...

Sigrid chewed her lip, trying to focus on a solution and not on the flaming beast.

Waves lapped onto the wide, rocky shoreline.

Hestur pawed the deck.

What if...

The hellhound paced in front of the tunnel, his flames continuing to jump from joint to joint like a spreading wildfire.

"If we want to get past him, we need a decoy," Sigrid said confidently, racing through a plan in her mind. "It's the only way."

Mariam looked at her sharply. "Like what?"

"Hestur and I can do it."

CHAPTER TWENTY-NINE

PLAYING FETCH
WITH GARMR

Mariam stared, eyes as round as the shields hanging on the sides of the ship, as if waiting for Sigrid to announce that she was kidding. "What—is—wrong with you?"

"Watch the way Garmr moves. He can catch a drifting ship, but he won't catch Hestur at a gallop. We've got the whole cave perimeter to work with."

Mariam gaped. "You make it sound like you've out-galloped fiery hellhounds before."

Sigrid shoved a barrel aside with a loud scrape, freeing Hestur, and he wasted no time in springing through the opening. To Fisk, she said, "As soon as I've lured Garmr away from the passage, sail into it. Hestur and I will catch up—even if we have to jump in the water."

Fisk gave a jerky nod.

She clucked at Hestur, inviting him to follow her to the back of the boat. "This way, buddy."

He obeyed, following her as closely as a trained herding dog. He was so alert, with his neck stretched high and nostrils flaring. Was this cruel? The cave and fire made him nervous, and he wanted her guidance, and rather than protect him, she was leading him straight into danger.

But this was the role of a valkyrie.

When she fulfilled her cosmic destiny and joined the valkyries, riding to other worlds and facing danger together would be what they did as a team.

It sent a bolt of determination through her.

A valkyrie shows no fear.

Sigrid chanted the words in her mind as she scanned the cave one more time. "I need to get to shore," she called out. "Fisk, can you keep the ship facing Garmr so he can't see us slip off the back?"

Fisk raced for the helm, moving like one flitting shadow among many. "Hang on. I'll get you closer."

Sigrid rubbed Hestur's ear, eyeing their path. "See the bumpy racetrack running along the wall, buddy? That's where we're headed. Breezy gallop."

She put on her helmet and Hestur's bridle. Would it be a help or a hindrance to have a saddle on? Probably a hindrance, given the extra weight. Speed was the priority. She left the saddle behind and removed her boots. Those wouldn't help when she had to swim.

Mariam hurried over. "Are you sure about this?"

Sigrid swallowed hard and tried to put on a brave face. *Valkyries show no fear.* "It'll be okay."

Once Fisk steered them as close to shore as he could without hitting ground, Sigrid leaned over the railing and touched the water. *Not bad.* The hellfire must have warmed it up.

"Okay." Not allowing her dread to build, she swung her legs over and plunged in.

Though a couple of years had passed since her last swim, her muscles remembered what to do. She would have to tell Peter when she got home that all of their time spent jumping in the river came in handy.

Hestur nickered, watching curiously as she treaded below him.

"Hand me the reins," she said to Mariam, who hesitated.

"Please. This is the only way."

Mariam rocked from foot to foot, seeming to weigh their options. She must have come to the same conclusion, because she pulled the reins over Hestur's head and leaned over to pass them to Sigrid.

"Only because I know how fast Hestur is." She said it lightly, but there was a tremor in her voice.

Sigrid tugged the reins, doing her best to hide how much the turbulent water mirrored what was going on inside her stomach right now. "C'mon, Hestur. The water's nice. Even better than Vanahalla's moat."

He stepped forward until he leaned against the railing, and as she kept pulling, he let his neck stretch as long as it would go without having to face the inevitable.

Mariam clucked to him and clapped a hand on his hindquarters. With both of them encouraging him, he began to dance on his hooves. He shuffled sideways, considering his approach, then gathered his legs and jumped.

The leap into the water was ungraceful. A deluge soaked Sigrid's face and helmet, and she spat out a mouthful that tasted like charcoal. By the time she finished coughing and rubbing her eyes, Hestur was already swimming for shore, nose in the air.

"Go now," she called to Fisk.

"You got it! See you in the tunnel," he yelled back from the helm.

Mariam leaned over the railing. "Sigrid." Her mouth opened, but no more words came. Trembling and gaunt, she looked ready to faint.

Sigrid nodded, her heart in her throat. She would get Mariam through this.

Fisk sailed the longship back toward Garmr and the passage he guarded. The hellhound fixated on the approaching longship, failing to notice the little horse swimming away behind it. She silently thanked Hestur's dark coat and the camouflage provided by the water.

Hestur got to the shore first and shook himself off. He sniffed the ground, maybe searching for a familiar scent. Sigrid found the rocky bottom with her bare toes and trudged up to meet him. Water dripped from her hair, and she plucked at her heavy tunic, uncomfortable. Maybe it would have been worth the embarrassment of jumping in wearing her undergarments.

Garmr paced, watching the ship sail nearer. A low rumble came from him and filled the cavern.

Sigrid shook out her trembling hands and vaulted onto Hestur's back. She scanned the barren shore for a refuge. Ahead, a hollow in the stone wall would be big enough to keep them out of reach of those fiery paws.

The longship drew nearer to Garmr, looking smaller and more insignificant by the second. He snapped his jaws, crouching in front of the tunnel.

Sigrid tightened her grip on the reins, heart about to pound right out of her chest. "Ready for another mission?"

Hestur's ears turned back, listening.

When she nudged him, they sprang into a canter, drumming a steady beat on the stone shoreline. They headed toward the flaming beast.

Garmr still focused on the ship. He entered the water, snarling in warning, stalking it like a cat spotting a field mouse.

Sigrid's pulse sped up in time with Hestur's strides. As they galloped, moving steadily toward the hellhound, the barrier between them disappeared. She and Hestur became one mind, responding to each other's movements.

Advancing on the ship, Garmr didn't notice them approaching on the shore. But they couldn't go much nearer to him before it became too dangerous.

Sigrid was back to sweating buckets from the heat coming off the beast. It was foolhardy to invite him closer, but that's what she had to do. "Hey!" Sigrid shouted. "Look here, you flaming piece of—"

Garmr snapped his head around so fast that the light took a moment to catch up, leaving an orange trail in the darkness. Though he arguably had no eyes, those black holes looked right at her.

He opened his fiery jaws and barked. Sigrid winced, tightening her grip on the reins. The sound echoed so loudly that rock chips and dust fell from the ceiling, and a wave of heat billowed at them.

Hestur galloped faster, ears flattened against his head, positively diving into danger.

Garmr's paws sloshed through the water as he abandoned his pursuit of the ship and stalked toward Sigrid and Hestur.

Sigrid leaned back and pulled the reins, surprised to find Hestur facing Garmr so boldly. Responding to her cue, he came to a jerky stop.

Garmr barked, both sound and heat wave blasting toward them.

"Run!"

Hestur spun on his haunches so fast that Sigrid had to grab his mane to stop from toppling sideways. If she'd thought he was fast during their gallops in Vanaheim, it had nothing on how he moved now. Sigrid fought the urge to close her eyes as the hot air whipped across her face. She gasped, forcing her breaths to steady.

"Good boy!"

Hestur's ears stayed flat and his nose stuck out, streamlining him as he powered onward.

Another bark reverberated, and a *whoosh* like a gust of wind. Water splashed. The light on the cavern walls flickered. The hot wind blew harder, whirling like a storm.

They pounded back along the shore at top speed, reaching the hollow in the wall in far less time than it took for them to leave it.

Sigrid steered Hestur inside, needing a firmer hand than usual. "Whoa!"

He stopped before he hit the wall, halting so abruptly that she nearly flew over his head. He pivoted to face the entrance with an agility that pitched her off-balance. She extended a hand to brace against the wall, breathing hard, pulse pounding in her ears.

Garmr appeared, barking and snarling. He reached a fiery paw inside, trying to get them, but Hestur shrank out of reach against the back of the cavern.

"Good boy," Sigrid whispered again, voice shaking. She stroked Hestur's neck. They'd done it. They'd distracted Garmr to let the ship through.

But they were trapped.

She hadn't thought things through at all.

Something crunched beneath Hestur's hooves, and Sigrid immediately regretted looking down. *Skeletons*. The charred remains shattered as Hestur recoiled from the flames reaching toward them.

Sigrid's chest tightened, her mind foggy. The heat was sucking out all the air, and she struggled to draw in a steady breath. They had to get out of here and catch up to the ship, but how? If Garmr would look away, even for a second, it would give them time to blast away without ending up engulfed in his flaming jaws.

The water dripping from her and Hestur sizzled dry from the intense flames, but streams of sweat took its place. Her legs stuck uncomfortably to Hestur's sides. The familiar scent of his sweat met her nose, oddly comforting, triggering memories of galloping across Vanaheim on sunny days.

Garmr swiped with his paw, leaving scorch marks on the walls.

Sigrid jerked back, letting out a scream. Hestur skittered, responding to her fear. "It's okay," she murmured, stroking Hestur's sweaty neck. "We'll be fine. We're going to get out."

Look away. Look back at the ship.

But Garmr continued to growl and swipe his paw at them with no signs of losing interest. His frustration rose—no one escaped him, after all—and he became frantic.

Sigrid wiped an arm across her sweaty face, suffocating in the heat. Would the fire suck the oxygen out of the little hollow? Or would the crevice collapse in on them first?

Then a cry rose across the cavern. Mariam or Fisk—she couldn't tell who—yipped like a coyote.

Garmr froze. His fiery ears turned back, listening to it.

The yipping increased, but Garmr ignored it. He thrust a paw into the cavern again, reaching for them.

Hestur pressed farther into the wall. Sigrid's heart ached as he quivered. Valkyries were supposed to show no fear, but how was that possible right now? It coursed through Sigrid's veins, scattering her thoughts and seizing her muscles.

She'd been naive to think she could do this on her own.

A shattering explosion and a blast of heat filled the air, and Garmr yelped and shrank back. He howled and snapped as great chunks of rock fell from the ceiling and splashed into the water.

Like the snap of a whip, Sigrid's mind cleared. She grabbed Hestur's mane and kicked him into a gallop. He surged forward and hit full speed in three strides, shooting between Garmr's front legs.

Flames licked toward them, the heat pulling sweat through her pores.

They were almost clear of Garmr's back legs when a deafening bark sounded overhead. The hellhound turned, one of his back legs skittering toward them. They dodged it, barely, but there was no escape from his swiping tail.

Sigrid cried out as the line of fire that formed his tail arced toward them, covering too much ground to dodge. "Jump!" she shouted, crouching into position.

Hestur needed no urging. His hooves lifted from the ground, and his powerful haunches took them soaring over Garmr's tail. The key to jumping was to avoid looking down, but Sigrid couldn't help it this time as the flames disappeared beneath Hestur's belly.

The landing almost unseated her, but Sigrid clamped her legs tighter to avoid bouncing off Hestur's side. "Go!"

Hestur galloped toward the ship with all his heart.

Garmr barked, the noise reverberating. Light flickered across the cavern walls.

Sigrid leaned closer to Hestur's neck, moving with him as he opened his stride. Far ahead, the ship coasted into the tunnel. The open-mouthed serpent at its nose disappeared into blackness.

They tore over the rocky shoreline toward it, the ground flying beneath them. Hestur dodged boulders, jumped over crevices, and swept past the skeletons on the shoreline, snapping bones beneath his hooves. He ran for his life.

"Almost there, buddy," Sigrid yelled over the rushing wind and Garmr's frustrated growls.

The ship became a shadow, the dark pit swallowing its outline.

The ground rose as they neared the tunnel, lifting them off the waterline.

Garmr's fiery hot breath washed over her back. He was a step behind them. In another second, his jaws would snap closed over them.

They were three strides from the tunnel.

A chasm of water sloshed below.

The jump was impossibly wide.

All of Sigrid's years of riding didn't prepare her for the fear seizing her lungs. They would never make a jump this big.

They were two strides away.

One stride.

She closed her eyes and held on.

There was a deafening bark, a blast of heat that seared her back, and Hestur's muscles gathered beneath her.

CHAPTER THIRTY

TURBULENT FEELINGS

Hestur went airborne, and the force of his jump launched Sigrid upward so hard that she separated from his back. She clung to his mane and clamped her legs tighter.

The deck rushed toward them.

They hit the moving surface.

Hestur jerked to a stop, and she lost her balance.

Sigrid hit the deck shoulder-first, a pained gasp wrenching from her. The crack of her helmet rang in her ears a second later. The world spun, and her stomach roiled as she tried to get up. *We made it?*

Fisk's voice bounced around the tunnel. "Hold on! The waves might push us into the walls."

Hestur's hooves clattered away across the wooden deck. He blew his nostrils, making that saw-like sound.

Get up. Locate Garmr. They weren't in the clear yet.

She sat up, fear for her companions overtaking the urge to squeeze her eyes shut and roll into a ball. Garmr's huge body covered the mouth of the passage, swirling like a fire caught in the wind as he tried to follow them in. His booming barks shook the tunnel walls.

Mariam appeared at Sigrid's side, holding her arms as they fought to stay still against the high swells carrying the ship onward.

"We're almost through!" Fisk shouted. "The passage widens ahead."

The current pushed them steadily into darkness, until the hellhound turned into a yellow flicker that grew smaller and smaller.

"Slow. Take it easy." Mariam made a distressed sound when Sigrid tried to stand. But the shaking in her limbs was so bad she couldn't get her feet under her. Why had she wanted to ride into danger like that? What was wrong with her?

She was beyond lucky to have made it away from that monster alive. But Hestur…the whites of his eyes showed, and he kept pacing the deck. That had probably given him a permanent fear of fire.

"Hestur, I'm so sorry," she croaked.

Mariam helped Sigrid to her feet, and Sigrid leaned on her, unable to walk without the support.

Panting and sweaty, Sigrid made her way over. Her eyes welled with tears as she took in his blowing nostrils and sweat-soaked neck.

"He'll be all right," Mariam said. "I think he's mostly worried that you fell off."

As if to confirm this, Hestur bumped Sigrid's chest with his nose. She wrapped her arms around his neck, burying her face in his mane. She clung to him as he danced sideways, letting herself be dragged across the deck. "We're okay."

"By golly, you got us through!" Fisk said in his usual chirpy tone. "Your plan worked."

Sigrid didn't want to hear it. She'd nearly gotten everyone reduced to ash. "I shouldn't have put Hestur through that," she said into his mane. "He trusted me, and I failed him."

"You didn't fail him." Mariam settled a hand on Sigrid's

shoulder and squeezed. "You led him into battle like a valkyrie, and he came through. He's doing fine. Look."

Sigrid peeled her face off Hestur's neck. Sure enough, his ears were perked, and though he was catching his breath, his eyes were bright.

Like a valkyrie.

Was that what being a valkyrie was like? Pure terror?

Sigrid rubbed her arm. It throbbed where she'd landed on it.

As she and the others stood panting, sweat and water shining on their faces, the ship floated down the passage. With no one steering, it bumped and scraped against the walls. The fact that they'd made it past Garmr sat hollow, the lingering terror overtaking any sense of victory.

With a jolt in her chest, Sigrid spun to Mariam. "What was that explosion? Did you throw your spear at him?"

Mariam grimaced. "Yeah. I doused it in lantern oil first. I was going for as big a distraction as possible."

Sigrid gaped at her.

Mariam held out her forearm. A pink, bubbling burn was etched across it.

Sigrid sucked in a breath. "Did Garmr get you?"

"The ship was rocking when I tipped the lantern. It's just oil."

Fisk pushed past Sigrid so abruptly that she nearly fell over, her limbs still weak. He cupped his gloved hands beneath Mariam's arm, studying the burn. "Does it hurt?"

Sigrid waved an arm. "Of course it hurts. Look at her skin!"

Mariam didn't argue. "Do we have anything to put on it?"

"There'll be ointment somewhere." Fisk flitted to the crates and barrels at the front, leaving the ship to bob along and scrape the walls.

Sigrid and Mariam caught their breaths in the ringing silence.

"Now both of us lost our spears," Sigrid said, throat tight.

"Worth it."

Sigrid offered a smile, but her eyes landed on the burn again. "The lanterns on Ratatosk's ship aren't made of, like, magical fire or anything, right?"

Mariam shook her head. "Just a normal, painful burn. Are *you* okay?"

Sigrid swallowed hard. She nodded once, cradling her arm. Had Mariam really launched that bold strike for her? "You didn't have to do that."

"Of course I had to." Mariam crossed her arms, wincing. "Your plan worked, and you needed a way to get back to us."

"No one was supposed to get hurt."

"That's the way life is on this side of your cushy stables," Mariam said, without heat or meanness behind it. Just a fact. "Sometimes you need to make risky decisions and sacrifices. Get used to it if you want to be a valkyrie."

Sigrid stared at her, finding the words too real to be offended by them. She was naive to have expected otherwise. Riding into battle was probably even more grim and terrifying than this.

Sigrid stepped aside when Fisk returned with a bucket of medicine and bandages. "Hold out your arm," he said, ignoring Sigrid as if she were another crate on the ship.

"You were amazing," Mariam said, and Sigrid's heart flipped over before she realized the words were directed at Fisk. "The way you steered us into the tunnel like that? Are you sure you haven't captained a ship before?"

"My father was a sailor," Fisk said. "He never taught me anything, but I wonder if this sort of thing can be part of someone's nature, you know?"

Scowling, Sigrid moved away to check on Hestur's legs. They could swell up after that hard ride over uneven stone.

While she fetched Hestur and tied him to the mast, she cast furtive glances at the others. Why was Fisk so weird about Mariam? He held her hand tenderly, dabbing something on her forearm. Their voices were too low to hear. Then he looked up at Mariam with those empty animal skull eyes and put a hand on her cheek.

Mariam smiled back at him.

A knot formed in Sigrid's belly, made worse by the adrenaline still raging inside her. Why was he caressing Mariam's face? Had they suddenly bonded over facing certain death in the jaws of a hellhound?

Sigrid's stomach twisted with undeniable jealousy. Her feelings toward Mariam hadn't exactly been platonic—the way she'd been drawn into her beautiful features, and kind of maybe wanted to kiss her, and got hopelessly fluttery inside when they touched.

There had been a few moments when she'd thought Mariam felt the same, but...

She shook her head, dismissing the secret wish that she was the one touching Mariam's face and receiving that stunning smile.

They were hours away from Helheim.

That meant they were closer to finding Aesa and closer to Sigrid fulfilling her cosmic destiny. Maybe this was good reminder to focus on those more important things.

CHAPTER THIRTY-ONE

BLOOD MARKINGS

Sigrid leaned over the side and filled four buckets with spring water for Hestur's legs, pain shooting up her arm with each lift. Praying she hadn't broken or sprained anything, she brought the full buckets to the center of the deck and made Hestur stand in them. The water came up to his knees, and that was the best she could do. She rubbed the liniment she'd packed all over his legs and dumped more in the buckets, which would help his circulation and hopefully stop him from getting sore.

Hestur had a bemused expression as he stood splayed in the buckets.

"Twenty minutes and you can get out." She rubbed his forehead and fed him a carrot from Ratatosk's endless food supply.

Fisk and Mariam sat close together on a crate, legs touching. He inspected her bandaged arm, holding her hand, even though he'd obviously finished with it.

A knot tightened in Sigrid's stomach. Fisk wasn't allowed to like Mariam in that way. This would distract her from the mission.

Then a darker thought struck her.

Mariam had commanded an army of Night Elves before, and

Fisk had played a trick on her so his group could capture them. They'd both promised to help Sigrid, but they'd also come on this quest with their own agendas. Alliances could change. What if they made some kind of alternate plan for themselves? One that worked against Sigrid?

Bile burned in her throat. Had they been pretending to help her all this time? In her early years, before she knew better, the junior valkyries had done that. They'd pretended to be her friends one moment only to stab her in the back with lies to General Eira.

Sigrid shook her head, hating how the trickle of doubt had suddenly become a puddle of worry. "Should I confront them?" she whispered, but Hestur's only answer was a snort and a nibble.

When his legs had soaked enough, she helped him step out of the buckets and let him wander around the deck again. He seemed calmer, his anxiety dissipated.

Sigrid couldn't say the same for herself. She hadn't stopped shaking yet. Hestur's companionship was the only thing stopping her from breaking down and crying.

Finally, Fisk left Mariam to tend the helm. *About time.*

Sigrid seized the opportunity to go to her. She adjusted her tunic, cleared her throat, and then said with forced casualness, "What did he want?"

"Just making sure I heal properly."

"Hm." Sigrid didn't believe it. "How do you feel?"

Mariam turned her arm to inspect the bandage. "Not bad."

"You could've been killed, playing with fire like that." Her stomach tightened with worry, even though Mariam sat safe and sound in front of her.

"Really?" Mariam snorted. "This coming from you? Sigrid, what you did was…" She shook her head and dropped her gaze, leaving Sigrid to wonder what she was about to say. Foolish? Reckless? Brave, maybe?

Mariam shuffled over, leaving room for her to sit on the crate.

She did, putting a more respectful distance between them than Fisk had.

"I *was* brainless, thinking I could outrun Garmr," Sigrid admitted.

"You succeeded," Mariam said, tilting her head, "ergo it was brilliant."

Sigrid almost smiled. "I got lucky. That plan could have easily gone wrong."

"It's not the worst plan I've seen."

"Please. When did you see something worse?"

Mariam chewed her lip, her cheeks going pink. "I once tried to train a stray dog to steal food for me. He ended up teaching his packmates everything, and they ransacked the local market and the butcher lost two fingers."

Sigrid covered her mouth with a hand.

Mariam shrugged weakly, as if in apology. Her expression was so earnest, even bashful. "Have you ever seen a sheepdog running down the street with an entire roast in its mouth and a shouting butcher running after him? It was horrible."

Laughter burst from Sigrid's lips. She couldn't help it. After what she'd been through, the story struck her funny. In a universe where a hound as terrifying as Garmr could exist, stray sheepdogs were stealing roasts from butchers.

Mariam's eyes widened at first. Then her lips pulled into a grin and she started laughing, too.

The giggles took hold of them. When Mariam leaned in and gripped Sigrid's shoulder for support, the exhilaration was the best feeling she'd had in weeks. Her heart expanded with every glimpse of Mariam's playful, carefree side. Despite everything the valkyrie had been through and all the pain she must be feeling—not only from her burns and scrapes, but also the soul sickness from losing Aesa—she was determined to keep living. Never had Sigrid met anyone so strong, so inspiring, and with a smile this contagious.

When they calmed down, Sigrid sat up and wiped her tears, skin dancing where they'd brushed against each other. She nudged Mariam gently with an elbow, a shameless excuse to lean into her for half a second longer.

Something glimmered behind Mariam's dark eyes. But instead of jumping to conclusions, Sigrid would give her saddle to know what she was thinking.

"You're still shaking," Mariam said, eyebrows pulling down.

Sigrid drew a breath. Was it that obvious she still brimmed with adrenaline? She rubbed her sore arm. "I always thought that if I could choose how I died, I would want to go out in battle like a valkyrie. Now I'm not sure. That wasn't glamorous... I nearly peed myself."

When Mariam said nothing, Sigrid cringed. That had been insensitive of her, talking about dying to someone who... "I'm sorry. That was—"

"Don't," Mariam said, frowning at her bandaged arm. "Of course it would be nice to choose how you die. We'd all like that. But nothing happens as we think it will."

More than ever, Mariam's past stood between them like a locked door. How had she ended up dead and at the gates of Helheim? Sigrid searched for a tactful way to ask about it. Already she'd managed to mess up this conversation, and she didn't want Mariam to think she was being nosy.

"Was it...?" she began, then stopped. "If you want to talk about anything, I'm here."

Mariam said nothing. She made no motion, like she hadn't heard.

Sigrid's insides twisted uncomfortably. Ugh, she'd said the wrong thing again. "You don't have to—"

"Aesa and I were fleeing after I stole food," Mariam said, keeping her gaze down. "I'd stolen from that shop owner a few times, and he was ready for me. He took Aesa down..." Her throat seemed to close, and she swallowed hard and waved a hand. "Well, you saw the blood markings on her side. When I fell off, he came after me with the first blunt object he could get his hands on."

Sigrid didn't need her to elaborate. She didn't want to be the reason Mariam had to relive the pain. "I'm so sorry," she whispered. What else could she say?

Mariam sighed and shifted her seat. "I didn't want to tell you because I didn't know what you would think of me. I died because I was a thief. I'm not proud of the way I lived, but I'm also not sorry for finding ways to survive."

"It's not your fault. You were born into that life." Far from judging Mariam for her mistakes, she was full of admiration, because Mariam lived a life full of hardship and managed to stay strong through all of it. Even now, with her soul ripped away from Aesa, she was as bold and fierce as the day Sigrid had met her.

"Thank you for sharing that with me." Sigrid's cheeks warmed. Hopefully, it was too dark for Mariam to notice the rising color. She *was* grateful Mariam had shared this, but it left her sad, because she was powerless to fix the pain. She had the urge to say more, to say that Mariam shouldn't be ashamed and that she'd never met a girl so smart and interesting.

"Are you still glad the Eye showed you that vision?" Mariam said.

"Oh—" Sigrid searched for the right answer, surprised by the question. Truthfully, this thought had bubbled in the back of her mind since the moment Garmr cornered her, because she wouldn't have put Hestur or anyone else through that if not for the vision.

The thing was, even though the path to fulfilling her destiny was terrifying, it didn't deter her. Good things came out of facing fears. And now she knew she was capable of facing something as fearsome as Garmr. She could fulfill what the Eye had shown her, no matter what it took to get there.

"I like knowing what my future is." The certainty of it burned in her veins. "It gives me something to work toward, even if the path to get there is scary."

"You think you wouldn't have anything to work toward if you hadn't seen the vision?"

Sigrid shrugged. "No one's ever told me that I can be anything other than a stable hand."

Mariam searched her face. "If someone had shown me my future, I think I would have been paralyzed with fear. I would rather not know what lies ahead. The future could be good, or it could be bad, but it's probably going to be a bit of both—and I don't want to know what bad stuff is coming."

This made sense, especially given what happened to Mariam, but Sigrid couldn't agree.

A scuffle and a squeak came from the mast. They turned to see Fisk disentangling his lemming teeth from a rope hanging from the sail. His mask went lopsided as he pulled himself free.

Mariam's hand settled over Sigrid's forearm. "Sigrid, I—"

Sigrid met her gaze, finding a deep, troubled expression. What was she thinking about? The idea that Mariam wasn't telling her something lingered in the pit of her stomach.

Mariam opened her mouth, hesitated, then said, "We're docking soon. It's…a long walk to the gates, so I'll go pack our bags." She jumped from their seat and made for the crate of food, leaving Sigrid to stare longingly after her.

From the moment Sigrid met Mariam, the girl had been calculating, shrewd, and hard to read. Her confident posture and assured movements stemmed from a lifetime of being a valkyrie. She was graceful in a way Sigrid would never be—and could not stop admiring.

A flood of warmth invaded her body the longer she stared.

Sigrid exhaled and shook her head, then went to collect empty water flasks to fill them up for the journey ahead.

At the helm, Fisk was also watching Mariam. At least, his mask was turned in her direction.

For a moment, Sigrid had forgotten, but now she narrowed her eyes, anger igniting in her chest like Garmr's flames. She leaned over the ship to fill the bottles and flasks with spring water, tamping down that tight knot that formed every time she thought of them together.

We're only going to be together for a few more hours. Then they would get to Helheim, fulfill the vision, and they would all go off to live their separate destinies.

She stuffed their belongings into the saddlebags, punching them into place.

The most important thing was to get Sleipnir and save the Eye of Hnitbjorg. As long as Mariam and Fisk didn't interfere with her plan, their flirting shouldn't matter. Right?

The ship shuddered. A scraping sound came from below.

Fisk stepped away from the helm. "We're here."

Sigrid shot to her feet so fast that she dropped several bottles, their clattering sound matching her jumpy heartbeat. They rolled across the deck. "What?"

She'd been too distracted, seething in jealousy, to notice the brightening surroundings.

Mariam strode toward her, anxiety pulling her features tight.

"Welcome to the realm of the dead, Sigrid."

CHAPTER THIRTY-TWO

THE PATH TO HEL

Overhead, the cave came to an end. Sigrid ran to the longship's railing, half expecting the goddess Hel to greet them on the shore. But only a barren, endless landscape of red sand welcomed them.

"Slow down, lightning bolt," Mariam said, coming to stand beside her as the ship ground to a stop, mooring against the sloping shoreline.

A pang went through Sigrid's chest at the nickname. She hadn't thought of home much. Would Peter be preparing a meal right now for the mares left in the stables? Maybe tricking Roland into helping out? Whatever the chore, she would have been helping if she hadn't left.

Instead, she stood at the edge of a wasteland with a banished valkyrie and a treacherous Night Elf.

Sigrid gripped the railing hard. "Where do we go?"

Across the expanse of nothingness, the dunes hid the horizon from view. There were no distinct landmarks, no signposts or helpful markers. The sight left her desperate, like everything she wanted lay just out of reach, if only she could get to it.

"It's a few hours across the desert to the gates of Hel." Mariam reached out, but then stepped back. "Come on."

They quickly gathered their supplies, loaded Hestur with the bags, and disembarked.

The surrounding emptiness sat uneasy in Sigrid's stomach as they crossed the red desert, sand crunching beneath their feet and Hestur's hooves. With no map, no compass, and no sense of direction in this unfamiliar world, they could easily go the wrong way into oblivion. How long until they ran out of water and food? They'd brought as much as they could by using Hestur as a pack horse instead of riding him, but it wouldn't last them more than a few days. Ratatosk's refilling crate, unfortunately, couldn't be pried from the ship, no matter how much weight they applied to Fisk's unbreakable sword.

The hot, red landscape was like nothing on Vanaheim. Even the sky was different, permanently in a state of twilight, with no sun or moon. The light came from a glow on the horizon, like the sun had just set—but as the hours passed, the glow didn't change. It was as if time didn't exist here to push the celestial bodies across the sky.

"Pee break!" Fisk said and flitted behind the nearest dune.

"Oh, come on!" Sigrid threw her arms up.

They'd already stopped multiple times for him. Apparently, he drank too much water before leaving because he was afraid of getting dehydrated along the trek. Given his problem with light exposure, it was a several-minute ordeal each time he had to relieve his bladder.

Exasperated, Sigrid shouted after him. "Careful you don't burn off your—"

"Sigrid!" Mariam giggled, punching her in the arm.

While they waited, Sigrid rummaged for snacks.

"He's funny," Mariam said, pulling apart the scone Sigrid handed her.

Sigrid grunted, rethinking the snack as her stomach tightened.

She offered an apple to Hestur, who devoured it sloppily, then sighed and searched for something for herself.

Mariam chewed her scone while Sigrid decided on an oatmeal cookie.

"I think he likes you," Sigrid blurted. Her cheeks burned, so she focused on breaking apart the cookie.

"He's just curious about me."

"He touched your face."

Mariam arched an eyebrow. "Making sure I didn't have a fever."

Sigrid didn't believe that for a second. Why couldn't Mariam just admit that Fisk had something for her? "He looks at you a lot."

"So do you."

"I—what?" The heat in her cheeks rose. "I don't."

She did. She really did. Had Mariam been creeped out by it though? Ugh, why did she have to be so awkward?

"Just about done!" Fisk shouted from behind the dune. "I think this is the last time we'll have to stop. The flow is lighter than before."

Mariam snickered and nibbled her scone. "Did not need to know that."

Sigrid ignored their exchange, heart still racing at being called out. She couldn't stop the next words. "Why did you say all of the stable hands must have a crush on me?"

They were too close to the end of their journey to Helheim for her to spend time deliberating over what to say. Even if Mariam and Fisk had grown closer, that didn't erase all the moments Mariam and Sigrid had. She had to know why Mariam had said and done all of the things that made her heart flip over and her lips tingle over the last few days. Was she imagining the way Mariam looked at her, touched her, spoke to her?

Mariam met her eyes, then looked back at her scone. "Oh.

Just—you're a girl. And they're boys."

"Right." Mariam had assumed the stable hands would be interested in her for that reason before, when she had spied Peter waving farewell as they escaped. But plenty of couples weren't necessarily a *boy* and a *girl*. Relationships might be different in Niflheim though.

Unless Mariam was fishing for a specific response. Did she want Sigrid to correct her—maybe to admit that she'd never been interested in boys?

No, I'm reading too much into this.

Mariam was just stating a fact.

Except then Mariam blurted out, "And, I mean, you're pretty."

Oh. A jolt in Sigrid's chest sent a thrill through every part of her body. Her cheeks started to burn, as they always seemed to do around Mariam. There was a chance she wasn't overthinking this.

Mariam pointedly avoided her gaze, a flush in her perfectly shaped cheeks.

Pretty. Mariam had called her pretty. Sigrid's chest expanded until she could have floated into the sky.

She opened her mouth, ready to tell Mariam where her interest lay, but the words wouldn't come out. Nerves sealed her throat shut. What would come next? They weren't even from the same world. After fulfilling the vision, they would probably part ways forever.

Fisk came back, trudging through the sand and carrying the cloak he used to cover up. "I know you're not happy with the amount of times we've had to stop, but I feel really invigorated after flushing my system with all that water. I think that spring is full of healthy vitamins and minerals."

Mariam pointed a finger at him. "Don't you dare put that cloak anywhere near us."

"I only used it to cover my body!"

"What if you splashed?"

They walked on, Mariam and Fisk arguing over the "pee cloak."

The words *"you're pretty"* bounced around Sigrid's mind, sending a flutter through her middle. No one had told her that before.

Well, Roland had, but he didn't count.

You're pretty.

She bit her lip, hiding a smile.

They trudged through the red desert in silence except for the occasional dry cough and Hestur's snorts. Mariam went glassy-eyed, as if in a trance. Fisk shuffled along in his leather and chainmail, probably sweltering. Sigrid fell into a rhythm, one that helped her ignore the heat and the achiness that remained in her arm. She tried really hard not to think about the number of steps they had yet to take before reaching Helheim.

With the sky in a fixed state, the only indication that they were making any progress was in the slowly changing red landscape, which became flecked with black stone.

"Lava rock," Mariam said, breaking a several-hour silence. "We're getting close."

Sigrid gave a half-hearted, "Woo."

They kept walking.

She was waiting for Fisk to go off and pee again, to talk to Mariam and maybe figure things out. Like, what to do when they got to the gates of Hel, and how she would get Sleipnir. Equally important to discuss was why Mariam's compliment had put such a flutter in her belly, and why she got angry toward Fisk whenever he showed Mariam attention.

Sigrid didn't want to misinterpret her own feelings or Mariam's. She wanted them to be close, to share experiences and laugh together.

To kiss her?

Heat sparked in her midsection.

She wasn't kidding anyone, not even herself. What she felt for Mariam was more than friendship.

She'd never felt this way about anyone before. The stable hands were like her brothers, and the valkyries paid her no mind, and besides, her interest in horses had always eclipsed any interest in making out with someone in the hay room. But she'd never met anyone quite like Mariam.

The thought of kissing her sent Sigrid's heart racing. She wanted to take hold of it inside her chest and force it to calm down.

A couple of paces ahead, sweat glistened on Mariam's warm-toned skin, her black hair cascading down her back. Sigrid imagined sliding a hand around the curve of her waist, the way she'd seen a valkyrie and her wife leave the barn after training a few years ago.

Flashes of memories shot through her mind, as if each one was a puzzle piece she'd held onto and didn't notice until now. She'd been more intrigued than anyone to find out those two valkyries were married, stealing glances when they touched and kissed. She'd blushed and dropped the subject when Peter asked why she was posing so many questions about them.

And what about the way specific valkyries caught her attention once in a while? Her stomach would twist in a knot whenever they interacted, and she would clam up and blush for no apparent reason. Once, a beautiful, willowy nineteen-year-old kissed Roland on the cheek, and something like curiosity and excitement bubbled up inside Sigrid. She lay in her hammock that night with her pulse racing, imagining rescuing that valkyrie from danger and winning her own kiss on the cheek.

She'd always thought her awkwardness around pretty girls was because of shyness and a lack of confidence. But with Mariam it was more than that.

None of it mattered right now though, not when they were

close to the end of the journey. Getting distracted now would help no one.

Sigrid had traveled worlds to fulfill the vision and save the Eye with the valkyries. Once Mariam and Aesa were reunited and that was done, only then would she consider what came next—and whether a kiss might be in their future.

CHAPTER THIRTY-THREE

CONFESSIONS AT
THE GATES OF HEL

Sigrid wiped her sweaty forehead with the edge of her tunic, but as the cloth was already soaked in sweat, it didn't help much. Mariam's tunic didn't fare any better, the back of it just as drenched. The familiar scent of Hestur's sweat met her nose as he trudged beside her.

In the few hours that had passed, the temperature had risen steadily and the lava rock became more prominent. And soon enough, the black rock gave way to bubbling red lava. The dusky sky hadn't changed, making it impossible to tell how long they'd been walking.

The whole way, no signs of the junior valkyries marred the sand. They would've had to stop to rest somewhere, but the desert sand was untouched. Could Sigrid have gotten here first? Triumph swelled inside her as she imagined securing her place on Sleipnir in time for their arrival.

Then, in a vision so odd that Sigrid wondered if it was real, something dark rose in the distance.

She plucked her sweaty tunic from her chest and squinted. "Anyone else see that?"

"The gates of Hel," Mariam said, voice strained.

Sigrid exhaled, her eyes suddenly stinging with tears, although none made it out. They'd done it. They'd crossed worlds, found a way down the spring without Ratatosk, gotten past Garmr, and made it to the entrance to Helheim. She wasn't sure whether to jump in celebration and sprint the remaining distance or cower in fear at the ominous sight.

Fisk whimpered. "Why did the gods have to make it so creepy? Couldn't they have added ivy and flowers?"

"You should write to them and request a renovation," Sigrid absently said.

"I will." He paused. "As soon as I figure out how to send the gods a letter."

Mariam gave no indication she heard them, her eyes glassy and unfocused. Had the soul sickness worsened? She needed to hold on a bit longer. Soon, she would reunite with Aesa and be whole again.

They stepped over black rocks and skirted hissing lava pools, nearing the dark shape. A double wrought-iron gate towered in the middle of all the nothingness, big enough for Garmr to pass through. The iron bent and swirled in intricate designs—serpents, hounds, horses, and gods. The gates creaked as if swinging in the wind, but they remained still, slightly open as if to invite someone in or let something slip out.

Sigrid fought the urge to back away as they arrived at the base. Something about that towering structure in the middle of this empty landscape made her legs weak and her steps falter.

"This is where Elina met me when I arrived on Aesa," Mariam said, wrapping her arms around her middle.

Fisk tapped the iron, which made a *clang* that resonated through the desert. "Indestructible. Infinite. Interdimensional. Golly, there's a lot of magic on this."

A stream trickled out of the gate, materializing from a haze of nothingness and ending in a pool the size of a garden pond.

The pool remained constant, apparently seeping into the sand at the same rate as the creek flowed. On the banks of the stream, grass grew in a pale green perimeter. A single dandelion bloomed within it.

If they followed that stream through those empty gates, they would end up in the land of the dead—Helheim.

Hestur sniffed around and ate the dandelion. Then he took a long drink from the stream and began nibbling the grass.

Sigrid's chest tightened in anticipation. Sleipnir waited for her beyond those gates. "Do we go through to get to Elina?"

Mariam grabbed Sigrid's arm, stopping her before she could move. "If you go through, there's no coming back."

Fisk shot backward so fast that he tripped over his own feet and tumbled into the sand with a squeak.

"What do you mean?" Sigrid asked, stepping closer to her.

"Passing through the gates of Hel is a one-way journey meant for departed souls. If someone among the living goes through, it's over for them."

Sigrid recoiled, a little more composed than Fisk, but with no intention of accidentally dying by stepping through a gate. "What, then? We have to wait for Elina to decide to come out here?"

Mariam crossed her arms, trembling and sunken like she was about to vomit. "She'll come. She knows we're here."

Sigrid shifted uncomfortably. "What about Sleipnir?"

Mariam frowned, studying the gate. "She'll be riding him."

Sigrid had assumed that if she followed the vision, it would become obvious how she was supposed to get Sleipnir. But here she stood at the entrance to Helheim with no idea whether she should politely ask Elina if she could have him, or challenge her to a duel or something.

"Don't you dare try anything," Mariam said as if reading her mind.

Sigrid drew a deep breath, summoning patience.

Mariam stared at the gate again, and it dawned on Sigrid what she was looking for. "Do you think Aesa's waiting for you in there?"

Mariam looked at her sharply, as if caught off guard by the question. She worked her jaw, then said in a strained voice, "Elina will be able to tell me."

The gates stayed empty.

They'd not come across any signs of them, but...What if the valkyries had gotten here first, and they'd already fought and defeated Elina and took the Eye of Hnitbjorg back?

"She'll come," Mariam said again. "Just wait."

They stood before the gates, gazing through them to the black-and-red desert on the other side, waiting to be acknowledged. This was the realm of the dead. Everything they'd journeyed for was beyond whatever portal these gates represented—Sleipnir, Aesa, the Eye, and a promising future.

At once, she was both desperate to see the other side of those gates and terrified. Her heart pounded so hard that she was sure Mariam and Fisk could see her pulse in her throat. Hestur kept raising his head from the patch of grass and looking around nervously, no doubt sensing Sigrid's tension.

Fisk stepped between her and Mariam. "I just want to thank you both for letting me come with you. I feel like I've really been able to discover myself over these last couple of days."

The black holes that would be his eyes gawked at Sigrid, unblinking bottomless pits. She snorted with laughter. "I'm sorry, I just can't take you seriously behind that snout."

Mariam cracked a smile as Sigrid doubled over.

Fisk stamped his foot. "Stop it!"

"All right," Sigrid said between giggles. "What have you discovered about yourself, Sir Lemming?"

"I mean it!" His voice broke, which made her stop.

"You're being just as mean to me as the Night Elves," he said, voice high. "I thought I was leaving that behind when I decided to come with you, but apparently not."

Her stomach gave a guilty lurch. Was he right? "Fisk, I—"

"You know, I figured out you lied to me about being a valkyrie. Hestur is yours, and you did something bad to make Mariam lose her mare, and now you're trying to fix it. Right?"

Sigrid said nothing.

Fisk stood taller. "But you know what? I decided to keep helping you, because I thought you were a nice person. Now I'm wondering if I was wrong."

He huffed and stomped away, plodding through the sand until he disappeared behind a dune.

She made to follow. "Fisk!"

Mariam grabbed her hand and held her back. "Give him a minute."

Divots in the sand showed where he stomped away, like deer tracks in the freshly raked training arena.

Sigrid *had* been unfair to him. She'd been determined to not trust him since they escaped on Ratatosk's ship, and that had manifested through teasing and snappiness. She'd doubted his allegiance even when he'd proven himself by safely sailing them down the spring and past Garmr.

"I feel like the biggest jerk in the nine worlds," Sigrid said. "I know what it's like to be teased. I should know better." The valkyries had made her life impossible, mocking her and making her feel worthless every day. How could she have behaved this way?

Admittedly, being jealous about Mariam hadn't helped.

"I laughed at his expense, too, so I didn't do any better," Mariam said and pulled at Sigrid's hand. "We'll talk to him when he comes back."

Sigrid nodded.

They seemed to notice their hands remained clasped at the

same moment and let go.

Sigrid tried to think of something wise or witty to say—they had minutes left before their lives changed—but nothing came to mind.

Fisk was silent behind the dune, which itself seemed to be brooding.

Behind them, the gates creaked softly. No one was there.

Sigrid's palm tingled where Mariam's had been.

As their gazes locked, a shadow passed over Mariam's expression. It carried an ache with it, like fear, or sadness, or something else.

They'd only been in each other's lives for a couple of days, but cold dismay rippled over Sigrid's body at the thought of saying goodbye. She might never see Mariam again.

Mariam bit her lip.

Sigrid caught herself doing the same.

Maybe they didn't have to part ways.

What if they returned to Vanaheim together with Aesa and Sleipnir? Mariam could be pardoned for helping to bring back the Eye of Hnitbjorg. There could be a place for her in the stables, and in Sigrid's life, if she wanted it.

Before they faced whatever awaited, she needed to know if this was possible.

"Mariam…" She cleared her throat, trying to summon courage. For the sake of something to do with her limbs, she kicked a lava rock down the dune they stood on. It rolled and bounced, moving quietly over the deep sand. "Mariam, I was thinking that after we—"

"Wait." Mariam's lips parted, and she hesitated, as if searching for words. "I need you to know something."

Sigrid stepped closer and searched Mariam's desperate face. "What is it?"

"I—" Mariam swallowed hard. "I've been lying to you."

Her brain seemed to stutter. These were not the words she'd hoped to hear. "Lying how?"

"When Elina sent us to Vanaheim," Mariam said, voice trembling, "the Eye of Hnitbjorg wasn't our only mission." Pain raged behind her deep brown eyes, as frantic and desperate as when she'd lost Aesa.

Sigrid swallowed, gut clenching, bracing for impact. "What was the other mission?"

Mariam didn't answer.

What was she talking about? What else could they have been after?

Fisk's footsteps crunched behind the dune. He peeked out at them and, seeming to sense the change of tone, remained quiet.

"What was it?" Sigrid said fiercely, like Garmr's flames were licking at her words.

Mariam choked the words out. "Elina sent us to bring back her daughter."

CHAPTER THIRTY-FOUR

VALKYRIES ARE LIARS

Sigrid's mouth went as dry as the sand at their feet. The surrounding heat seemed to thicken, making it hard to breathe. "What?"

Footsteps crunched as Fisk walked closer, wordless.

"Sigrid, I'm sorry," Mariam said.

"Her daughter? What's that supposed to mean?" Sigrid's lips seemed to move on their own, without her conscious choice of words.

"She gave us a description," Mariam said. "I didn't think we'd find her, but it all fit when I met you. It has to be you. You're—"

"No." Sigrid stepped back, shaking her head, which didn't help the spots cropping up in her vision. She needed air. "I'm no one's daughter."

"She said the girl would be sixteen and living with the valkyries. She would be the only one with a Midgard horse." Mariam stepped closer, but stopped when Sigrid raised a hand in front of her. "When I saw you and Hestur, I wondered. Then you came to the infirmary, and you told me you were an orphan and that you saw a vision of you on Sleipnir—and I knew it was you. You look so much like her, Sigrid."

Each word was like a spear piercing Sigrid's chest, making her bleed inside. Betrayal and embarrassment burned in her. She'd been searching for information about who she was, and all along, Mariam had known. *Mariam.*

"You tricked me. You agreed to bring me to her." Her words came out strangled.

Mariam stepped closer, eyes streaming in earnest. "I wish I hadn't. Please. I didn't think...I mean, I didn't expect you to be..."

Sigrid shook her head faster. Whatever Mariam thought about her, or about the two of them, didn't matter. Not anymore. It was ash in the wind. "What does Elina want with me?"

"To meet you, I guess."

"Sixteen years after she abandoned me? What if I don't want to meet her after what she did?" Sigrid glared. "I guess that's why you had to trick me into it."

"Please, Sigrid. I'm sorry I lied to you. I've been thinking about telling you." She reached out, and their fingers caught before Sigrid pulled back.

"But you waited until now. When we've arrived and it's too late." Her eyes burned. Out of her two companions, she hadn't expected Mariam to be the one to slide a knife between her ribs like this. Her suspicions about Fisk had masked the real betrayal happening before her eyes.

"I didn't know how to tell you! I didn't want you to be mad at me." Mariam's voice was high, her breath stuttering.

Sigrid didn't care. "Of course I'm mad! Has anything you've done or said been real?"

Mariam's brow pinched. "What do you mean?"

"I wanted to help you, Mariam. I wanted to fix what I did to you and Aesa. I liked you! I even thought..." She waved a hand, swallowing hard. None of that mattered.

Sigrid blinked until her eyes stopped burning, dreams of returning to Vanaheim with Mariam collapsing to dust. She kicked a black rock at her feet, watching it roll into a lava pool and disappear with a *blub*.

"How was I supposed to know that?" Mariam said finally, voice breaking. "I thought you only cared about getting Sleipnir and fulfilling your destiny."

"Then you're not very good at reading people." She kicked another rock, but it was too big and barely moved, adding to her frustration.

Mariam's expression contorted to anger. "You agreed to take me with you because you knew I could get you here—not because you cared about me."

Sigrid pointed a shaking finger at her. "That was before I knew you." Before they'd ridden through forest and Sigrid helped bandage her arm. Before Mariam had taught her about the nine worlds and shared her childhood. Before they'd escaped from Night Elves, ridden Jörmungandr's terrible waves, fought Garmr and won.

Before Sigrid realized that going back to a life without Mariam would be her worst decision ever.

Mariam, however, scoffed. "So you're less obsessed with your self-centered journey now that you've known me for a couple of days?"

Sigrid reeled back. "Self-centered?"

Mariam opened her arms. "Here we are, oh great and powerful Sigrid. We've crossed the nine worlds so you can feel important and fulfill your cosmic destiny because the nice life you had just wasn't enough. But go ahead. Your steed, Sleipnir, awaits you. Go get him." She dipped into a mocking bow and opened a hand toward the gates.

Sigrid clenched her jaw tight enough to make it ache. How could Mariam belittle her ambitions? It wasn't wrong to want something greater, to want to find a better place in the world, especially after a lifetime of being treated like a barn rat by a stable full of self-righteous valkyries.

"You know why I wanted…why I *want* a better life! How can you—"

A roar escaped Sigrid. In a fit, she grabbed a rock from the sand and threw it at the iron gate. It bounced off with a deafening reverberation. Hestur startled and looked at her in surprise. As the rock thumped back into the sand, the sound dissipated across the barren landscape.

Mariam's expression twisted into terror as she backed away from Sigrid.

Before Sigrid could process what was happening, Fisk jumped between them, hands up as if to block Sigrid from advancing.

Behind Fisk, Mariam swayed like she might faint.

"I wasn't going to hurt her," Sigrid said, glowering. What did he think she was going to do, throw the rock at Mariam's head?

"No, but that was a pretty insensitive thing to do given how she…" Fisk waved a hand, but his words were firm. "Just be more considerate, all right?"

Mariam's wide, glassy eyes shifted between them.

Sigrid dropped her arms, chest heaving as she pieced together Fisk's words and Mariam's reaction. In Niflheim, the butcher had used a blunt object against her. *A rock.*

Sigrid's insides turned to ice. How could she have done that, after learning how she'd died? She hadn't been thinking. She'd completely forgotten. She opened her mouth, but instead of the apology she wanted to make, she said, "You told Fisk how you died?"

Mariam said nothing.

An ache shot through Sigrid's chest. She thought Mariam had confided in her. She thought they shared this secret—something Mariam trusted her with, which she wouldn't share with anyone else.

How naive of her.

She wasn't special. She meant no more to Mariam than Fisk did.

She wanted to shout at Mariam for this, but what could she say? This was her own fault for misinterpreting what she and Mariam meant to each other.

Voice shaking, she finally said, "I'm glad we cleared up that I'm nothing more to you than a parcel to be delivered."

Mariam said nothing, looking fainter than ever. Her silence was an admission, like twisting the dagger she'd lodged in Sigrid's ribs.

That settled it.

The gates creaked louder.

They all whirled around.

The double gates swung away from them, opening wider, and from the middle, materializing as if from fog…a horse appeared.

The beast was steel gray with a coal black mane, twice as thick as Hestur and several hands taller. Sweat foamed on his neck, and his nostrils blew loudly, bright red inside, like he'd galloped hard to get here. He stopped between the iron gates like a half-formed vision—standing tall on eight powerful legs.

CHAPTER THIRTY-FIVE

SOMETIMES,
BIRTHRIGHTS GET STOLEN

Sigrid's breath hitched when she raised her gaze to the woman sitting astride Sleipnir. Her nose, mouth, and even her build were as familiar as Sigrid's own reflection. Her long braid was the same shade of blond, her eyes more gray than blue. Amber gems glinted across her inky black robe, as striking as the night sky. On her forehead rested an amber diadem.

The truth grabbed Sigrid's heart, squeezing it inside her chest. This wasn't possible. She didn't want to believe Mariam, but how could she deny it?

Queen Elina tightened the reins as Sleipnir danced between the open iron gates, refusing to stand still on his eight massive hooves. Her commanding stare said plainly that she never doubted that Sigrid would come to her.

Rage struck at Sigrid's core like a lightning bolt to a tree, not just at being manipulated, but at this woman's certainty that Sigrid would willingly follow. Clenching her jaw and lifting her chin, Sigrid stood squarely, ready to stand up for herself.

Sand crunched as Mariam and Fisk flanked her, but Sigrid did not allow herself to soften. Beside the gate where the little stream trickled out, Hestur snorted, standing as rigidly as a wooden carving, no doubt trying to process the eight-legged thing standing before him.

"Sigrid," Elina said. "I've waited for you for so long." Her voice was deep, warm—and despite the sound of it, despite the likeness of her features, Sigrid could react with nothing but fury.

"How *dare* you?" Her anger was a vise around her throat, making her choke on her words. "How dare you use my name when you abandoned me so soon after giving it to me?"

Elina's eyes widened, and she looked past her to Mariam. Whatever she saw made her expression fall. Was this not how she imagined their reunion? What did she think would happen after sixteen years? Her disappointment was all the more infuriating.

"Please," Elina said, sounding pained, "listen to why I did it."

Sigrid's last thread of hope that Mariam had been wrong snapped. She'd clung to that feeble wish, praying her mother wasn't the woman sitting before her, alive, a *queen*, because this hurt worse than if her mother were a peasant who died after giving birth.

"How could you do this to me?" Sigrid shouted, voice carrying across the barren landscape.

"Sigrid, listen—"

"You left me, a stable hand with no family—"

"Sigrid!"

Beneath Elina, Sleipnir tossed his steel-gray head, agitated.

Sigrid ground her teeth, every muscle coiled for a fight. "You *abandoned* me."

"I did it to protect you!" Elina shouted, her words ringing. She swelled, chin high, looking every bit a queen.

Hestur left his tuft of grass to trot over to Sigrid and the others. She backed closer to him and rested a hand on his neck, wanting his comfort as much as he wanted hers. The sweltering heat, bubbling pools of lava, and dusky sky pressed in on her, suffocating.

Sigrid narrowed her eyes, waiting for some pathetic explanation of how abandoning a newborn could possibly be for protection.

Elina touched her temple, running her fingers back over her ear as if fixing her hair. "Before I came to Helheim, I was a Vanaheim royal," she said. "I grew up within the walls of Vanahalla."

Sleipnir flicked his head like a winged mare raring to take off. Elina twitched the reins, her long black sleeves fluttering, and let him pace back and forth in the open gates. His eight hooves made a strange, irregular beat on the sand.

"When I was twenty-six, Vala came to me in private with a vision from the Eye of Hnitbjorg. It showed me in Myrkviðr, having just given birth to a daughter. Sleipnir lay on the forest floor, curled around us like a guardian."

Each time she turned around in the gates, the stallion's body dissipated and reformed, as if in a thick fog. They were half here, half there.

"Vala and I agreed on what this vision meant." She stared at Sigrid for a beat, then said, "I was destined to birth Sleipnir's heir."

Sigrid's heart leaped. Behind her, Mariam and Fisk gave a sharp intake of breath.

Sleipnir's heir. Just like she'd read in Vala's study. But if this was true, then Vala had known all along who Sigrid's mother was. Yet she'd said nothing, letting Sigrid believe she had no parents and no future.

Sleipnir's hooves continued their eight-beat crunching over the red sand.

Sigrid clenched her fists. "Why didn't Vala tell anyone else about this?"

"She felt it best to keep Sleipnir's heir a secret. Power-hungry gods and men have sought him since his birth." Elina shook her head, her diadem glinting in the eerie light from beyond the gate.

"We wanted to protect you."

The life promised by this vision flashed across Sigrid's mind. She should have spent it as the powerful and fearsome rider of the eight-legged horse—like Odin. She should have ridden with the valkyries instead of suffering their petty insults.

Fury and longing roiled inside her. "So you stole him from me?"

"Sigrid, do you know what kind of life you would have had?" Elina said in a tone like she was speaking to a child. "Imagine an infant girl with Sleipnir waiting for her in the barn. You would have been murdered in your cradle. I chose to keep him worlds away from you for your safety."

"You could have sent him away. You could have stayed with me," Sigrid said, voice cracking. How ironic that now, after a lifetime of wishing for a mother, the sight of the woman filled her with disgust.

Elina shook her head sadly. "Sent him where? Who could I trust to keep the most powerful stallion in the nine worlds without stealing him or abusing his power?"

Sigrid wanted so badly to argue. Of course trustworthy people existed. She would trust Peter with such a responsibility. But maybe her mother had lived like Mariam, with no real friends and no one to rely on.

"He's my birthright," Sigrid said. "You had no right to decide that for me and steal him away."

"It was a decision I had to make as a mother." She lifted her chin. "I weighed the risk of letting you keep Sleipnir against taking him away until you grew old enough to carry the responsibility. I had the right to decide on behalf of my child. And I picked the choice that would keep you alive and safe."

Sigrid crossed her arms, not knowing what to make of the story. Had her mother been trying to protect her for all these years? Did she steal Sigrid's birthright—her entire upbringing—

out of love?

"I don't believe you," Sigrid said, spitting like the pools of lava between them.

Elina opened her mouth, hesitated, and let Sleipnir pace between the gates a few more times before she spoke. "Sigrid, I understand more than anyone how it feels to have your birthright stolen. As firstborn, I should have been queen. But the Vanaheim throne goes to the firstborn male." Her face took on an ugly expression, like she ate something rotten. "At twenty-four years old, I was skipped over in favor of my twelve-year-old brother."

"King Óleifr is your *brother*?" Mariam asked, startling Sigrid. After concentrating so hard on her mother, she'd forgotten about the others behind her.

"Unfortunately," Elina said, bitterness seeming to coat her tongue.

"But then you're..." Mariam said.

Elina inclined her head.

The king sitting on Vanaheim's throne is Elina's brother?

Sigrid gasped. "You're the eldest princess. The one who went missing."

"My birthname is Helena. My sister used to call me Lena, and so..." She lifted a shoulder in what would have been a casual shrug, but the movement was heavy. Was it the mention of her sister? "Now you understand what I mean when I say the Eye of Hnitbjorg is rightfully mine—along with the throne of Vanaheim."

Sigrid's breaths came fast, like she was trying to lead an unruly mare. Princess Helena, who'd been missing for sixteen years, stood in front of her. All of Vanaheim should know about this.

Or Sigrid could bury whatever dark secret she'd stumbled upon.

Whatever she'd expected to learn by following the vision to Helheim, this wasn't it.

Beneath Elina, Sleipnir snorted impatiently. Hestur

responded by puffing out his chest and stomping his front hoof, as if to say, *Don't come any closer.*

Sigrid stroked his neck, paying careful attention to her horse's body language. Was he trying to tell her that Sleipnir was dangerous, or was he just uncertain about seeing a horse with eight legs? She'd ignored his judgment once before and gotten caught by elves—a mistake she wouldn't repeat a second time.

"The royals said you were kidnapped," she said to Elina. "Everyone thinks you died."

Elina's lips curled in amusement. "I made a bargain with Hel and arranged the attack to make it look like my kidnapping. When the army came, I left with them for the underworld."

"And your family never figured out what happened?"

"Oh, they know. Cowards," she spat. "They would sooner lie than admit I fled Vanaheim to serve the goddess Hel."

Sigrid shifted. As firstborn, fine, Elina should have inherited Vanaheim's throne. The rule about the throne going to a male was ridiculous, and she would be angry, too, if she'd been in Elina's position.

But was it right to hate King Óleifr for it? The memory of the king taking care with the little valkyries outside the infirmary showed he was a kind man. And as a ruler, Sigrid never had reason to think him unfair, and no reason to want someone else in his place.

An ache formed in her temple even as tears threatened to spill. It was all too much to process. If Princess Helena was her mother...

Sigrid almost choked on the words. "You mean to tell me that I spent my life as a stable hand when I could have been—"

"You still are a princess," Elina said gently. "You're the Princess of Hel."

CHAPTER THIRTY-SIX

MORE THAN A VALKYRIE

A princess? Sigrid's heart beat faster as emotions clashed within her at the revelation, but anger prevailed.

Her nails dug into her palms as rage flared in her stomach—but she didn't know where to direct her anger anymore. She hated Elina for abandoning her to a life of loneliness. She hated the valkyries for treating her like a servant her whole life. She hated all of Vanaheim for regarding her as nothing more than the lowest class of society, a peasant who shoveled manure for the noble class.

"I'm nothing but a stable hand," Sigrid said, her words like venom. "I'm not even a valkyrie."

"You're right. You're not a valkyrie." Elina pulled her shoulders back, her expression arrogant. "You're Princess Sigrid Helenadottir, heir to Sleipnir, descended from Odin."

Sigrid blinked, eyes stinging. She had a name. She had a family tree. This was supposed to have been her place in the world, but it had been ripped away.

Elina leaned on the reins, forcing Sleipnir to halt. "Sigrid, I have always loved you with all my heart. Leaving you behind was the most difficult thing I have ever done. But I had to if I wanted you to stay in the land of the living." Her mother's gaze was tender, remorseful. She seemed to take in every inch of Sigrid, from her braided hair down to her well-worn boots. "You're even more beautiful than I imagined. You're strong, and there's a fire in your eyes—your father's eyes. They're the same shape."

Sigrid's throat tightened. Here was everything she wanted to know about where she'd come from, standing in front of her in an otherworldly fog. Memories drifted forward—the way, in recent years, some adults seemed to stare for a bit too long. General Eira had done it once. The doctor in the infirmary had done it. Sigrid assumed they were silently critiquing her, but maybe they were trying to place where they'd seen her before. Maybe they were trying to understand why they saw hints of Princess Helena in her appearance.

She stepped closer to her mother, away from Mariam, Fisk, and Hestur. They didn't stop her. She moved until she was a stride away from the gates, and the smell of Sleipnir's sweat drifted toward her. Through the haze, the stallion's black mane and tail rippled, his eight legs dizzying. Elina sat regal and confident, her features painfully like Sigrid's, and yet garnished with a real diadem and robes with amber beads.

"What was my father like?"

"He was a wonderful man," Elina said warmly, and her blue-gray eyes filled with tears. "Not a day goes by that I don't miss him."

Sigrid swallowed hard. She was tired and overwhelmed, but she desperately wanted to learn more. She wanted to pry every detail from Elina while she had the chance.

Elina smiled. "Sigrid, darling, are you ready to claim your birthright?"

The question startled Sigrid and she furrowed her brow. "You want to *give me* Sleipnir?"

"You're sixteen now. You've found your way to Helheim. I

would say you've earned him."

Sigrid's heart beat faster. Was this how she came to ride Sleipnir in the vision? She didn't need to fight for him or steal him, because her claim was written in the cosmos. She only had to step forward and accept her birthright.

She rocked from foot to foot, aching with longing. She was both unwilling to trust the woman in front of her and desperate to get answers.

Finally, she could ask the question that had burned on her lips since the vision. "What do I do once I have him?"

Elina's lips pulled into a wide smile, like she'd waited for this. "Sleipnir has the power to travel the nine worlds, entering places none other can pass—Asgard, Helheim, and everywhere in between. He carried Odin through the worlds this way."

"Then why can't you leave Helheim? You're standing on the threshold, but you can't come through the gates."

It hadn't escaped her that Elina seemed blocked by an invisible wall. Sleipnir tossed his head and snorted, agitated. He wanted to keep going but couldn't.

"When I decided to enter Helheim, I sealed my fate," Elina said, a flicker of sadness crossing her face. "I cannot return to the land of the living. At least, not without help."

Sigrid frowned. "Then it isn't true that Sleipnir can take people through the nine worlds. You can't get through on him."

At the sound of his name, his black eyes burned into her—and her heart leaped. Even when she stepped sideways, his head moved to track her. Did he recognize his true rider?

"Sleipnir can travel the nine worlds, but only his heir can pass through on him—I am not his heir."

I am, Sigrid thought, a flare of triumph in her chest. Keeping her voice even, she said, "So if I come into Helheim, I'll be able to leave on Sleipnir."

"You alone can cross all nine worlds. You, and whoever you

choose to lead, of course. No one since Odin has had this power." Elina swept an arm toward the red desert. "For example, you could lead the dead through these gates and into the land of the living."

The dead? I can lead the dead out of Helheim?

At the image of a group of decaying corpses following her through the gates, her breath quickened. "Are you saying I can bring the dead back to life?" she said, desperate for clarification. The idea was more scary than exciting.

"Not *back to life*, exactly, but you can raise Hel's army," Elina said, and when Sigrid stayed puzzled, her lips quirked into a little smile. "The goddess Hel began assembling an army of the dead who could be raised for one conquest. They can follow Sleipnir into the land of the living and fight as well as any living soldiers. It's an army bigger than any other, trained by a goddess, and waiting for your command."

Sigrid's eyes widened. The book in Vala's study had told of Sleipnir's heir being able to lead armies across the nine worlds. This must be the army it referred to. Hel's warriors could be at her command. Except—

"I don't want an army to kill for me." Sigrid wanted to be a valkyrie to protect, not to kill, unless absolutely necessary.

"They don't have to kill. They'll do whatever you ask— conquer peacefully, forcefully, or not at all. It's up to you what you want to do." Elina shifted in the saddle, and the stallion shook his head, forelock fluttering over his dark eyes. "But you asked what you're supposed to do with Sleipnir, and this is the answer."

Sigrid studied the two of them, calculating them like the strides before a jump. She'd assumed Sleipnir was her means to ride with the valkyries—that was why she'd come. But if her destiny was simply to ride with the valkyries, wouldn't the Eye have shown her on a winged mare?

Sleipnir was in her future, not any ordinary winged mare.

If Sleipnir's power was to raise Hel's army, then was she meant to raise these warriors and bring them to Vanaheim? And if so, for what purpose?

A cold sweat passed over her. This was more than she was ready for. She'd never been a leader.

"Okay, what if I lead Hel's army to Vanaheim?" she asked, putting as much skepticism as she could into her tone. "What would they do there?"

"Returning to Vanaheim with an army at your service would make you a valkyrie and more," Elina said. "They might make you a general of your own division. If that's what you want."

"My...my own valkyrie division?" Sigrid asked, numb. She'd never even dreamed of such a thing.

"If the other generals and the king want it, that is. This is where we can help each other, Sigrid." She tilted her head and offered a little smile, as though in sympathy. "If you raise Hel's army and we claim my place on the throne, we can also claim your royal title as Princess of Vanaheim. I'll become queen, and you'll become princess. I'll tell everyone who you are." Elina grinned, her eyes twinkling. "*This* is how you become more than just a valkyrie."

CHAPTER THIRTY-SEVEN

ROYALTY SOUNDS NICE

The title *Princess of Vanaheim* dangled before Sigrid like one of Ratatosk's ship's delicious blueberry tarts. The things that would come with such a title... A proper bed. Her own room. Real purpose and belonging.

But it comes with a price.

Claiming Elina's place on the throne meant storming Vanahalla and overthrowing King Óleifr. She couldn't do that. Her was a kind man and a just leader. She couldn't support a plot to overthrow him.

Sigrid inhaled deeply, hoping to calm her frantic heartbeat and find clarity.

She'd come to Helheim expecting to find Sleipnir, save the Eye of Hnitbjorg with the valkyries, and ride home. It was all to prove to the general she was worthy to be a valkyrie. Instead, she'd found her mother and a cosmic purpose more powerful than she'd imagined. She was meant to do great things with Sleipnir—but the exact path forward was as turbulent and unpredictable as the spring of Hvergelmir.

Was she supposed to go along with her mother's treacherous plan and claim her royal title? Or was she supposed to use Hel's army on her own to do…something? Or maybe she was supposed to leave the dead where they were, take Sleipnir, and get her and her friends out of here.

How could she know which destiny to pursue?

If she could go through the gates and learn more about Hel's army, maybe she could figure out the best way to use them and Sleipnir to protect the nine worlds.

"Sigrid," Mariam whispered behind her.

Sigrid started.

Mariam stood right there, arms crossed like she was cold. "Can we talk for a second?"

Fisk and Hestur remained where she'd left them.

Elina inclined her head and let Sleipnir keep pacing.

Sigrid took this as permission. "All right."

She followed Mariam back to the others, and they stepped behind another dune, different from the one Fisk had used as a toilet. After Mariam peeked around it to ensure Elina was out of earshot, she whispered, "I'm not so sure of this."

Sigrid crossed her arms, still furious at her for lying. "Why not?"

"Raising an army of the dead?" she said emphatically. "Doesn't that sound…wrong to you?"

"Sounds pretty much terrible," Fisk said. "Like, more terrible than when I tricked you into saving me and you almost got kill— ahh—and we teamed up. What I'm trying to say is this army could have disastrous consequences for all of…um, us…you know?" He gulped.

Sigrid shot him a withering glare.

The nose of his mask drooped down.

"*If* raising Hel's army is my destiny, there's nothing to worry about because the army will be under my control." Hopefully.

"So you're going to do it, then?" Mariam asked with a withering glare.

"I don't know," she snapped, frustration tightening like a fist around her diaphragm. "I need to figure out what I'm meant to do."

Mariam raised an eyebrow. "I think you need to figure out what you *want* to do, not what you're *meant* to do."

Sigrid waved her off. "Same thing. I followed the vision here, thinking it was showing me the way to ride with the valkyries, but it's apparently not as simple as just taking Sleipnir and turning around. The vision led me to Helheim for a reason."

"Uh huh."

"I just found out I'm a princess," Sigrid said, flinging her hands out for emphasis. "Not Sigrid the stable hand, but Sigrid Helenadottir, Princess of Vanaheim, descended from—"

"Yeah, yeah. What about getting the Eye back?" Mariam said.

Sigrid frowned, slightly confused. "What about it? I'll still return it to Vanaheim. And it's through those gates, in case you didn't realize. All the more reason to go."

Mariam and Fisk exchanged a look.

Sigrid had the urge to slam a door in their faces. Things were finally starting to fit into place and make sense. She had a place in the world as a princess and a purpose to join the valkyries. They didn't understand how overwhelming this was. "The Eye of Hnitbjorg doesn't lie," she said, backing away. "It showed Sleipnir in my future. I need to figure out what this means, and that involves going into Helheim."

Mariam grabbed Sigrid's arm. "At least be careful of Elina's motives. I know she said she abandoned you because she was trying to save your life or whatever. But she could have taken you with her, or any number of other options that wouldn't have meant leaving you an orphan."

"I know." Sigrid was very aware how Elina's excuses didn't change that she'd spent sixteen years an orphan. She didn't have to trust her mother. She didn't even have to regard her as anything more than a means to get information.

"Also, overthrowing King Óleifr is sort of treason," Fisk said in a small voice.

"Yeah," Mariam said. "You'd be executed."

Sigrid sighed. *Obviously, I won't be doing that.* "Noted."

When Mariam still didn't release her, Sigrid pulled her arm free and stepped out from behind the dune, leaving the others to trail behind. Facing Elina once more, arms crossed, she said, "If I come through those gates, I'm not making promises. I want to learn about Sleipnir and Hel's army before I decide what I want to do with them."

Elina nodded. "Fair. I'll teach you how to ride him so you can see what power you're dealing with. He's not a child's pony, and I can save you a lot of tumbles and frustration."

A spark of excitement flared inside her at the thought of riding lessons on Sleipnir, but she smothered it, staying vigilant. "First, I need you to prove to me that if I go through those gates, I'll be able to get out again. I want to know that I really am Sleipnir's heir before I step into Helheim."

Elina laughed, then stopped on seeing that Sigrid didn't find humor in the situation. "How am I supposed to prove that you can get back through the gates if you won't come through?"

Sigrid tapped her fingers on her arms, scowling.

Elina deliberated, then swung a leg over the saddle and dismounted. "Invite him to you."

Wait, what?

CHAPTER THIRTY-EIGHT

THROUGH THE
GATES OF HEL

Calling Odin's massive eight-legged stallion to her wasn't risky, right?

Sigrid hadn't imagined Sleipnir's attention on her before. He fixated on her, dark eyes unblinking, ears forward. He tensed, ready to spring through the gates and into the hands of his heir.

"Go on. He wants to come to you," Elina said, crossing her arms with remarkable calmness.

Sigrid extended an arm to beckon him. Her hand trembled, so she drew a steadying breath and clucked like she would to Hestur. "Here."

Hestur nudged her in the back as if to tell her that he was already here.

"It's okay, buddy," she murmured, scratching his neck with her other hand. "He's going to be our friend."

Hestur rested his nose on her shoulder, as if in solidarity. His presence was calming.

Without a backward glance to Elina, Sleipnir left her side. He trotted through the iron archway and over to Sigrid, his hooves making that irregular beat on the sand. His body became solid and real as he left Helheim behind.

Having grown up in a stable full of winged mares—plus Hestur, a gelding—Sigrid had never seen a stallion. Up close, Sleipnir was all power, wild and majestic, and more stunning than the drawings had depicted. He stopped in front of her, nostrils making a deep *whoosh* as he took in her scent.

She rested a hand on his dark gray forehead. He was hot to the touch. A lick of flame seemed to pass from his skin to hers.

Hestur sniffed the air, his breath warming the back of her tunic. He didn't shy or get defensive in the stallion's presence, which boded well.

"Mount up," Elina said, standing between the gates with a smile still dimpling her cheeks.

Sigrid thumbed the reins, a thrill of nerves sending a tremor to her toes. "He'll listen to me?"

"As long as you know how to ride."

"Ha," Sigrid said, taking the reins in one hand and stepping up alongside the saddle.

His back seemed a mile up, at least eighteen hands tall, compared to Hestur's fifteen. Even getting on Hestur was difficult if she didn't have momentum to vault up, which was why she taught him to bend a knee to help her mount. Sleipnir wouldn't know that trick, and she didn't trust him enough to take a running leap.

"Uh, can you give me a boost?" She spoke vaguely in Mariam and Fisk's direction, hoping one of them wasn't so mad as to ignore her.

Fisk stepped forward. He linked his fingers and turned his palms up so she could place her knee in them.

"Sigrid," Mariam whispered, eyeing the stallion's nose as if he might bite. "This doesn't prove anything. He could have come to anyone."

"I'm just going to get on," Sigrid said stubbornly. "I want to see if I feel anything when I'm on him."

Then what?

If she was Sleipnir's heir and could lead people through those gates, then—if she chose to—she could command Hel's army to do whatever she wanted. Once she got everyone home safely, including the Eye of Hnitbjorg, how many other worlds could use her assistance? How many people could she help? The harsh conditions in Niflheim that Mariam had told her about came to mind, and that was just the start.

The prospect of this bigger cosmic destiny than she'd imagined filled her with a wild combination of desperation and panic.

Mariam's eyes narrowed, and she nodded past Sigrid. "She's going to ask you to use Sleipnir to lead her through the gate next."

Sigrid placed her knee in Fisk's palms and bounced on one foot. "I know."

Elina would want to be led back into the land of the living to test Sigrid's ability, but an option occurred to her. She had Sleipnir now. What if she galloped away from here with Mariam, Fisk, and Hestur? Elina was stuck in Helheim, a result of her own choices, and she couldn't stop them from leaving.

Elina stood between the gates, watching them intently, the likeness in her features that Sigrid saw when she looked in a mirror. She and Sigrid both had their birthrights stolen, and they'd both come to Helheim wanting to find something greater.

If Sigrid left now, she would never discover if the cosmos had led her here for a reason. She would never figure out what she was meant to do with Sleipnir's power and how much potential lay ahead. She couldn't leave now, not when so much of her purpose remained a mystery.

"Whenever you're ready," Fisk said, drawing out the syllables. He stood awkwardly crouched at Sigrid's rear, fingers linked together.

"Just a second," Mariam snapped. "Sigrid, after you've proven you can do it, your next step will be to go with her and raise Hel's army. You'll be raising the dead."

"And what if Aesa is among them?"

Mariam's eyes widened. She swallowed hard, as if her next words lodged in her throat. "That's beside the point."

Sigrid hadn't forgotten her promise to reunite them. If she could find Aesa inside the gates, Mariam would have her mare back, and their bond would be healed. But she couldn't do anything without stepping through the gates on Sleipnir.

"First of all," Sigrid said, "I might decide I don't want to raise the army. I don't even know what I'd do with them. Second, they'll be in my command if I do."

Sure, the idea of raising the dead was less than comforting, but everything great came with discomfort, didn't it?

Fisk sighed pointedly, rolling his neck.

Sigrid bounced again, ready for him to boost her into the saddle. "On the count of three."

"Sigrid, don't!" Mariam said, pulling her away so hard that Fisk stumbled.

"Oh, come on," he said, adjusting his mask.

"Raising the dead should not even be in your list of things to consider," Mariam said.

They were nose to nose, Mariam's warm breath tickling her lips.

"You're making it sound worse than it is," Sigrid said, ignoring the heat building inside her at the closeness. "Wouldn't you want to learn more if you found out your mother was a princess? Wouldn't you want to know more about Odin's stallion if someone handed him to you? I have the potential to save worlds here."

"Mariam," Fisk said quietly. "It's okay. Sometimes people need to go discover—"

She held out a hand to silence him. "You've been letting a vision tell you what to do all this time, but you won't accept a word of caution from an actual person who cares about y—" She looked away, the color in her face deepening.

From this distance, Sigrid could count every freckle dusting her nose. "I will be cautious. But how can I go back to life as a stable hand now that I know I should have been a princess? I need to at least try to figure out what I'm supposed to do."

Mariam said nothing, eyes searching.

"I'm going," Sigrid said, pulling away.

"Don't!"

"Stop it, Mariam!"

In the span of a heartbeat, Mariam's soft hand cupped her cheek, her breath grazed Sigrid's lips, their noses brushed—

Sigrid pushed her away. Mariam stumbled back, brown eyes wide with surprise.

A moment passed where they stared at each other, Sigrid's pulse pounding in her ears, struggling to make sense of what just happened.

Did Mariam try to kiss me?

The hurt on Mariam's face told her everything.

She'd been so angry, so overcome with frustration for having to justify her decision, that she hadn't considered what Mariam was trying to tell her—that she cared about Sigrid and didn't want anything to happen to her in Helheim. She'd pushed away the very kiss she'd wanted.

"Mariam, I…" She swallowed hard, skin dancing where Mariam had touched her. "I promise I'll turn back if anything bad happens."

Before she could change her mind, she turned away from Mariam's pained expression.

This wasn't the time to let emotions cloud her judgment. She couldn't forget why she came here, and she couldn't let anyone, not even Mariam, make her doubt herself.

An ache in her chest constricted her airway. She wanted to

run to Mariam and apologize and grab her face and kiss her—

She lied. She tricked me.

Steeling herself with a deep breath, Sigrid placed a knee into Fisk's linked palms once more and counted to three.

Grumbling about back pain, Fisk hoisted her onto Sleipnir.

As she settled in the saddle, nothing mystical happened. The cosmos did not speak to her about her destiny. Instead, she might have been straddling a tree trunk, her splayed legs barely reaching down the stallion's rib cage. His ears looked elephantine compared to Hestur's. Even his mane looked twice as thick and long.

Sigrid cast Hestur a guilty glance. He stared at her and Sleipnir with his ears forward and his eyes wide. *You're still my number one.*

Letting out a slow breath, she nudged Sleipnir into a walk. His enormous strides lumbered compared to Hestur's airy, delicate movements. She tried to let her hips go with the back-and-forth motion of his spine, but no amount of experience had prepared her for how to ride eight beats instead of four. It left her clumsy and off-balance, like a novice who resorted to gripping the saddle with her knees.

"Good boy," she said, hoping to put Sleipnir at ease. His ears didn't turn back to listen to her. They stayed forward, focused on the iron gates.

She asked Sleipnir to stop before they got to Elina. Or she tried to. He kept walking. She pulled harder on the reins, leaning back until all her weight was on the stallion's mouth. Finally, his ears turned back to her and he stopped.

"His mouth is a little hard," she said, letting out a breath.

"Don't forget he used to have Odin on his back."

"I haven't." She sat tall, ready to cross into Helheim. She only had to ask Sleipnir to step toward her mother.

Her *mother*.

The thought tingled through Sigrid's insides. Never in her life had she imagined that her mother was a royal—that *she* was a royal.

Mariam ran after them, clumsy in the deep sand. Fisk clattered along behind her. After a pause, Hestur trotted to catch up.

Elina's eyes narrowed, unfriendly. But then she seemed to recognize Mariam. "Your mare is Aesa, is she not?"

Mariam stopped in her tracks. "Yes. Is she here?"

When Elina shook her head, Sigrid's caught Mariam's flinch and her heart plummeted.

"Her rider's soul was not honorable enough to pass through into the afterlife yet," Elina said. "You'll find her out here, wandering, waiting for you. Once you find her, your soul will be redeemed. You served me well in Vanaheim, Mariam."

Mariam lifted her hands to her mouth. Her eyes filled with tears.

Fisk turned his eye holes between Mariam and Elina. "But the desert is huge. Endless. What if we never find her?"

"We will," Mariam said fiercely, wiping her eyes with the palm of her hand. "Come on, Fisk."

Sigrid's chest tightened. Despite Mariam's lies and betrayal, Sigrid had still promised to help her find Aesa. The valkyrie had been deteriorating without her mare and would continue to do so until they reunited.

But Mariam lied to me this entire time. She could do it again.

Sigrid chewed her lip, a mix of longing and uncertainty clouding her mind like fog. Their paths were taking them in different directions too soon.

She tried to kiss me.

I pushed her away.

"What'll you do with Hestur?" Mariam snapped.

Sigrid opened her mouth, but Elina spoke. "I can ride the Midgard horse."

Something rose in Sigrid's gut—a fierce "*no*." She shook her head, and guilt burned her cheeks when her mother raised an eyebrow. But she didn't like the idea of Hestur coming with her into the underworld, and she didn't like the idea of Elina riding him.

"I—I want him to go with Mariam and Fisk," Sigrid said. "They need him to carry their stuff."

Elina scrutinized Mariam, Fisk, and Hestur. "Very well."

"You're leaving Hestur?" Mariam said loudly.

"I can't go with you, but Hestur will help you cross the desert and find Aesa," Sigrid said, pushing down the ache in her chest. "Besides, it's only temporary. We'll see each other again when the vision is fulfilled."

Mariam rolled her eyes and scoffed.

Ignoring this, Sigrid said, "Take Hestur back up the spring with you if you go. Keep him under the canvas. Bring him to Vanaheim for me, all right? Fisk?"

She must have looked desperate, because Fisk quickly nodded and cupped a hand over Hestur's neck. "Don't you worry. I'll keep him safe."

Mariam threw her arms up. "You can't abandon Hestur! Not after everything you've been through together."

"I'm not abandoning him!" How could Mariam even suggest it?

"It sure feels like it."

They stared each other down. Mariam looked more drained than ever after so much time away from her mare.

"You need to go find Aesa," Sigrid said patiently. "You can't be apart from her for much longer."

"And you need to—" Mariam drew a breath, leveling her voice. "Stay with Hestur."

Sigrid swallowed around the knot in her throat. "Stop telling me what to do."

Sleipnir flicked his head impatiently and danced on the spot, not helping to calm her irritation.

Mariam turned around and raised an arm, waving at Sigrid with the back of her hand. "Guess this is 'bye, then."

"It's not," Sigrid said, because despite everything Mariam had done, despite her betrayal, a sick feeling rose at the thought. "I saw us riding together in the vision."

Mariam spun around, her expression twisted in anger. "Don't be naive."

"Mariam—" Fisk said.

"The future changes, Sigrid. You know that as well as I do."

Sigrid didn't believe it. She'd chosen to follow the future she'd seen in the vision, and so far, it was coming true. Mariam would go on to find Aesa and they would ride together again.

"Be careful in the desert. There might be—"

"Fisk and I have each other," Mariam cut in. "We'll be fine."

Sigrid ground her teeth. "Where will you go once you find Aesa?"

"What do you care?"

"Your plan just sounds a little vague—"

"For gods' sake, are you doing this or not? Stop stalling and go through the gates," Mariam shouted. She sat in the sand with her legs and arms crossed, glowering.

Sigrid huffed. *Fine.* It was time to do what she came for.

"You're sure this won't be a one-way journey?" she asked Elina.

Elina smiled. "Darling, how are we supposed to use Sleipnir to our advantage if you can't get back through? Trust me. Neither of us stands to benefit if you get stuck in Helheim."

Sigrid drew a breath. No sense in stalling any longer.

She nudged Sleipnir gently and braced for whatever was about to happen.

The stallion stepped confidently through the iron archway.

The air instantly cooled. Sigrid's belly swooped, from nerves or from passing through the gate. It caught her in the moment of weightlessness between rising and falling.

Elina grabbed Sleipnir's reins before he could keep walking, stopping him and guiding him a few steps sideways. "Good," she said, and her voice sounded clearer than before.

Back the way Sigrid came, the desert was hazy. Mariam and Fisk had the same foggy aura that Elina had a moment ago.

Sigrid viewed the flickering and cloudy landscape ahead—Helheim. It was a vast, open, and muted world. The only clear and colorful figures were the horse below her and the woman beside her.

Without the barrier between them, Elina came into full focus, her features real and solid.

"Hi," Sigrid said in a small voice, not knowing what else to say.

Elina beamed. The glimmer in her blue-gray eyes sent a trickle of warmth through Sigrid's chest. "Ready to lead me back?" she said, crisp and clear.

Though Sigrid could have stayed like this for a while, the two of them hovering in the space between worlds, she nodded. "Do you need to be touching Sleipnir or me?"

"I only need to follow you."

Swallowing hard, Sigrid nudged Sleipnir back toward Mariam and Fisk.

Please work. Her heart beat frantically, as if struggling with the enormity of what she was about to do. And then it was done.

With one step of Sleipnir's hooves, they emerged back into the hot desert.

Elina stood behind Sigrid on the sand, fully out of the gate, looking around as if taking in a view. "Honestly, I told you it would work."

She spoke so casually, like Sigrid had hopped over a log in the woods and not just pulled someone out of the realm of the dead, which was *impossible*.

Her friends all stared at her, her ride, and the queen she'd helped cross the iron archway. Mariam gaped from her seat on the sand. Fisk and Hestur were frozen in place.

"Onto Helheim?" Elina said.

"Um," Sigrid said, stammering. "Yeah. Sure."

I'm Sleipnir's heir. The truth bounced madly around her brain. She could lead Elina in and out of the gates, which meant she would be able to command Hel's army. The possibilities of having that kind of power and respect were more than she'd ever dreamed.

She opened her mouth, wanting to share her excitement with Mariam and Fisk. She wanted to tell them she was determined to see them again soon. But after Mariam's angry words, all she managed was, "Goodbye."

Blinking her burning eyes, she turned Sleipnir around and faced the gates.

Hestur whinnied, a purposeful, desperate note usually reserved for horses calling to their stablemates.

Her eyes welled. She couldn't look back at him. If she did, her heart would burst. "It's okay, buddy," she called out. "I'll see you soon!"

It had to be this way. He would be safer on this side of the gate.

Sigrid nudged Sleipnir onward. With Elina on foot beside her, they followed the trickling stream through the gates of Hel.

CHAPTER THIRTY-NINE

STUBBORN STEEDS

Riding Sleipnir into Helheim, Sigrid's stomach swooped as if she'd jumped off a cliff. Her breath caught, and she scrunched her face, and then she blinked a bright, cloudy sky into focus.

They stood on a dirt path in a vast meadow. In front, to the sides, and behind the gate at their backs, waist-high grass swayed in a warm breeze. The pale green and yellow blades were less lush than on Vanaheim, but the afterlife wasn't a dismal place. A stream ran down from a snow-capped mountain beside them, trickling past and out into the desert.

For all its reputation of being the lowest world, a place of corpses and sins and regrets, Helheim was, above all, peaceful.

Elina set off along the dirt path, and Sleipnir followed without urging. Far ahead, nestled in a valley, cottages and stables were scattered like wildflowers through the rolling fields.

"I didn't know souls could be turned away at the gates," Sigrid said, remembering what Mariam said of the time she was recruited, and how Aesa now wandered that endless red desert.

"One way or another, we all have to repay our sins in the afterlife. Only then can we move on."

"On? To where?"

Elina cast her a crooked smile. "Everywhere."

Sigrid tried to process this, until her attention caught on a passing farmhouse. Lights were on, but it looked empty. The front door creaked.

"Where is everyone?"

"They're here." Elina flicked a hand. "Living in these houses, tending the fields. You won't be able to see them."

This sounded too creepy for her liking. "What does that mean? You can see them?"

"Like the goddess Hel, I'm halfway between the living and the dead. I can see both and be seen by both."

The hairs on the back of Sigrid's neck tingled. It was not a nice idea that unseen departed souls were all around her.

"Don't worry, darling. Hel's army will materialize for you on your conquest," Elina said, like Sigrid had already come to a decision.

As Elina walked ahead, she brushed her fingers over the long grass beside the path. Did Sigrid walk with the same straight spine and smooth grace, or did that come with being born a royal?

She nudged Sleipnir to catch up. "Am I supposed to believe that people who spend their days tending fields and living in cottages are actually Hel's army?"

Elina laughed, a warm sound that made Sigrid wonder how different her life would be if she'd grown up hearing it. "Those people aren't your army, darling. Helheim is a world like any other, with farmers, tailors, merchants, and the like. Hel began training a proper army of departed souls who wished to become warriors, and when I became queen, I continued her legacy. That's who you'll be leading through the gates."

Actual warriors trained by Hel. Sigrid's breaths came shallow. Would they really follow her? She'd never led anyone anywhere. She tried to imagine herself at the front of this fearsome army but couldn't complete the picture. She only saw herself on Sleipnir, the world behind her vacant.

The seriousness of her decision wrapped around her like a bandage, tighter and tighter. "You said you'd teach me to ride Sleipnir."

"Of course," Elina said. "Have you ever ridden a horse besides your own?"

Sigrid shook her head. A valkyrie letting her ride her mare sounded as likely as Hestur learning to fly.

Elina waved a hand. "You'll just need time to adjust. Let's practice the basics first."

They walked toward a wooden barn at the base of a sloping hay field. A vegetable garden sprouted in front, which Elina nodded to.

Sigrid furrowed her brow. Did her mother just greet some tomato vines?

No, she nodded to the people tending them.

A chill rippled up her spine.

Behind the barn, the open hay field begged to be galloped in. Sigrid tightened her reins, a nervous flutter in her gut. This was happening. She was getting a riding lesson on the infamous Sleipnir. What would Peter say when she told him about this?

A ball of anxiety tightened in her stomach. Seeing Peter would mean leaving Helheim one way or another—with or without Elina's support, with or without Hel's army at her back. Next time she saw him, she would be a different person.

"Take him to the far end and back," Elina said. "Let him open up his speed. Practice bringing him down to a walk before you turn around."

"Okay." Her mouth twisted into a little smile. Practicing slowing to a walk could only mean one thing: he preferred to go fast. "Ready, Sleipnir?"

He was.

But Sigrid wasn't.

And then Sleipnir surged, almost unseating her, and everything from her past life dissipated in the wind howling past her ears.

Sigrid let out a noise somewhere between a laugh and a scream. The raw power beneath her straddled the line between exciting and terrifying—like cliff-jumping into a black lake or climbing the steeple of the highest barn at midnight or asking Hestur to jump a fallen tree that was a little too wide.

Unlike Hestur, who galloped long and flat like a feather on the wind, Sleipnir traveled upright, head high, charging like a war horse. They could probably crash through Vanaheim's stone wall if he decided he wanted to be on the other side. He snorted with each stride, his hooves slamming into the ground with enough force to shatter stone. Sigrid wouldn't have been surprised to see flames erupt from his nostrils.

Halfway up the hill, her heart was ready to burst through her chest from the effort of riding him. He needed a constant pull on the reins to stop him from bolting faster, maybe as a result of having Odin on his back for millennia, or maybe it was in his nature. She asked him to stop long before they reached the crest, leaning on the reins harder and harder, using all the strength in her arms, abdominals, and legs.

"Whoa, Sleipnir!" His responsiveness would need some serious work.

When she finally brought him down from a gallop, she slumped in the saddle, gasping. She wanted to drop the reins and shake the tension out of her hands, but Sleipnir pranced sideways, tossing his head, ready to gallop again. Resigned, she nudged him to return to Elina. Fighting him would accomplish nothing.

Galloping down the hill was more exhausting than galloping up it. All Sigrid could do was stay in the saddle and not tumble off the side, bracing against the slope and praying that Sleipnir had enough self-control not to stumble as gravity pushed them faster.

By the time they returned to the old brown barn, Sigrid wheezed for breath, sweat running down her temples.

"How was that?" Elina said, beaming.

"P-powerful."

Elina laughed and patted Sleipnir's neck. He tossed his head again. Sigrid wished he would stop doing that. It unseated her every time, making her feel like she'd temporarily lost control.

"If I'm his heir, shouldn't he be easier for me to ride?"

"You're doing wonderfully," Elina said. "Odin rode with a firm hand."

"Apparently." She used her shoulder to wipe the sweat beading down her temple.

She'd never doubted her ability as a rider. But with Sleipnir, she might have an easier time trying to ride a lion.

"It's a little hard to believe an army will follow me," she said, intending to make a self-deprecating joke but instead sounding a little pathetic. After a lifetime of being told she wasn't enough to join the valkyrie ranks, she barely believed she could ride Odin's steed, let alone raise Hel's army.

"Leadership is about confidence," Elina said. "If you believe you'll be victorious, then so will they."

"I guess that's the part that needs work."

Elina cupped her long fingers over Sigrid's knee. "You're a leader like your mother. By the time we're finished training you on Sleipnir, you'll believe you can lead an army. Trust me, Sigrid."

Trust me. Like she hadn't permanently lost Sigrid's trust sixteen years ago.

She must have seen Sigrid's expression cloud, because she said brightly, "Ready to keep riding?"

After practicing serpentines across the field, Sigrid returned to Elina jittery, tense, and with a boulder of frustration in her gut. With Hestur, asking him to slow meant relaxing her body. Asking him to turn meant looking in the direction she wanted to go. Asking him to speed up meant the slightest, visibly imperceptible twitch of her ankle. With Sleipnir, asking him to slow meant leaning back with all her strength, pulling the reins with the same force she used to lift a hay bale. Asking him to turn meant hauling on one rein, turning her full body, pressing his ribs with every bit of strength in her leg. Asking him to speed up—well, he needed no urging for *that*.

"I should've allowed you to rest first," Elina said with a slight frown and a tilt of her head. "You must be exhausted after your journey."

"I'm fine," Sigrid said, wheezing. "Just need a bit more time with him."

It wasn't like she'd expected to magically bond with the stallion, but that had been harder than expected. How was she supposed to lead an army when her horse couldn't follow her commands?

And speaking of armies. "Where is Hel's army, exactly?" she said, looking around the sloping land, expecting to find them camped out somewhere.

"They're a crypt beneath the palace. I've been continuing Hel's work for years."

"They've...been in a crypt under the palace for years?" A warning pinched in Sigrid's stomach.

Elina's mouth twisted in a little smile. "It's a big crypt. The palace holds more than you know. We'll be able to raise them as soon as you're ready."

Except Sigrid was now less sure about that part of the plan.

CHAPTER FORTY

UNCONVENTIONAL
RIDING LESSONS

Hel's palace probably held a lot of secrets, but Sigrid hoped the army of the dead beneath it was the worst of it.

She shifted in the saddle. *And how am I supposed to believe I have power over all those warriors?*

Elina searched her face. "What's wrong?"

Sigrid chewed her lip, then said, "How do you know I have the power to raise the dead? Even Vanahalla's best sorcerers can't do that."

Elina hesitated, seeming to choose her words carefully. "When you bring the army through the gates, you're bringing them temporarily into the land of the living. The dead stay dead, and their souls belong in Helheim. They will have to return here eventually."

Elina's words cinched around her heart, and the next question tumbled out. "What about Mariam?" Sigrid asked.

Elina frowned. "What about her?"

"Does her soul belong here? Will she have to return? Why is she visible among the living?" Not knowing was a void in her chest, sucking out all the air.

"When I stopped her at the gate, she never crossed into

Helheim," Elina said simply. "Even though she lost her life and ended up here, without crossing she is, in essence, still alive."

Her pulse jumped. "So, you saved her life."

"I suppose you could say that. I stopped her from dying in exchange for her service?"

Reluctant gratitude overcame Sigrid. *Elina saved Mariam's life.* If not for her, Mariam would be permanently gone from the land of the living, and they would never have met.

Mariam's lie still made Sigrid's stomach writhe, but with less intensity. Would Sigrid have agreed to the same mission in exchange for her life? Would she have risked the mission by telling the truth?

I think I would have.

Sigrid shook her head and got back to her original question. "So, Hel's army is temporary?"

"Correct," Elina said. "That's why it's important that we have a plan before we leave Helheim."

"I see." If Hel's army could only be raised for one conquest, what conquest was she meant to go on? Well first, they could help her and her friends get back home safely, especially with the Eye of Hnitbjorg in their possession. But then what? What was she supposed to *do* with this army?

Elina obviously wanted her to use the army to seize Vanaheim's throne. Mariam wanted her not to raise it at all. Sigrid only wanted everyone to see it for long enough to decide she was worthy of becoming a valkyrie. But that couldn't be the army's sole purpose.

The memory of the hostile Night Elves who'd captured them on the way here swam forward. Fisk had basically admitted they were interested in controlling the spring and more groups were out there, so it was possible that she hadn't seen the last of them. The mystery of what they'd done with Ratatosk remained unsolved.

"Is Ratatosk here?" Sigrid asked.

A question formed behind Elina's expression. "No."

"So he's still alive."

"Why wouldn't he be?"

"On the way here, we almost couldn't get down the spring of Hvergelmir because we were captured by a group of Night Elves who'd taken it over. We thought they might've killed him."

Elina watched Sleipnir's legs, gaze unfocused. After a long time, she said, "That's interesting."

Hostile Night Elves were still out there, and Ratatosk remained lost. Maybe this was a problem that required the help of Hel's army. They could search the nine worlds for Ratatosk until he was found, liberating any areas overtaken by elves along the spring. The valkyries would be grateful for the extra help.

Sigrid smiled to herself.

"Do you want to ride a bit longer?" Elina motioned to the field.

Sigrid nodded. Before any raising, marching, or liberating with an army, she needed to learn to ride Sleipnir. So she drew a breath and gathered the reins.

Elina pointed to a wooden fence dividing this field and the next. "Try a jump."

Sigrid's heart did just that. "It's huge!"

Her jumping experience consisted of logs and hay bales. This fence rose higher than Sleipnir's chest.

Elina grinned. "Sleipnir can jump twice as high as the average horse."

"How long did it take you to be comfortable on him?" Sigrid said, shifting in the saddle. Sleipnir pranced on the spot.

"It was a few months before I felt confident, but unlike you, I wasn't born with a natural gift for riding." Elina motioned behind Sigrid. "After the fence, come and take this line."

Flushing at the compliment, Sigrid looked over her shoulder.

A wide garden box sat adjacent to the barn, full of evenly spaced cabbages. Beyond it, a few strides out, was a waist-high pile of chopped wood.

"Four strides?" she said, trying to gauge the distance between the jumps.

"Probably three for Sleipnir. But don't you worry about that. Let him take care of working out the distance."

Sigrid nodded firmly, afraid her voice would come out as a squeak. She jittered like she'd eaten too much sugar, and the stallion's energy built like a geyser ready to erupt.

She clucked him onward, and they galloped toward the fence. She breathed into the beat, moving with the up-and-down of his neck. As they approached the fence, she counted down the strides.

Three…two…one.

His hindquarters tensed as his weight shifted to his four hind legs. His front ones came up, up, up, until his four knees peeked up on either side of his neck. She sucked in a breath.

They weren't just airborne, they were flying. This was what being on a winged mare must feel like. Weightlessness twisted her stomach at the top, like when she was a kid jumping from stacks of hay bales into a pile of loose hay on the floor.

When she came back from her little course, beaming, Elina made her jump again and again, until she stopped fearing it. By then, Sleipnir was so excited that he wouldn't stop prancing and snorting no matter how hard she pulled the reins.

To her relief, Elina waved her over. "That's enough for today. I'm sure you could use the rest after such a long journey." She smiled tenderly at Sigrid. "Let's have supper and give him a chance to calm down."

Sigrid relaxed in the saddle, her legs cramped and trembling. "That was fun!" Her voice came out louder than intended, like the ride had energized her. She wanted to gush about this to Mariam, Fisk, Peter, Roland—but they weren't here, of course.

I'll see them soon. I'm not here forever.

Her fingers tightened over the reins and her calves around Sleipnir's ribs, gripping her ride out of the underworld a little tighter. The fact that this stallion was her only way back through the gates of Hel put a little jolt of fear in her chest.

They walked past the vegetable garden, more freshly raked than when they'd passed it the first time, and back onto the path. Sleipnir marched onward with no signs of tiring. Did he ever lose energy? Maybe this was part of his power. His four front legs thumped over the dirt, appearing and disappearing ahead of his shoulders in a hypnotic way.

She couldn't believe Sleipnir was hers, and that she'd proven she could ride him.

Elina caught her staring and smiled, cheeks dimpling. Her eyes gleamed with excitement, like she'd gotten as much thrill out of the ride as Sigrid had. They could've shared years of moments like this, but Elina had chosen to leave.

Sigrid could not forget that.

"You said you got here because you made a bargain with Hel," Sigrid said, hopefully sounding curious and not like she was trying to pry Elina open. "How did you do that?"

"The towers of Vanahalla are full of magic. You can feel it when you walk through the halls, like static. If you know where to look, you can find a sorcerer." Elina shrugged. "I persuaded one of them to help me."

"Was he a friend?" *An accomplice, maybe? My father?*

"Him? No. I needed him to help me get here. He was a business deal." She winked. "I don't think my dear brother Óleifr ever noticed the small fortune that went missing. Anyway, it's quite beautiful inside Vanahalla. You'll love it there."

Sigrid didn't miss the repeated implications that she would, in fact, lead Elina and the army out of Helheim. And staying consistent, she was careful not to agree.

If she did decide to help Elina take Vanaheim's throne, she could someday walk that beautiful hall as a princess, join her mother for a pancake breakfast, and sleep in her own room while Hestur enjoyed a bigger, brighter stall. She would have a real bed with pillows, clothes, a bathroom, maybe even access to a library. Maybe she could convince Elina to bring Peter to Vanahalla and give him a higher role of his choosing. He could bring Roland if he wanted.

But it was still an *if* and not a *when*.

On either side of the path, the lush grass became sparser as the landscape changed to dry dirt and rock. The hills felt endless thanks to her exhausted body. It felt like she hadn't slept in days, much less eaten.

When they crested another hill, and Elina gestured ahead. "Welcome home, Sigrid."

The landscape before them stole the breath from her lungs.

CHAPTER FORTY-ONE

ELINA'S PLANS

Across the valley on a barren hill stood a dark brown palace. It rose from the ground like a fungus, with four pointed peaks and a wet, mud-like texture to its walls. The base of the hall had dozens of angled pillars, fanning out like a spiderweb anchoring it to the ground.

As they approached, the hall loomed larger and larger, until Sigrid gaped at its vastness. Muddy waves oozed down the walls, like the whole palace was slowly sinking.

An empty stable sat to the right, tangles of weeds creeping up the sides. Sigrid dismounted to lead Sleipnir toward it.

Elina touched her arm to stop her. Her long fingernails grazed Sigrid's skin like claws. "I keep Sleipnir inside the hall with me, darling."

"Oh."

Sigrid changed course and led the horse to the front doors, feeling absurd. He marched inside, evidently accustomed to this arrangement because he knew where to go.

The inside was cold, dank, and as muddy-looking as the outside. The lobby was a vast space with a vaulted ceiling and a balcony along the second-floor perimeter. Beyond the iron railing were a few closed wooden doors.

With no portraits or furniture, the place had obviously been decorated with little sentimentality. Had it always been this way? For all Sigrid knew, Elina might have improved on it.

"Sleipnir's room is on the main floor," Elina said, voice drifting eerily across the lobby.

The stallion clip-clopped over the stone floor. Sigrid followed at his shoulder, letting him pull her by the reins.

They came to a closed door with tack hanging beside it, all of it black and shimmering with gemstones. Bronze hooks held a bridle with a padded noseband and crystal browband, a halter with Sleipnir's name carved into a gold plate on the cheek piece, and a tangle of leather that was probably spare reins and stirrup straps. On the floor beneath it sat a pile of tendon boots lined with fur. In all, there must have been enough tack to dress several horses.

The bit attached to the fancy bridle snagged her attention. The metal piece was thin and twisted with a rectangular paddle in the center, designed to press against the inside of the horse's mouth with maximum force. She winced, never having seen a bit so harsh in the valkyrie stables.

Sleipnir pawed the door, his hoof rattling it so hard that it was a wonder he didn't break it. Elina opened it and let them inside.

Whatever the room looked like before, the stallion had destroyed it. The muddy walls were warped and indented with hoofprints the size of dinner plates. Dirty straw and hay covered the chipped stone floor, so the room smelled like a barn. The only furniture was a vanity with a dusty, cracked mirror, and a four-poster bed, rumpled and dirty, as if Sleipnir actually used it. The wood on both of these was chewed and splintered.

Amid the wreckage, Sigrid and Elina untacked and groomed Sleipnir while he munched on an entire bale of hay that had been hauled inside and placed by the bed. Sigrid worked a curry comb in slow circles over his coat, distracted by the vastness of the room.

"Upstairs is more suitable for humans," Elina said with a wink.

Sigrid opted not to mention that this felt normal, as she'd spent her whole life in a barn. A pang of yearning for Hestur stung her heart at the thought of their shared stall back home.

"Who lived here before you?" She returned the curry comb to the brush box and grabbed the hoof pick, wanting the experience of cleaning out eight hooves on the same horse.

"Hel," Elina said simply. When Sigrid looked at her sharply, she went on. "Helheim had no queen, only a goddess. When I gained favor with Hel, she accepted my offer. I imagine ruling this world was becoming tiresome for her. Now, she is free to do as she pleases."

Before Sigrid could ask what the goddess of the dead was like, Elina tossed her brush in the box and sighed. "Come. I'm starving. The stable hands will finish this for us."

She exited the room, leaving Sigrid with the icy realization that departed souls shared the room with them—the same ones who had deposited the hay bale. She threw the hoof pick in the brush box and ran after Elina.

The dining room was another vast space, as cold and untouched as if it had never been inhabited. A rainbow of roasted vegetables, mashed potatoes, and fruit already covered the table.

"Is this what it was like to live in Vanahalla?" Sigrid said, aching to learn about her family.

"Oh, it's much nicer there," Elina said, leaning in as if clinging to the opportunity to talk about royal life. While they dined, she told Sigrid what it was like to be a princess on Vanaheim—the beautiful robes and jewelry, extravagant meals, private suites, important engagements, and the interactions with her parents and siblings. The age gap between her and her younger siblings was enough that she saw them as nuisances rather than friends. But her parents—Sigrid's grandparents—had been so fixated on

Óleifr that Elina and Kaia got into all kinds of trouble.

"I remember one time," Elina said, laughing, "Kaia and I snuck into the slaughterhouse and stole one of the pigs. We put a horse halter on it like a harness and took it for a walk around the courtyard. The thing wouldn't stop squealing."

There was a spark in her mother's eyes when she talked about her younger sister that Sigrid longed to have herself. But the more stories Elina told, the more living as a royal seemed like a whole other world. Poise and appearance aside, her mother even dined like a royal. Sigrid did her best to mimic it, noting the order to use the cutlery, the delicate way to hold them, what size portions to cut, how often to dab her lips with her napkin, and the special skill of eating slower.

As Elina leaned forward to put down her goblet, the Eye of Hnitbjorg swung from a chain around her neck. She saw Sigrid watching and tucked it beneath her shirt. "The Eye was the reason I knew you were coming. It showed me a vision of you galloping past Garmr. You're talented, Sigrid. Gods have failed to get past Garmr." She put a long-fingered hand to her mouth and said in a conspiratorial whisper, "The gods can be egotistical idiots, though. Don't tell them I said that."

First praise, and now a joke. Her mother was trying very hard to win her favor.

Elina rose and slipped through the kitchen door. "I'll be right back."

Sigrid leaned away from the table, full to bursting but unsatisfied. Despite crossing the nine worlds, claiming Sleipnir like she'd wanted, and finding answers to some of her questions about where she'd come from, a layer of misery coated her insides like molasses.

Something was incomplete. The vision had shown her with Mariam and the junior valkyries, but how did they fit in with raising Hel's army? And was Sigrid meant to bring the Eye of

Hnitbjorg home around her mother's neck, or steal it back? Elina didn't make up part of the vision after all.

Ugh. The future was still frustratingly foggy.

Her mother returned with dessert—a plate of blueberry pastries. Sigrid's chest tightened at the memory of the last one she'd eaten. Where was Mariam now? Had she found Aesa? Would Sigrid ever be able to rekindle what she and Mariam had after parting ways so coldly?

Elina's long fingernails clinked a rhythm on her goblet. "What's wrong, darling?"

"Nothing." Sigrid grabbed a pastry, avoiding her mother's eye.

"If you don't like this, I can have—"

"It's not the food. The food is great."

"Then what is it?" Elina said, voice sharp.

"It's...I was thinking about Hestur and Mariam. And Fisk." Sigrid pulled the pastry in half so the blueberry filling oozed onto her plate. "Do you think they'll be all right out there?"

Elina leaned back in her chair. "Sigrid, you can't live your life worrying about everyone else. You have to keep *your* destination in mind."

Yet, when she'd done exactly that, Mariam had called her self-absorbed and selfish.

She stuffed the dessert in her mouth.

"Your friends were holding you back." Elina continued, giving a tight-lipped smile, as if struggling with her calm tone. "Why did you bring them along, anyway?"

"They helped me get here," Sigrid said, a little defensive.

Elina pointed knowingly at her. "This is why it's important to make a distinction between business deals and friendships. They helped you get here. That makes them a business deal. Right?"

Hestur aside, it was true that Mariam and Fisk had made it hard to think. Sigrid had come a long way and finally found her cosmic purpose on Sleipnir, yet the moment she decided to fulfill it, all Mariam could do was beg her not to.

Pushing down her guilt, Sigrid nodded.

"Good," Elina said. "Now that you're away from them and can form your own opinions, *you* get to decide what you want to do."

"What do you mean?" Sigrid said, searching her blue-gray eyes.

"As Sleipnir's heir, do you want to fulfill your purpose and raise Hel's army?"

"Is raising Hel's army my purpose, though?"

Elina tilted her head, a dimple in her cheek. "I don't see why else the cosmos gave you Sleipnir. You're the first and only heir he's had since Odin."

That seemed like a very…narrow purpose.

"I want to be a valkyrie," Sigrid said. To protect her home and the people in it.

"Just a valkyrie? Or a general in charge of your own division?"

Sigrid shifted in her seat, goose bumps prickling beneath her tunic. "I…don't know. I never thought about becoming more than a junior valkyrie before today."

"You were born to be so much more. If not for antiquated laws, you would have been a royal, a valkyrie, and who knows what else."

Images sparked in Sigrid's mind—racing across the Bifrost, galloping to Alfheim to liaise with the Light Elves, meeting with officials on important royal duties, all as a high-ranking valkyrie in a white-and-gold uniform. It was the deepest, most private dream she held close in the dark hours of the night.

"But instead," Elina said, "we're both here, all because my little brother was given the crown instead of me."

Sigrid made a face. "Valkyries are the best warriors in the cosmos. I don't understand why women are allowed to be warriors but not queens. It isn't right, and that rule is absurd."

"Exactly." Elina raised her goblet to toast these words.

"How would you take the throne from King Óleifr?" Sigrid said, careful to keep this hypothetical.

Elina refilled their goblets with a sweet cloudberry liqueur that had Sigrid's head buzzing. "That decision…can be yours," she said slowly. "What would you like to do?"

"Not kill him," Sigrid said at once.

"Then we won't."

They sipped their drinks in silence.

If Sigrid found a way to make sure the stable hands didn't get involved…if there was a way to do this swiftly…Elina could be queen, and Sigrid would be her heir. She could live in Vanahalla as a princess instead of sleeping in a hammock at the back of a horse stall. All she had to do was lead Hel's army to Vanaheim and help her mother take the throne. The means to do it was right here.

Still, could she commit treason? Did she trust her mother enough to put her on the throne instead of King Óleifr, who'd always been fair and kind? Was she willing to do that to Vanaheim?

The answer was clear.

As angry as she was at Vanaheim for tamping her down all these years, that world was home. Maybe it took visiting Helheim to realize it, but she loved the green hills and the golden hall and the sprawling valkyrie stables more than anything. Everything about that world was beautiful, bright, and *hers*.

"I want to find my cosmic purpose and join the valkyries," Sigrid said, tracing the rim of her goblet. "It's why I came here. I also have my fr—my companions who I promised to return home. And Hestur. I think if I raise Hel's army and get us back to Vanaheim safely with the Eye of Hnitbjorg, I'll earn my place with the valkyries. But I don't want to overthrow the king. That's treason, and the conquest would hurt Vanaheim."

For the briefest moment, Elina's expression twisted. The candles lining the muddy walls flickered over her face, and something dark passed behind her eyes. Then it was gone. "It's your decision as Sleipnir's heir."

They stared at each other. The thick, muddy walls amplified the underworld's absolute silence.

"Then I'd like to continue learning how to ride Sleipnir," Sigrid said. "I want to raise Hel's army to protect the people I care about and get everyone home. If we have the Eye with us, the journey will be dangerous. The Night Elves I told you about are trying to control the spring of Hvergelmir and have done something with Ratatosk. Once we're all safely home, I'm going to use Hel's army to go after the elves."

The words were out. She'd made her decision. It unfurled inside her like the start of a valkyrie charge, a rush of adrenaline and determination.

She braced for Elina to argue and deliver another lecture about how the throne was stolen from her. But to her relief, Elina nodded. "They're ready when you are."

Heart pounding, Sigrid said, "Five days. I want five days of lessons, and then I'll do it."

Elina nodded, reaching across to place a cold hand over Sigrid's. "Tomorrow, we'll do some mounted combat training. You can throw and recall a valkyrie spear, I presume?"

"I've spent my life practicing it in secret."

"That's my girl," Elina said. "Combat is only the beginning. When I'm finished with you, you'll be the most formidable woman in all the nine worlds."

CHAPTER FORTY-TWO

BECOMING A WARRIOR

Sleipnir's power was like nothing Sigrid had experienced. After four days of training, it became clear that the jitters from the first ride weren't nerves, but an energy seeping through the saddle and into her. Whether they practiced dressage movements or combat stunts, each ride left her on edge for hours.

All the while, pressure from Elina built like water boiling beneath a steam column. She tossed around phrases like "when we're in Vanahalla" and "if you change your mind about my place on the throne" and, worst of all, "I'm proud of you." She was *proud* of Sigrid for coming to Helheim, for searching for a greater destiny, for wanting to be a valkyrie, for raising Hel's army.

You don't get to feel pride because of me, Sigrid wanted to say. *You lost that privilege when you decided you didn't want to be my mother.*

Soon, the steam would erupt—but as much as the explosion might come from Sigrid, it might also come from Elina. Sigrid avoided agreeing whenever Elina made these assumptions, tossing around her own phrases like "when I'm a valkyrie" and "when I command the army."

My army. My plan.

Elina let these reminders pass with the subtlest flickers of disappointment in the line of her mouth.

Sigrid channeled the building pressure and Sleipnir's energy, working up a sweat as she trained her hardest, determined to make his eight legs an extension of her own.

One day left. She'd given herself one more day of training to master this stallion.

After stampeding through what must have been her hundredth jumping course while throwing a spear at targets, she rode back to find her mother wearing an odd expression. She looked Sigrid up and down, forehead creased, lips puckered. Even in her casual brown tunic and riding trousers, with her diadem and jewelry left back at the palace, she carried a regal air. Sigrid sat taller to match it.

"You ride him well," Elina said slowly. "And your skill...if I didn't know any better, I'd say you spent your life in valkyrie training."

Sigrid fiddled with her leather gloves, chest expanding as she breathed in the compliment. All of her secret practice sessions on Hestur had been worth something, after all.

She swallowed as she thought of Hestur. Where was he? How was the desert treating him, Mariam, and Fisk? The urge to gallop out the gates and check on them increased daily, but she dared not voice this to her mother. She just needed to get through training, and then she'd be able to find them and use the army to get everyone to safety.

"Now you'll need to work on your confidence," Elina said. "You've got too much youthful innocence working against you."

Sigrid pulled her attention back. "Youthful innocence?"

"You're pure," Elina said, petting the stallion's shoulder. "It's hard to imagine a face like yours leading an army."

With that, she walked back toward the palace, leaving Sigrid flustered. Was Elina talking about her expression or her actual face? Would it help if she looked angry all the time? Maybe she would have more confidence if she hadn't spent her life being told she wasn't good enough.

Exhausted and wound tightly, she rolled her neck and let Sleipnir take them back.

That night, she tossed in bed for a while before tiptoeing down to Sleipnir's room. Again. Sleep had come terribly since arriving in Helheim. Her room was as cold and empty as the rest of the hall, and though the bed was as soft as a mound of feathers, she would have chosen her hammock in Hestur's stall over that dank room any day. Plus, as she lay shivering each night, she couldn't stop wondering if departed souls shared the room with her.

She slept better on Sleipnir's destroyed bed, the familiar smells and the sound of stomping hooves and a swishing tail feeling like home. And in the pre-dawn hours, she awoke to do groundwork with him before breakfast. She might be able to ride him, but she didn't *know* him. Their connection was a shadow of what she had with Hestur. If she was going to command Hel's army, she first had to command the horse she would be riding.

As she worked on the usual exercises—using oats to train him to respond to his name, asking him to follow at her shoulder, and using pressure and release to cue him to move sideways—her attention wandered back to Elina's comment.

How am I supposed to look less pure? People had to fear her. That was how leading an army worked—like the valkyries swooping down in a storm of wings, hooves, and weapons. People respected them. They respected General Eira.

Leaving Sleipnir to chew on a bedpost, Sigrid crossed to the splintered, dusty vanity. The girl in the cracked mirror had a soft, smooth face and a mess of blond hair over one shoulder. Her hair was frizzy, like when a child comes back from playing outside. Her eyes, too colorless to be called blue, were wide and uncertain.

She cringed.

This was not the image of a leader. Did she really believe she could raise Hel's army and become a valkyrie general?

In the upper ranks and in all of the illustrations from legends and sagas, valkyries wore armor, emblems of Vanaheim, and practical attire that wouldn't hinder them in a fight. Sigrid looked nothing like them.

She ran her hand along the side of her head with three braids running front-to-back—the style she wore to free her fighting arm.

A little smile pulled at her lips as she flexed. Finally, she could call it a fighting arm.

Sleipnir's brush box held oils, combs, and a razor blade for trimming his mane and tail. She grabbed the razor, brought it up to the braided side of her head, and let out a breath.

Do it.

She sawed at the base of the braids. Working carefully, she shaved the majority of the left side down to bristles and left a clean line to separate the shaven part and her tangled blond mats. She swept those over the crown of her head and let them fall heavily down her right side.

She dropped the razor in the brush box and let a fistful of hair drop to the floor. The girl in the mirror looked a little fiercer, with bristles instead of frizzy braids on her left side. It was practical, but not enough for the Princess of Hel.

Behind the vanity, the wall's muddy texture oozed downward in that endless flow, warped and dented by Sleipnir's hooves. It was as if the palace were a fountain that slowly pulled mud from the ground and let it trickle back down.

Hesitantly, she reached for a ripple. The warm, gritty substance coated her fingers. *Mud?* A reddish tint caught her eye, but that could also be the candlelight playing tricks.

If she was to be the Princess of Hel, then Hel's palace should be a part of her.

She grazed the wall and stripped off more.

Sigrid swept the warm, sticky soil over her face, making an asymmetrical pattern, then drew more around her eyes. When she was done, she stepped back to admire her work.

A rush of warmth spread through her chest. Now *this* was a leader. She looked like she could jump onto a horse and ride into battle at any moment. She looked fierce.

One more step.

Out the door, where Sleipnir's spare tack sat against the wall, she rummaged through the pile of tendon boots. Choosing two boots made of hard black leather and lined with gray fur, she placed them over her forearms. They were meant to wrap the lower part of Sleipnir's legs for protection, which made them sturdy, but too loose on Sigrid's small arms. She pulled a set of reins from the tangle of leather straps and wrapped them over top, crisscrossing them over the leather and between her thumb and forefinger. Satisfied, she flexed her fingers to study the effect.

"Sigrid?"

She gasped and jerked back, almost losing her footing. Not fierce at all.

Elina stood across the lobby holding a dish of scrambled eggs.

"Sorry, you scared me," Sigrid said, taking a breath to calm her racing heart.

"What are you doing?"

Sigrid stepped closer and lifted her chin, trying to exude confidence. Suddenly the grit on her face felt sticky, the side of her head felt cold, and her forearms sweated beneath the fur boot lining. "What do you think?"

Elina's gaze flicked from her makeup, to her hair, and down her body. She grinned. "You look like a warrior."

CHAPTER FORTY-THREE

DANGEROUS TRICKS

Sigrid entered the fifth day of training with her shoulders square and her calves tight to Sleipnir's sides, determined to make him listen. She became a conduit for the power pulsing through his veins, and when she cued him to kick, strike, and stomp his front hooves, that power exploded from his muscles with deadly force.

A winged mare could never fight this hard.

"Good!" Elina said, eyes gleaming like someone had gifted her a cart of Alfheim's finest wine. She came to stand at Sleipnir's shoulder. "Let's try something. Shorten your reins."

Sigrid sheathed her spear and worked her fingers up the reins, confused because they were already so short. Sleipnir began to back up.

"Nudge him," Elina said. "Shorter reins. More pressure. Give him nowhere to go."

She shortened the reins until she might as well have skipped them and held onto the bit. All the while, she nudged Sleipnir so he wouldn't back up. Unable to go forward or back, he curled his neck and pranced to and fro like a rocking horse.

"Now lift your hands."

Sigrid did, tensing. The stallion raised his arched neck higher and pranced more quickly. His front end bounced, light on the ground.

"Now give him a nudge and—" Elina whistled, and as Sigrid pressed her heels to his ribs, his front end lifted from the ground.

She gasped, heart in her throat. "Oh!"

Sleipnir reared so high that Sigrid grabbed his mane to avoid slipping off the saddle. His front hooves thrashed with deadly force, like four flying boulders. Then he touched down with a gentle thud and tossed his head, seeming proud of himself.

Elina clapped. "Well done! Never taught a horse to rear before?"

Sigrid loosened the reins, limbs tingling with adrenaline. "It's one thing I never taught Hestur because it's so—"

Dangerous, she finished in her head. It was a dangerous move. She didn't want to say it in case it made her sound timid and not like a fierce valkyrie ready to lead armies.

"Difficult, I know. Now, when you cue him, position the reins like—" Elina reached for Sigrid's hands.

The stallion tensed, every muscle coiling. Sigrid reacted instinctively, tightening her legs to brace against whatever was coming.

With speed that belied his size, Sleipnir spun into Elina, his front legs a blur, thrusting his head out so hard that Sigrid pitched forward. His teeth clamped where the woman's hand had been. Elina stumbled backward. She tripped and fell, hitting the ground with a gasp.

"Sleipnir, whoa!" Sigrid pulled the reins and rooted in the saddle, struggling for control as her hands trembled.

Rather than scream or cower, Elina roared. "No!"

The stallion snorted, prancing as if ready to strike again.

As Sigrid calmed him, Elina jumped to her feet and marched forward. She grabbed the reins and yanked them hard, jerking the bit in his mouth.

The stallion made a guttural sound, as if in pain.

"You—will—not—do—that!" Elina jerked the bit with every word, causing him to toss his head higher to avoid the pain.

"Stop!" The word tore from Sigrid's throat like one of Garmr's fire blasts. Her lifelong role as a stable hand—a protector and caretaker of horses—erupted from her like a shield around Sleipnir. No matter his crime, this wasn't the right way to correct it.

She didn't recall drawing her spear, but suddenly it was in her hand, pointed at Elina. She nudged Sleipnir, and he reared, pulling back with enough force to break away from the woman's grip. As Elina stumbled and caught her balance, he stood facing her, nostrils blowing.

Sigrid trembled in the saddle, in numb shock.

Elina's chest heaved. "This stallion needs firm discipline. He can't behave like that."

"He was protecting me," Sigrid said. "It's his instinct. I won't let you hurt him."

Elina's expression darkened. Her gaze flicked between Sigrid and Sleipnir. Was it wrong to have shouted at her?

No. *She* was Sleipnir's heir, not Elina. She was his rider and guardian.

An icy feeling surged through her at what Elina had done. She'd hurt a horse. She'd used the bridle to inflict pain and punish him.

"Walk in a circle," Elina said, dusting off. "Practice rearing on cue."

Sigrid sheathed her spear, frown firmly in place. "Are you—?"

"I'm fine. Let's keep practicing."

Drawing a breath to try and stop trembling, Sigrid nudged Sleipnir forward. He was wound up, ready to explode.

"It's okay. You're okay," she cooed, hoping her voice was low enough that Elina couldn't hear.

She swallowed her disappointment in Elina's training methods. It was a harsh reminder of the divide between herself and her mother. Elina had admitted she wasn't a naturally gifted rider, hadn't she? Maybe no one had taught her any better. Maybe Sleipnir had tried to hurt her before, and without anyone to guide her through how to discipline him, she'd resorted to any means to stay safe.

The stallion was a difficult ride, but cruelty was not the answer.

When she got her nerves back under control, she cued him to rear again. He obeyed her commands without a fuss.

"Good boy," she whispered as victory flooded her veins. His behavior was obvious—he had put his allegiance and trust in her.

Sigrid was ready to ride him better than Elina had, and better than anyone since Odin. But she was also aware she had to harness the consequences that came with having such a powerful horse before riding him to Vanaheim.

She rolled her neck and flexed her fingers, mentally tracing the journey back through the worlds. Walking Sleipnir in a circle, she inhaled deeply, trying to curb the stirring sensation in her chest before it sent her heart beating too quickly.

"Will the army fit on Ratatosk's ship?" The initial group that was sent to retrieve the Eye had been a fraction of the size of Hel's army. A thousand people wouldn't fit on deck.

"Enough of them will. If not, we can make more than one trip." Elina tapped her chin. "Of course, this is only if your travel companions haven't already taken the ship."

Sigrid flushed. "Oh."

Elina waved a hand, still deep in thought. "We'll send valkyries ahead to fetch it. We'll just be delayed a few days."

Valkyries. Hel's army had valkyries. How could Sigrid have forgotten that?

"I can still raise the army tomorrow?" Sigrid said, swelling with excitement.

"Whenever you feel ready."

Sigrid swallowed, unaccustomed to adults wanting her opinion on important matters. She'd worked hard in these five days of combat training. It was time to start the next stage of her life. A life that would begin with getting Mariam, Fisk, Hestur, and Aesa back home safely to Vanaheim. And once they were there? A whole new world would be waiting for her. A life in which she was finally a valkyrie...and more.

"I'm ready," she said, breathless.

Elina beamed. "And so, the Princess of Hel becomes the Princess of Vanaheim."

CHAPTER FORTY-FOUR

A COSMIC DESTINY

"I'm so proud of you and your decisions, Sigrid," Elina continued. "When I'm queen, we can go after the Night Elves you told me about. We could launch a conquest in Svartalfheim."

Sigrid reined Sleipnir to a halt when Elina started her usual monologue about claiming the throne, becoming queen, and leading conquests to Svartalfheim and other worlds. Did she even listen to herself? Because she clearly did not listen to Sigrid.

And Sigrid was beyond tired of it.

The pressure had been building, and now it reached a peak.

"I need to make something clear," Sigrid said, lifting her chin. "I'll bring you back to Vanaheim with me so you can assume your role as a *princess*, but I will not use Sleipnir and Hel's army to commit treason and make you the queen. I want to get everyone home safely and to be a valkyrie. I will remove the elves from where they're causing trouble, but I don't intend to invade their home world.

"That's all. If you don't like that, you can stay in Helheim."

Elina's expression darkened with each word. Her fists clenched, knuckles whitening. But looking down at her from atop Sleipnir, she was no more than an angry chickadee.

Eyebrows knitted, mouth a thin line, temple throbbing, Elina might have been choosing which precise words she wanted to use to shout at Sigrid. But when she opened her mouth, her words were flat. "It's your army. You get to decide."

A charged silence formed between them, like the static sensation in the air before lighting hit. Sigrid opened her mouth, searching for words to bring them back to where they'd been a moment ago, when Elina said shortly, "Are you going to keep training, or are you done for the day?"

Sigrid shut her mouth and gathered the reins. "Let's keep going."

They finished the day's training with an agility course that included jumps, targets, stunts, maneuvers, and ended with a fierce rear that had Sleipnir thrashing his hooves. It was her best round yet, validating her decision to raise the army tomorrow. She was ready. She could get everyone home, claim her birthright, and use Hel's army to protect the worlds from the elves.

Beaming, she trotted back to Elina, but the woman merely nodded and walked back to the palace.

Sigrid caught her breath and followed a moment later.

"That was great, buddy," she said, scratching Sleipnir's neck. His ears turned back to her. The movement was almost, but not quite, as familiar as Hestur's usual response to her voice. She swallowed hard, the Hestur-shaped hole in her heart growing painfully big.

Back in the palace, she untacked Sleipnir and brushed him alone. She rewarded him for the great ride with treats and smiled when he nudged her gently for more.

"Glad you still know how to act like a horse."

As she rubbed his wide forehead, his abnormally high temperature seeped into her palm. When her pulse began to accelerate, she took her hand away.

"What is it about you?" she murmured.

Sleipnir blinked, and she hoped she wasn't imagining that his eyes seemed softer and more curious than when she'd first met him.

When Sigrid arrived in the dining room, Elina wasn't there. Food waited on the table, but Sigrid sat for half an hour before deciding her mother must have already eaten. She ate alone, reflecting on what she'd said. Was it too harsh?

Maybe a little, but Elina needed to know Sigrid's intent. They couldn't march to Vanaheim with separate goals in mind.

The problem was that Sigrid kind of did want her mother on the throne instead of King Óleifr. Guilt burned her cheeks at the mere thought. She didn't want to commit treason, but if she was going to be a princess and a valkyrie, she would rather serve under her mother, a powerful woman and the rightful queen of Vanaheim.

As long as Elina kept working for forgiveness, it was possible that their future could include a loving relationship.

Sigrid just needed time.

In the morning, she found Elina at the breakfast table, sitting back with a cold expression.

Sigrid took a seat, keeping her chin up and her eyes on her mother. "I'm ready to raise the army."

"I wish you all the best," Elina said flatly.

Sigrid had expected a response like this. "I like the idea of being a valkyrie under your rule instead of King Óleifr's." She drew a breath. "But I want to get to know you first. If we go to Vanaheim together and live in Vanahalla, maybe we can discuss what's next. I wouldn't mind that. It...it would be nice to have you in my life, Mother."

It was the first time she'd called her *mother*. The word tasted strange.

Elina's breath hitched. The familiar dimples appeared in her cheeks and she looked at Sigrid. "I would like that very much."

Sigrid's heart leaped, as light as if she'd jumped a stone wall on Sleipnir. "Good."

"Good." Elina smiled warmly. "Sometimes when you turn your head a certain way, I see glimpses of your father. He was talented on horseback, like you."

The mention of him sustained Sigrid, like a sip of water after a ride in the sun. *He rode horses.* What was it about her face, exactly? Did they have the same nose or cheekbones? She ached to ask a thousand questions about him, but before she could, Elina spoke.

"Tack up and meet me in the lobby."

Sigrid's insides flipped over. They were marching to Vanaheim on her terms. She was going to ride home with Sleipnir beneath her and an army at her back. The people she cared about would be safe.

For a moment, she felt like a true valkyrie, capable and confident.

And if all went well, she'd be more.

After a quick sandwich, Sigrid brushed and readied Sleipnir, this time using the bridle with the crystal browband. It shimmered on the stallion's steel gray forehead, glints of light peeking through his thick black forelock. At Elina's suggestion, she fitted him with a steel breastplate, which made him look twice as large. Finally, she fastened eight fur-lined boots around his legs to support his tendons while they galloped.

With the stallion ready to go, Sigrid donned a hard leather vest over her red tunic, which Elina had given her as armor. She wrapped her forearms and painted her face with a fresh layer of mud from the palace walls. She put on her helmet and gloves, then grabbed a spear and sheathed it in a quiver across her back.

Elina changed into a robe as magnificent as the black-and-amber one she'd worn to meet Sigrid. This one was sky blue with a boar's head embroidered on the breast—the emblem of Vanaheim. She'd probably been saving this robe for the day she returned home. The amber diadem glistened on her forehead.

"Are you not wearing armor?" Sigrid said, suddenly conscious about her wrapped forearms.

"Darling, the entire army is our protection. Our job is to lead. However…" Elina rapped on her stomach, which made a hollow knock. She must have worn a similar vest beneath her robe. "I am prepared in case we run into trouble."

"Right." Sigrid was being dramatic. It's not like they would head into a real battle yet. Sleipnir's breastplate and the leather vest were more for show.

Confirming this, Elina said, "It's important for us to look like royals when we arrive in Vanaheim, not berserkers. Your choice of bridle for Sleipnir is beautiful, by the way."

The crystals glimmered through the stallion's forelock, unquestionably royal.

A strange calm settled over Sigrid as they left Sleipnir's room. The situation was so far from anything she'd ever experienced that it was like watching it happen to someone else. Someone else took Sleipnir's reins. Someone else mounted up. Someone else followed Elina outside.

"Remember, darling, this is about confidence. They'll trust you if you trust yourself."

Sigrid nodded and sat taller in the saddle.

I'm the Princess of Hel. I have Sleipnir. I can lead an army.

His energy trickled into her, tightening her chest and quickening her pulse. Being on his back made her want to gallop, to fight, to feel a sense of victory.

Her heart raced with ideas and she imagined her new life

in the shimmering royal towers, where she could roll over in her plush bed and gaze at a tapestry of her ancestors instead of twisting around in her creaking hammock to look at a mound of horse poop. She could have blueberry pastries any time, especially while she learned everything there was to know from Vanahalla's scholars. She'd learn about the nine worlds and how to protect them.

The promise of this new, better life drove her onward.

She followed Elina, not toward the rolling fields as usual, but around the back of the palace. There, they came upon the most dismal garden in existence. Gray ivy snaked across a shattered stone walkway, around a cracked wooden arch, and over a smattering of dead shrubs. Black roses bloomed on an unkempt bush with oversize thorns, its stems strangling the row of pale hedges lining the garden perimeter. A gray fountain in the center had dark mud oozing from the top and bubbling like poison in its pool. The place had the pungent smell of decaying plants.

"Among the warriors are trained war horses whose riders haven't yet joined us in the realm of the dead," Elina said. "I'll ride one of them."

"All right," Sigrid said, pleased to find her voice loud and bold.

They crossed the garden to the palace wall, where a section dripped more quickly than the rest, like a brown waterfall pouring down and seeping into the ground.

Elina stopped in front of it, arms crossed. "The door beyond this leads into—"

"The big crypt," Sigrid said, still in awe that an entire army had been beneath the palace for years, waiting for her to raise them.

Elina cast her a sideways smile. "Very big."

Where the dripping wall of mud hit the ground, it bubbled and frothed before disappearing.

Sigrid nudged Sleipnir closer and asked him to stand sideways so she could touch it. The warm liquid poured over her fingers for a second until it stopped flowing. The last strings of thick, opaque mud hit the ground, and a wooden door stood in its place. It was wide enough to fit two of Sleipnir if he stood sideways, and tall enough that Sigrid wouldn't even hit the frame from her towering perch on his back.

A wild sensation constricted her lungs and pulled her muscles taut. A tremor passed from Sleipnir into her and back again, each stoking the other.

She cast a confirming glance to Elina, who nodded. "They're ready for you."

Done waiting and more than ready to fulfill her cosmic destiny, Sigrid leaned down, seized one of the round handles, and pulled the door open.

CHAPTER FORTY-FIVE

THE DEAD
HAVE AN AGENDA

Until that moment, Sigrid's stay in Helheim had been lonely, without so much as an otherworldly breath on the back of her neck. The supernatural had never particularly spoken to her, and even in this world, she wouldn't have known that departed souls existed alongside her if Elina hadn't said so.

Now, as Hel's army marched from the crypt, invisible to her eyes, a chill swept over her like a wintery wind blowing from the open door. The hairs on the back of her neck rose, a tingle going down her spine. She sensed them in the same way she sensed Elina stood behind her.

"Departed souls of the nine worlds!" Elina shouted. "Elves of light and darkness, giants of fire and ice, humans of soil and sky. After centuries of training, your final test is here!"

*Elves, giants, humans…*Sigrid mapped Elina's words to the nine worlds, imagining Mariam explaining Yggdrasil. Hel had recruited people from all worlds into this army. All except Asgard, of course, where the gods had kept to themselves since ancient times.

"The goddess Hel commends you for your service, warriors. On this day, your dedication will be rewarded!"

She gestured onward, and Sigrid took her cue.

"This way to the gates!" Sigrid galloped to what she intuitively knew to be the front of the army. There, she slowed Sleipnir to a brisk walk and rode him up the grassy hill.

The gates became visible in the distance, like a tick on the green hillside, while a steady beat rose like drums in her ears.

Elina had told her this would happen, but her breath still caught.

Behind her, the army materialized as if from fog, a thousand people from all worlds marching in grid formation. They carried wooden shields, swords, axes, spears, javelins, and bows and arrows. The humans and giants among them wore chainmail and helmets, indistinguishable from each other except for a foot or two in height. The Light Elves, ethereal and petite, wore shimmering white robes, while the stout Night Elves looked as she'd come to know them in dark leather, chainmail, and skull masks. Soaring overhead were armored valkyries on white mares.

The afterlife had to be the only place where all these people from different worlds would march together.

As they approached the black gates, Elina flew ahead on a winged mare and touched down in front of them. She faced the army, chin high, looking as much a queen as ever with her amber diadem glowing in the sunlight. The mare beneath her nervously pawed the grass.

Sigrid rode up and stopped beside her, pulse drumming at the gathered army. The hillside rendered them above everyone else, and when Elina spoke, the landscape's acoustics magnified her voice and carried it over the crowd.

"Congratulations." She opened her arms and inclined her face, giving off more confidence than Sigrid had ever felt in her life. "You've been waiting a long time for this day. It has arrived, as I promised. Together, we will march through the gates and be liberated from the confines of Helheim."

Sigrid scanned the faces before them. Her heart jumped as even a dire wolf pushed forward in their midst. It had mangy brown fur with patches missing and red eyes that gleamed like flames.

She drew a breath. They would be under control. They wouldn't run amok and attack everyone.

"The battle will be quick," Elina said, returning her hands to the reins, brow pinched in a serious expression. "We are bigger and stronger than any living army. We are the fearless dead, and because of that, we are unstoppable."

The battle? It seemed a little soon to be firing them up when they didn't know what battle they would have to fight, but it must have been the right thing to say, because cheers erupted.

Sigrid shifted in the saddle, struggling against a sense of drowning dread. This army was huge, and she was younger than all of them, not to mention underqualified.

To her horror, beneath the cheers, murmurs rose and gazes lingered on her. *Are they thinking the same thing?*

Elina met Sigrid's eye and gestured to the crowd, inviting her to introduce herself.

Sigrid lifted her chin, hoping no one could see how shallow her breaths were. "My name is Sigrid Helenadottir," she said, the volume straining her vocal cords. "I am the heir to Sleipnir, and I will be leading you through the gates of Hel and on to Vanaheim. Once we are safely home with the Eye of Hnitbjorg, your conquest will be to defend Vanaheim from the Night Elves who—"

"My daughter," Elina said, speaking over her, "is the only one who can lead us through the gates and back to the land of the living."

The murmurs grew louder, drowning out the cheers, and her insides turned icy. What was going on? A tremor of nerves ran through her, causing Sleipnir to shuffle sideways.

"You said *you* were Sleipnir's heir," a Light Elf in front said to Elina, his tone soft but challenging. He had a handsome face with high cheekbones, dark skin, and piercing brown eyes.

Several voices rose in agreement.

"I was," Elina said. "Now he has passed on to my daughter."

The lie was so smooth that Sigrid would have believed it if she hadn't known better. Why did Elina lie to them? Maybe she needed them to follow her until Sigrid came?

It would have been nice to get this warning before raising the army.

"Again, we are expected to serve Vanaheim's royals," the Light Elf said. "It was never my home. Óleifr was never my king, and you and your daughter are not—"

"This isn't a choice," Elina snapped. The mention of Óleifr seemed to act like kindling, sparking anger in her tone. "I am your queen, appointed by Hel, and you will serve *me*."

With those words, a hush fell.

"You want us to follow a young girl through the nine worlds to claim Vanahalla?" a Viking man said, placing a stinging emphasis on the words.

"This young girl is the Princess of Hel," Elina said sharply, "heir to Sleipnir, and heir to the throne of Vanaheim."

Insulting word choice aside, what did the man mean, *to claim Vanahalla*? What did he think they were going to do? Sigrid's pulse quickened. Raising the army wasn't supposed to be like this. They were supposed to be in her control, like the way a herd instinctively obeyed the alpha mare.

Maybe she'd misunderstood. She was panicking for nothing. Of course they wouldn't instinctively obey her like a herd of animals. These were people with goals, wishes, and families. They'd traded a peaceful afterlife and agreed to be in Hel's army so they could have one more conquest in the realm of the living, before being pulled back into Helheim. They needed to be motivated.

King Óleifr came to mind, who had been patient and compassionate around those little valkyries in the courtyard. Though Sigrid would never admit it to Elina, she'd always been happy to call him her king.

Elina opened her mouth to say more, but Sigrid cut her off.

She was supposed to be leading this army, not her mother.

"Like Queen Elina, I traversed the nine worlds to get to you," she said, doing her best to inject power into her voice. "The cosmos showed me where I needed to be, and I followed that vision."

"Right," Elina said, "the cosmos—"

"I didn't know where it would lead me or why," Sigrid said, determined to speak. "But now that I'm here and I see all of you, I understand. I'm here because you deserve to walk among the living again, even if for a short time, and on Sleipnir, I have the power to give that to you."

As resolved as she was to get a few words in, they tumbled from her lips, clumsy and forced. If only she had the eloquence and charisma of a real royal, like the way King Óleifr addressed crowds on special occasions.

Sleipnir pawed the grass, charged by the army's energy. She let him tread in front of the gates, recalling when Elina first appeared on this massive stallion, pacing beneath the iron archway like a half-formed vision.

"I crossed worlds to get to you. Are you willing to follow your queen and Sleipnir's heir back to Vanaheim—"

"On the conquest you were promised," Elina said.

Sigrid glowered. If Elina wanted Sigrid to lead Hel's army, then she should be letting her do it instead of constantly interrupting.

Also, what conquest had she promised them?

The warriors glanced to those beside them, murmuring and shifting. It wasn't the cheering approval King Óleifr would have gotten.

"Are you ready to walk among the living?" Elina said.

"For our children and grandchildren!" a woman shouted, to cheers and applause.

"Some of us have debts to collect," another said, and dark laughter broke out.

The laughter sent a shudder through Sigrid.

Debts? Did these people know that their conquest was temporary?

Shouts and stomping rose, until the hillside sounded like a river gaining momentum. The army lifted their weapons and roared.

Sigrid's pulse reached a peak, causing Sleipnir to snort and toss his head. This wasn't the control Elina had promised. The air hummed like a static charge, the crowd growing frenzied.

Why isn't this as simple as Elina led me to believe? And what did she promise them?

Dread built inside Sigrid as she recalled Elina's original plan. *Treason.*

The shouting surged to a chant, the noise taking a moment to congeal into words.

"Let us out! Let us out!"

Desperate for control, Sigrid spotted a dozen or so valkyries perched on the hillside beside the army, the calmest of everyone. The mares' wings twitched in response to the uproar, fanning over their bodies in the way the ones back home did to cool down after a ride. Would they follow her? If they'd been noble warriors in Vanaheim, she could trust them. But if they'd been exiles from Niflheim…

Among them was a solitary mare, tossing her head, agitated. Her rider must have still been among the living. She turned, dancing on her hooves, and Sigrid's heart stuttered.

Sweeping down the mare's shoulder was a reddish-brown marking.

A chill rippled down Sigrid's back and her lungs seized.

"Aesa?"

CHAPTER FORTY-SIX

LEVERAGING POWER

The loud chants from the army faded as every other thought melted away. What was Aesa doing in Helheim? Hadn't Elina told Mariam she was on the other side of the gates?

Sigrid's gaze landed on her mother, sitting regally on her mare and looking out at the gathered crowd, as if savoring her moment of triumph.

"You said Aesa was in the desert."

Elina peeled her gaze away from the roiling crowd. "What?"

Sigrid pointed wordlessly at the cluster of valkyries. She wanted to be wrong. She had to be. The mare bore a new marking, a red patch on her ribs that hadn't been there before. But it was no mystery where it had come from.

Elina sighed. "We can clarify this matter at a later time. Now isn't the moment."

Her words were like a punch to the stomach, leaving Sigrid breathless and dazed. Elina hadn't denied it. She'd lied this whole time.

Nausea overcame Sigrid, and she had to fist Sleipnir's mane and feel his steady energy to ground herself. "You said Mariam's soul wasn't honorable enough to enter the afterlife, so Aesa—"

Elina laughed, the tone forced, like she hoped Sigrid would get the joke. "There is no *honorable* and *dishonorable*. Everyone acts for a reason. Everyone comes to the afterlife to work off their sins before passing on."

"But…" Sigrid blinked, trying to work this out. What about Mariam being turned away at the gates? This didn't add up. "Mariam, Fisk, and Hestur are wandering around the desert trying to find Aesa."

"A little lie that worked out in your best interest."

Sigrid tightened her fingers, Sleipnir's energy rushing into her. Elina had blatantly deceived Mariam, then lied to Sigrid about it. *Mariam*, who'd been weak and hurting because of her broken bond. "You sent them away for nothing?"

The army grew louder. "Let us out! Let us out!"

Elina frowned. "Darling, we can discuss this more *later*."

Fury ignited in her chest at Elina's flippant tone. This wasn't something to be discussed later. This was a matter of life and death for Mariam and the others. This lie had consequences beyond them.

"We'll discuss it now!" Sigrid said with such intensity that Sleipnir tossed his head. "What about the army you sent to Vanaheim? I thought you turned them away at the gates because they weren't honorable enough to enter."

Elina shrugged. "I needed to send an army to fetch you and the Eye. I simply saw an opportunity in departed souls who hadn't yet passed through the gates."

"That's an abuse of your power!"

"No. It's *leveraging* my power."

Bile crept up Sigrid's throat as she glared at Elina. The woman had no care about what harm came to others as long as she got her way. All this time, Mariam thought her soul wasn't good enough to pass into the afterlife, when Elina just needed her services from the other side of the gates. Now, Mariam continued to believe that lie, wandering across that barren landscape in search of her mare, her body deteriorating by the minute.

"You denied people entry to the afterlife for your own gain. You lied to Mariam about the purity of her soul so she would go fight a battle for you. And then lied again so she couldn't find her mare!" Sigrid choked on her anger, then growled. "Why?"

The crowd pressed closer. "Let us out! Let us out!"

Elina shifted in the saddle, expression darkening. "Sigrid, I thought you learned this lesson already. Mariam and that elf were a burden to you. They were stopping you from following your ambitions. I had to give them a reason to turn around. What better motivation than the fate of one's own soul?"

"They could be lost out there. They could be—"

"It doesn't matter. I don't know how many times I need to stress that you can't afford to care so much." Elina looked skyward, as if praying for patience. "Look, darling, you're best forget them. The desert is a ruthless place."

Sigrid's face tingled, like all the blood had rushed out of it. Sleipnir danced on his feet as her legs tightened over the saddle. "They're my…" Fire burned in her throat. "They're my friends!"

"I thought they were a business deal."

Shame burned Sigrid's cheeks.

"If you want to succeed, you need to put yourself first. Others will only impede you." Elina gave her a sad smile before she turned back to the crowd. "Let's march!"

The crowd roared and pressed forward. The sea of bodies surged up the hill at them, a blur of armor, shields, and weapons.

Sigrid sat taller in the saddle, trying to channel Sleipnir's power. She swayed, vision narrowing like she'd spent too long in the hot sun. The crowd pushed closer to the gates, mouths open to bare chipped teeth and wet tongues, faces contorting. It forced to mind the illustration from Vala's study of all those grotesque faces trying to claw out of Helheim behind Odin.

The reality was worse.

Every sensation sharpened—gloved fingers tightening around the reins, scalp tingling inside her helmet, sweat prickling beneath her leather vest and cuffs. How could Elina have done this? She claimed to care about Sigrid while sending her friends off to die. She'd promised Sigrid an army as a means to become a valkyrie, but these warriors were clearly not ready to serve her. She'd lied about Aesa, and she'd lied about Sigrid's control over Hel's army.

Elina had made it clear that she didn't care about others. This was Sigrid's fault for failing to grasp what that meant. She'd naively trusted her mother's word, and now she stood ready to unleash Hel's army upon the living. Though the future was foggy, one thing was certain—these warriors would not accompany them on the journey back to Vanaheim as peaceful allies. Beyond the gates, the dead had an agenda of their own.

Sleipnir whinnied and tossed his head as Sigrid's breaths came fast. What had she done? After all of the decisions that led her to this spot, was she any better than her mother? She'd walked away from Peter and the stable hands, then used Mariam and Fisk to help her get to Helheim. Her obsession with Sleipnir and Elina had taken over, and she'd told Mariam and Fisk to leave. She'd even sent Hestur away, the most loyal friend she'd ever known.

What was the point of being Sleipnir's heir and raising Hel's army if losing her heart was the cost? Nothing was worth losing Hestur over—or Mariam, whose company she'd enjoyed more than anyone in her life and had awoken an exciting new feeling inside her. She even wanted Fisk back.

Sigrid ground her teeth, nostrils flaring as she sucked in a breath. Sleipnir responded to the change by pawing at the ground, his hooves making it rumble. She refused to be like her mother, using those around her with disregard, even her own daughter.

Sigrid had people who cared for her, people who needed her to defend them from the hellish army she'd unleashed.

She had to find her friends.

Tightening the reins, Sigrid kicked Sleipnir's sides and cued him to rear. She drew her weapon. The spear glinted in the sunlight as the stallion raised himself on his back legs, thrashing his hooves to force the crowd back.

"Stop!" Sigrid roared.

CHAPTER FORTY-SEVEN

VANAHEIM'S ORPHAN

Sigrid's cry and Sleipnir's hooves had the nearest warriors screaming, skittering backward and bumping into each other as they tried not to get trampled.

Elina nudged her mare closer, reaching out. "Sigrid!"

"Get back!" She directed the tip of her spear at Elina. Without prompting, Sleipnir rounded on her, ears pinned, teeth gnashing.

Elina's mare responded by backing off in a flurry of wings and legs, nearly unseating her.

After regaining control, Elina raised a hand in surrender. "Darling, can't we talk about this? What are you doing?"

Sigrid kept Sleipnir planted before the gates, refusing to lead anyone through. Their tempers bled into each other until they both quivered. "I'm taking control, *mother*," she spat, letting her anger bleed into her words. "Now tell them all to back up. I want them away from the gates."

When the queen hesitated, Sigrid curled her lip. "I'm not taking a step until you do."

Elina's gaze lingered, and whatever she saw on Sigrid's face made her nod. She made a shooing motion. "You heard the princess. Give us space."

Those nearest hissed and bared their teeth, and a Viking woman even spat on the grass, but they obeyed. In a noisy shuffle, the army backed off, pushing and shouting as they bumped into each other. A couple of horse strides away and sufficiently out of earshot, they stopped.

Sigrid's breaths matched the harsh bellows coming from Sleipnir's nostrils. She'd seen and heard all she needed to know and wanted to leave. Immediately.

But something kept her from bolting out the gates.

After all the talk of wanting to get closer and be her mother, Elina had manipulated Sigrid without a second thought, and for that alone, Sigrid would never forgive her. Nonetheless, she wanted the truth this time.

"You planned to use the army to take the throne," Sigrid said, voice cracking. "No matter what I chose… Why?"

Elina searched her face, her eyes such a frosty shade. An ache drove through Sigrid's chest at how many of her own features reflected back. She hadn't realized how much she wanted a future with her mother until now, when that promised life broke apart like a crumbling wall.

"Darling, I hoped to use the journey home to change your mind. I hoped to convince you of what we can achieve if we work together. I see so much of myself in you. You want to find your place in the nine worlds, same as I did. You came to Helheim seeking it, same as I did." Elina reached out, palm up. "Please, darling. With the Eye of Hnitbjorg and the magic in Vanahalla's towers, we'll be the leaders Vanaheim needs. We can reign over *worlds.*"

Sigrid shook her head, stomach churning at the thought of what kind of leader Elina would be. Had she ever loved, or had she always used others for personal gain?

"What other lies have you—" She swallowed around the lump in her throat. Dread trickled through her, cold and numbing, as a question rose to her lips. "Why did you take Sleipnir and leave me behind as a baby?"

Elina furrowed her brow. "I told you. I had to protect you from—"

"Tell me the truth!" Her words came out strong, carrying across the hillside.

The army was silent, probably straining to listen. *Let them hear.* They needed to know who they were serving. *Do they even care?*

Elina's gaze lingered. She looked unsettled, even queasy. Clearly she was not used to people fighting back.

Sigrid nudged Sleipnir, threatening to gallop away.

Elina responded to the movement, extending a placating hand once more. "I left you in Vanahalla's nursery, Sigrid, because it was the only way I could become queen."

Sigrid's chest tightened, a hollowness eating her insides at the confirmation. Another lie uncovered. This was not what Elina had told her the other day in that soft, motherly tone. But it fit. Of course it fit. This woman had one goal.

"Do you understand the struggle I went through?" Elina whispered, her eyes taking on a wild look. "Can you imagine what it feels like to watch a little brat take the throne instead of you, just because he's male?"

"No. I don't know a thing about thrones, remember?"

"I'm twelve years Óleifr's senior," Elina said passionately. "When he was made king, I'd already spent years carrying myself like a queen and living with the dignity of one. *He* had spent those years playing with toy horses in the mud."

The mare responded to Elina's tension, dancing and flapping her wings as if wanting to take flight.

"I spent every day searching for a way to take the throne. I tried making him ill so the throne would fall to me. I tried to persuade the valkyries to take my side. I tried everything I could think of—until finally, my answer came when I received a visit from Vala."

"And Vala said that you would give birth to Sleipnir's heir," Sigrid said, mouth dry.

A flicker of a grin pulled at Elina's lips. "Sleipnir's heir. Hel's army. With both under my control, I would be able to take not only Vanaheim, but worlds beyond it."

Nausea bubbled in Sigrid's stomach, all of the lies Elina had fed her curdling. "And my father? I guess it didn't matter who he was. You only needed him for one thing."

"I met him once, the day I seduced him. He was a commoner. A tailor, or maybe a smith. It didn't matter. He served his purpose." Elina rolled her shoulders as if shrugging off an uncomfortable sensation. "Nine months later, I gave birth to you in the woods, like the vision had shown. Sleipnir came hours later, stalking toward us through the trees like a mountain lion drawn to the scent of a kill. I took him for myself and returned to Vanahalla. I left you in the nursery, where I knew you would be cared for if I put you with the newborn valkyries."

Sigrid's blood pounded in her ears. "None of it was to protect me from greedy gods and royals."

"Protect you?" Elina scoffed. "I gave birth to you *because* I wanted Sleipnir. The only reason you exist is because I needed to fulfill the vision. Believe me, I wouldn't have had you if there was another way to get Sleipnir."

The words were like a slap to the face.

Sigrid trembled as she struggled to keep her temper. Beneath her, Sleipnir shook his head, agitated. "Why did you bother bringing me to the nursery? You could have just left me to die after you took Sleipnir."

"Darling, I wasn't sure if I would need you someday. And it's a good thing I had the foresight. Imagine if you hadn't come to lead us all back into the land of the living. I would be stuck here with a useless eight-legged horse."

Sigrid's insides boiled and churned like the water in Garmr's cave. Her whole life had been a setup. Her existence was a strategy to get Elina into power. She'd planted Sigrid in Vanahalla's nursery at birth, like a shrub, and left her to grow until she was ripe enough to pick. Then, when Elina was ready to finish her plan, she had sent Mariam to fetch Sigrid and bring her to Helheim.

"You used me," she whispered.

Elina waved a hand, dropping her voice. "I used you, and you used me, and we'll both use this army. It's the hardest lesson to learn, Sigrid, but you need to understand it if you want to be an effective—"

"Where did Hestur come from?" Sigrid asked, cutting her off.

"Who?"

"My gelding, Hestur." If she'd been left in the nursery right after birth, where had her best friend come from?

"Well, I couldn't leave you in the valkyrie ward without a horse. They would have kicked you out with the commoners, and I wouldn't have been able to retrieve you when I needed you. Since I couldn't acquire a winged filly, I decided to take a foal from a racing stable on Midgard. He's a fine horse, you know. Excellent bloodlines—"

"How could you do this to me?" Sigrid screamed.

At no point in her life did she have control over her destiny. She was not so much a daughter as a stepping stone.

"Sigrid, if I didn't take that vital step in getting Sleipnir, all of my efforts would have been wasted. Hel's army was the only way for me to seize the throne that should have been mine—the power, the world, the *relics* that should have been mine."

Elina pulled the string around her neck, producing the Eye of Hnitbjorg from beneath her tunic. "They could be yours, too, if you'll help me take the throne."

Her eyebrows pulled down, pleading, like she hadn't torn a hole in Sigrid's heart. Did she not understand the unbearable pain she'd caused?

Elina hadn't loved her then and didn't love her now. She'd used Sigrid, in the same way she was using every soul in Hel's army. And Sigrid had obediently done everything she wanted, full of hope that they could build the relationship they'd missed out on.

"When I arrived at the gates of Hel," Sigrid said, voice trembling, "and you said you'd been waiting for me, you were only waiting for what I could do with Sleipnir. It wasn't about me being your daughter."

Elina offered a small, pitying smile. "I warned you not to get attached to others."

Sigrid gritted her teeth, fighting back tears. Elina had betrayed every family member she had, and she hadn't flinched at the thought of sending Mariam, Fisk, and Hestur to die. This woman was not worthy of becoming the Queen of Vanaheim. With the Eye of Hnitbjorg and the rest of Vanahalla's magic at her command, there was no telling what she would unleash on the nine worlds.

The word "mother" had never rolled comfortably off her tongue, and now it was clear why. The woman birthed her, but her motherhood had ended there. The truth had been rotting beneath the surface of their relationship all along.

The worst part of all of this was not Elina's abandonment, but Sigrid's own decision to abandon Hestur. He'd been stolen from another world and left by Sigrid's side. He'd been her home, her comfort all these years. Yet she'd been so smitten with the idea of Sleipnir that she hadn't cared what that meant for Hestur.

Or Fisk. Or Mariam.

The hollowness in her chest expanded.

She'd left her heart behind when she decided to cross into Helheim.

With or without the army, she had to find them. She had to

save them, before Mariam—

Sigrid raised her voice. "Aesa!"

The mare looked but didn't move.

Elina laughed. "She won't come to you."

Sigrid gritted her teeth and nudged Sleipnir. *Fine.* Then she would go get her.

"No, you don't," Elina said, blocking her path.

Without urging, Sleipnir lunged, aiming to bite Elina's leg.

Elina shouted and kicked her mare, who launched into the air at full speed. She made a wide, dizzying circle overhead. "Don't lose sight, Sigrid!" Elina yelled. "You wouldn't have Sleipnir if not for me."

"I owe you nothing," Sigrid said, snarling. "Don't pretend like you've done anything for me."

Elina stopped the mare so she hovered overhead. Voice tight with anger, she said, "Enough time wasting. We've got a job to do. March!"

The army roared, the sound blasting with force as they started forward. For how wild they'd been before, they now formed an impenetrable wall of shields and weapons that got closer with each step. Elina had not lied about training them.

"Stop!" Sigrid nudged Sleipnir. He reared, having nowhere to go as the army advanced. She directed her spear at them, baring her teeth. "Come any closer and you'll be dust beneath Sleipnir's hooves."

Some hesitated, their battle-ready expressions flickering, but others advanced, closing in and smothering her.

"I said stop!" She cued Sleipnir to lunge. He struck out, gnashing his teeth. Four shields shattered beneath his front hooves, the warriors behind them buckling to their knees. Others shouted and backed up, tripping over each other.

"So keen to give up your title as princess," Elina called out from the air.

Sigrid scoffed. The title meant nothing anymore. "I don't want to be a princess if you're the queen."

She nudged Sleipnir onward, but though he tried to push through, the warriors formed a wall, trapping her in front of the gates. A spear glanced off his breastplate. Sleipnir was eager to plunge into the line and do battle, but Sigrid held him back, afraid he would get hurt.

"Aesa!"

Still, the mare didn't come.

She cursed under her breath. There was one exit through the gates at her back, but if she used it, the whole army would try to follow. She would have to be quick.

"See you on the other side," Elina said.

"You won't," Sigrid said, forcing confidence into her words. "I'm closing the gates behind me."

Elina laughed. "Already your ego is inflated. You have no control over the gates, darling. They'll stay open for a minute after you and Sleipnir pass through. A helpful way to let you lead departed souls back, don't you think?"

Sigrid's pulse quickened. The army blanketed the hillside like ash.

Elina made wide circles overhead, the mare's wingspan blocking out the sun as they passed overhead.

She considered calling for Aesa again, but it was useless. The mare wouldn't come to her. Valkyrie mares only heeded the call of their riders. She needed Mariam here.

With the army pushing her and only one way out, Sigrid had no other choice. If the gates stayed open for a minute after she passed through, then she would spend that minute fighting them back.

Odin, give me the strength to do it.

CHAPTER FORTY-EIGHT

BACK TO LIFE

Sigrid tugged the reins with one hand, the other brandishing her spear, and backed Sleipnir through the gates. Her stomach swooped with the pull of gravity as he crossed the threshold.

The army swarmed, pushing and clambering over each other to follow her out. She held her breath as the sensation of freefall gripped her insides.

The fading sight of Aesa put an ache in her chest.

I'm coming back for you, she vowed. She would find Mariam, Fisk, and Hestur, and they could figure out how to retrieve her.

A wave of hot desert air hit her.

The daylight changed to a muted red.

"Don't be meek, warriors!" Elina shouted from somewhere distant. "How badly do you want this?"

The army pushed hard, their cries deafening, using their shields to shove Sleipnir in their efforts to get to the land of the living.

Sigrid spun him so he was parallel to the gates, a wall stopping them from moving any farther. "Whoa!"

Sleipnir halted. She raised her spear and cued him to strike.

"Get 'em!"

Sigrid used her spear like a sword, slashing at the oncoming horde. She hooked the tip around the wooden shields, yanking them away and exposing the people behind them. Sleipnir struck and kicked, sharp cracks ringing through the desert air as he made contact. They could do this. With Sleipnir as a blockade, only two or three warriors could squeeze through at a time.

They fended off as many as they could, waiting desperately for the gates to seal.

"You—belong—in—there!" Her balance tipped as she swiped her weapon while staying atop the fighting stallion. "Sleipnir, strike!"

He thrashed, pawed, and bit.

Over the warriors' heads, a flash of white wings and hooves descended. Sleipnir reared to meet it, tipping Sigrid off-balance. She clamped her legs tighter as he gnashed his teeth and struck out with his forelegs.

Elina hovered between the warriors and the top of the gates, flickering in and out of focus. "Sigrid, I'm trying to save you from your miserable life as a stable hand."

Sigrid kept urging Sleipnir to strike, sweat pouring down her temples. A sharp pain in her arm brought a cry to her lips, and she nearly came unseated. As she hooked another shield and sent it to shatter beneath Sleipnir's hoof, something long and pointed soared back to Elina's open palm.

Elina had thrown a spear at her.

Anger burst through Sigrid, raw power seeming to surge up from the stallion, through her core, and into her fighting arm. Without pausing to look at her injury, she redirected her own spear.

"My life will *never* be as miserable as yours, Elina!"

As the mare soared closer, becoming less foggy as she left Helheim behind, Sigrid aimed for Elina's shoulder and hurled her spear with all her might.

Elina ducked too late. The spear clipped her hard enough that she pitched sideways, screeching like an angry cat. She parted from the mare, who spun and disappeared back into Helheim. Elina hit the ground with a crunch, flickering in the space between worlds. A line of bright blood seeped through the shoulder tear in her elegant blue robe.

Sigrid had the briefest flash of remorse. Had she really drawn her mother's blood? When her own wound seared with pain, warm and wet, seeping down her upper arm, Sigrid quashed that feeling.

The army pushed forward, and Sleipnir gave another bold strike. Sweat steamed from his neck and shoulders, adding to her sticky face. She couldn't fight much longer. Both arms were heavy, one from controlling the stallion and the other from swinging her weapon. Her lungs screamed for air.

Swords and spears slashed dangerously close to Sleipnir, one slicing a lock of his mane, while Elina got to her feet with her spear raised again—

A gust of air blew from the gate, like a door had closed.

Sigrid gasped, faint in the sudden desert heat.

Elina vanished, and so did the roaring army behind her. Silence fell. No one else pushed toward her.

"Is it—closed?" she panted.

Sleipnir snorted. His hooves thumped dully on the sand.

Sigrid lowered her spear. The opening that had been roiling with bodies showed the empty red desert speckled with lava rock. The stream babbled beside her.

Coughing and trembling, she let go of the reins and collapsed against Sleipnir's neck.

"We did it," she croaked, trying to catch her breath.

He let out a huff.

On this side of the gates, the world was so quiet that the sounds of battle still echoed in her ears. She braced herself to sit up. Resting could come later. Right now, her friends were out in the desert and she needed to find them. She *had* to—

"Sigrid?"

The familiar voice rose above the silence, swimming into her ears as if from the bottom of a pond.

Sigrid followed the sound and froze at what she saw.

CHAPTER FORTY-NINE

FRIENDSHIPS
SPANNING WORLDS

Sigrid blinked a couple of times to make sure her tired eyes weren't deceiving her.

Beside the stream leading into Helheim were Mariam, Fisk, and Hestur. Hestur stood frozen like a startled deer, a blade of grass sticking out of the corner of his mouth. Mariam and Fisk sat cross-legged on the ground, patterns drawn in the sand between them. Both were so covered in red sand that they almost blended with their surroundings.

Sigrid struggled to form words. "Wh-why are you—?"

They stood in a rush. Hestur chewed the blade of grass once, but made no other move.

"Are the dead coming?" Mariam said, facing the gates with her fists clenched. Her voice was gritty, like even her throat was coated in sand.

"I—no. They're not," Sigrid stammered. Her heart beat so hard it ached. "You stayed."

"Hestur wouldn't leave," Fisk said. "No matter what we did, he wouldn't leave these gates."

Mariam's eyes were bright beneath all the sand on her face. "We talked about it and decided Hestur was right. We would wait here, where it was safer, and where you would eventually come back."

"We've been rationing food," Fisk said, gesturing to their pile of stuff. "You have golly good timing, Sigrid. I don't know if we would have lasted another day."

Hestur still focused on Sigrid, blinking his large, dark eyes as he processed the sight of her. He looked thin.

Unable to wait a moment longer, she leaped off Sleipnir and ran to him. She threw her arms around his neck, tears gushing as if supplied by the spring of Hvergelmir. Hestur gave a low nicker, lips flapping on her back as he tried to eat her hair.

"I'm sorry," she said, voice muffled in his mane. "I messed up."

She let go of Hestur and faced her friends, wiping her face dry. "And I'm sorry to both of you. I was greedy and selfish. I'm grateful for both of you, and I should have listened to your advice."

It hurt to meet Mariam's gaze, but she forced herself to. Had her eyes always been such a rich shade of brown? She also tried to meet Fisk's eyes, settling with a tentative glance through the holes in the lemming skull.

"You don't have to forgive me," Sigrid said, face burning as the silence stretched.

"We understand," Mariam said at last. "You came here in search of your cosmic purpose, and you found it and more. You found a chance to get to know your mother. Of course you made that decision."

Sigrid swallowed hard. An apple-sized lump in her throat prevented her from speaking, so she nodded. Away from Sleipnir, his power drained from her and left her tired and diminished. How had she faced an entire army? Facing her friends was hard enough at the moment, and she clung to Hestur's neck to help her stand.

Mariam opened her mouth to say something, but Sigrid wasn't done. She'd messed up in more ways than one and needed to admit it.

"Fisk, I never should have teased you," she said firmly. "I was mean and—"

Fisk waved a hand. "Don't. I'm used to it."

"But that's exactly it. No one should poke fun at who you are."

Fisk nodded, mask wobbling. "I know. I've had a good think about it, and I decided I'm not going to let it bother me, because people can judge me all they want for wearing a jerff on my head—"

Sigrid was about to ask what a jerff was when he pressed on, louder and more confidently.

"But golly, I'm so much more than that! I'm a hard worker, and I'm clever enough to captain Ratatosk's ship, and not many Night Elves can say that."

"No, they can't," Mariam said, clapping him on the back.

Sigrid grinned. "You're brilliant, Fisk."

"I'm sorry for making *you* feel bad," Mariam said to Sigrid. "You had every right to want to escape a life where you're bullied."

"No, I get it," Sigrid said. "My life in Vanaheim was good. A bit of teasing was nothing compared to what Fisk endured or what you faced in Niflheim."

"That doesn't make it okay! Being treated like that depletes your soul, too, even if you're in the nicest place in all the nine worlds. I shouldn't have made you think you were wrong to feel upset."

Sigrid nodded. "Thanks."

Even coming from different worlds and circumstances, they'd all dealt with the same thing. Who would've thought that she'd find such friends across the nine worlds?

Fisk poked at her arm. "You're bleeding."

"Oh." Sigrid studied the wound her mother had left. It stung a bit, especially with Fisk touching it, but the flow had slowed to an ooze.

Mariam stepped in to examine it, her soft fingers grazing Sigrid's skin. She'd removed the bandage from her own arm, and the burn from their Garmr escape looked more healed.

"Really, I'm fine," Sigrid said. Next to Mariam's injuries, this was a sliver.

Mariam didn't seem to hear. She traced her gaze over Sigrid's face, clothes, and new haircut. "You look, um, wow."

Sigrid wiped an arm across her sweaty forehead, hoping the *wow* was a compliment. "Thanks."

Mariam's cheeks took on a rosy flush. "I'm sorry again for lying to you. I really, really—"

"I forgive you," Sigrid said, holding her gaze. "You were following an order. I made the mistake of trusting Elina, too."

Mariam's eyebrows pulled down. "What happened?"

Sigrid drew a breath, unable to stop the quaver in her voice. "Elina was keeping you on this side of the gates for her own gain. Aesa is in there."

Mariam stepped back, the news seeming to weaken her legs. She studied the towering black gates, chest heaving.

"We have to get her," Sigrid said.

"That isn't right," Fisk said. "Hel should know about this."

"But Sigrid, why did you come back?" Mariam said, eyes brimming.

"Everything seemed off when I saw Aesa. That was when I got the truth from Elina. Including…" She drew a steadying breath. *Might as well admit the whole truth.* "She never wanted a daughter."

Mariam's shoulders slumped. "Really?"

"I'm just a means to get Vanaheim's throne."

As she spoke the words, blood rushed in her ears, a storm of anger and shame.

"Sigrid, you deserve so much better," Mariam said.

Those few words were enough to relieve the heaviness in her

muscles. After everything, they were allies, and not just because circumstances forced them together. Mariam's friendship was all she needed.

"We have to go back in," Sigrid said. "Aesa will come to you, right?"

The mare was so close, and that meant they could save Mariam from wasting away of soul sickness. It was worth the risk of reopening the gates.

Mariam nodded. "What about the Eye of Hnitbjorg?"

The Eye? It was like the relic had to wade through mud to get to the front of Sigrid's mind again.

"As long as we're in there, we have to get it," Mariam said. "It belongs in Vanaheim."

Getting Aesa was one thing, but how dangerous would it be to try and take the Eye from around Elina's neck? This was beyond her skill set. The entire fleet of junior valkyries had been sent to get the Eye for a reason. The three of them would be smashed to pulp trying to fight that army, even with Sleipnir.

"What harm can Elina do with it if she's stuck in Helheim?" Sigrid asked, a pathetically hopeful attempt to brush away Mariam's suggestion. But she remembered Vala's warning. It could become a dangerous weapon in the hands of those unworthy of prophetic knowledge.

"It's not about what she'll do with it, but what Vanaheim will do *without* it," Fisk said, to Sigrid's surprise. He might've had a jerff on his head, but he was perceptive.

"He's right," Mariam said. "You've got to get the Eye, Sigrid. Vanaheim sent the valkyries to retrieve it, but what are they supposed to do? They don't have Sleipnir to get them through the gates and back."

It was true. Vanaheim wouldn't let Elina keep holding onto its greatest source of power. The junior valkyries wouldn't be able to come home until they recovered it, and without Sleipnir to lead them back out, they would not succeed.

"You and Sleipnir are the only way to get the Eye from Helheim without getting stuck in there," Fisk said.

Sigrid crossed her arms. Fine, they were right. They couldn't leave without the Eye and it had to be her who stole it back.

Sleipnir dropped his head and sniffed the sand. Hestur watched him plod around on his eight legs, ears perked.

"What's wrong?" Mariam asked Sigrid.

Out of the saddle, the rush of energy that had been guiding her actions was gone. Sigrid could think better without that constant hum through her skin. The worry that had lingered in the back of her mind for days pushed forward.

"I don't like riding Sleipnir," she admitted. "His power does something to me. I feel it in my blood when I'm riding him. It's like he's making me evil."

Mariam's mouth opened, and the word "evil" swelled in the silence before she said, "Sigrid, nothing can *make* someone evil."

Sigrid kicked a lava rock. She didn't understand the way his energy bled into her when she rode him. It was a power outside of her control. If she let that take hold of her, would she become like Elina?

Mariam stepped closer. "When we decided to wait here by the gates, I had this moment where I thought, *I don't want to be dishonorable. I deserve to pass into the afterlife.* I thought about the life I'd lived in Niflheim, and I felt remorse. I thought that maybe if I became honorable, it would draw Aesa back to the gates so we could pass through. Do you understand what I'm saying? I decided to be good, and so I was."

Sigrid blinked at her. "You're saying a person can decide who they want to be, no matter what Yggdrasil throws at them?"

Choosing to be good seemed simple, but there was something cosmic about Sleipnir, something beyond her control. The power of the gods of war and death surged through his veins, and that power was not necessarily a good one. Sleipnir might be better classified as a weapon than a horse.

"You're the most talented rider I've ever seen, stable girl." Mariam nudged her and smiled. "Yggdrasil threw you the most powerful horse ever to exist. Now what are you going to do with him?"

CHAPTER FIFTY

A RIDER,
NOT A VALKYRIE

Sigrid flushed at Mariam's compliment, which was probably overstating her abilities. "That's just it. I'm a rider, not a valkyrie."

Mariam let out a note of laughter. "I know you think that not being a valkyrie is a flaw, but it's your strength, Sigrid. You wouldn't be the person you are today if it weren't for Hestur and all of the work and training that you've done with him. Sure, you could be an ordinary valkyrie, same as all the other girls—but with him, you're special."

Sigrid turned toward Hestur, if just to hide her burning face. No one had put it quite like that before. She drew a breath to calm the wild galloping and bucking going on inside her chest.

Back when they'd sailed down the spring, when she'd traced her gaze over the sky to make a constellation, she chose to see the shape of herself and Sleipnir among the infinite stars. What if she'd chosen to make a different constellation? Just like she could choose what connections to make between stars, she could choose her own destiny.

Sleipnir and Hestur touched noses, evidently trying to figure out whether each other was a threat. Hestur puffed out his chest, but nothing dramatic ensued, and then they began sharing the little grass patch.

Sigrid faced her friends and nodded. If Sleipnir was good enough for Hestur, he was good enough for her. "All right. Let's get the Eye back."

Mariam straightened. "It's settled. Come on, Fisk."

They marched over to the horses, and Sigrid trailed behind, analyzing the towering gates like she would find a secret etched in them. Was this reckless? She'd be risking her friends getting stuck on the other side or killed by that massive army. There was also the issue of Ratatosk's ship. It was still moored, and if the army escaped, she risked letting them sail all the way to Vanaheim.

"Hold on," she said.

"If you tell us to stay here," Mariam said sharply, pausing in the middle of re-braiding her hair, "then so help me, I'll—"

"I won't. But I don't like our odds against the army."

Mariam had no argument. She finished her braid and tied it off aggressively.

"I'm just wondering if there's a safer way to do this," Sigrid said, moving to scratch Hestur's wither. "Maybe we shouldn't all go at once. Someone can stay here to stand guard by the gates."

"I have an idea," Fisk said. "Elina came part way through the gates to talk to us, right? She stood between worlds on Sleipnir, not in one or the other. Maybe you can do the same, you know?"

This was true. If Sigrid stopped before she walked all the way through, she could do as Elina had. She could talk to her and figure out what bargain she was willing to make in exchange for Aesa and the Eye of Hnitbjorg—and at the very least, distract her for long enough that Mariam could call Aesa.

"I can stand guard here on Hestur," Fisk said. "You can go in, and while you talk to Elina, Mariam can call Aesa to the gates."

This seemed to win over Mariam, who perked up. "Let's do it."

The plan was better than the three of them simply storming

through the gates. If she stayed in the space between worlds, Elina and the army wouldn't be able to follow her out.

Sigrid nodded, unable to think of a better idea. There was no turning back. They had to succeed. Failure meant their death and the death of countless others in her world.

"Fisk, are you sure you want to fight?" she said. "There's nothing in this for you. You'll be risking your life for a relic of Vanaheim."

He shook his head firmly, mask clattering. "I want to help. I've always done stuff because I've been told to, and now I would like to decide to. Because — because you're my friends." He trailed off on the last word, as if uncertain whether this was the wrong thing to say.

"You're my friend, too, Fisk," Sigrid said, smiling.

"And mine!" Mariam said.

Sigrid poked Hestur, and Hestur gave a low nicker.

"See?" Sigrid said. "Hestur's, too."

Fisk laughed. "Good. I'll gather our things." Their belongings lay scattered around the sand where he and Mariam had stayed put over the last several days. As he struggled to pick up Hestur's saddle, Mariam cleared her throat.

"It's good to have you back," she said. "I...I missed you."

Sigrid's heart stammered, and she could barely hold Mariam's gaze. It was like looking into the sun on a beautiful summer day. "I kept thinking about you while I was there. About Fisk, too, but... mostly you."

A smile broke across Mariam's face, accentuating the apples in her cheeks more than ever, and Sigrid couldn't help grinning back. She wasn't sure who moved first, but suddenly they were hugging, their arms tight around each other.

"Thank you for waiting for me," Sigrid whispered.

Her heart seemed to miss several beats as she stood wrapped in Mariam's arms, wanting to stay there for a while. Mariam's soft cheek grazed hers. The moment stretched on, and she waited for the tiniest cue that Mariam was ready for the hug to be over. It didn't come, and where Mariam's arms wrapped around her waist, her fingers trailed up Sigrid's back—a subtle, private touch that Fisk wouldn't see.

Mariam's arms loosened, and they stepped apart. She dropped her gaze, cheeks flushed.

Sigrid's insides did a celebratory barrel roll. Maybe she hadn't permanently messed everything up.

Fisk coughed. "So are we going to get Aesa and the Eye, or what?"

Sigrid and Mariam jumped, turning to him. He'd finished tacking up Hestur.

"Right," Sigrid said.

"Onward!" Mariam cheered, no doubt eager to get Aesa back.

The two of them mounted Sleipnir, Mariam in the same position as when they'd fled Vanaheim on Hestur. Except this time, when Mariam's body pressed against Sigrid's back, chin leaning over her shoulder, arms wrapping around her waist, Sigrid nearly melted right out of the saddle. Was Mariam holding her this closely on purpose? Was her palm intentionally grazing a sliver of bare skin at the base of Sigrid's tunic?

Sigrid bit her lip, summoning every bit of willpower to pull her attention away from Mariam and onto the gate in front of them.

Fisk mounted Hestur and came to stand beside them, wooden sword in hand. Mariam unsheathed a dagger, which Fisk had apparently made out of metal scraps from their belongings.

"No matter what happens," Sigrid said, "we have to make sure everyone stays on that side of the gates, all right?"

Her friends nodded.

Fisk raised his sword, and Hestur stood taller than usual, his chest puffed out and his neck stretched high.

"That's my boy," Sigrid said, leaning over from her perch on Sleipnir to scratch Hestur behind the ear.

There was no trace of the fear he'd shown days ago when they approached Garmr. He was ready to face whatever the nine worlds threw at him—and so was she.

CHAPTER FIFTY-ONE

MAKING A
FAIR EXCHANGE

When the gate's swooping sensation began, Sigrid squeezed the reins to ask Sleipnir to stop. He seemed to know what she wanted and stepped sideways, taking her and Mariam to the place where they could stand safely between worlds.

Her stomach twisted, caught in the moment of weightlessness between rising and falling. It left her slightly nauseous. She would have to do this quickly.

The fog between worlds cleared to reveal Elina, regal in her elegant blue robe and amber diadem. She wore a sour expression from atop a white mare, whose wings opened at their sudden appearance in the gates. Elina reined her in with a firm hand, looking like nothing could unseat her. Behind her, the army fanned out like a dark forest.

Whatever drop of satisfaction Sigrid felt at seeing the rips in her clothes and the diadem sitting crocked atop her messed up hair quickly evaporated as she noticed the distinctive red markings.

Mariam let out a cry. "Aesa!" Her hands tightened over Sigrid's waist.

The mare's front hooves lifted, and her wings flapped. She

whinnied desperately, eyes rolling, nostrils flaring.

"You found your friends quickly," Elina said in that deep, calm tone, at odds with the mare throwing a fit beneath her.

Warriors rushed to help restrain the mare, who seemed about to flip over in desperation.

"Don't hurt her," Mariam shouted. "Aesa, whoa!"

Aesa obeyed, calming enough that the warriors didn't need to fight her. Sweat foamed on her neck. Elina adjusted her seat and smirked, pointedly scanning her guard. They held the mare in place so she couldn't bolt for Mariam.

Sleipnir tossed his head, reacting to the rising tension. Sigrid let him pace between the gates like Elina had done days ago.

"Pleasure to see you again, darling," Elina said.

"I can't say the same."

"I fetched you the mare you wanted and that's how you thank me? Someone failed to teach you manners, Sigrid."

Sigrid ignored the taunt. "You brought her, now give her to me."

"And in exchange?" Elina said coldly.

No bargain could make Sigrid agree to lead Hel's army through the gates. But what else would Elina settle for? Even as she thought it, the answer came to her. The trade was obvious. Odin's steed was probably the only thing Elina would accept.

When Sleipnir snorted and flickered his ears back as if to check on her, Sigrid's heart sank. She'd come to like the stallion over these last few days and hated the idea of passing him back to Elina. Especially when her answer to his high-strung energy was cruelty.

But Mariam's life was at stake.

Sigrid motioned to the stallion beneath her, hating what she was about to do. "He's yours."

Elina gave a half shrug. "That's all?"

Sigrid narrowed her eyes. "I wouldn't have considered an

eight-legged stallion to be a meagre offer," she said shortly.

"What about his heir? Sleipnir is worthless without his heir."

"He isn't. He was Odin's horse."

"And he will be stuck in Helheim with no power or purpose."

"He's the best war horse in all the nine worlds!"

"What war will I be using him in?"

They glared at each other. Elina wanted Vanaheim, and Sigrid had nothing to offer that would appease this. Would they have to fight her? They would never win against this army.

"There are two things you want, are there not?" Elina said. The Eye hung from its chain around her neck, tantalizing. "I want you and Sleipnir both. In exchange, you get something from me. I'll give you either the Eye or Aesa. Make your choice."

"Despicable," Sigrid said through her teeth. How could she be related to this awful woman? "You deserve to rot in Helheim—"

"We'll take the Eye," Mariam said. "The Eye for Sleipnir. One for one. That's our bargain."

"Mariam!" Sigrid said. How could Mariam say that? Aesa was everything to her.

Mariam's hands tightened around her waist. "Saving the Eye is about saving all of Vanaheim. It's about the cosmic balance."

"But—"

"It's more important than me getting Aesa back, and I won't be selfish."

Elina inclined her head, considering Mariam's offer.

"No," Sigrid shouted, refusing to accept it. "I won't let you leave Aesa here. There must be a way—"

"All right," Elina said.

Sigrid spluttered. "What?"

"Give me Sleipnir, and I'll give you the Eye."

Sigrid's eyes burned. This wasn't the bargain she wanted to make.

"Sigrid, it's okay," Mariam whispered in her ear, arms

wrapping tightly around her. "I'll enter Helheim to be with Aesa, like I was meant to do long ago. My cosmic destiny led me right back here where I need to be."

"Don't say that—"

"My last few days among the living have been a bonus that never should have happened. You need to get the Eye and take it back to Vanaheim."

"Your life is more important than that!" Sigrid said, voice high.

"The cosmic balance is more important. I'm destined to be in Helheim, and you're destined to save the Eye. We're exactly where we're meant to be, Sigrid, and you know it."

Sigrid wanted to fight Elina, to convince her of any other deal. More than anything, she wanted to make the choice that would keep Mariam alive. But Mariam's words held some truth. She had to think about the bigger impact than one valkyrie reuniting with her mare. The Eye needed to return to Vanaheim, and a lot more lives would be at stake if it didn't. If Elina was willing to make this trade, she had to accept it, didn't she?

Mariam dismounted.

Sigrid blinked, eyes brimming, wanting to say so many things to her.

"I suppose you'll have to lead me through the gate in order to make this exchange," Elina said, a cold smile pulling at her cheeks.

Sigrid scowled at her. It was the only way she could hand over Sleipnir without getting stuck in Helheim. Elina had to come to the land of the living.

Behind her, Fisk and Hestur flickered in and out of the haze, standing guard.

"Fisk is waiting on the other side, and he's armed. If you try anything, we'll push you back." Sigrid's voice was weaker than she intended, diminished by the weight of Mariam's decision.

Elina raised her hands in surrender. "We'll make a fair exchange."

The army loomed behind her, unnervingly ready for action.

Sigrid's stomach twisted, and this time it wasn't because of the gate. It did nothing to help her unease. "If they take one step forward, I'm out."

Elina nodded once and dismounted Aesa. To her guard, she said, "Make sure the mare stays here."

Mariam let out a hiss.

This was Mariam's decision, then. She would go with Aesa into Helheim, and Sigrid would trade Sleipnir for the Eye and go home. It didn't feel like a victory at all as loss plummeted in her stomach. She was giving up everything for a relic.

Before Sigrid could change her mind, she nudged Sleipnir the rest of the way through the gates. With a final swoop in her gut, they stepped onto solid ground, Helheim looking clearer than it had a moment ago.

Elina grinned.

Something in the back of Sigrid's mind stiffened, expanded, like a mare opening her wings before a predator. This wasn't right. It was too easy.

Movement blurred in Sigrid's periphery. Armed giants approached from both sides.

"Sigrid!" Mariam shouted.

It was a testament to how un-horse-like Sleipnir was that he didn't shy at their sudden appearance. He spun and gnashed his teeth at one side and kicked his back legs at the other.

They must have hidden behind the gates where Sigrid hadn't seen them. They swarmed, and she could do nothing but hold on because Sleipnir fought with everything he had.

"Darling, you're our ride out of here," Elina sang out. "We aren't letting you go that easily."

The warriors rushed Sleipnir, even those who had backed off, and struck at him with their weapons. His steel breastplate clanged. They weren't trying to kill them, but force them back through the gate.

"No!"

Sigrid fought with Sleipnir, throwing and recalling her spear in short range and swinging it wildly. Without time to aim, more of her shots struck armor than flesh. The warriors swarmed like angry wasps, a hundred times more desperate than before.

Mariam's voice rose above all others. "Aesa!"

The sound was desperate, frantic, like her life depended on it.

Sleipnir backed away, having no choice amid the slashing weapons. He tossed his head and reared. Sigrid wrapped her fingers in his mane to brace against his abrupt movements.

A swooping sensation pulled at her gut. She cried out, helpless. Too soon, hot, dry desert air blew against her. They'd backed through the gate, the magic leaving it open for the warriors who followed. A sword bounced painfully off her wrist cuff, leaving a groove.

The gates moved forward in her periphery, and still Sleipnir backed up.

Fisk appeared at her side with Hestur, shouting and slashing in an effort to keep the warriors in Helheim. He cracked a Light Elf in the chest, sending her toppling into everyone behind.

From within the gates, Mariam shouted for Aesa again, growing distant. She disappeared beyond the wall of shields and weapons.

"Mariam!"

But Mariam's voice—the sound that had brought Sigrid joy and comfort during their travels, one she could have spent the rest of her life hearing—became a breath on the wind. With a last cry, it disappeared through the gates of Hel.

"Mariam, no!"

Sigrid's insides turned colder than the land of the Ice Giants. After all they'd been through together, that they'd missed a goodbye felt like a cruel joke of the cosmos. The way they'd met and the way they'd parted were painfully symmetrical—Mariam calling for her mare, the purest part of her, the only constant in her turbulent life.

Her eyes burned as she clung to Sleipnir.

Let her go.

The army poured out like a dam had broken, pushing Sigrid and Fisk away from the gates. Among them, Elina stepped through and inhaled deeply, like her first breath of fresh air after a long imprisonment.

"Keep fighting!" Sigrid shouted to Fisk, kicking Sleipnir so he would stop retreating.

Sleipnir fought hard, shattering shields, striking the warriors behind them, and biting anyone within reach. Hestur seemed to understand the goal, because he dodged and shifted to help block everyone from advancing. Fisk had to grab his mane with his free hand to stay on.

They would never win.

Two people on two horses had no chance against this army of a thousand.

Sigrid wheezed for breath, her lungs aching with the effort, not sure how much longer she would be able to fight. Her arms were sore like she'd heaved hay bales all day.

"Watch your back!" Fisk shouted.

Enough warriors had passed through to surround them. Multiple pairs of hands closed around her arms, and she had no energy to throw them off. She roared as they hauled her out of the saddle. A blur of people swarmed, a skull mask with a broken tooth in their midst. The air left her lungs as she hit the ground. Sleipnir whinnied.

Overhead, a winged mare burst through the gates like a bolt of white lightning, and a gust of wind signaled its closing.

The valkyrie bellowed a war cry, and her mare's wings spread like a wall before the charging horde.

Sigrid could only answer with a cry of her own, feeling it burst like sunlight from her chest. "Mariam!"

Mariam descended on the group attacking Sigrid, Aesa's hooves cracking against their heads. Fisk fought with her to push everyone back.

Amid the mob, someone grabbed Sigrid's ankles and dragged her across the red sand. It bunched under her tunic and scraped against the soft skin of her stomach. She was headed back toward the gates. As she scrambled for grip, the black rocks weren't enough to hold onto, and her fingers left grooves in the sand.

She twisted and found Elina dragging her, teeth gritted with the effort. "I'm nothing if not persistent, Sigrid. Maybe after a few hundred tries you'll finally let the rest of my army out. What do you think?"

Sigrid shrieked, rage bursting incoherently from her lips. Her kicks grew wild, anger giving her enough power to fight back, but Elina held on.

Aesa's wings blew sand into Sigrid's eyes and mouth as Mariam fought to get near, shouting, "Fisk! They've got Sleipnir!"

Several Night Elves restrained the stallion. He battled fiercely, trying to break free and return to Sigrid. They held the reins and hit him in the chest, forcing him back.

"Get him to Sigrid!" Mariam shouted.

"Don't!" If she was going to be dragged into Helheim, she refused to give Elina the ability to follow her out again—even if it meant trapping herself inside. "Keep him out here—"

Elina twisted Sigrid's ankle, jolting the words from her as they struggled over the sand.

"Don't make a mistake," Elina snarled. "You're useless without him."

"Useless to you, maybe."

Hestur whinnied. Sigrid's heart squeezed in regret. But he wasn't looking at her. He was looking at the sky. He whinnied again, louder and more desperate.

Something approached, growing larger in that strange, dusky sky.

Winged figures. Arms raised, spears ready.

Valkyries.

CHAPTER FIFTY-TWO

VALKYRIE SWARM

Sigrid's heart roared in triumph as the flock of white mares soared toward them.

Elina cursed and tried pulling Sigrid harder, but in the next moment, the valkyries were upon them, diving like birds of prey. They held formation as they swooped low and drove spears into their attackers. Mariam and Fisk raced out of the way so as not to get hit.

"Edith!" Sigrid shouted, recognizing the mare sweeping overhead.

From Mjöll's saddle, Edith waved at her with a look of mild surprise before turning her focus back to Elina.

Elina shrieked and covered her head with her arms, letting go of Sigrid. Free, she scrambled away from the flying spears. The queen gave up and sprinted for the gates of Hel, cursing. Her army was less lucky as the projectiles made contact, knocking down the ones wearing armor and piercing them where they were exposed.

Sigrid opened her palm to summon her spear from wherever it was. It soared back, and she barely caught it in her trembling, scraped hand.

The valkyries had seized control of the fight. Dive after dive, they executed flawless maneuvers, pummeling their opponents, swerving in alternating directions, merging back together in time to make another dive. The assault flattened those of Elina's army who had crossed over.

Mariam and Fisk joined them atop their mounts, and they worked with the valkyries to push the remaining warriors back to the gates of Hel. On Hestur, Fisk swung his wooden sword with abandon, catching the few souls who tried to escape unnoticed.

She hoped he had enough control not to hit Hestur.

Sigrid picked herself up from the hot sand and ran to help him, but it was like an ant trying not to be crushed by a stampede. She needed to mount up.

In the midst of the roiling battle, she raised her voice and pinned her hopes onto one word. "Sleipnir!"

The mess of bodies around her was too dense. She couldn't spot him. Was he still restrained?

"Sleipnir!" she called again, coughing from all the sand the fight kept lifting.

A collective cry rose to her right. Something snapped. Hooves pounded. A group of warriors dove out of the way as the stallion charged through, reins and stirrups flapping. He skidded to a stop in front of her, nudging her with enough force to push her back a step.

"Yes!"

She ran for momentum, slid a foot in the stirrup, and swung her leg over his back.

The moment she was in the saddle, the familiar sensation of his power bled into her, vibrating through her muscles. She grinned.

"Go!"

When Sleipnir launched into a gallop, tossing his head, she was ready for it, engaging every muscle and moving with him.

They fought together, pushing back hard with the others until the battle pressed nearer to the gates of Hel.

"Don't go through the gates!" Sigrid shouted to Runa, who was nearest. She pointed to the gates for emphasis, roaring at the top of her lungs. "Stay on this side. Pass the message!"

She threw her spear at a charging dire wolf while Runa ascended to spread the warning to the other valkyries. So much chaos had broken out that Sigrid wasn't sure if anyone heard.

The offense worked. Any surviving warriors had started to retreat back through the gates.

"Hey!" Gunni shouted, pointing at Mariam.

As Mariam looked in confusion, Gunni reached into her bag, withdrew a spear, and tossed it in the air hilt forward. Mariam stretched out a hand and caught it.

Sigrid's heart lifted as Mariam whooped and sheathed her metal dagger. "Let's get 'em, Aesa!"

Elina was steps away from the gates. She stumbled on a lava rock, and the pink stone swung from its chain on her neck.

No. She tensed all over. They were about to lose the relic again.

"Wait! She's got the Eye!"

It was no use. Nobody heard her amid the beating wings, shouted commands between valkyries, and thumps of weapons.

"Break Elina away from the group!" she shouted desperately, urging Sleipnir onward.

Ylva shot her a confused look. "Stay back! We've got this under control."

"We can't let her—" Sigrid ducked as a mare swooped low and hooves nearly struck her head.

Elina lunged through the black gates and fell to her knees, pausing to catch her breath. That otherworldly fog half obscured her as she lingered between worlds. Around her, the last of the warriors pushed through and disappeared into Helheim.

Sigrid brought Sleipnir to a stop next to Fisk and Hestur. She breathed hard, insides rioting, muscles clenched with the need to move. But she couldn't go after Elina without opening the barrier again.

A gust of wind blew Sleipnir's mane, and hooves thumped behind her as the junior valkyries landed.

Elina looked back at Sigrid and sneered. She stood and raised a finger to stroke the pink stone around her neck. Then she vanished beyond the gates of Hel.

CHAPTER FIFTY-THREE

ORDERS FROM
A STABLE HAND

Sigrid wiped her eyes, coughing up sand, as the desert fell into a ringing silence. She patted Sleipnir's neck and took in the view left behind by the battle—shattered shields, weapons, and bodies. Would these souls already be back in Helheim, ready to come through and fight again?

Fisk and Hestur were beside her, seemingly unharmed. With a gust of wind, Mariam and Aesa landed on her other side. All of them stared at the flock of mares that had come out of nowhere.

The junior valkyries were *here*. They'd saved her from being pulled into Helheim. As they dragged the casualties into a pile beside the gates, subdued and without their usual chatter and giggles, Sigrid urgently counted the mares.

Twenty-one.

She counted again to be sure, then let out a breath.

Everyone made it.

Mariam dismounted and wrapped her arms around Aesa's neck, dissolving into tears. "I missed you. I missed you," she said, voice muffled.

Aesa nuzzled into her with such force that she stumbled back with a laugh. Her wings flapped delightedly, bringing to mind a dog wagging its tail.

Sigrid grinned, her heart lighter than it'd been in days. They were together again. Already, Mariam seemed brighter, healthier, happier. And she was here, on this side of the gates. A lump formed in Sigrid's throat at how close they'd been to separating forever.

She cleared her throat and said to Fisk, "Hestur's all right?"

Fisk nodded and patted Hestur, who tossed his head proudly.

She dismounted and checked Sleipnir. The breastplate had done its job, but a few cuts had opened and reddened the gray hair around it. Her heart squeezed for the stallion, who was more stoic than any horse she'd met. She kissed his neck.

Sensing everyone gathering around—probably waiting for an explanation of why they'd found her in the midst of battle with such a motley team—she drew a breath. How could she ever explain? She inspected Sleipnir for another moment before facing them.

Up close, the junior valkyries looked less groomed than when she'd last seen them. Their faces were smudged in dirt, their cheeks hollow, their hair matted. Their uniforms and mares were not so much white as a dusty, patchy brown. Whatever they'd faced over the last several days had not been kind to them.

She hobbled over and bent to check Oda's legs for signs of swelling. A lifetime of grooming responsibilities made the task comfortable, rooting her in reality. "How's she doing?"

"Good, I think," Gunni said. "Thanks."

Sigrid rubbed Oda's forehead. The mare closed her eyes and leaned into the touch.

"All right, Runa?" Sigrid said, going to smooth Tobia's ruffled feathers.

From Tobia's saddle, Runa nodded, offering a little smile. The mare gave Sigrid an affectionate nudge.

The mares' wings rustled, the only sound in the thick silence as Sigrid checked them like usual. Her heart still pounded, but the familiarity of the routine helped focus her racing thoughts.

After all of that, Elina had gotten away with the Eye. If the valkyries had listened to what she was trying to tell them, they might have seized it before she fled.

She let out a slow breath. *No point in being frustrated.* They could still get it if they all worked together.

Sigrid returned to Sleipnir and mounted up. How strange to look across at the junior valkyries, even down from Sleipnir's towering height, instead of gazing up from her usual place at their feet. And rather than finding sneers and haughty expressions on the line of warriors, she found defeat.

"The Eye of Hnitbjorg is on the other side of those gates," she said. "I know this isn't how you planned to get it back. You planned to face the thief in a clean, coordinated attack, like you've trained for. Nowhere in your plan did you imagine you'd be taking orders from a stable hand."

A couple of girls scoffed. Sigrid sat taller in the saddle.

"I don't intend to give you orders. I only want to tell you what I know. We're all after the same thing right now. If we go through those gates united, we can win. But if you go without listening to what I have to say, then you're going through those gates on a one-way journey."

She expected more scoffing and eye rolling, but that didn't happen. Every valkyrie stared at her, silent and attentive.

"The woman we just chased back through the gates is the Queen of Helheim, and as you just saw, she has an army. She's the one who sent the attack the day the Eye was stolen, and she has it now. She's—" Sigrid searched for a way to describe Elina. "She's an ordinary woman who was born into royalty. She might have an army, but so do we. We can beat her if we work together."

The valkyries fidgeted with their reins and exchanged nervous glances.

"Isn't the goddess Hel the ruler of the underworld?" Runa asked, barely loud enough to hear.

The others nodded and mumbled their agreement.

Sigrid swallowed hard, nervous about delivering all this news to the valkyries who tended not to believe her. "Hel is its goddess, but Elina is its queen. She made a deal with Hel to become queen of this world, but before that, she was the eldest princess of Vanaheim—Princess Helena."

They gasped and turned to whisper to each other. Relieved they didn't challenge her word, Sigrid continued with more volume.

"I don't know if you saw it, but she's wearing the Eye around her neck. It's a pink stone. If she isn't with the army, she'll be in the palace—"

"I didn't see her," Gunni said. "Which one is she?"

A couple of other valkyries murmured and nodded.

"She's wearing a blue robe and..." Sigrid tasted the sour words on her tongue before she spoke them. "She's my mother. You'll know her when you see her because she looks like me."

Another gasp passed over the valkyries like a breeze. The whispered word passed between friends. *Mother. Mother. Mother.*

When no one else raised a question, she pressed on.

"We've got to find her, take the Eye, and turn back. Those gates are usually a one-way journey for anyone from the land of the living, but we have Sleipnir, and he's how we get back through."

"Specifically, Sigrid on Sleipnir," Mariam said.

Sigrid held back a wince. She wasn't sure how much she wanted to reveal about her connection with the stallion. "Right. You need to follow me and him. This means we can't let Elina take him from me, or it's over. Without Sleipnir, we'll be stuck in Helheim forever."

The silence was absolute. Were they afraid?

"So if we die in there, you'll just be able to lead us back out, right?" Runa said, sounding hopeful.

Sigrid shook her head, wishing she had a different answer. "The dead stay dead, and they belong in Helheim."

"But those warriors weren't ghosts," Gunni said.

"That's because they're Hel's army. I, um—" Sigrid hesitated, trying to put this delicately. "I sort of raised them. Temporarily. I was going to have them come with us back to Vanaheim, but... well, you saw how they are."

This was met with a profound silence. Sigrid swallowed and searched for words to ease the magnitude of what she had done. Maybe she shouldn't have brought that up.

Ylva tossed back her long braid and sat taller. "How big is the army?"

The confidence in her voice seemed to bolster those around her. They, too, sat taller, lifting their chins and gathering their reins.

"Their numbers are more than ours," Sigrid said. "Much more. And they have valkyries, too. But you're trained for this. All of you."

Elina's voice echoed in her memory, telling the army they were unstoppable because they were the fearless dead. Sigrid disagreed.

"We have something Hel's army doesn't," she added. "We have the will to live. We're fighting for our lives and our home, and that makes us stronger than them."

She nudged Sleipnir to pace before the valkyries and held eye contact with each in turn. "Let's use the blood in our veins and the breath in our lungs to fight our hardest. Let's bring the Eye of Hnitbjorg home and leave Hel's army where it belongs."

The line of girls sat tall in their saddles, chins high, looking more ready to fight than a minute ago.

Bracing for what was to come, Sigrid gathered as much confidence as she could muster. "Who's coming with me?"

After a brief pause, Edith and Runa whooped. Others echoed. Soon, a cry went up from all twenty-one junior valkyries, and the sound carried across the vast red desert.

Beside her, Mariam vaulted up and cast a radiant smile that made Sigrid's stomach flip over. Sleipnir paced more rapidly, responding to her adrenaline.

"We've got the element of surprise," she said. "They don't know how many of us are going to come through, and they don't know when. Once we're on the other side of those gates, our only goal is to get the Eye from Elina. Fight the others off, but stay focused on her. Got it?"

Everyone nodded. The mares tossed their heads, rustled their wings, and stomped their hooves.

"The two most important things are to follow me and Sleipnir out when we're done, but to not let Hel's army come through with us."

The valkyries exchanged looks, not of fear or hesitation, but of determination. They squared their shoulders and nodded, tightening their reins in preparation.

"Together, then."

The group turned to face the gates of Hel.

Sleipnir tensed beneath her, ready for what was coming. Sigrid's hands remained steady on the reins and around her spear.

With everyone gathered on the red-and-black landscape, the moment's familiarity hit her. She'd seen this before—but suddenly, fulfilling the vision became less important than whatever came next.

Sigrid raised her spear and roared, the fierceness in her own voice surprising her.

"Charge!"

Sleipnir responded to her aggressive call, lifting his four front hooves off the ground. Behind her, the valkyries echoed the war cry. A gust of wind from their wings tangled her hair and Sleipnir's mane.

They charged.

CHAPTER FIFTY-FOUR

BATTLE CRIES
AND BARREL ROLLS

Lava rock cracked beneath Sleipnir's hooves as he stampeded over the dark, fiery landscape. Sigrid roared astride his back, holding her spear high. The junior valkyries followed on their white mares, wings beating the sand with the force of a windstorm. Among them was Mariam on Aesa.

The red sand steamed. Lava bubbled. Black rock blistered the sand like battle scars.

Over Sigrid's shoulder, Fisk brought up the rear on Hestur, who tossed his head and champed at the bit, raring to go faster. His eyes rolled, and sweat frothed on his neck. She'd never seen him so worked up.

They burst through the gates of Hel and into the midst of Elina's army. The warriors shouted in surprise, leaping to attention and raising their weapons. As Sigrid and Sleipnir hit the wall of bodies and half-raised shields, the junior valkyries shot overhead and past them. Elina's valkyries took flight in response.

Sigrid urged Sleipnir through the crowd, hunched close to his neck, throwing and recalling her spear to take out anyone who challenged her. Everyone dove out of Sleipnir's way as he stampeded through, and those who didn't were knocked over and crushed beneath his eight massive hooves. His steel breastplate deflected weapons like they were made of straw. Shields shattered, fragments billowing like leaves in the wind.

Fisk roared behind her, following in her wake and slashing at the encroaching army with his sword. She flinched when a lance got too close to Hestur's side.

"Stay close!" she shouted, not wanting to place an unarmored Hestur at the points of these weapons.

They burst through the army and into the open meadow. Elina seemed to have decided fleeing was the best option, because she sprinted toward a riderless winged mare. The mare skittered sideways, but Elina grabbed her mane and vaulted on before she could take flight. They launched into the sky, shooting straight up as if aiming for the clouds.

Sigrid cursed, too far to do anything.

The junior valkyries converged overhead.

Sigrid caught Gunni's eye and motioned upward. "Get above her! Push her down and pin her between us!"

They shot after her like white lightning bolts in the cloudy sky. While Sigrid and Fisk followed from the ground, the valkyries rose above Elina. Elina was skilled, though, and she rolled and pitched to avoid their spears. Her own valkyries followed like a swarm of wasps, making it hard for the juniors to aim.

From the ground, Sigrid checked her speed, keeping Elina in view overhead. Looking up made her head dizzy and her pulse spike. She ground her teeth and hurled her spear, taking aim at the woman's back.

The spear missed as Elina did a full barrel roll, the mare's wings tucking in so she turned over in the sky. Cursing, Sigrid opened her hand and summoned her weapon back. How did Elina know so many stunts? She must have taken valkyrie training back in Vanaheim.

Sigrid's team showed off their own skills without restraint. As

Elina retaliated, they dodged each shot and fired back in harmony, their mares staying in formation.

Rhythmic snorting came from Sigrid's left. Hestur and Fisk kept pace, charging alongside her. Hestur's dark eye fixed on her, waiting for a command.

"She's getting lower!" Fisk shouted. "We'll go left. You go right."

"All right!" She steered Sleipnir right while Fisk and Hestur veered left. The valkyries continued to press Elina downward.

Ahead, the muddy brown palace loomed like a mountain. Elina flew straight for it, the valkyries in close pursuit.

"She's headed for the balcony!" Sigrid shouted.

"Drat. Where's Mariam?" he called back.

Mariam was high overhead with the others, their formation scattering as Elina's valkyries surrounded them.

Sigrid nudged Sleipnir faster, tracking Elina toward an upper-floor balcony. Beyond its railing was a closed wooden door and an open window. It looked big enough for the mare to slip through if she tucked in her wings and legs.

"Meet me inside, Fisk!"

Sigrid sheathed her spear in the quiver on her back, then tied a knot in the reins and laid them on Sleipnir's neck. As he galloped toward the palace, she brought her legs up and planted her feet on the saddle. Nerves tightened her stomach. She'd done this on Hestur plenty of times, but Sleipnir's eight-beat stride was so different.

Above, Elina roared at her mare, who seemed to hesitate. She flattened against the mare's neck and pulled her knees up. Startled by Elina's aggression, the mare folded her wings, tucked in her legs, and shot through the open window like a spear. The curtains flapped as they disappeared inside the palace.

Sigrid crouched in the saddle, planting her hands and feet to stay balanced. The ground rushed below her, sending her heart galloping. *Must not fall.*

"What are you doing?" Fisk squeaked.

They were strides away from the building. Sleipnir headed for the front door, but not Sigrid. She was headed for the balcony.

"Just get inside and meet me upstairs!"

Two strides away. She tensed up. *This is going to hurt.*

Fisk and Hestur shot into the palace in a clatter of hooves on stone. Sleipnir followed. Sigrid leaped from the saddle and reached for the balcony railing.

Wham!

Her body slammed against it hard enough to reverberate through every bone. She cried out in pain but held on, arms clamped over the railing. With a grunt of effort, she heaved herself over and collapsed onto the balcony.

Wheezing and coughing, she got to her feet. She opened the wooden door and stumbled into a large bedroom. Elina's mare stood beside an armoire, nostrils red and flaring as she caught her breath. She hopped nervously on the stone floor, wings flapping.

Elina was gone.

Somewhere below, hooves clattered, echoing like a stampede.

"Sigrid!"

She didn't respond in case Elina was close, instead putting out a hand to calm the dancing mare. The mare snorted, staring across the room to the right, where an open door led to another room—maybe a bathroom or closet.

She ran quietly toward it.

Before she got there, footsteps thumped from the hallway to the left, and Fisk blasted in and stopped with a hand on the knob, panting.

Sigrid motioned for him to follow her through the door on the right. A soft noise rose beyond it, like the scuff of a boot. Fisk nodded, and together, they hurtled through.

They barged into a study like Vala's circular room. Elina was at the far wall—or half of her was.

What in Odin's name...

Sigrid blinked. Between two bookshelves, Elina extended both arms toward the wall. No, not *toward* it. *Through* it. Elina was pushing right through the muddy wall. Where it would lead, Sigrid had no idea. But they couldn't lose her.

She and Fisk sprinted across the room, Fisk moving like a shadow in her periphery. She leaped over an armchair and wrapped her arms around Elina's waist, stopping her from going farther. Elina shrieked. Sigrid pulled her back, grunting with the effort. The wall seemed to have a suction, like it wanted to pull her through into the room beyond.

Fisk grabbed Elina's arms, and their combined force pulled her out of the wall and sent all three of them toppling to the stone floor.

"Sigrid," Elina said, grunting as she struggled under the weight of both of them. Her muddy arms made her slippery. "You're—making—a mistake."

Sigrid sat on her chest and used her knees to pin the woman's wrists to the floor. "Get the stone, Fisk!"

Fisk seized the necklace and pulled it over Elina's head with such force that he ripped out a clump of her hair.

She shrieked in pain. "I swear, elf. This'll be the—"

"Oh, shut up," Sigrid said, clapping a gloved hand over her mouth. "Fisk, round up the others."

"Yes, ma'am." He sprinted from the room, leaving Sigrid to contemplate how best to get away from Elina.

When Elina didn't struggle, Sigrid removed her hand from her mouth. She'd left a splat of mud.

"Sigrid, darling, you could be a princess," Elina said calmly.

"I don't want—"

"Think of the wealth and status, the beautiful hall, the luxurious lifestyle that could be yours. As my daughter, you have a right to all of that," Elina said. "Do you want to claim your place at my side? Or do you want to stay an orphan stable hand?"

Breathing hard, Sigrid met her mother's blue-gray eyes. No matter how true her words were about wealth and luxuries, beneath the decorated shell, what did it mean to be a royal? Elina's amber diadem sat crooked on her forehead, her blond hair tangled around it. Mud coated her skin and that magnificent blue robe, which was twisted and bunched. This *royal* demanded respect by force rather than earning it, seized power by starting wars, and thrust the cosmos into imbalance.

After the atrocities Sigrid had nearly committed at her side, and knowing the kind of person Elina expected her to be, the answer was clear.

Sigrid snarled. "I would rather be a stable hand."

Leaving Elina looking stunned, she leaped up and sprinted out the bedroom door. She emerged in the lobby on the second-floor balcony. Below, Fisk galloped toward the front door on Hestur, the Eye swinging from the same hand that held his wooden sword. Sleipnir stood across the lobby at his bedroom door, apparently waiting for someone to let him in. The distant shouts of the battling valkyries rang from somewhere outside.

Before Sigrid made it to the stairs, Elina's footsteps pounded closer. Sigrid spun, adrenaline surging through her limbs, ready for a fight—and her insides turned to ice.

Elina drew back her arm for a throw, a spear in her fist.

"No!" Sigrid reached for her own to retaliate—and it wasn't there. It must have fallen out of her quiver in the study. Was that her own weapon in Elina's hand?

Elina aimed past her and released. The spear flew through the air toward Fisk and Hestur.

Sigrid gasped, opening her palms to summon it back. It wouldn't come. She willed it to miss or to hit an invisible wall and fall to the floor—anything but meet its target.

The weapon struck Fisk's shoulder outside of his chainmail, and the tip disappeared beyond his thick leather clothing. He let out a strangled cry and tipped sideways. Hestur shied. Fisk hit the stone floor with a crack, and his sword went flying. The Eye of Hnitbjorg rolled, the brightest color in the dark lobby. Hestur bolted out the door and disappeared from sight.

"Fisk!" Sigrid leaned over the railing, waiting for him to sit up. When he remained still, her heart plummeted. *Don't be dead!*

How deep had the spear gone? She couldn't tell how thick the leather was and whether it had protected him at all.

Sleipnir whinnied after Hestur and pawed the floor, agitated by the commotion.

Elina pushed past Sigrid and sprinted down the stairs. Sigrid followed, thundering behind her.

At the bottom, they both lunged for the Eye. Sigrid whacked Elina's arm out of the way and got her fingers around it first. She was grateful for her leather gloves because Elina's claw-like fingernails dug into them so hard that she would have drawn blood.

Sigrid brought her knees to her chest, hugging the Eye to her stomach. She braced for Elina to try and pry her apart, maybe kick her.

Nothing happened.

Fisk groaned. Sigrid risked a peek. He was sitting up, whimpering. Elina held onto him by his mask, which had a crack in the nose. The spear stuck grotesquely out of his shoulder.

Sigrid reached for them. "Stop!"

With a movement like a strike of lightning, Elina yanked the spear from Fisk's shoulder. He screeched in pain, rolling over to cover the wound.

Lip curling, Elina pointed the weapon at Sigrid, who froze. "Give me the Eye, or this Night Elf stays in Helheim forever."

CHAPTER FIFTY-FIVE

CHOOSING A PATH

Sigrid's breaths sawed in and out of her as she faced Elina. Her mother held Fisk in an unforgiving and dangerous grip. Fisk's breaths sounded like whimpers, his hands hovering between the wound in his shoulder and Elina's hand on his mask.

Could Sigrid get them both out of this and keep the Eye?

Elina tugged.

Sigrid lunged, closing her fingers over Elina's wrists, stopping her from pulling off Fisk's mask. "Don't!"

He grabbed it, desperately trying to keep her from removing it. "Please," he whimpered. "Please don't. I'll burn."

Elina's gaze darted behind Sigrid, and she grinned. Sigrid's insides plummeted as she realized her mistake. The Eye lay on the stone floor. Elina dropped her hold on Fisk, ready to lunge after the relic.

Zing.

A spear whipped between them, grazing Elina's cheek. She recoiled with a yelp.

Sigrid pulled Fisk away, and he cried out from the jostling move.

Mariam swooped into the lobby, Aesa folding her broad

wingspan so she fit through the door. She landed with a clatter, and Mariam jumped off. She opened her palm and summoned her spear back, then pointed it at Elina. "Let my friends go."

Elina glared, clenching her spear. A line of blood oozed on her cheek where Mariam had caught her.

"The valkyries are busy luring your army away from the gates," Mariam said. "You've got no allies to protect you."

Elina sneered. "This is how you thank me?"

Sigrid took the opportunity to snatch up the stone. She wrapped both hands around it and hugged it close.

Fisk hobbled to his feet. Blood glistened around the gash in his leather. "Golly, what great timing, Mariam."

Mariam sent him a quick smile.

Elina stood tall. Despite being surrounded by all three of them, she looked calm and confident. "Mariam, I can change your mind."

Sigrid stepped forward. "Don't listen to—"

"I knew your mother."

Sigrid and Fisk froze.

Mariam's surprise melted to defiance. She narrowed her eyes, crouched in a fighting stance. "Obviously. You both lived in Vanaheim."

"Haven't you ever wondered why you had to grow up in Niflheim?"

Mariam didn't answer. She stayed still, nostrils flaring. Behind her, Aesa backed away, wings twitching and the whites of her eyes showing, as if shying away from a predator. She was afraid of Elina.

"Did she ever tell you why Vanaheim banished her?" Elina said, pacing closer.

Mariam straightened. Fisk looked between them, silent. Sigrid gripped the stone in both hands and glowered. She wanted to grab her friends, the Eye, and run. But Mariam had a right to know about her mother.

Elina moved steadily closer to Mariam, the spear in her fist. "Your mother was one of four valkyries who sided with me during my campaign for Vanaheim's throne. When the royals discovered the treachery, they banished all involved." She paused, letting the words hit full force. "Your mother was my dear friend, Mariam. She chose to ally with me. She would want you to do the same."

She stopped at arm's length and held out a hand in truce.

Mariam stared at her, wide-eyed.

Sigrid wanted to shout at Elina for lying again, because all she did was lie and trick and deceive, but something told her this story was the truth. She had known Mariam's mother.

Mariam blinked. She looked to Sigrid, Fisk, Aesa, and back to Elina. Her eyes narrowed. "You tricked my mother into trusting you, just like you tricked me, and just like you tricked Sigrid."

Elina swelled. "There was no trickery involved in—"

"You got her banished! I won't fall into the same trap, and I won't forgive you."

"She chose to ally with me at her own will."

"I don't care. I'll never side with you after what you've done."

Elina lunged for her, spear raised. Mariam raised hers to meet it, and the hilts collided with a crash that echoed off the mud walls. Elina pushed hard, and Mariam gasped as she stumbled backward. Elina slammed into her, and they fell to the stone floor.

Aesa snorted and unfurled her wings, sending a gust of wind through the lobby.

"Get off her!" Sigrid shouted, taking a step forward. But Mariam's cry stopped her.

"Go," Mariam grunted. "Take—the Eye—out of here."

With a roar, Elina pinned Mariam and pressed a hand over her throat, holding her down. Fisk swept toward them, bellowing, but Elina swung the point of her spear around to face him. He skidded to a stop.

"Give me the Eye, Sigrid!" Elina shouted, teeth bared.

"Don't," Mariam croaked, frantically prying Elina's fingers.

Sigrid clutched the small pink stone, breathing hard. Her friends' lives hung in the balance. The delicate chain of the stone dug into her palms. Panic threatened to suffocate her.

Elina pushed harder into Mariam's throat. She looked deranged, blond hair falling out of its braid, face blotchy and distorted with anger. "Give it to me!"

Mariam's face changed color, growing darker, her eyes bulging. Her legs kicked, fingers working to pull Elina away from her throat.

Sigrid let out a strangled sob, her grip on the Eye loosening.

"Stop it!" Fisk shouted.

"The Eye, Sigrid!" Elina roared.

Mariam's eyes rolled back. Aesa grew frantic, wanting to go to Mariam but clearly terrified of Elina. Sleipnir responded to the energy, pawing the floor.

Mariam made a choking sound as Elina leaned all her weight into her throat.

"You can have it!" Sigrid shouted, her words shrill and panicked.

The hall fell into a silence that echoed her words.

"It's yours! Let her go." Sigrid held out the Eye, which swung on its chain.

Elina didn't pause to negotiate. She let go of Mariam, who let out a rattling gasp and coughed violently, and was over to Sigrid in two strides.

The moment the weight of the Eye left Sigrid's grip, Sigrid sprinted to Mariam and dropped to her knees. "Are you okay?"

Mariam touched the place where Elina had strangled her, staring blankly at the ceiling as she caught her breath.

"Sleipnir!" Fisk said.

Sigrid froze. *No.*

Elina grabbed Sleipnir's reins and spun him to face the exit. She vaulted on while he sprang into a canter.

Sigrid cursed and jumped to her feet. "Sleipnir!"

But Elina had a firm hand, and she pulled the reins so hard that Sleipnir's eyes rolled in fear. With the Eye of Hnitbjorg swinging from its chain in her hand, she and Sleipnir raced out the door.

The stallion's hoofbeats faded into the distant clash of battle.

CHAPTER FIFTY-SIX

SURRENDERING
TO CHAOS

E lina galloped away from the palace on Sleipnir, leaving Sigrid numb and depleted. Never mind losing the Eye again, she'd also lost their ride back to the land of the living.

She knelt beside her friends on the stone floor of the lobby, more overwhelmed than if she'd been dropped in the middle of Niflheim without a map.

"Mariam, are you okay?" Sigrid asked, helping her sit up.

Mariam coughed, gulping down air, a hand over her throat where Elina had choked her.

Sigrid held a hand to her back, rubbing soothing circles until Mariam nodded. "Fisk?"

He was trying to stop the shoulder would from oozing, but his hand was trembling too much. "I'll be okay."

How had everything gone so wrong? They'd had the Eye, they were making their escape… She had to go after Elina, who would no doubt be with an army at her back once more.

But retrieving the Eye and Sleipnir would have to wait. Her friends needed her and she would not abandon them again.

She exhaled. "I'll find bandages. We need to stop the bleeding."

Fisk extended a hand to stop her. "Don't worry about us! You need to go after Elina."

Sigrid shook her head. "You two are more important."

"You can't afford to lose her," Mariam said, voice raspy, her dark eyes full of fire. "I meant what I said about the valkyries luring her army away. You've got a clear path to the gates."

A clear path.

She swallowed hard. "But you… I don't know if I can—"

"Go, Sigrid. Fisk and I will follow." Mariam nodded toward the door to where Hestur had gone. "You're fast enough to catch her." Her chest rose and fell as she caught her breath, the panic in her eyes clearing as she located Aesa.

Sigrid rocked back on her heels, inhaling deeply. They were right. After all this, she couldn't give up. Her friends and allies were with her, and Hestur wouldn't have gone far. She had everything she needed to beat Elina.

"I don't know how many more times I can handle almost losing you," Sigrid said, the words catching.

Mariam's brown eyes blazed with determination. "I'm okay, Sigrid. Really." She reached out to squeeze Sigrid's hand. After all of the pain she'd experienced, physical and emotional, she managed to sit tall, energized and ready to keep fighting.

Sigrid squeezed back, heart thrumming at the feel of their entwined fingers.

How is she so impossibly beautiful, inside and out?

Without pausing to consider, Sigrid leaned forward and kissed her. Their lips touched gently, urgency making her pull back sooner than she would've liked. Mariam's sweet taste and the cushiony feel of her lips lingered and made Sigrid's head swim.

Surprise slackened Mariam's jaw—and then a smile broke across her face like a ray of sunlight blazing through the dark palace.

"See you soon," Sigrid said, chest fluttering. She bit her lip, aching for a longer kiss.

Mariam opened and closed her mouth, apparently lost for words.

"Okay!" Fisk said with forced casualness.

Sigrid jumped to her feet and instinctively reached for her spear, then remembered with a sinking feeling that her quiver was empty.

When Elina had thrown the spear at Fisk, why hadn't it obeyed Sigrid? It was hers, and Mariam had told her that was a fundamental rule of spears. *Unless that was a different spear. Unless mine is still in the palace.*

In all the panic, she hadn't been able to think earlier.

Sigrid opened her palm, focusing on the study in the upstairs bedroom.

A heartbeat passed, and then her spear soared over the railing toward her. It clapped into her hand with a satisfying *thwap*.

"First rule of spears," she murmured. "Hestur, come!"

A clatter of hooves came from outside. He trotted into the lobby, looking around tentatively.

"Let's race, buddy." She grabbed Hestur's mane and swung onto his back, marveling at his delicate bone structure and light, agile movements after spending so much time on Sleipnir.

"You two get on Aesa. Round up the others and get ready to follow me to the gate." She waited until her friends nodded, then steered Hestur toward the door. "Yah!"

Hestur responded to her command, springing into a gallop. They charged out the door and away from the palace. Sigrid leaned forward, moving with him. Her heart was ready to burst with the joy of riding him again. His strides were smooth and weightless, taking them over the terrain like a gust of wind.

At the end of the muddy, cobweb-like structures reaching out from the palace, Hestur veered right. Sigrid trusted his guidance. Sure enough, Elina and Sleipnir headed that way, galloping down a dirt path toward a little town. They weren't too far.

Sigrid and Hestur could catch up.

"Let's get her." They seemed to meld into one as they galloped flat-out, responding to each other's movements, Hestur obeying her commands before she made them.

As Sleipnir and Elina converged on the town, Sigrid urged Hestur faster, afraid of losing them among the buildings and streets.

She twirled her spear in her fingers, waiting for an opportunity. Elina was too far ahead to hit. What if she misfired and killed Sleipnir?

Fear closed around her throat at the image that brought up, but she gritted her teeth. All of her training was worth something. Her skills were better than ever, and she was more familiar with a spear's power and velocity. *I can do this.*

Focusing on her target, she let the world around her fade into the background. Where did Elina's protective vest end? She had to strike higher than it, but not so high as to clear her shoulder.

With a steadying exhale, Sigrid threw with all her might, roaring as the spear left her hand.

The golden weapon flew through the air in a straight trajectory.

With a sickening thud, it hit Elina in the shoulder blade. She shrieked and pitched forward, the spear lodged. Sleipnir's stride hiccupped at the sudden shift in weight, but with eight legs, he didn't lose balance.

A surreal haze clouded Sigrid's brain as the spear wobbled in the woman's back, dark blood gushing down her elegant blue robe. *I did that. I shot her.*

Elina tipped and struggled to stay in the saddle, using the reins for balance. Sleipnir tossed his head and grunted in pain.

Sigrid's anger surged back. This woman had caused enough suffering. It was time to end this. She urged Hestur faster, waiting for the inevitable. "Come on. Fall."

Finally, the Queen of Helheim came unseated from Sleipnir. As she hit the ground, a *crack* rang out, and Sleipnir shied away from her and kept galloping. The pink stone rolled and bounced before coming to rest in a tuft of grass. It peeked through the swaying blades.

"There!" Sigrid and Hestur closed the distance, aiming for it.

Elina rolled over, struggling, the spear sticking out of her back. Her gaze fell to her own spear, which lay cracked in two, and then to the Eye. She was within reach.

Sigrid cursed. She wouldn't get there in time.

"Sigrid!"

A shape darkened the sky above. Mariam and Fisk rode double on Aesa, who nose-dived toward the Eye at a speed that would surely end in them crumpling in the dirt.

Feet from the ground, Aesa leveled out, and Mariam grabbed Fisk's good arm and flung herself off Aesa's back, swinging beneath the mare.

Sigrid's heart jumped into her throat at the maneuver.

Elina lunged for the Eye, but Mariam got there first. Hanging from Fisk, the toes of her shoes grazing the grass, she kicked the pink stone in Sigrid's direction. The Eye bounced across the ground and landed out of Elina's reach.

"How *dare* you betray me after I gave you your life, Mariam!" Elina shouted, laboring to her feet.

Mariam let out a note of defiant laughter as Aesa dipped a wing to help her back up.

Sigrid's lip curled. She leaned into Hestur's bobbing neck, galloping straight at the Eye. His proximity to the ground and small stature wasn't always an advantage, but she relished the times when it was.

"No!" Elina shrieked.

In all their training, Sigrid had proven what she was capable of, and there was no denying what was about to happen. This was one of her favorite tricks.

Sigrid wrapped one hand in Hestur's mane and leaned over,

gripping his rib cage with all the strength in her legs and core. He powered onward, snorting evenly with each stride.

Four strides away. Sigrid tipped sideways so she was horizontal, clinging to the saddle with her legs.

Three strides. She reached down.

Two strides. She opened her hand, fingers grazing the grass.

One stride.

Elina let out a wail of rage.

Sigrid's fingers closed around the Eye, and she swiped it off the ground, its chain swinging around her hand.

"Good boy!"

Sigrid heaved herself upright as Hestur continued galloping. His ears pricked forward in response to her praise, and he galloped faster. Elina's wail faded into the howling wind.

"We got it!" she shouted, voice cracking with exhaustion.

Overhead, Mariam and Fisk whooped. Mariam was back on Aesa, and they soared above her like a guardian, wings stretching wide enough to cast a shadow.

A thunder of hooves closed in beside her. She tensed, expecting an attack, but it was Sleipnir. He'd evidently turned around after finding himself without a rider, and now he fell into stride beside Hestur. His reins flapped loose, at risk of getting caught and snapping beneath a hoof. The stirrups banged against his sides, kicking him faster.

"Nice of you to come back," Sigrid said.

At her words, his black eye fixed on her, finally seeming to hold a glimmer of personality.

"Let's go, boys!"

Sigrid's lips pulled into a smirk as she leaned into Hestur's neck and let him open up to full speed. He galloped like he had never galloped before, powering back toward the gates of Hel.

They had the Eye. All they had to do was get out of Helheim with it.

Sleipnir kept pace, galloping hard beside her.

Sigrid searched the sky for the others, and her heart lifted when white mares descended from the clouds and merged from the sides. They came together into their *V* formation, ready to follow.

Any sense of relief was smothered by what came behind them. In the sky and in the valley below, Hel's army gave pursuit. The valkyries had done their job luring the army away from the gates, but now, a mass of foot soldiers, valkyries, and dire wolves raced back toward them, steadfast in their plan to follow her to the land of the living.

A sick feeling plunged into her gut.

I can't pass through the gates on Hestur. I need to be on Sleipnir for this to work.

The eight-legged stallion galloped tirelessly beside her.

"We're going to try something tricky, boys," she said, voice bouncing with Hestur's strides.

Hestur's ears flicked back, listening. She clucked to him, guiding him closer to Sleipnir, and reached out to the stallion. "Here."

Sleipnir responded, and the two horses converged until they were less than an arm's length apart.

Hestur sped up without her asking, chewing up the ground at an eye-watering speed. Beside him, Sleipnir kept pace. They powered over the grassy field neck-and-neck, moving faster and faster, each horse's nose taking its turn bobbing ahead of the other. Hestur lunged forward with a renewed burst of energy, and then Sleipnir surged to catch up.

They're racing each other, Sigrid thought, startled.

The speed was wild, crossing right over the wall between control and chaos. She wouldn't be able to stop them if she wanted to.

She leaned over and reached for Sleipnir's mane. Though

Hestur's long, flat strides ate the ground at the same speed as Sleipnir's upright ones, the two horses couldn't have been more different. She couldn't stay synchronized with both at once. This would have to be quick.

She let go of Hestur with both hands, holding on with just her legs. With one hand wrapped in Sleipnir's mane and the other on the back of his saddle, she pushed off and flung herself over. His galloping strides jolted her as she lay across his back.

With a roar of effort, she heaved her leg over Sleipnir's back and pushed upright.

Hestur kept galloping beside her. He fixed his eye on her, waiting for instruction.

Over Sigrid's shoulder, the valkyries flew low in *V* formation. Beyond them, Hel's army followed like a dust storm rolling over the land, the dire wolves at the forefront.

But her allies were in the lead. Could she bring them through with enough time for the gate to seal behind them?

The gate was strides away.

"Let's go!" she shouted and leaned into Sleipnir's mane.

Hestur's nose was ahead of them. She couldn't let him try to go through first. She reached over and grabbed his flapping reins, pulling him back so his head fell behind Sleipnir's.

Sleipnir charged through the gates without checking his speed. Sigrid shouted in relief and let go of Hestur's reins, fighting for balance.

A wave of heat blasted her face as they left Helheim for the red desert beyond it. The difference in footing made Sleipnir stumble, and even with eight hooves, he couldn't restore his balance. Before she could brace, he fell to his knees and sent her flying.

She screamed. As she toppled off Sleipnir, she caught a glimpse of Hestur bursting out of the gate in her periphery, stumbling in the deep sand.

Sigrid landed in a dune and everything went dark as the hot sand buried her. She sat up, spluttering.

"Hestur! Sleipnir!"

She wiped an arm across her face. The momentum had sent the horses rolling across the sand. Hestur and Sleipnir lay with their legs curled under them, snorting sand from their nostrils and shaking their heads.

Overhead, what looked like white lightning bolts shot through the gate and into the dusky sky.

Sleipnir rose, shaking a cloud of red sand from his mane. He was okay.

But Hestur…

Sigrid stumbled to her feet, losing her balance from exhaustion.

"Hestur!"

He lay in the sand, breathing harder than she'd ever seen him. His nostrils were bright red inside. His rib cage rose and fell frantically as he caught his breath. His whole body foamed with sweat.

She fell to her knees in front of him and held his face.

"Buddy, are you hurt?"

He isn't getting up. Why isn't he getting up?

He snorted. She traced her eyes over his body, breaths shallow and panicked. Would she find a broken leg, bent and twisted?

Please, no. She would never forgive herself.

Mariam landed a few strides away and leaped off Aesa. "Sigrid! Are you okay?"

"I think he's hurt!" As Sigrid ran a hand over Hestur's knees, he stretched out his front legs—and then he rose to his feet with a deep groan. He shook the sand off his coat and looked at her. He wasn't favoring anything. Nothing was bleeding.

He was all right—just out of breath.

Letting out a sob, she threw her arms around his neck and

pressed her face into his gritty, sweat-soaked neck. "I love you, Hestur."

A booming bark and several screams tore the air.

A dire wolf bounded through the gates with a spray of sand, mangy brown with missing patches. It snarled and looked around, drool flying.

Mariam grabbed Sigrid and pulled her backward. "Look out!"

Sigrid cursed. They weren't ready. Her muscles couldn't take another fight, and neither could her horses.

"No, you don't!" Fisk raced toward the wolf, a flash of moving nightfall, unsheathing the wooden sword from his back.

Mariam dashed toward him. "Fisk, no!"

He was closer to the wolf than anyone. No one else would make it in time to help.

"Back to Hel with you!" he shouted.

The wolf's red eyes gleamed as it locked onto Fisk. It crouched, and when Fisk was two strides away, it leaped at him.

Mariam screamed.

Fisk roared.

Hestur whinnied.

Fisk disappeared beneath a flash of claws and gnashing teeth. A dull, wet crunch sounded. The wolf landed on top of him, and they fell hard into the sand.

"Fisk!" Sigrid cried.

She and Mariam ran to him, shouting his name.

A gush of dark blood pooled out, seeping into the sand and trickling with a *hiss* into a nearby lava pool.

Then the beast's head separated from its body. It rolled into the sand and lay motionless, red eyes open, black tongue lolling.

"Oh!" Mariam squeaked, crouching at its side.

Sigrid followed, and together, they heaved the dire wolf's decapitated body off Fisk.

Fisk gasped for breath, wiping blood from his lemming snout.

"You're okay!" Mariam said as a wave of relief cascaded over Sigrid.

They all stared at each other and then up at the gates. There'd been too much chaos to notice whether that gust of wind came to indicate the closing barrier.

A long silence passed, in which every junior valkyrie, every horse, Mariam, Fisk, and Sigrid all stared at the empty gates of Hel. As before, they creaked softly, like they were moving.

"Did we do it?" Gunni said.

"I think so," Sigrid said. "I don't think anyone else was quick enough to follow us."

They all stared for another minute.

When nothing else tumbled through, a numb feeling trickled over Sigrid. *We did it.*

"We got the Eye back!" Edith shouted.

Everyone gaped at her. She jumped from her saddle and stooped to pick something up. She held the light pink Eye high overhead, letting it swing like a pendulum. Sigrid must have dropped it when she'd fallen off Sleipnir.

Runa whooped. The others joined in. They cheered, laughed, and shouted to each other.

"I did a barrel roll!" Ylva shouted. "Did you see?"

Mariam brushed her fingers against Sigrid's, a subtle, gentle touch that awoke a battalion of wings inside her. The girl's face split into the most radiant smile, and Sigrid decided she could spend her whole life watching her look this happy.

Not only did they get the Eye of Hnitbjorg back, but Sigrid had also gotten Sleipnir. He stood looking around at all the mares with interest, as different as if he were a whole other species. This magnificent, eight-legged anomaly was hers, and he was with her on this side of the gate.

A twinge of uncertainty rose inside her. She would rather have Sleipnir in her power than in Elina's, but the stallion's godlike power still made her uneasy.

She brushed sand off her front, drawing a deep breath.

Mariam and Fisk stared at the dire wolf's head, where it lay in the sand with the severed part thankfully facing down. Fisk walked over and picked it up with his uninjured arm, gazing at it through his big lemming eyes.

Mariam walked over and clapped a hand on his shoulder.

"Well, Fisk. I think you just found your new mask."

CHAPTER FIFTY-SEVEN

AN EIGHT-LEGGED SECRET

Sailing up the spring of Hvergelmir on Ratatosk's ship was less daunting with the company of twenty-one junior valkyries and their mares. The air buzzed with energy like being back at the stables, except the barn was rocking in the waves.

Unlike being at the stables, Sigrid laughed along with the valkyries as they recounted their misadventures through Midgard over a meal of cake and pastries. Fisk sat in silence, focusing on carefully skinning and cleaning his new dire wolf mask. Thankfully, he and Mariam had been welcomed without question after their involvement in recovering the Eye.

Sleipnir relaxed in the presence of other horses, and Hestur nuzzled him a few times as if to reassure him that he was safe now. He towered above the herd with all the subtlety of a rooster among hens.

Mariam giggled. "Where are you going to put that giant?"

"I'm not sure, yet. Can't exactly put him in the main stable." Sigrid still didn't know if she wanted anyone else back home to see she had Sleipnir. But she did want the others to meet Mariam. "When we get to Vanaheim, I can show you my stall. It's not that big, but it's cozy," she said. "There's a village nearby where I shop—"

"Oh, I…" Mariam said, avoiding her eyes. "I'm going back to my mother. It's been…a long time now."

"You're flying all the way back to Niflheim?" Sigrid said, stunned. "By yourself?"

Mariam shook her head. "Fisk will come with me. He said he's not ready to go back to Svartalfheim."

Sigrid's chest ached like she'd swallowed a stone. Obviously, this was going to happen. Why should their feelings for each other change anything? It was selfish to think she was enough reason for Mariam to stay when her whole life was back in Niflheim.

Sigrid should be grateful that Mariam had stayed with her for this long when she could've said goodbye and taken a fork in the spring yesterday.

Still, it hurt to think they would part forever in a matter of hours.

"Right," she said, forcing a smile. "Well, I'm sure your mom will be happy to have you back."

Mariam returned a sad smile. She looked like she was about to say more, but Sigrid couldn't handle hearing any parting words.

"I should check on Hestur and Sleipnir." She stood and walked away, blinking back tears.

The journey past Garmr was easier with an entire fleet of valkyries as a distraction. Mariam and Aesa worked great along with the junior team. While they twisted and turned in the cavern, Garmr became frustrated, and before he realized a ship was passing through, they were gone.

When they docked in Vanaheim, the Night Elves had abandoned camp and taken the mounds of stolen belongings. Mud and litter haunted the place.

Sigrid jumped off the ship and flopped into the long grass, blissfully happy to see Vanaheim. Hestur trotted down the gangplank behind her and set to work on a patch of dandelions.

As everyone disembarked, the abandoned camp sat uneasy

in her gut. Were the Night Elves still in Vanaheim? She had no army to root them out and chase them back to their world. And where was Ratatosk?

The valkyries took flight at a leisurely pace, while Sigrid rode Sleipnir and Fisk rode Hestur through Myrkviðr. Hestur seemed fine with this arrangement, though Sigrid continually checked that Fisk was riding him properly. He was. In fact, he seemed to be a good rider. He sat tall and confident in his new dire wolf mask. The mask was ridiculously big but didn't seem to clatter around too much, so it must have fit all right.

"What kind of horses do you have in Svartalfheim?" she said.

"Ponies," Fisk said. His mask tilted downward. "And they're a lot closer to the ground than Hestur."

Sigrid grinned at the idea that someone considered Hestur to be far from the ground.

A shadow eclipsed them, and Mariam landed between them on Aesa, cheeks flushed from the wind.

"Vanaheim is amazing," she said with a wistful groan. Her dark eyes gleamed with delight. She looked so much healthier and happier than a few days ago. It made her all the more beautiful.

You could stay, Sigrid wanted to say, but the words wouldn't come out. Her heart ached with the knowledge that it was too soon to say goodbye.

"When I was a lad, I had a good steed…" Fisk sang under his breath, slipping into a hum. The uneven tune bounced with Hestur's strides.

Mariam searched Sigrid's face. "Wishing you were on Hestur?"

She scowled. "How could you tell?"

"You've been watching him like a dire wolf watches a baby."

"Nice."

"Don't you want to look all tough and ride into Vanaheim on Sleipnir?"

Sigrid grimaced. "It's just—I know we proved that I'm his heir, but there's still something about him that gets to me. I feel so tense when I'm on him, and he's hard to control."

Mariam studied the stallion. "You look like you're controlling him fine."

"But when I ask him to stop or turn, sometimes he just doesn't. He has the will of a horse ridden by a god."

Mariam chewed her lip over this as she let go of the reins and stretched her arms. "Wasn't Sleipnir said to be birthed by Loki?"

Sigrid smirked. "I read something like that."

"Well, what do you expect from the God of Mischief's son? Total obedience?"

Sigrid laughed. She had a point.

"If you don't want to ride him, what'll you do with him?" Mariam said.

Sigrid had thought about this. Ideally, she would set Sleipnir free to gallop through the nine worlds and do as he pleased, but given his power, this wasn't an option. Anyone could capture and ride him. Elina was proof of that. She could give him to Mariam or Fisk, but they would have as difficult a time keeping him out of the wrong hands, maybe more, in a dark world like Niflheim.

"I'll keep him somewhere secret." Maybe a clearing in the forest far from any roads or paths. "I'll set up a corral and go take care of him before I do the valkyrie mares every day."

Mariam looked startled. "That sounds like a lot of work."

"I know. But if I keep him in the stables, then General Eira, the royals, and everyone else will see that I have him."

"I think the whole of Vanaheim will know you have him, anyway, once this flock opens their mouths." Mariam pointed skyward, where the valkyries soared above the treetops.

Sigrid shrugged. "I told them you two are taking him and I have no idea where you're going. As far as they're concerned, Sleipnir is about to leave Vanaheim forever."

Mariam smirked. "You're going to break everyone's hearts."

Sigrid almost smiled at the image of General Eira's face upon finding out that she'd sent away the most powerful horse in the nine worlds.

They reached the edge of Myrkviðr and stopped. Beyond the lush meadow, Vanahalla's gold towers touched the sky, more majestic than she remembered. Mariam gave a wistful sigh.

Overhead, the junior valkyries turned back to check on them.

Sigrid waved them onward. "I'll catch up!"

They watched them grow smaller, and then Sigrid dismounted Sleipnir. After so long on his back, she had to shake her head to get rid of the jittery feeling he gave her. Was it getting worse?

"Meet me at this spot at nightfall," she told Mariam and Fisk. "I'll bring you enough food and supplies to get you back to Niflheim."

They agreed, wanting to rest before starting the next leg of their journey. While they dismounted and flopped in the grass, Sigrid left them with Sleipnir and rode Hestur up to Vanahalla. Her insides twisted at the thought of the goodbye that must come later.

CHAPTER FIFTY-EIGHT

EMBARRASSING FANFARE

Sigrid didn't have time to fret for long, because when she arrived in the courtyard, everything was in a total uproar. The junior valkyries had attracted the attention of the entire hall, and by the time Sigrid arrived at the edge of the crowd, General Eira, King Óleifr, and a jumble of courtiers waited. Even the cook from her daily lunch runs, Gregor, was there, and when he saw her ride up on Hestur, his eyes twinkled behind his bushy beard. She cast him a smile.

To her disappointment, Vala wasn't among the crowd. The number of people was probably too much for the old Seer.

"The queen of the underworld had it," Gunni said loudly, holding the Eye of Hnitbjorg aloft. It swung on the end of the chain, catching the light for all to see. "We had to go into Helheim to get it back."

King Óleifr cupped his hands and accepted it gently, like a father being handed his newborn. He looked sicker than when Sigrid had left, eyes tired, skin sallow, and that lustrous, sun-colored hair and beard wispy and dull. His delicate amber crown was the brightest thing about him.

"Thank you," he said breathlessly, turning the Eye over in

his hands. After a moment, he addressed General Eira. "We'll have medals created. Every junior valkyrie will be awarded for her service."

General Eira clapped. "Well done, girls!"

The court applauded the junior valkyries. The noise spread, growing louder, until the golden towers themselves seemed to be applauding their success. The valkyries glowed, exchanging grins.

When the applause died, Ylva said loudly, "And Sigrid."

Sigrid startled, unable to stop her mouth from opening in surprise or her cheeks from flooding with heat.

"Yeah!" Gunni said, and the other valkyries nodded and voiced their agreement.

To Sigrid's horror, all of the valkyries turned to her and Hestur at the edge of the crowd. King Óleifr and the rest of the courtyard followed. Sitting astride Hestur with a view of them all, she had the urge to dismount and sink into the cobblestones.

"Sigrid was the one who got it back from Princess Helena!" Runa said.

Sigrid's heart jumped at Runa's unfiltered mention of the missing princess. Not that Sigrid had planned to keep it a secret, but she had wanted some time to consider how to bring up the fact that the princess now ruled Helheim.

"Helena?" someone said sharply. "Helena is Queen of Helheim?"

It was Princess Kaia, who stood behind King Óleifr. Sigrid scrutinized her amber diadem and sky-blue robe with new perspective. She resembled Elina only in her slim stature, with straight dark hair and large, innocent eyes.

When several valkyries nodded, Princess Kaia and King Óleifr exchanged a serious look.

"And she sent that army to take the Eye of Hnitbjorg?" King Óleifr said.

Everyone turned back to Sigrid.

She cleared her throat. Now was as good a time as any. "She's after the throne. She planned to raise Hel's army to attack Vanaheim."

King Óleifr stepped back, ashen. "What... Is that true? Where is she now?"

"Helheim," Sigrid said. "She's there to stay."

His shoulders relaxed a little.

Princess Kaia's gaze darted over the cobblestones as she considered Sigrid's words.

"Well," King Óleifr said, straightening his jacket. "Thank you, Sigrid and the valkyries, for your tremendous service to Vanaheim. You will be rewarded and commemorated."

Sigrid endured an embarrassing round of applause before the crowd dissipated, buzzing with the news. She lingered as the king and his sister—her family, technically—leaned in to talk in low voices. No one seemed to notice her, and she would gladly keep it that way. She'd had enough of royal life.

Having no desire to spend any more time up here, she turned Hestur around and rode back to the stables. The valkyries glided overhead, chatting brightly like they'd finished an exciting day of training and not a multi-day mission across worlds and into Helheim.

They entered the barn to an uproar of cheers from the stable hands. Chickens flapped everywhere, startled by the noise and sending an explosion of feathers across the aisle. The familiar blend of hay, wood shavings, tack, and horses drifted under her nose, as soothing as a bouquet of lavender.

"Sig!" Roland shouted as she led Hestur through the cluster of horses and stable hands. "Good to have you back. Peter told me what you were doing and—wow. I knew you'd be back. Nice haircut. You look strong. Hey, we left Hestur's stall clean for you. I'll oil your tack tonight. My treat."

By the time he finished talking, she was halfway down the

aisle toward Hestur's stall. "Thanks! Missed you, too, potato sack."

He grinned and went to help untack the mares.

Hestur's stall was spotless, as promised. While everyone talked and shouted over each other at the other end of the barn, she untacked quickly and upended her saddlebags. Among the belongings that tumbled out, she discovered the woolen sack of coins she'd taken from the Night Elves during their escape. She'd completely forgotten about that. Inside, it stowed more riches than she'd ever seen.

She grabbed a rucksack and filled it with food and supplies for Mariam and Fisk's journey. The sack of coins, too. They might need the money as they crossed the worlds, whereas Sigrid had everything she needed here in Vanaheim.

With the rucksack stuffed to bursting, she hid it beneath her hammock for later. Then she went to get Hestur as much hay as she could carry and dumped it in the corner for him to get started on.

Something tugged her pant leg. A chicken strutted over the clay by her boots, searching for dropped grain. It looked up at her and clucked loudly before resuming pecking at her ankles.

"Oh, get off," she said, nudging it aside. "You'll get your dinner soon."

She couldn't help smiling. *It's good to be home.*

A scuff of boots on clay made her turn. A familiar figure stood outside the stall door, hands in pockets, head tilted a little.

"Well, did you find what you were searching for?" Peter said.

Sigrid nodded firmly. "And I decided I didn't like it."

He narrowed his brown eyes. "What, your destiny?"

"Yep."

Peter stared at her before letting out a bark of laughter.

She ran forward and threw her arms around him. She'd forgotten how hugging him felt like hugging a tree trunk. "I'm sorry I left."

He let out a breath at the impact of her hitting his chest. "Hey, it's okay, lightning bolt. I ran away from home once, too. It just—well, it wasn't to go to Helheim and unleash Hel's army on the nine worlds. But everyone's different."

Sigrid laughed and stepped back. "You heard?"

He motioned with his head to where the valkyries and stable hands were still buzzing. "We *all* heard."

She wrinkled her nose. Couldn't the valkyries keep what she did a secret for more than a few minutes? Far from wanting to be recognized as Elina's daughter, she wanted to melt back into her life as a stable hand—an orphan with no ties to the Vanaheim royals and no relation to that awful woman.

"You really sent away the eight-legged horse?" Peter shook his head.

A smirk pulled at her lips. She'd told the valkyries that lie, but as for Peter?

"Actually," she said, "I might need your help with something."

CHAPTER FIFTY-NINE

A PROPER GOODBYE

W hen the sun began to set, Sigrid grabbed the overstuffed
rucksack from beneath her hammock and went on foot
to meet Mariam and Fisk. The hills and tall grass hid her as she
picked a weaving path down to the woods. The rucksack was
heavy, maybe too heavy, but they needed enough food to last the
long journey.

She'd dreaded this moment since they left Helheim. Saying a
simple goodbye would be hollow and unsatisfying after all they'd
been through.

Mariam waited at the edge of the woods like a vision, as
lovely as ever. They exchanged a smile.

"Fisk is back there with Aesa and Sleipnir," Mariam said,
jabbing a thumb over her shoulder.

Sigrid followed her deep into the tangle of trees and bushes,
hoping the place she'd picked to keep Sleipnir was hidden enough
that no one would wander by.

The stallion stood in a corral made of branches, trees, and
logs. Fisk worked on the fence, wedging pieces together to form
a barrier that rose past her head.

"Wow! Thanks, Fisk."

"Masters of craftsmanship," he said, throwing out his chest. "I siphoned magic from the trees, so the fence will keep growing and become sturdier over time."

Sigrid whistled in admiration. He'd done so much for her. "Don't you have an injured shoulder?"

He patted the place where he'd stitched up the leather. "I'm fine. Honest."

Sleipnir's tack rested on the ground outside the corral. The harsh metal bit glinted in the fading daylight. That bit was going straight into the junk pile.

She shrugged out of the rucksack and leaned it against a tree. "Here. I packed you—well, lots of things."

"Blueberry pastries?" Mariam said, a playful gleam in her brown eyes.

"Maybe..." Sigrid's cheeks burned, and she fussed with a strap on the rucksack.

Fisk came over to rummage through it. "Golly, this'll be a huge help. Thanks." He straightened up and hugged her.

She hugged him back, vaguely surprised at the bony figure beneath the layers of leather.

"You're going back to the spring, then?"

"We've got to get to Niflheim somehow," Mariam said.

Of course. Silly question.

Silence stretched between them. Sleipnir snorted.

"Well," Sigrid said, swinging her hands awkwardly by her sides. "Bye, I guess."

Mariam grabbed Aesa's reins and handed them to Fisk. "Will you take Aesa to the forest edge so we can have a clear spot to take off? I'll be along in a second."

Sigrid's heart skipped, something like panic rising inside her.

Fisk jumped into action with the energy of someone who had not been to Helheim and back. "Sure!"

Sigrid patted Aesa goodbye and hugged Fisk one last time.

As he led Aesa away, she tried to think of something clever to say to Mariam.

"Before we go…" Mariam seemed to struggle for words, then drew a deep breath. "You weren't just a parcel to be delivered. I'm sorry I ever treated you that way."

Sigrid's cheeks warmed, and she kicked a toe into the dirt, hoping Mariam didn't notice. She was ashamed of her outburst when they'd stood before the gates. She'd been hurt, and she'd tried to hurt Mariam back. "It's okay. I understand why you did it."

She meant it. Of course Mariam was right to accept Elina's terms when her soul was at stake. Anyone would have done the same. It just hurt to think it might have ruined what could have formed between them.

Not that it matters now. She's leaving.

Mariam drew a breath, as if steeling herself, and reached forward to grab Sigrid's hand. "You made me want to dream, Sigrid. To want a brighter future and go after it. You made me want to be better." She slid her fingers between Sigrid's. "I think we were meant to cross paths."

At the sensation of their entwined fingers, Sigrid's heart ached worse than ever. She swallowed a lump in her throat, unable to hold back one last plea. "If you stay in Vanaheim, you can join the valkyrie ranks."

Mariam's eyebrows pulled down. "You're forgetting how we met."

"The royals will forgive you. I'll tell them how you helped us fight. We can convince them…" Her words faded, more hopeful than truthful. Mariam's help in getting the Eye back didn't change the fact that she'd attacked Vanaheim in the first place and then escaped captivity in the dead of night. Her decision to leave Vanaheim made sense for her safety.

But living without Mariam at her side? The thought of this future was deflating, like a spear puncturing her heart. They'd been through so much and had just begun to know each other.

"I have to get back to my mom," Mariam said, Sigrid's sadness reflected in her expression. "She needs to know I'm alive. And now that I have a second chance at life, I want to go home and…"

She trailed off, searching Sigrid's face. What did she see there that made her stop talking?

"I care about you. A lot," Mariam said. "I need you to know that."

"Oh. That's good," Sigrid said, barely audible. She cleared her throat. "Um, why do you need me to know that?"

"Because…" Mariam looked around as if searching for an escape. Or maybe she was checking if Fisk was listening in. Her ears reddened. "I like you."

Sigrid's heart hammered against her ribs. *Like.* The word was so ambiguous. Were her feelings about Mariam so fierce that she misinterpreted the word *like*? Did Mariam *like* Sigrid the same way Hestur *liked* apples?

If you like me, don't leave me, she thought, leaving those selfish words unspoken. She kept her fingers as still as she could in Mariam's hand, as if moving them might make her let go.

"And when you say '*like*'…" Sigrid bit her lip, sinking into the deep pools of Mariam's eyes.

Mariam stepped closer, until the world became just her. "I mean…"

Her breath tickled Sigrid's lips. Every freckle dusting her nose became distinct.

Something erupted inside of Sigrid as she inclined her head to meet Mariam's lips. Every emotion since she first laid eyes on Mariam acted as kindling to a fire burning in her middle. She opened her lips and put a hand on Mariam's waist, wanting to hold onto her for however much time she could.

One of Mariam's hands tangled in her hair, the other pulling their hips together. Sigrid's mind seemed to dissipate, leaving this world for another one entirely—Asgard, maybe, or higher yet. Their bodies pressed closer as their lips moved, exploring each other's mouths with a need Sigrid had never known. It made her pulse race, her hands tremble, her lungs—

She pushed Mariam back and gasped.

Mariam looked at her with a mixture of surprise and concern, the color high in her cheeks.

"S-Sorry," Sigrid said, gulping down air. "You're the first person I've kissed. I forgot to breathe."

Mariam laughed.

Sigrid's insides tingled at the sound. "I think you're the only person in the nine worlds who can make me forget to breathe, Mariam."

With a wicked grin, Mariam stepped closer, allowing Sigrid to pull her in and kiss her again. She ran her fingers through Mariam's soft hair and down the back of her neck.

After a blissfully long time, they stopped and let their foreheads rest together. Sigrid's lips felt deliciously tender.

"I'll come back," Mariam said, breath hitching. "I need to go to my mom, but after that, I'll come back to you."

The words floated into her chest, inflating like a bubble of hope inside Sigrid. "You will? But—"

"I'm about as safe here as I am in Niflheim. Even if I have to live in hiding, we'll make it work." Mariam pecked Sigrid's lips once, twice. "I want to be with you."

Sigrid nodded as she stepped in and kissed her again, stomach swooping like an entire fleet of winged mares had gotten loose inside her.

They kissed and clung to each other for another moment until they agreed that stalling any longer would make this worse. Besides, they had to consider poor Fisk, who held Aesa while they stood there making out.

"Bye," Sigrid said, holding Mariam's hand as she stepped back.

"See you soon, stable girl."

Then her hand was empty, palm tingling where she already missed Mariam's touch. *It won't be long. She's coming back.* And although it didn't make the goodbye any easier, it did give her something to look forward to.

As she began the long trek back to Vanahalla, Mariam, Aesa, and Fisk rose over Myrkviðr and flew away into the cloudless sky.

In the morning, after spending half the night reinforcing Sleipnir's secret corral and bringing down bales of hay, Sigrid rode Hestur up to the golden towers to see Vala. She used the same means as before to get inside, swimming through the moat and pulling herself through the window. She was, after all, still a stable hand with no permission to be inside the hall.

"Sigrid! I saw you coming." Vala stood with the help of her walking stick and motioned to the pink stone on her desk. "First thing the Eye showed me when it was back in my hand. And I'm prepared."

She ushered Sigrid to a seat beside the fire, where she'd folded a stack of towels. Sigrid thanked her and did her best to dry off. It was good to see her doing so well.

"What brings you to me, Sigrid, other than your love of swimming?"

Sigrid suppressed a smile. "I wanted to tell you what happened in Helheim. I think you should know."

Vala gave her an encouraging nod and sat across from her in front of the fire. Her white hair fell around her like a curtain, wayward strands quivering in the breeze from the open window.

Sigrid told her everything she'd learned since leaving Vanaheim—how Elina was the missing princess, how she sent the army to steal the Eye, and how she tried to use Sigrid and Sleipnir to try and take back Vanaheim's throne.

"Given the chance with Hel's army, I think she would take more than just Vanaheim," Sigrid said.

Vala stood, brow furrowed, a deep frown adding more lines to her wrinkled face. "I would not have expected this of Princess Helena. This displeases me. Then again, she has surprised me many times."

"And she's not the only one who wants control over the worlds." Sigrid relayed how the Night Elves seemed to be trying to gain power, starting with controlling the spring of Hvergelmir and capturing Ratatosk.

"Ah. This, we suspected," Vala said gravely. "All evidence pointed to it. The senior valkyries should have returned by now, but with Ratatosk gone, they'll be stuck in Jotunheim. I am afraid we have a power struggle on the horizon."

Sigrid turned back and forth, letting the fire dry her clothes. This news of the senior valkyries would have directed her next question, if she didn't have a more personal matter squeezing her heart.

"You knew," Sigrid said, the words bursting out after having been trapped inside her for days. "You knew that Elina was my mother and I was destined for Sleipnir all along, and you didn't tell me."

Vala leaned heavily on her walking stick, looking so old and sad that it became hard to hold on to anger.

"And so we get to the real reason why you came to see me," Vala said, sounding fragile.

Sigrid said nothing, waiting for her to explain.

"Do you intend to act on your title as a princess of Vanaheim?" Vala said.

"No. I intend to ignore it."

Vala almost smiled.

When she said nothing more, Sigrid said, "I just wanted to know why you didn't tell me about Elina or that vision."

"*A measure of wisdom each person shall have, but sharing it must be restrained. For the wise person's heart is seldom content, if wisdom too great he has gained*," Vala recited. "When the gods wrote this verse of Hávamál, Sigrid, I believe they meant for Seers to take heed. Knowledge of the future is a burden. I don't share most of the visions I see because they can be harmful. I learned that lesson seventeen years ago."

Sigrid furrowed her brow. Seventeen years would have been shortly before her birth. "You mean the one you told my mother about?"

"One of my biggest regrets is telling Helena—Elina—about that vision. It caused her to abandon you, and for that, I will never forgive myself. After all the damage I caused, I did not want to burden you with the knowledge of an old Seer's mistake."

A mistake. The word seemed too benign for what it was. That "mistake" had changed Sigrid's entire life. She had the right to be furious with Vala for what she did—but she wasn't. After everything she'd learned in Helheim, she was certain that growing up as an orphan was better than growing up under Elina's shadow. Her life had changed because of Vala's actions, but maybe not for the worse.

Besides, if Elina hadn't abandoned her, she wouldn't have ended up with Hestur.

"I wonder," Sigrid said, "do you think that by not telling someone about a vision, it's just as bad? You're denying them the knowledge of their destiny."

Vala tilted her head and hummed thoughtfully. "I think that the journey to discovering your destiny is more important than the thing itself."

Sigrid stopped moving. "What do you mean?"

"Don't be so hasty about reaching your destiny that you

forget the most important part of life—discovering who you are by living from moment to moment."

Sigrid chewed her lip. Maybe there was a reason the gods gave the power of Seeing to so few. "Vala, if you'd been the one to see the vision that I saw—the one of me riding Sleipnir—?"

"Then I would not have told you about it."

She pondered this in silence beside the soothing warmth and sounds of the fire, unsure how to feel. Vala offered her tea, but she shook her head and made her way out.

She descended the spiral stairs, uncertain whether it was right or wrong for her to have seen the vision. Did it matter, when the cosmos wanted so badly to lead her to Helheim? Was there a point in thinking about a universe in which she hadn't seen the vision?

She climbed through the window and onto Hestur. No, there wasn't a point, because there was no such universe. The only universe was this one, and it had led her to be here in this moment.

Instead of returning to the stables, Sigrid went for an easy gallop beside the stone wall surrounding Vanahalla. Hestur's ears were forward, his neck bobbing enthusiastically. He seemed to enjoy the relaxed pace and lush green footing as much as she did.

As for what she would do with Sleipnir, she didn't know. She would take care of him in his secret corral on the edge of Myrkviðr until the next step became obvious. By then, she hoped to better understand the uneasy feeling the stallion gave her— the sense that he embodied gods, wars, and power she couldn't comprehend. Was she meant to embrace that feeling, or was she meant to tame it?

When she returned to the stables, the junior valkyries were zipping around the training field. They took the day casually, playing games rather than flying drills.

"Morning, General," Sigrid said as she stopped to watch.

"Afternoon." General Eira glanced at the position of the sun.

It was, indeed, noon. "Sigrid, I wondered—"

She gathered her reins, pointing Hestur back toward Vanahalla. "Lunch? I'm on it."

"Well, yes," the general said. "But there's something else."

General Eira studied her so closely that a jolt of panic went through Sigrid's middle.

Don't mention Elina. Don't mention Elina.

"Please grab an extra serving for yourself. We hoped you could join us for this afternoon's training session. We're being sent to Svartalfheim to investigate Ratatosk's disappearance, and if I might be frank, we could use you on the ground."

Sigrid stared at her for a long moment, her pulse picking up as she absorbed the general's words.

"Me? Why?"

"I heard from the valkyries what you did in Helheim. It also hasn't escaped me that in order to get there and back, you would have had to get past Garmr twice."

She swallowed, her insides churning. "Yeah, but I had help…"

"Sigrid, do you want to go or not?"

"Yes!" The word burst out of her, surprising them both. But Sigrid recovered quickly and squared her shoulders. "I mean, yes. Of course I do."

The general's lips twitched. "Very well. Lunch, please."

Before the general could see how wide her smile was, Sigrid nudged Hestur into a gallop. A valkyrie mission in Svartalfheim! Her chest filled with joy as she and Hestur raced up the grassy hill.

The journey would be full of risks, but weren't all journeys like that? Hestur was brave, and *she* was brave. Hestur had come through in Helheim and faced the battle like he'd trained his life for it, and so had she. Together, they would be able to take on this mission like the valkyries.

Galloping up the hill to Vanahalla, Sigrid and Hestur moved as a team, navigating through boulders, molehills, and the herd of fluffy sheep, shooting toward those shimmering gold towers.

She wrapped her fingers in his mane and braced for the transition between a gallop and that flat-out speed—the stone wall separating control and chaos. The best in all the nine worlds.

Mariam was right. They were stronger for not having wings.

Finally, this world understood it.

AUTHOR'S NOTE

In all of my research for *The Valkyrie's Daughter*, one fact stood out above all else: we don't know a whole lot about Norse mythology. Other than a small collection of poems called the *Poetic Edda*, Norse religion had no scripture and nothing to tell us how they worshipped the gods. In fact, most of what we know about Viking society comes from medieval Christian historians and records kept by their opponents, and it's safe to assume this information is a little biased.

In the Middle Ages, an Icelandic historian named Snorri Sturluson compiled the *Prose Edda*, which is the second most informative Norse mythology source with one big caveat: it has a lot of inconsistencies. Snorri probably took creative liberties to fill in gaps, made some mistakes, and let his Christian faith influence how he wrote about the Norse religion. For example, we don't even have a definitive list of the names of the nine worlds. The realm of the dead might have originally been called "Hel," sharing its name with the goddess, or "Niflhel," and it's possible that Snorri interpreted it too much like the Christian hell.

Here's an example of an interesting translation by Snorri: he wrote that the Aesir (gods of Asgard) came from Asia. This could be a mistake or a misinterpretation, but it could also refer to an Asian migration into Scandinavia. Robert W. Rix wrote an article about how Odin might have been a real person who migrated from Asia, if you're interested in reading more about this theory. (Thanks to Dr. Kyle Frackman of UBC for referring me to this paper.) We'll never know the truth, but there is a lot of evidence that Scandinavians in the Viking Age were a racially diverse society. I like this theory, so this is how I wrote Sigrid's world.

Because medieval Christian historians likely filtered what they recorded, we also can't be sure how the Viking society viewed sexuality. Evidence points to strict gender roles, but on the other hand, their mythology includes a lot of stories about genderfluid gods. Odin, the manliest war god of all, practiced sorcery, which was considered a feminine activity. Loki was a shapeshifter and happens to be Sleipnir's mom. I chose to write about a society that sits somewhere in between, giving the characters the chance to challenge gender-based jobs and titles while living in a culture where queer relationships are widely accepted. I like to imagine a world where queer kids are spared from thinking, "What will others think?" and instead just focus on, "How do I feel?" How liberating that would be! I might have come out as a teenager instead of in my twenties, if we lived in such a place.

Like others who have written about Norse mythology, I made a few adaptations when writing *The Valkyrie's Daughter*. For example, in the *Edda*, valkyries were women who decided who died in battle, Ratatosk was a squirrel, and the afterlife is more complex than everyone simply going to Helheim. I also took the liberty to fill in gaps, like naming the royal hall of Vanaheim "Vanahalla" (following the naming pattern of "Valhalla," the hall of the slain). For the underworld, I chose the name "Helheim" to differentiate the location from the goddess.

If you're interested in learning about Norse mythology, I recommend reading the *Poetic Edda*. I like the Jackson Crawford translation because he wrote it in a modern tone. I also recommend *Norse Mythology* by Neil Gaiman, which is an entertaining adaptation of a few of these stories.

Thanks for coming with me on Sigrid's journey! I hope you find the nine worlds and their inhabitants as interesting as I do, and I can't wait to explore more of it with you in the next book.

- Tiana Warner

ACKNOWLEDGEMENTS

Thank you Stephanie and my Crit Coven for the feedback and masterminding, Amy and the Entangled team for believing in me, and my wonderful support team—Toshi, my friends and family, and of course Mom and Dad, who always have my back.

Let's be friends!

🐦 @EntangledTeen

📷 @EntangledTeen

👍 @EntangledTeen

♪ @EntangledTeen

📰 bit.ly/TeenNewsletter

entangled teen

an imprint of Entangled Publishing LLC